# TOM DEITZ

"A MASTER OF MODERN FANTASY"
Brad Strickland, author of *Moondreams*

"DEITZ'S CHARACTERS ARE AT ONCE
VERY HUMAN, AND SOMETHING MORE."
Diana L. Paxson,
author of *The Dragons of the Rhine*

"A COMPELLING CRAFTER OF
CONTEMPORARY NOVELS"
*Dragon*

"A MAJOR FANTASY WRITER"
*Booklist*

"ONE OF THE BEST"
*OtherRealms*

"HE DRAWS RECOGNIZABLE,
BELIEVABLE CHARACTERS
AND THROUGH THEM
MAKES FANTASTIC SITUATIONS REAL"
M. R. Hildebrand

"TOM DEITZ IS WRITING
BETTER THAN EVER"
Mercedes Lackey, author of *Magic's Price*

D0058961

*Other AvoNova Books by*
**Tom Deitz**


*The* SOULSMITH *Trilogy*

SOULSMITH
DREAMBUILDER
WORDWRIGHT


WINDMASTER'S BANE
FIRESHAPER'S DOOM
SUNSHAKER'S WAR
STONESKIN'S REVENGE


*AvoNova Hardcovers*

ABOVE THE LOWER SKY
DREAMSEEKER'S ROAD

Avon Books are available at special quantity discounts for bulk purchases for sales promotions, premiums, fund raising or educational use. Special books, or book excerpts, can also be created to fit specific needs.

For details write or telephone the office of the Director of Special Markets, Avon Books, Dept. FP, 1350 Avenue of the Americas, New York, New York 10019, 1-800-238-0658.

# GHOSTCOUNTRY'S WRATH

# TOM DEITZ

AVON BOOKS • NEW YORK

If you purchased this book without a cover, you should be aware that this book is stolen property. It was reported as "unsold and destroyed" to the publisher, and neither the author nor the publisher has received any payment for this "stripped book."

GHOSTCOUNTRY'S WRATH is an original publication of Avon Books. This work has never before appeared in book form. This work is a novel. Any similarity to actual persons or events is purely coincidental.

AVON BOOKS
A division of
The Hearst Corporation
1350 Avenue of the Americas
New York, New York 10019

Copyright © 1995 by Thomas F. Deitz
Cover art by Steven Adler
Published by arrangement with the author
Library of Congress Catalog Card Number: 94-96776
ISBN: 0-380-76838-0

All rights reserved, which includes the right to reproduce this book or portions thereof in any form whatsoever except as provided by the U.S. Copyright Law. For information address Avon Books.

First AvoNova Printing: July 1995

AVONOVA TRADEMARK REG. U.S. PAT. OFF. AND IN OTHER COUNTRIES, MARCA REGISTRADA, HECHO EN U.S.A.

Printed in the U.S.A.

RA 10 9 8 7 6 5 4 3 2 1

This novel is especially, and obviously, for
Greg Keyes,
and also, and nearly as obviously, for Russell Cutts.
But it is likewise for the other great guys and gals of
the
University of Georgia Flying Rat Toli Club Na Hollo:

Tracy Abla and Chip Baker
Nick Banchero and Jamie Bishop
Grant Blankenship and Randy Brooks
John Burrows and Kristine Burrows
Billy Caldwell and John Chamblee
Eric Clanton and Gene Crawford
Jim Dana and Joel Dukes
Jason Edwards and Brittney Euliss
Frank Farrar and Mark Fowlkes
Dee Fraker and Jessica French
Todd Frizzell and Kevin Gaston
Jeff Gwathney and Walter Gwathney
John Guy and Cary Hardwick
A. J. Hoge and Dan Iorio
Heather Jacobs and Kit Johnson
Kevin Jones and Scott Jones
Scott Keith and Ray Knapp
Hyla Lacefield and Vince Lang
Peter Leary and Reid Locklin
Matt Lusk and Greg Matthews
Kohl Matthews and Paul Matthews
Gina Matthieson and Dave McMichael
Scott McMillan and John Mincemoyar
Georgia Moore and Jason Moore
Lawson Moore and Ascha Newt
Kevin O'Neil and Mike Paul
Robert Philen and Gordon Respess
Joel Respess and Frank Reynolds

Justin Seufert and G'Anna Weissinger
Brian Willoughby and Mark Wise
and
Sandy Wompler

(also Kay, Roy, and Tom, whose last names have
eluded me—and anyone I've misplaced altogether) . . .
. . . none of whom laughed at an old guy
past his (physical) prime, who runs stiffly,
shoots crooked, and all-too-frequently breaks.

Thanks, folks!

# *ACKNOWLEDGMENTS*

thanks to:

Davy Arch
Gordon Campbell
Charles Hudson
Scott Jones
Adele Leone
Reid Locklin
Buck Marchinton
Chris Miller
Klon Newell
Valerie Spratlin
Jean Starr
B. J. Steinhaus

and a special appreciation to:

Gordon Respess,
who played natural history consultant
when he should have been
playing guitar and chasing bats

and to:

Russell Cutts and Greg Keyes,
who showed me that Galunlati
is not nearly as far away
as I'd imagined!

*Wado!*

*Oh Lord, my name is Calvin, an' Indian blood runs
through my veins.*
*Yeah, my name is Calvin Fargo, an' Cherokee blood
be pulsin' in my veins.*
*I've had some strange adventures; seen an awful lot
o' wond'rous things.*

*I've been to Galunlati; I've been right near a place
called Tir-Nan-Og.*
*Yeah, I've been to Galunlati, an' I've been pert nigh
a place called Tir-Nan-Og.*
*They're both a kind of heaven; but the only way to
go's through magic fog.*

*I've seen the great* uktena; *my friends an' me, we
killed that monster dead.*
*Yeah, I saw that old uktena; three friends an' me, we
shot that serpent dead.*
*There's a jewel grows in his forehead; that'll show
you what's a-comin' up ahead.*

*I've also fought Spearfinger; she'll steal your liver
gone before you know.*
*Yeah, I've fought that bitch Spearfinger, what eats
your liver up afore you know.*
*I shot her, an' I drowned her; but 'fore I did she laid
four good folks low.*

*Werepossum Blues*
words: Calvin McIntosh
music: Darrell Buchanan

# PART ONE

# Rewards
# and
# Promises

# Prologue:
## Hyuntikwala Usunhi and Asgaya Gigagei Discuss Nunda Igeyi, Edahi, and Other Enigmas

*(Walhala, Galunlati—high summer—dawn)*

Hyuntikwala Usunhi was afraid to look at the sky.

For as long as he could remember—which was nigh as long as the Ani-Yunwiya had dwelt in the underlapping Land he had at last conceded should be called the Lying World—he had been fearless. But where the wise among The Principle People might wonder what a god could find to fear, Hyuntikwala Usunhi knew that he was no god, or less so than was was his father, Kanati, the Lucky Hunter. And he likewise knew that when last he had gazed at the heavens, yesterday at sunset, they had held something terrible indeed.

As for this morning . . . Well, either that which disturbed him would remain or it would not; and loitering on the cool, dim threshold of his cliffside home would tell him neither. And yet he lingered, shoulders against the splatter-damp granite of the man-wide ledge that fronted his dwelling, feeling Ugunyi's song thrum and

rumble up through his bare feet as he stared at the ever-
falling veil that filled his ears with its thunderous roar,
even as it flicked tiny darts of cold the whole tall length
of his body.

*Water*, it was: a river's worth of it. The Long-Man,
the Ani-Yunwiya called it; but he had always considered
it an endless blue-brown serpent that coiled among the
ancient forests of Walhala before plunging down the
face of the granite cliff called Hyuntikwalayi, at whose
base it smashed apart, only to ooze together again and
slither on to the fire-laced seas at the edge of the world.
An arm's reach before his face it fell, and ten times their
span to either side. And by the paleness awakening in
it, and the sparks of red and orange that lurked and laced
among the gray and green, he knew that beyond it lay
dawn.

"It would seem, Uki," a voice hissed from beside his
left ankle, giving him the familiar form of the name that
in the tongue of the Ani-Yunwiya meant *Darkthunder*;
"it would seem, oh Weathering-One, that you have
learned, these last few weeks, that even one such as you
may be afraid."

"It is a good thing *to* know," Uki answered calmly,
sparing the most disparaging of downward glances at the
fat black-and-gold diamondback that blinked slit-eyes at
him from the arching cave mouth that was gateway to
his home. "—But when the vermin of the Underworld
seek to counsel me, Walhala must surely fare ill indeed."

And with that he turned right and followed the ledge
into the light of first day. Not until he had traversed the
tight trail to the top of the cliff, however, did he dare
look at the sky, masked as most of it had been, first by
steep stone ledges, then by the towering beeches, hickories, and chestnuts that crowned them.

And even then he shrank from seeking Nunda Igeyi, the Day-Dweller: the sun.

It found him, though, relentless as he was not; and sent its breath to stain his chalk-white flesh the color of fading fire. It gleamed off long legs and strong arms, off a flat-muscled torso and a narrow hard-lined face that wore the cast of the Ani-Yunwiya, if not their rusty hue. It struck skin that was bare save for a white knee-length loincloth painted with serpents and quilled with lightning, and armbands in the shape of *uktenas* that coiled like quickened gold about his biceps. Finally, it found his hair and bound bloody highlights into the waist-long braids that by noon-light were black as ravens.

But, to his vast surprise, Nunda Igeyi's breath was cool! Cooler, far, than when last he had sampled it, yesterday at sunset. Uki sighed his relief, and—finally—dared let his eyes seek eastward, to the dawn.

The last of his tension faded with a second sigh.

Where yesterday, as for days before, Nunda Igeyi had flared and flickered, and at times had bloated so huge as to blot out all the heavens, so that the rains he sang up dried before they reached the earth, and he could hear leaves crisping where they hung; now it shook no longer. Now it was back in its proper place, with its proper light and heat.

And Uki no longer had cause to fear the sky.

"*Edahi!*" he cried, his voice like a clap of joyous thunder in the misty air. "Edahi: Calvin Fargo McIntosh! You who are my apprentice and like a sister's son to me, know that I see what you and your friends in the Lying World have done, and it is very well done indeed!"

"Indeed it is!" a voice boomed behind him: a thunder of bronze, where his was brass. And with that Uki snapped his head around and beheld a man walking from the woods to the east.

He was exactly as tall as Uki and precisely as well formed; his face as hard and handsome and lined. But his skin was red as blood—redder far than the tint sunrise had smeared across Uki's flesh. His loincloth was blood-hued, too, and bore a likeness of the rising sun and birds that might have been gulls.

"*Siyu*, Uncle!" Uki cried in turn: "Greetings, *Asgaya Gigagei*! Greetings, Red Man of the Lightning, Chief of *Nundagunyi*!"

"*Siyu* to you likewise, brother's son! *Siyu* to Hyuntikwala Usunhi, Chief of Walhala!"

"It is long since you visited, Uncle," Uki noted placidly, as he embraced his kinsman.

"It is long since I had call to visit," Asgaya Gigagei gave back, with a mischievous twinkle in his eye. "You serve your Quarter well." He paused then, stared up at the clear blue sky. "Though for a time," he continued more seriously, "I feared you would delay too long— or your apprentice would."

"How is it that you know of him?" Uki asked carefully.

"He passed through my Quarter once," the Red Man replied. "It was a year ago and more, when he and his Nunnehi friend fared east in search of the Burning Sand. I have been following his progress ever since. I also feared that this last undertaking of his would fail."

"But it did not!" Uki cried. "Nunda Igeyi no longer shakes. Edahi has ended the war in that other Land which upset it."

The Red Man scowled—an expression with which his brow looked unacquainted. "Do you *know* that it was Edahi who wrought this wonder? Men from the Lying World do not commonly have influence in Lands not their own."

"He—or one of his comrades," Uki answered flatly. "But only Edahi knew how to breach the World Walls;

he therefore must have played a major role.''

The Red Man's brows lifted in curiosity. ''You are proud of this mortal boy? This son of the Lying World?''

''Not all who live in the Lying World lie themselves!'' Uki snorted.

The Red Man ignored him. ''He wants to be an *adawehi*?''

''A *magician*, as his folk would say? So it appears. I have tried to direct him as best I could.''

The Red Man chuckled. ''*Edahi*: He-Goes-About—that was your name for him?''

Uki shook his head. ''His mother's father was a man of Power; when the boy was born he foresaw that the lad would travel far and called him accordingly—in both our tongue and his.''

''Names can be important,'' the Red Man observed thoughtfully. ''And they can mark important things as well.''

Uki's eyes twinkled conspiritorially. ''What are you thinking, Uncle?''

Asgaya Gigagei's cryptic smirk became a grin. ''I do not need to tell you what I am thinking.''

Uki's response was to gaze once more at Nunda Igeyi, which had now fully cleared the horizon, still amazed that he could trust it. ''Perhaps,'' he murmured, ''we should *see* how things fare with my apprentice.''

''Perhaps,'' the Red Man laughed, slapping his nephew on the back, ''we can use your Power Wheel—though of course we will use my *ulunsuti*.''

. . . a clearing in a forest, perfectly circular and as wide as three hands of men are high; paved with white sand across which no wind wanders; the whole bordered with watchful laurel; vigilant cedar at its back . . .

. . . four trees, lightning-blasted, twist skyward at the

cardinal points: red at the East, white to the South, black marking West, and blue in the North; and running from them to the center of the wheel, lines of darker gravel that cross the circle into quarters . . .

. . . a crystal like an uncut diamond as big as a man's fist, split by a septum the color of blood: the ulunsuti—the jewel from the head of the great uktena . . .

Two men gaze into it, there where the Quarters meet in Uki's Place of Power. Blood films it: perhaps the blood of men. Or perhaps the blood of spirits—or even gods.

The ulunsuti drinks its fill of their might—and still the men stare into it.

And then . . .

. . . *mountains. The soft-edged ridges of the Lying World, blazing purple and blue and green in the midday light. Lakes sprawl among them, cold man-made mirrors of a summer-hot sky. And amid those hills and long-drowned hollows a round knoll rises, carpeted in new-cut grass. Objects circle it like bright beetles: cars—for Edahi has taught Uki that word. But these are empty; the folk who rode them to the knoll have gathered around its summit, where, beneath an arch of pure white roses an aging man in night blue robes addresses a brown-haired youth clad in stiff white clothing that clinches close about his throat and strains tight across thick muscles. A white-veiled young woman stands be-side him, her dress likewise of white, though it is loose and flows like foam among the grasses.*

*At her left more women wait; in pink, pale blue, soft green, lavender, and yellow: fair as the flowers in their hands.*

*To the young man's right, five youths likewise linger, all in snug white garments accented with color at throat and waist. Three of them have bound their long hair back in tails, and two of the five Uki does not recognize:*

*one compact, dark-haired, and shortest, the other thin, gold-crowned, and tall.*

*The others Uki* does *know, for they have guested with him in Galunlati.*

*There is the slender, brown-haired youth named Alec McLean—once called by Uki* Tawiska: *the Smooth One—whom Edahi brought with him to Galunlati, where he helped slay an uktena and nearly died thereby; and who, reborn, was thereafter named* Tsulehisanunhi: *the Resurrected One.*

*Beside him stands his brother-close friend, David Sullivan; called* Sikwa Unega—*White 'Possum—for his grin and the fairness of his hair; who journeyed once to the sacred lake* Atagahi *in quest of healing water with which to save Tsulehisanunhi from that same uktena's poison.*

*And finally, there is Edahi. Dark and handsome, strong and black-haired, and alone of the young men gathered there also of the Ani-Yunwiya, that the folk of the Lying World call Cherokee.*

*The White Man and the Red Man watch fascinated, as some ceremony—Edahi has said something about attending a wedding—lapses into merriment and feasting.*

*"Very well," Uki whispers at last, nodding at his uncle. "As soon as we can summon the others, we will proceed!"*

# Chapter I:
# The Boy in the Stone

*(near MacTyrie, Georgia—
Saturday, June 21—late afternoon)*

Mad David Sullivan snugged a worn leather belt around his narrow waist and vented a grateful sigh. "Well," he announced to the log-walled room at large, "I feel like my old self again."

Shirtless, barefoot, and inclined to stay that way for a spell, given how hot the bunk room in Aikin Daniels's unair-conditioned mountainside cabin had become in the few hours since he and his MacTyrie Gang buddies had deserted it, he scooped a pile of mostly-white clothing from the oiled pine floor and began transferring his wallet, keys, and checkbook from the tuxedo pants he had so eagerly abandoned to the faded cutoffs that replaced them now.

Amid the chaos of sleeping bags, backpacks, pizza boxes, beer bottles, and X-rated videotapes that updated the otherwise rustic room, that same Aikin "M. H." (for Mighty Hunter) Daniels whose parents owned the cabin was likewise transforming himself from groomsman to civilian; moving, as always, with the near-absolute silence that was his stock-in-trade. A low, steady hiss to

David's right was Calvin McIntosh showering in the adjoining john. The faint odor of Coast soap wafted between the diagonal planks of the ill-fitting door. David wished he'd hurry. They needed to talk—badly. Not here, of course—with Aik's overly eager ears alert and starved for secrets. But soon—real soon.

"Yeah, thank *God* it's over," Aikin agreed, oblivious to David's subtle agitation, as he stuffed the tail of his black *Sandman* T-shirt into his own cutoffs. He retrieved his silver-framed glasses from the scarred oak dresser in the corner and raised inky eyebrows into like-colored bangs in relief.

"Guess it's your turn now," David chided. He unbound his "formal" ponytail, turned to the single mirror, which hung between the windows, and applied a comb to his thick, white-blond hair.

Aikin bared his teeth at the taunt, then flung his tux jacket straight at him.

David observed the attack in the glass, plucked the garment neatly from the air, and whirled it back whence it came, then flopped against the rough-hewn wall. Aikin wadded the forsaken formal wear into his backpack and eased toward the greatroom door.

Before he reached it, however, it flew open, and Alec McLean stomped in, likewise (and atypically) barefoot, and with his purple satin bowtie undone and trickling down his shirtfront, but otherwise still fully clad in the regalia the Gang had endured for Gary Hudson's wedding. He lugged a duffle bag: as gray as his eyes and almost as elegantly slim. In line with his abrupt entrance, he also looked very harried.

Aikin flicked an unclaimed pair of Enotah County 'Possums gym shorts at him—which he dodged. "So what's the deal, Mach-One? You don't look like a happy camper."

Alec shook his spiky dark head as he advanced into

the room, releasing shirt studs in the process. "How'd *you* like havin' a dog-drunk Darrell Buchanan vomit red velvet wedding cake all over your dashboard, then pass out cold?"

David rolled his eyes. "That's our Runnerman."

"What about Cal's lady?" Aikin wondered. "Sandy, or whatever? I thought you were gonna lead her up here."

Alec flung down his bag and commenced to undress in earnest. "She needed to pick up a couple things in town but said she'd come up after that if she got antsy— assuming she can pry Liz away from the other brides- maids long enough to show her the way. Otherwise, we're supposed to rendezvous at the Pizza Hut in MacTyrie. Me and Dave and Cal are," he added apol- ogetically to Aikin. "Sorry to stick you with K.P. man."

"I'm *not* stupid!" Aikin growled. "I know you guys've got some big secret you're hot to download. It's no big deal."

David shot Alec a wary glance. "Sorry—*really*. I'll tell you what I can when I can, I promise."

"Yeah, like ten years from now," Aikin muttered. He stared at them a moment longer, then grimaced sourly and slipped out of the room, silently as always: the qui- etest person David knew—save Calvin. He also made an obvious point of closing the door. David wondered what he was thinking.

"So, where *is* young Mr. MacIntosh?" Alec asked offhandedly.

David dipped his head toward the loo. "Made a bee- line for the shower as soon as Aik got the door open. Said he couldn't stand himself a minute longer. Seems the A.C. in Sandy's truck died right when they hit the road this morning."

Alec laughed out loud. "Six hours in this heat? No wonder he was so ripe at the wedding!"

"I can't believe he actually changed in the middle of the field!" David giggled. "No, actually I can, knowin' Cal. And we *were* standin' guard around him—sort of."

"He say why he was late?"

David shook his head, suddenly serious. "Just what he told us when he called to say he was on his way."

"It's complicated, and I only want to have to tell it once," a new voice called above the fading hiss of the shower expiring.

Once again Alec and David exchanged glances: blue and gray eyes locked in quizzical resignation. While David collected his finery, Alec resurrected his civilian persona. An instant later, the bathroom door squeaked open, releasing a cloud of steam around a muscular, rusty-skinned young man who stood there applying one end of a long blue towel to shoulder-length black hair, while the other flirted with his thighs.

David stared fixedly at the opposite wall as Calvin continued drying himself. "So, Fargo," he drawled, "when *are* you gonna reveal this great secret of yours?"

"Besides the one he's already revealing?" Alec chuckled. "Doesn't look so great to me!"

"Eat me, White Boy!" Calvin snarled.

"Don't have a fork that small," Alec shot back.

Calvin bent over to dry his legs—which not so coincidentally mooned him.

"Neither does your tattoo, actually," Alec observed coolly, refusing to be baited. "—Look good, I mean."

"*Eat me!*"

David glanced at Calvin's bare backside reflexively, in quest of the cross-in-circle tattoo that had always graced—if that word was appropriate to such a referent—his friend's upper right "cheek." "God, he's right!" he gasped. "It's all . . . faded!"

Calvin straightened and craned his neck to peer over his shoulder, then gave up and padded to the mirror, where he proceeded to peruse his bottom critically. "Well, that's interestin'," he mused. "Not that I spend a lot of time lookin' at my butt, or anything. Gosh, I bet it's cause—"

He broke off, scowling, and unhooked a small, mud-colored leather bag from a peg by the door and slipped the thin cord over his head. It thumped against his chest and lodged against a glassy, palm-sized object wrapped in copper wire and depending from a wet and obviously brand-new rawhide thong. First things first, David noted: mojo before modesty.

"'Cause why?" he prompted.

"The door can be locked," Alec added. "Runner-man's out of it, and Aik'll forgive us—eventually."

"Poor Aik." David sighed, shaking his head.

"You guys still haven't told him . . . ?" From Calvin.

"Not much," David grunted. "'Course we don't know everything either," he added pointedly.

"Start with the tattoo," Alec suggested.

Calvin fingered the vitreous ornament between his pecs. "I . . . was gonna say that I bet it's faded 'cause of all the shapeshifting I've been doin' lately."

Alec looked stricken—as he usually did when such topics arose. David shot him a glare and gnawed his lip. "I thought you didn't like doing that," he ventured at last.

Calvin fished a pair of flowered boxer shorts from a battered khaki knapsack. "Not likin' something and not doin' something are two different somethings," he observed as he slipped them on. "But like I said, I've been doin' a lot of shapeshiftin'—and I guess every time I do, the tattoo loses something. I mean, it's not part of *me*, really. Like—"

"Oh, *I* see!" David broke in eagerly. "When you

change back to human, your body has to reconstruct you according to your genetic blueprint. Only the tattoo's not part of it, so it has to make do as best it can."

Calvin nodded. "And when you turn into something with scales—which I, to my regret, have lately done— it's kinda hard for a few grains of pigment to figure out where to go, 'cause there aren't any analogous structures. Like, rattlesnakes don't even have hipbones, much less asses!"

Both David's brows shot up. "*Rattlesnakes?*"

"A matter of necessity. I don't recommend the experience."

"Which is very interesting," Alec inserted. "But which doesn't explain why you're late—or all that B.S. on the phone. I mean, you called right after we discovered . . . *it*. And at the last possible moment before we had to split for the bachelor party. Five minutes later, and you'd have missed us."

Calvin stepped into a pair of jeans. "Sorry 'bout that," he mumbled. "Sorry I had to be so vague, too, but I didn't trust the phone not to be tapped."

"By whom?" David asked.

"By the police in Whidden, Georgia, for one; by the G.B.I., for another. Probably the feds as well. Shoot, for all I know, they're snoopin' now!"

"I would think it highly unlikely that this room's bugged," Alec intoned sarcastically. "And I'm not sure *anything* can snoop through solid log walls."

David folded his arms across his chest. "It's time you talked, Fargo."

"Okay, okay." Calvin sighed. "Well, to give you the quick and dirty version: I'm sure you remember our, uh, adventures of last week. . . . "

"How could we forget?" David snorted. "World-hopping like crazy, shapeshifting, daring rescues, Faery naval battles, you name it."

"There's something you don't know, though."

"What?"

Calvin took a deep breath. "You remember that night in Jackson County when I conjured up that fog, so I could summon Awi Usdi, the Little Deer, so he could call a *real* deer for me to get blood from? So I could use it to empower Alec's ulunsuti to open a gate to that place those guys were holdin' Finno?"

"Okay . . ."

"Well, I got something else as well," Calvin whispered shakily. "Or something answered, anyway. "Guys, I . . . I called *Spearfinger!*"

"*Shit!*"

Calvin nodded grimly. "The lady—if you can call her that—herself. Seems she'd been followin' us—you, in particular—ever since the first time we went to Galunlati. And when I opened the gate between Worlds for Awi Usdi, she sneaked through as well."

David's face was very pale. "And . . . you've had to deal with her."

Again Calvin nodded. "And she's *killed*, Dave! She . . . she even killed my dad!"

David sat down with a thud. "Oh, Jesus!"

An even grimmer nod. "And a woman and a couple of kids."

Silence.

"I killed her, though—I hope."

"You *hope?*"

A shrug this time. "She's a supernatural creature not native to this world. I'm not sure what to believe. But I saw her die. In *this* world I saw her die."

"Let's see," Alec mused. "She's that shapechanging, liver-eating ogress from Galunlati, right? The one with power over stone—"

A knock rattled the door, jerking David back to the present. "What're you guys doin' in there?" Aikin demanded. "Tonto's lady just drove up—and I'm stuck out here with a sot!"

"Tough," David called through the door, even as he moved to open it. "I'm in here with a Cherokee sorcerer!"

"I hope you know what a lucky son-of-a-bitch you are," David muttered to Calvin twenty seconds later, as they and Alec neatly sidestepped the resigned Aikin and the reeling Darrell (who had somehow achieved the porch) and bounded down the split-log steps into the sparse stand of pines that comprised the cabin's front yard. A laurel hell fenced it upslope to the right, beyond which the Enotah National Forest began in earnest. To the left, a narrow rutted road snaked up the wooded mountainside from MacTyrie three miles away. A motorcycle and two cars crouched near the porch. Cal's BMW bike, Aikin's old brown Nova, and the battered red '66 Mustang David called the Mustang-of-Death (as of the previous weekend, closer to simply a dead Mustang, he thought dully).

But a newish red-and-black Ford Bronco had joined them, knobby tires straddling the terminal ruts. Silver mylar on all side windows wrapped the interior with mystery and obscured the occupants, if any. "Now that raises an interesting question," Alec smirked, when they stopped beside it. "Is it an insult to call a shapechanger a son-of-a-bitch?"

"Only if he hasn't eaten dog," a new voice volunteered: low and musical, with a soft Carolina drawl— and definitely female. David whirled around, cheeks aflame with a mix of irritation and embarrassment. He'd seen no sign of Sandy, and then suddenly there she was: five feet away and grinning like a 'possum. She'd apparently been lying in wait behind the nearest pine.

"Hey!" David laughed, stepping forward to enfold

Calvin's lady in the properly hearty hug he hadn't had time for at the wedding because of preoccupation; or at the reception, where he'd had his hands full overseeing the degradation of Gary's getaway car. Now, though, he'd finally got a good look at her, and he liked what he saw.

Though a high school physics teacher in her middle-twenties, Sandy Fairfax looked little older than his own girlfriend, Liz Hughes, who had just turned eighteen. She was tallish and slim, with serious features, a gently arching nose, and a waist-length sweep of straight, sun-bleached hair that was presently confined in a ponytail, though she'd let it down for the wedding. She'd worn a flouncy spring green cotton dress, then, with a belt of linked silver dogwood blossoms. Now she was attired more typically: jeans, white Reeboks, and a scarlet T-shirt hyping a locally produced educational film called *Voices in the Wind*. She wore no makeup, but a pair of tiny dream catchers depended from her ears. Yeah, David thought, Calvin was a *damned* lucky S.O.B.

"Liz saw a bird she wanted to get a shot of," Sandy explained, in response to a concern David had not yet realized himself. "You're lookin' good," she added with an exaggerated twang, as she released him. "Not as good as a couple hours ago, though. Ain't nothin' like handsome lads in tuxes."

Calvin slid an arm around her waist and grinned. "Actually," he confided, "what she really means is there's nothin' like a handsome *man* in his birthday suit!"

"The operative word being *man*," Sandy countered smartly.

David grinned obligingly, then checked his watch and craned his neck, his gaze combing the woods.

Sandy saw him. "I don't suppose you'd be willing to fill in your part of this little conundrum while we wait for your gal, would you?" she ventured brightly.

"Liz didn't tell you?" David replied, surprised. "She hasn't seen . . . *it* either, but she does know about it, 'cause I told her."

"Called her in the middle of the bachelor party!" Alec confided to Calvin, sounding disgusted. "I—"

They were spared further digression by the emergence of a slender red-haired girl from behind the Bronco. Like Sandy, Liz Hughes was wearing jeans and a T-shirt (hers was dull burgundy), which to David looked exactly as smashing as the complex lime-sherbet bridesmaid dress she'd sported in the wedding.

"Sorry," she panted as she jogged up to join them, pausing to give David a perfunctory peck on the cheek. "I thought it was a red-tail, but then I realized it was a *peregrine*, which are really rare, and—" She broke off, looked at David with frank openness. "You're in a hurry, aren't you?"

" 'Fraid so," he admitted, and turned to give Aikin a silent farewell salute before steering Alec toward the Mustang. Aikin nodded sketchily, stuffed a shoulder under Darrell's armpit, and dragged him inside. "Catch you later," he grunted from the door.

"Yeah, thanks," David yelled back. "As for hurrying," he added to Liz, "well, it's a pretty big deal, at least to me, even if it's not a matter of life or death."

"Which it's not," Calvin agreed. "At least I hope not. But a couple days ago, it was a very big deal indeed." He did not add, David noted, that affairs still might not be settled—if Liz had really seen what she'd claimed. The peregrine was Cal's totem. And to see one anytime, especially so far inland, was cause for concern.

"You lead," Sandy told David, fishing in her pocket for her keys. "Me and Liz'll follow, in case we can't keep up."

"Yeah," Alec muttered, "and maybe old Cal'll finally set us straight about *his* mystery."

"They *are* related," Calvin told him. "But like I said, I don't wanta get into it until I can lay out the whole tale without interruptions. And I don't wanta do that till I've got a look at *your* surprise."

"Which we'll never do, if we spend all day jawing," Liz concluded practically. "Come on folks, let's travel!"

Thirty minutes later, Calvin, Alec, David, Liz, and Sandy were standing in a semicircle before a truck-sized outcrop of dark granite that thrust from a wooded slope behind David's parents' barn. Beyond rose forested mountains; behind was the farm proper, dipping to the Sullivan Cove Road, with, across it, another ridge. The highway slashed through the river bottom a hundred yards to their left.

But it was the rock face itself that focused their attention—something *in* the rock face, more precisely. Specifically, it was a life-sized simulacrum of David—wrought entirely of rounded pebbles and poised as if frozen in the act of striding from the stone: left foot and right arm extended, expression one of alarm or surprise. Little more was obvious, save that the naked (and, to David's embarrassment, excruciatingly anatomically correct) effigy was patently no work of nature—which, given what Calvin had said earlier about Spearfinger's mastery over stone, was not comforting at all.

"Well, it's a good likeness, anyway!" Calvin opined at last. "Even better than I remember, actually."

"I'm pleased you approve," David growled acidly. "Now, do you happen to have any idea what it's doing behind our burning dump?"

"Weatherin' away slowly," Calvin replied promptly, but his expression belied his flippancy.

Sandy eased forward to inspect the effigy more closely. "Hmmm," she murmured, "I see two weird things right off—not counting how it happens to look like Dave, of course.''

"Of course," David grumbled through his teeth.

Sandy probed the juncture of figure and cliff with a finger. "Yeah, well, the first thing is that it really does look like it walked right out of the stone," she observed, as if addressing her physics students. "See, if you look closely you can see how the granite matrix follows the contour of every pebble interface precisely—which means this wasn't just made and stuck on."

David shifted his weight and tried not to fidget. The damned thing gave him the world-class willies, appearing so suddenly, as it had, the evening before—or at least that's when he'd discovered it. "And the second thing?" he managed.

Sandy puffed her cheeks. "These pebbles aren't native to north Georgia."

"Of course not!" Calvin broke in. "Seein' as how that thing was put together three hundred miles south of here!"

David rounded on him, uncertain whether he was feigning anger or actually felt it. "*Okay*," he gritted, "you've had your fun, your little game of 'Prolong-the-Mystery'; I think it's time you laid things out straight."

Calvin's eyes flashed fire, but then he nodded resignedly. "Before I do, could you do me one favor?"

David shot him a skeptical glare. "What?"

Calvin glanced around, mouth set, normally dusky skin unaccountably pale. "Uh, well . . . could you tell me if it's normal for fog to completely surround this place in, like, two minutes? It was clear as day when we got up here—and now I can't even see your house!"

"I can't either," Alec added shakily. "But I *can* see a godawful big rattler."

# Chapter II:
# The Boys in the Earth

*(Sullivan Cove, Georgia—very late afternoon)*

"*Rattler?*" Liz gulped, blanching, but to her credit not bolting. "Where?"

"In front of Mr. Stony," Alec muttered, inclining his head subtly to the right.

A chill crept across Calvin's body that had nothing to do with the abruptly appearing fog, as he followed Alec's edgy stare. Yep, it was a rattler all right: eastern diamondback, if he had his eyes in straight. Big one, too; the largest he'd ever seen, in fact—at least in *this* World: pushing eight feet if it was an inch, and as big around as his upper arm, with scales that gleamed so brightly they seemed wrought of bronze and gold. A glassy clump ornamented its tail like a hand-sized pine cone cased in yellow ice. It had evidently just crawled from some hidden hole in the shadowed triangle between the effigy's legs and was now gliding toward them, its whole vast length sliding easily across the pine needles that comprised the ground cover thereabouts. But what really put the wind up him was that none of them had observed its emergence until, all of a sudden it was simply *there*.

Which was impossible.

And then a second realization made him shiver all over again.

That species didn't live this far north! Their territory ended at the fall line, a hundred miles to the south!

"*Adawehi!*" he whispered, tearing his gaze away to lock eyes with a troubled-looking David. Calvin imagined his friend was scared as shitless as the rest of them but trying not to show it. God knew he was fighting a very instinctive urge to get the hell out of there—yet feared to move abruptly lest that provoke the snake to strike.

"*Magician?*" Liz wondered, with a skeptical frown. She was tense as a wire but, like Sandy, showing no fear of snakes *as* snakes—which was the only good thing about their situation, he concluded.

"*Supernatural*, in this context," he corrected under his breath. "Cherokee think snakes are supernatural. And I'll bet this one *is*."

"What makes you say that?" Alec asked through his teeth.

"This fog, for one thing—as you should know."

Alec glanced around nervously. "You mean this is like . . . *that* one?"

Calvin started to shrug, but caught himself. "That'd be my top three guesses! I mean, fog's a *between* thing, neither water nor air, which is why it works so well as a gate between Worlds. And of course rattlesnakes *are* creatures of great power."

"Servants of Thunder, right?" Sandy murmured, as still as the rest of them.

"More often enemies," he corrected, gaze never leaving the reptile. " 'Cept that Uki sometimes uses them as messengers, probably 'cause they can slide between Worlds so easy."

The snake was no more than three feet away now, and

nearest Calvin. One abrupt motion, and he'd feel fangs in his leg. And though diamondback venom wasn't as virulent as most folks believed, one that big could still do serious damage. And it would hurt like hell and be inconvenient regardless.

It was then that he saw the second one. Like the first, it was oozing from the shadows between the statue's legs. But where the rattler had shone bronze, the newcomer was brass and copper, and maybe a tad slimmer of body, though still, at six feet, enormous for its kind. *"Wadige-daskali,"* he groaned. "Copperhead. Now I *know* we're in deep shit."

Yet no one moved. Perhaps it was because, inured to magic as they had become in the last few years, they all sensed that *something* was about to happen, and that if they fled no good would come of it. Or perhaps it was the uncanniness of the fog that swirled and eddied less than a yard behind them, and so far above their heads they could see neither mountains nor trees but only a disc of sky. And that, much worse, ended with impossibly well-defined abruptness, to describe a perfect cylinder around them and the scrap of cliff that held David's pebbly twin.

The only sound was the swish of scales across pine needles, and of shallow breathing.

The diamondback was less than a yard from Calvin's boots now; but where it had been steering straight at him, it suddenly veered toward the bank of fog, lifting its front fifth a finger's width as it progressed. But instead of entering the white barrier, it turned again, to parallel its arc, until its whole length lay just inside it, measuring one-fourth of the circle's circumference on the ground.

The copperhead was following, too, matching the rattler's path precisely. Calvin stared as if ensorcelled.

—Until a sound startled him: a grinding thump that

almost made him flinch—which could have proved disastrous. He tore his gaze from the serpents—and saw that the rock that had formed the statue's right kneecap had fallen off and now lay beside one foot. And even as he watched, more pebbles crumbled from the arms and chin.

And then another rattler emerged, as large as the first, followed by a second copperhead. They were moving faster, too, just as the pace of the statue's disintegration was accelerating. There was deliberate intent at work here, that much was clear, but Calvin knew in a way he could not explain that in spite of the presence of these denizens of the Underworld, no hostile power was involved. His friends seemed to sense it too, even Sandy, who'd had least exposure to the arcane. Still no one moved, but growing uncertainty was evident in more than one pair of eyes.

"Oh, shit!" Alec blurted out suddenly. "I see what they're doing!"

Calvin started to shush him, but then he too noticed what his friend had. For, alternating diamondbacks and copperheads, the reptiles were defining a Power Wheel: four formed the rim, and four more had crawled inward to comprise the spokes, their blunt, triangular heads barely touching. Unfortunately, he and his companions were also enclosed by those quarters.

The pebbles were falling in a regular torrent now, the David effigy decaying at a shocking rate, until finally the fist-sized stone that had lain where its heart would have been thumped to the ground, sealing the hole from which the fourth and apparently final copperhead had just emerged.

Liz yipped in spite of herself. Calvin scowled at her—and felt another chill, for the unnaturally cool air abruptly filled with a dry, low-pitched buzz, as first one, then the other diamondbacks began to shake their rattles.

Louder and louder—and something cold brushed his hand. He jerked away reflexively—but whatever it had been was already moving past him. A downward glance identified it: the too-solid fog drifting past his knees like water filling a glass.

"Christ!" Sandy cried beside him, as it flowed in from all sides to engulf them. Already it was waist-high, but the rattling continued, though he could no longer see the snakes.

Chest high, and he gasped, for the fog was as cold as death.

Neck high, and then . . .

"Grab hands!" he yelled as he felt some *force* tug at him.

—And barely had time to feel Alec and Sandy seize his left and right wrists respectively before the world turned to white and the buzz of rattles.

And then there was pain, as if every cell in his body had been struck by a separate bolt of lightning and boiled to vapor.

Darkness and cold . . .

Then warmth and light again . . .

The fog was gone. But neither was there a defunct statue of David, nor any rock face to support one, nor a mountain for that outcrop to thrust from. Nor was there any sign of snakes forming a Power Wheel on a carpet of pine straw.

But there *were* pines—a few—mingling with a great many more cedars and laurel, all ringing a perfectly round clearing paved with fine white sand.

Head still awhirl, Calvin eased free of Alec's grip and squinted past his companions (all present and accounted for, he noted absently) toward the palisade of trees. By the position of the sun, they were facing north. "Galunlati!" he whispered at last, almost to himself. "And if this isn't Uki's Power Wheel, it's a damned fine copy.''

"We've . . . been here before," David added shakily to Sandy and Liz. "That is, me and Cal and Alec have."

"Some way to travel!" Sandy breathed. Her voice sounded reasonably steady, though the hand that clutched his was trembling. "I can see why you don't like it!" Her face, when he checked, was pale, and he knew she was working to hold off hysteria.

"You . . . get used to it," he managed as shock launched a sneak attack and made him reel.

"Galunlati," Liz mused softly, her face even paler than Sandy's, though Calvin knew she'd been world-hopping more than once. "But—but *why*?"

"Who knows?" he replied. "But this can't have happened accidentally. Watch and listen, and just go with the flow as much as you can."

" 'Specially as we've got company," David noted quietly, inclining his head to the left.

Calvin expected to see Uki—this was, after all, his Place of Power. But the figure that stood obscured by the shadows there was not the familiar bone white adawehiyu. Not by a long shot.

True, the man advancing toward him looked to be Uki's size, and mirrored his mode of dress—and, as he drew closer, showed features like enough to Uki's to brand him kinsman if not twin. But this man was blue! Saving his roach of slate gray hair, his ornaments of mica and dull-hued stone, and the troubling patterns shaved into the short fur of his loincloth and tattooed like killing frost across his skin, he was the cold, dark blue of winter shadows and icy water beneath thick-grown pines.

"*Asgaya Sakani*!" Calvin hissed. "It has to be: the Blue Man of the North, Chief of *Uhuntsayi*, the Frozen Land."

"Friend of yours, I hope," Alec muttered.

Calvin glared at him and shook his head, not daring to voice aloud that north was the direction of defeat and trouble. The rest held their peace, bodies tense, eyes feverishly alert.

"There's another one!" Liz murmured, nudging him with her elbow.

He scanned the perimeter—and saw a second unfamiliar figure emerge from the long shadow of the blasted tree to the west. Nor was he surprised to observe that this man's skin and garments were black as soot; his ornaments of jet, bear-claw, and iron. Otherwise, he differed from the Blue Man chiefly by having unbound silver white hair.

"And over there!" from Sandy, as a glance east showed yet another tall figure, this one red, even to his skin, which was the color of new-flayed flesh.

And then, finally, he dared look south—and relaxed. "Uki!" he mouthed at David, whose face was already lighting with recognition.

"Your . . . mentor?" Sandy whispered beside him.

He nodded, his hair hiding most of a troubled scowl. "This kind of thing isn't normal, though. I wonder what's up."

"*Siyu!*" Uki stated flatly, when he came to within speaking range. His face was unreadable, displaying neither pleasure, surprise, nor disdain.

"*S-siyu!*" Calvin gave him back uncertainly. "*Siyu, adawehiyu!*"

Silence, as the three other . . . whatever they were . . . joined Uki to form a line in the southeast quadrant of the Wheel. And still no words, neither from Calvin and crew, nor their visitors, though the latter's eyes spoke volumes, and little of it comforting. Doubt and contempt there was, mostly. Calvin was suddenly afraid.

"*Edahi,*" Uki said at last, his voice atypically sharp

and threatening, "Tsulehisanunhi, Sikwa Unega—you three will come with us." He paused then, as if seeing Sandy and Liz for the first time. "You women remain here," he grunted, almost as an afterthought. "My sisters will attend to you when we leave."

"Now wait a minute!" Calvin began hotly, his hands already balling into fists, as an anger he had never before aimed at Uki roared to life.

"*Silence?*" Uki spat. "You will keep silent until I say otherwise! The women will not be harmed, and if you act as you ought, you will see them again. No more will I say."

Calvin had to clamp his jaws down hard to keep from telling Uki he was full of crap—and from lashing out with his still-clenched fists.

"Cool it," David hissed through his teeth. "Go with the flow, remember?"

Calvin's reply was a wordless growl, but at a grim, resigned nod from Sandy, he fell in behind the Red Man as Uki led the way from the clearing. David came next, with Alec following. Then came the Black Man, with the Blue Man of the North bringing up the rear.

They did not head south, though, toward Uki's house in the cliffs beneath the rumbling waterfall Calvin could only just hear. Rather, they turned into the deeper woods to the north, where Calvin, though he had visited Uki more than once, had never fared.

Calvin did not know how long they trekked along, only that it was due north through unrelieved forest, that he was unaccountably hungry, given the food he'd scarfed at the wedding reception—and that he was bloody tired, which was not so unaccountable, seeing how little sleep he'd had the last week or so. He was also feeling guilty for not having told his friends about the statue when he'd had the chance. He could've given them the short form, for God's sake: how he'd watched Spearfinger construct it down in Willacoochee County, then send it marching into the earth in quest of Dave. Now . . . who knew when he'd get to lay out the whole tale?

Never mind that both Dave and Alec were probably pissed as hell at him. And certainly never mind whatever it was that had Uki's breechclout in a wad.

Uki. . . . His mentor had held ruthless silence since this journey began, as had everyone else in their odd party. And whatever was up had the feel of ritual.

Which could be either good or bad.

Not until sunset did the situation clarify even a little, but when it did, the switch was abrupt. One moment they were panting along the trail between close-grown maples, the next they were confronting a seemingly impenetrable barrier of laurel. Uki simply walked into it. The Red Man went next, whereupon Calvin gritted his teeth, closed his eyes, and followed.

The leaves did not prick as much as he'd expected, though, and as soon as a brush of clearer air touched his face, he was blinking across fifty yards of open ground at a mound. Three times as high as Uki was tall, he guessed it was, and close to thrice that across; conical and covered with grass, and with a more steeply walled projection thrusting to the right like the entrance to an igloo. A trickle of white smoke drifted from the apex— or was that steam? He relaxed a fraction. If this was what he hoped it was, maybe things would be okay.

Still no one spoke. And as the light faded, casting the whole site into a study in red and black, Uki led them to the east, toward what Calvin presumed was the entrance.

He was right. For when they halted, he could see a low, log-framed opening, beyond which a packed-earth tunnel pointed into darkness. He glanced at Uki, then at his stone-faced companions. None of them acknowledged his presence. His stomach growled. As if in sympathy, David's followed suit. Finally Uki eased around to stand between him and the dark archway. "Remove your clothing. Do not speak unless I tell you."

And with that, he and his fellows backed away.

Calvin rolled his eyes in resignation at his companions and fell to applying himself to buttons, snaps, and zippers. What choice did they have, after all? At least, he observed, when he'd stepped out of his gaudy boxers, it wasn't cold.

David was also naked now, but Alec was hesitating over his dangling-dagger earring. Calvin saw him catch Uki's eye and raise a quizzical brow. Uki spared him a curt, almost contemptuous, nod. Alec grimaced, but unhooked it and set it neatly in one of his sneakers. Calvin took the cue and lifted his medicine bag from around his neck. A thoughtful pause, and he likewise removed the uktena scale that had depended on a thong beside it.

Silence, still, but when Calvin straightened from depositing bag and scale, Uki pointed toward the mound's extension.

Calvin started that way, heard David, then Alec sigh and fall in behind. An instant later, he ducked through the opening he found there. The skin of a black bear hung beside it, he noted, probably to shut out cold and retain heat. A pause for a final deep breath of fresh air, and he continued on, forced by the low ceiling to walk hunched over.

Fortunately it required no more than nine paces along a narrow tunnel walled with fresh-made mats of woven cane: not so far that he couldn't see at all, but far enough that he ran head-on into a second bearskin marking the opposite end. Swearing silently, he eased it aside and paused on the threshold of a round chamber nearly thirty feet across and shoulder high at the sides.

Or that's what he thought it was; it was hard to be certain, for the air was so thick with cedar-scented steam it was like walking into burning fog. As best he could tell, however, the room was walled with more cane mats above a low earth platform that followed its circumference at sitting height. Four thick cedar trunks halfway in braced the conical ceiling and quartered the cardinal directions. A fire burned in the enter of the packed clay floor—or had; mostly it was embers now: embers that yet gave their heat to a number of large glowing stones, atop which a huge pottery vat of water boiled and bubbled with a violence that would have done Old Faithful proud.

Calvin swallowed hard, took a deep breath—and regretted it, for the heat seared his lungs. *Sweat lodge for certain, then*—as the beads on his skin were already proving. *Could be worse,* he added, one this big couldn't get *too* hot—whereupon he squared his shoulders and stepped in. As was proper upon entering such structures, he moved left, described a clockwise path, and took a place to the right of the entrance. David followed by example, and Alec, after a flurry of hand signs involving securing the door flap, as well.

As so they sat in the northeast quadrant, bathed in a steamy, golden half-light, and waited.

Very quickly the chamber grew dark, filled only with the dim glow of the persistent embers and the sounds of increasingly vocal stomachs and nervous breathing. Occasionally an ember popped or hissed, or a red-hot rock split with an explosive crack.

And still they waited.

Unfortunately, the heat was increasing by the second, the air becoming thick and close; presumably because the smoke hole in the ceiling had been sealed. Already reality was shifting away as Calvin's awareness focused on his senses, on his body and what it was experiencing. The sweat that had beaded him from the start turned to torrents. Streams of it gathered on his forehead and dripped into his lap, or slid like lazy waterfalls down his back, shoulders, and arms. Beside him, he could hear Dave and Alec stirring restlessly, and thanked whatever gods looked after him that they had sense enough not to act up. They'd been in similar situations before, after all, and had read at least *some* of the right books—or Dave had.

If this was what he hoped.

Liquid splashed onto his head—probably their own sweat condensing on the ceiling to drip back down. The air was beyond muggy: hot and dense, with more than a hint of tobacco smoke or resin incense wafting through it that made it doubly hard to inhale. He tried to calm himself, to take shallow breaths, to use as little energy as possible. He sought also to turn his awareness inward, away from the torments of the body to that place were his *self* dwelt, inviolate and secure.

Longer and longer, hotter and hotter; and Calvin found reality shifting ever further away. More than once he started awake, having drifted to sleep—or passed out. Several times he thought he heard voices or drums, or saw lights. But the reflexive twitches those instances prompted brought him sufficiently aware to conclude they were mere tricks of his mind.

Finally, however, he was roused by what he truly could not distinguish between heat on his skin, the twisting in his gut, the tightness in his lungs, or the throbbing in his head—and saw true light: a man-high rectangle to his right, whose glimmering surely marked an exit from this place of torment. And even as he saw it, he felt a breeze—a *cool* breeze—and with it came fresh, clean air. As he rotated his head to clear the stiffness, and breathed deep to fill his tortured lungs, he heard a voice.

One word it said—Uki maybe, or maybe not. And that one word was, "*Come!*"

# Chapter III:
# The Warriors

*(Galunlati—morning—high summer)*

Calvin rose stiffly, saw Alec and David doing likewise, their faces grim and apprehensive beneath their sodden hair and sheen of sweat. He blinked—they all did—as he pushed aside the bear skin and half-staggered up the now-sunlit tunnel and thence back into—not the *real* world, he told himself firmly, but at least one more tangible than that inside his skull.

Asgaya Gigagei, the Red Man of the Lightning, awaited them alone outside the earth lodge, his face as passionless as it had been since they had entered Galunlati. It was morning, presumably the one following their arrival—which meant that Calvin was now officially late for his final go-round with the Willacoochee County authorities regarding the Spearfinger affair.

Not that he could do anything about it. Not that he even wanted to on a morning such as this.

The sun had barely risen, its lower rim still masked by the treetops to the east, and the air—blessed respite—was cool and smelled of honeysuckle. Wisps of fog wove in and out among the more distant trunks like misty dancers tying the night to dawn with cobweb

35

scarves. *Their* clothes, however, were nowhere in sight, which neither surprised nor concerned him. "Follow," the Red Man grunted, striding eastward, where an opening between two hickories marked the beginning of a trail. Having no reasonable choice, they obeyed, first at a walk, then a jog, finally at a steady ground-eating trot. At some point the Red Man began to chant: *"Yo, yo, yo, yo . . ."* Calvin hesitated at first, then joined in, Uki's ban having been on speech, not obscure monosyllables. Apparently the Red Man approved, for he began to blend his tones with Calvin's, and eventually David and Alec chimed in.

Fortunately, they did not have far to go—no more than half a mile. And their destination was precisely what the pattern of the ritual so far had led Calvin to expect. David knew it, too, to judge by the increasing confidence with which he moved. And even Alec, though still tense and edgy, looked marginally more serene.

It was a river. Not the wide one that thundered over Uki's cliffside home, however; this one was no more than thirty feet across and, by the darkness of it, deep. Its banks were mostly overgrown with laurel, save where a strip of coarse-sanded beach marked the terminus of the trail. Calvin didn't need to be told what to do next. With a final "Yo, yo, *yo!*" he darted forward to launch himself into a flat dive straight into midstream.

The water was far colder than he'd expected, and made him gasp and shiver. But even as the cold stabbed into his heat-slackened muscles, it likewise reawakened his senses and brought tingling new life to his skin. For an instant he foundered, then found his depth and trod water while he waited for the others to join him. David did, whooping loudly. Alec followed more calmly, but likewise showed a relieved grin. The Red Man merely watched from a round-topped boulder on the shore—

and lit a long soapstone pipe with a cedar stem. The smoke was pink and did not smell of tobacco.

For maybe five minutes they sported there, silent as river rocks but, as they grew accustomed to the frigid water, enjoying themselves nonetheless. Eventually Calvin waded to the shallows, where he made a stab at scraping a day's worth of dirt off his body and at untangling his badly snarled hair. When the Red Man motioned them back onto the beach, the sun had cleared the trees and was warm on their skin. And by the time they had jogged another quarter mile—still chanting "Yo, yo, yo, yo . . ."—Calvin, at least, was quite dry. Eventually he realized that their cadences had merged with a pounding of drums that grew louder as they approached the lodge.

But the place they returned to was not that from which they had departed—not hardly! Instead of a small clearing centered by a single mound, he stared down from a low ridge at an open area of perhaps ten acres, enclosed by a palisade of sharpened, head-high stakes. A little way inside rose the east slope of the nearest of the four-sided earthwork mounds that marked the cardinal directions around a flat courtyard of roughly one acre, in the center of which stood a single wooden pole, easily twelve feet high and capped by what was likely a bear skull. Each mound was maybe fifty yards on a side, and all bore on their summits thatch-roofed, wattle-and-daub structures that Calvin assumed were temples—assuming this was some sort of ceremonial complex, which it almost had to be. The presence of staircases leading up the mounds' inner sides reinforced that suspicion.

He had never seen this particular place before, but it smacked of several historical sites in his own world: Etowah over near Rome, Georgia, for one; Kolomoki down by Albany, for another; Town Creek out past Charlotte, for a third.

But those were reconstructions; at least in part, this looked . . . not lived in, but perhaps *maintained*.

"This is *Otalwatadjo*," the Red Man said. "The Place at the Navel of the Earth. It is the center of Galunlati. Enter Otalwatadjo from the East." And with that he stepped into the woods and was gone.

Uki met them at the designated point—which was simply an overlapping of the walls like the entrance to a spiral. But where before the shaman had been simply clad, now he wore an elaborate headdress of white feathers that looked like egret, with more frothy plumes depending from quilled and painted bands around his arms and legs, while a complexity of lesser ornaments made mostly of incised conch shell clicked and winked from his ears and nose, at his throat, wrist, and ankles, and among the waving feathers. He also sported a gray-and-white finger-woven sash. Wordlessly, though with a ghost of a smile, he gestured to them to follow. Sighing, they fell in behind him and marched (still keeping time to the beat of the unseen drums) up the southern mound.

It was not all that high, but the pitch was steep, and Calvin's calves tightened painfully as he trudged up the split-log stair. The summit was level and grassy, maybe sixty feet on a side, and centered by one of the thatch-roofed buildings. A single opening faced the head of the stair. They dared it, entering a garage-sized room lit by four torches fixed to the four wooden pillars that stabilized the pitch-poles that supported the roof. A fire blazed in the center of the floor, fed by logs set along the primary axes, burning where they met.

Calvin bowed toward it, in obeisance to Sacred Flame, but as he raised his head, Uki stepped past him to pause before a low carved box of cedar wood set against the far wall. His body blocked Calvin's view, but when he turned back around, he held a pottery jar the size of a man's empty skull. "This is the fat of Yanu, the Bear,"

he said. "Annoint yourselves until Yanu's strength con-
ceals every trace of your paleness." Whereupon, he set
the jar between the bewildered young men. It contained
some sort of foul-smelling, red-tinged ointment.

Calvin squatted beside it, sniffed it, and winced at the
strong animal musk. But this was no time for shirking.
Rolling his eyes at his companions, he scooped up a
handful and smeared it across his chest. It was disturbingly warm.

The next few moments were a comedy of nervous
embarrassment as they slathered themselves from head
to foot until they were gleaming in the flickering light,
their skins now faintly scarlet.

Uki inspected them for a long ambiguous moment,
then returned to the chest. This time when he faced
them, he clutched three white leather bags, fringed with
engraved shell discs and egret feathers. "Take now the
first rewards of silence, of suffering, and of patience,"
he intoned as he passed them one each. Calvin opened
the drawstring that bound his and fumbled inside. His
fingers brushed soft leather. But there was more. He sat
down and rummaged about in earnest.

The first thing he drew out was his medicine bag; the
second, his uktena scale necklace. Next came a long strip
of white leather with thongs along either side that proved
to be a loincloth similar to Uki's, though shorter and
less ornamented. There was also a pair of low, pucker-
toed moccasins. He studied them briefly, then eased
them on, stood, and secured the loincloth about his
waist, noting that his friends had been similarly gifted.
When they had finished, Uki nodded an impassive, mute
approval and motioned them back outside.

The glare made Calvin squint, as they descended to
the court at the bottom. The drums were still pounding,
too: still invisible, but louder and with an indefinable
note of celebration infecting their rhythm. Calvin

couldn't stop his gaze from darting from one mound-top temple to another. But nowhere could he see anyone save Uki, who stood like a strange white bird at the crest of the southern stair.

Abruptly, the drumming shifted tempo, and this time along with it Calvin caught a shimmer of voices: the high, clear tones of women. *"Yo He Wah!"* they sang. *"Yo He Wah!"* over and over, hypnotically. He didn't recognize the language.

But he certainly recognized the singers! For just as the sun cleared the roof of the eastern temple, four young women danced into view from behind it, their slow, shuffling steps those of what Calvin knew from attending pow-wows was called a stomp dance. The first and last held turtle-shell rattles, with more clumped like barnacles around their ankles. These he identified with an impossible to suppress shudder as Uki's sisters, the Serpent-Women (he'd heard no other name for them). Both were almost as tall as their brother and as white-skinned. They had black hair, too, but Calvin knew that it was false, that beneath their waist-long tresses their heads were as bald as pumpkins. They wore kilts of snow white leather, but went bare-breasted—and would have been impossibly enticing, had their mouths not been bracketed by the gaping maws of tattooed serpents, the bodies of which curved around those breasts to sting the nipples with their tails.

And the middle two . . . could only be Liz and Sandy, clad much like their companions, if somewhat more modestly, with knee-length feather capes fastened around their chests. And they really *were* singing, right along with the Serpent-Women. More to the point, neither looked at all uneasy. Indeed, Sandy, in particular, looked like she was having a hard time not grinning, as if she knew something Calvin didn't—which she undoubtedly did. Liz's eyes sparkled as well, and Calvin thought she looked fine indeed, with her red hair set off by the white feather cape. Dave was a damned lucky guy.

The worst was over, then—he hoped. Why else would Liz and Sandy be carrying on so, perfectly relaxed as they were?

" . . . *Yo He Wah! Yo He Wah! YO HE WAH!*"

Three final beats of a drum, as the women ranged themselves at the foot of Uki's mound . . . then silence.

—Broken, from the North, by a jingling of bells.

Calvin nudged David with his elbow, and the three boys spun about—to see, standing at the top of the northern mound's stairs, the disquieting figure of Asgaya Sakani, the Blue Man of the North. He was dressed much like Uki, save that his clothing and feather ornaments were the blue of lizard tails, jays, and herons, accented with discs of mica and incised slate. In his right hand he bore an arm-long length of azure wood Calvin identified as an *atasi*, or war club.

"*Sikwa Unega!*" Asgaya Sakani cried. "White 'Possum, whom men in the Lying World name David Sullivan! Is it you that stands before me, arrayed for war, yet weaponless?"

Calvin was relieved to hear David reply clearly, "*Siyu, adewehiyu*: it is I!"

"Sikwa Unega," Asgaya Sakani continued, "was it you who came to Galunlati, where you had never been, and where your kind are no longer welcome, baring no weapon save a simple stick of wood?"

"It was."

"And was it you who fought the great uktena that threatened the peace of Walhala? Was it you who, when your friend was wounded nigh unto death, ventured alone to the Lake Atagahi, where you fought Yanu Tsunega and won the water which healed that friend? And was it you who put an end to a war in the land of the

Nunnehi that made Nunda Igeyi burn hot across Galunlati?''

"It . . . was," David said meekly.

"These are the deeds of great warriors," the Blue Man went on. "And by a warrior's name should you therefore be known! Henceforth you will be known as *Yanu-degahnehiha*: He-Wrestles-Bears! May warriors in every Land hear that name and despair!"

And with that, he strode down from his high place until he was an arm's length from David. "Wits are a mighty weapon," he said. "But a warrior must rely on his strength of arm as well." And with that, he passed David the war club. David took it awkwardly, but Calvin could see he was grinning like his namesake.

Asgaya Sakani studied him for a moment, then reached around and clamped his left hand briefly on David's bare shoulder. David flinched, and his eyes widened, but he did not cry out. "*Iaaai!*" the Blue Man whooped, and withdrew, staring at David as if awaiting some reply.

"*Iaaai!*" Calvin yelled, to fill the nervous void, and because it seemed right. After a moment, Alec followed. Finally David responded as well. "*Iaaai!*" he cried. "*Iaaai!* Hear me, Asgaya Sakani, and all of Galunlati. I am . . . Yanu-Degahnehiha!"

Calvin relaxed. They'd had no coaching on this, but as best he could tell, Dave had winged the right response. Or at least Asgaya Sakani looked pleased, before he turned and ascended the northern stair.

When he reached the summit, a second jingling sounded, this time to the West. As one they faced that way.

The Black Man stood atop the mound there: Asgaya Gunnagei, Chief of Usunhiyi, the Darkening Land. His loincloth still bore slick black fur, the feathers he wore were black, and his ornaments were of jet, obsidian, and raw iron. He too clutched an atasi.

"*Tsulehisanunhi!*" he shouted. "You, whom the Lying World names Alexander McLean! Is it you that stands before me arrayed for war but weaponless?"

"It is!" Alec said, far more forcefully than was his wont.

"And was it you who likewise came to Galunlati, though you fear to fare in such Lands? And yet you came, because your friends had need of you?"

"It . . . was." Alec sounded uncertain, and Calvin had a good idea why, though this was not the time to think on such things.

"Tsulehisanunhi, was it your spear that slew the great uktena when no other weapon could? Was it you who felt the fire of its poison and well nigh died by that, so that I thought to have you as my guest in Tsusginai?"

Alec's expression darkened. "It was."

"And did you likewise master the ulunsuti, and thereby help restore Nunda Igeyi, and thus save Galunlati?"

"I did."

"It is good that you did!" Asgaya Gunnagi cried. "For by those acts you mark yourself a warrior indeed, and by a warrior's name shall you hereafter be called: *Uktena-dehi*: He-Killed-An-Uktena! May warriors in every Land hear that name and tremble!"

The ritual that followed was the same as before. The Black Man descended, conferred the club, and clapped Alec on the back with his left hand—prompting a startled yip that provoked a frown from Asgaya Gunnagei before he whooped.

Fortunately, Alec recovered enough to respond properly, as Calvin and David added their cries to his.

By now Calvin was primed for what passed next. But

the jingling came not from the South, as he expected, but from the East.

He spun about and saw Asgaya Gigagei, the Red Man of the Lightning, clad as the others, though in scarlet, and likewise grasping an atasi.

"Edahi!" he shouted. "You who were named at birth Calvin Fargo McIntosh! Is it you who stand before me arrayed for war yet weaponless?"

"*Siyu, adewehiyu!* It is I!" Calvin called back with a grin.

The Red Man raised an eyebrow. "Was it you, Edahi, who sought the way of Ani-Yunwiya, though your father would have denied you that part of your soul?"

"It was!"

"And was it you who came to Galunlati and contrived the slaying of the great uktena? Was it you who first pierced its side, and thus awakened it?"

"It was!"

"Was it you who then fared to the burning sands at the edge of my Quarter so that you might aid your Nunnehi friend, and dared the perilous return alone?"

"It was!"

"Was it you who aided these others in fixing Nunda Igeyi once more in its proper place?"

"It was!"

"And—"

But a jingling interrupted, from the South. Calvin glanced that way uncertainly—and saw Uki, dressed as before with the addition of a club similar to the others.

"Edahi!" Uki cried fiercely. "You whom I, Asgaya Tsunega, whom you know as Hyuntikwala Usunhi, claim as friend and apprentice; is it you who comes before me arrayed for war yet weaponless?"

"It is—adewehiyu!"

Whereupon Uki frowned. "Was it you, Edahi," he began, "who studied my arts and my learning for more than a year, though it cost you great pain to fare to the place of my teaching?''

"It was!''

Uki's face turned even grimmer. "And, Edahi, was it you who then used those arts in the Lying World to open a gate to this Land?''

Something about Uki's face and tone made Calvin's heart skip a beat. "It . . . was.''

"And was it *you*,'' Uki asked louder, "who by creating that gate allowed Utlunta, whom your kind call Spearfinger, to enter the Lying World where she did not belong? Was it *you* who admitted one there who slew a woman who had done you no harm, and likewise your sire and a young man to whom you were beholden, and also a girl-child, whose brother befriended you? There, in that place where friendship is as strong as clan or kin?''

"I—''

"*And*,'' Uki thundered, "was it *you* who took the fault of all that upon yourself, as a warrior should? Was it you who tracked Utlunta, and shot her with arrows, and fought her in more shapes than one? Was it you who discovered her dread of water and drowned her at last, so that she is no longer a threat to the Lying World?''

Calvin's reply was no more than a whisper. "It was.''

Uki's eyes flashed fire. *"Was it then* you *who by this showed the men of the Lying World things they should not have seen and let them know things it is not good for Galunlati that they know?''*

Calvin could not reply. It was true. All of it, the bad with the good—and almost as much bad as good. Indeed, had he not overstepped his bounds the first time, though for a good cause, none of the rest would have happened.

*"Was it?''* Uki demanded?

"It was. I . . . wish it wasn't—but it's true."

Uki did not continue, but Calvin saw him exchange glances first with the Red Man, then with the Blue and Black.

"Well," he said at last, "whatever errors you have made, you are nevertheless a great warrior, and by a warrior's name should you be known. Therefore, you shall bear the name—"

"—*Nunda-unali'i*: Friend-of-the-Sun!" Asgaya Gigagei interrupted. "This shall you be called in Galunlati!"

"—*Utlunta-dehi*: He-Killed-Spearfinger!" Uki countered. "That shall be his name in the Lying World!"

*"And may warriors in both Lands hear that name with dread!"*

And as one Asgaya Gigagei and Asgaya Tsunega strode down from their mounds and caught Calvin between them. Each presented an atasi, one red, one white. Each clapped him on the back.

—Whereupon he realized why David had flinched and Alec had cried out, for that touch bit into his flesh like the hottest fire or the coldest ice. It was like being branded, or stung by hornets, or pressed by sub-zero metal. But as quickly as it came it vanished, leaving an itchy tingle.

"*Iaaaii!*" Uki and Asgaya Gigagei whooped as one.

"*Iaaaii!*" Calvin echoed. "Know, all of Galunlati, that I am Nunda-unali'i and likewise that I am Utlunta-dehi!"

"And that you are all great warriors!" the chiefs of the Quarters roared together.

*So what happens now?* Calvin wondered, as he watched Uki return to the top of his mound. By tradition there ought to be celebrating: singing, dancing . . . feasting—certainly that, after a day-long fast.

And perhaps there would be, for the drumming commenced again, and this time he saw who did it. There at the limits of the square ground a host of shadowy figures stood, each no taller than his waist, each dark-skinned and black-haired, clad in skins and feathers. Mostly he saw bright eyes and the flash and flicker of hands that beat with uncanny speed upon small drums.

"*Iaaai!*" came matching female whoops behind him, and Calvin turned to see Sandy and Liz rushing toward them to gift them first with hugs, then kisses.

"Yuk," Liz grunted, as she released David abruptly. "You're all—"

"—greasy," David finished with a laugh. "It's—"

"Warriors!" a shout broke in, from the South. Calvin looked up from smooching Sandy to see Uki once more at the top of his mound. "Warriors! Hear me! Tradition demands we celebrate. *Tradition* demands we feast; it demands we dance and sing, smoke and drink the White Drink! And yet that cannot be!"

"Warriors!" cried Asgaya Gigagei, from the East: "Many fine deeds have you accomplished, and much have you done to be admired. Yet these things have not always served Galunlati; some have threatened it! And this is *not* cause for celebration!"

"Warriors," echoed Asgaya Sakani in the North. "Gifts we have given you, as was your right. Yet gifts we withhold as well, and the chiefmost gifts we withhold are twofold. The first is that for a year you are all forbidden to come to Galunlati. If during that time you act as warriors and honor the trust we have given you by bringing you here, we will call you here again for the celebration that is due.

"And," he went on, "the second thing we withhold is our involvement in your affairs. You have all been gifted—some would say cursed—with knowledge few in your Land possess. Edahi, you in particular have access to arts none of your kind can claim—which you

have used more than you should. That knowledge, and
that power, could do great damage should they fall into
unwise hands—of which there are very many in the Lying World. You must be accountable for both—without
recourse to Lands beyond your own.''

"Know therefore, Edahi,'' the Red Man took up
again, ''that you must be much more careful how and
to whom and of what kind you make promises. Know
that you must be lord of your own mind and acts, and
accountable for your own thoughts and deeds.''

"And know, most particularly,'' Uki continued, ''that
the gift I made you of the scale of the great uktena, by
which you are able to shift your shape, may not be used
indefinitely. It permits but a certain number of changes,
and none can know that number. Be warned, then, that
if you continue to put on the shape of beasts, you may
find yourself one forever.''

"Therefore, warriors,'' came a final voice, though not
a shout but a whisper: the whisper of the Black Man of
the West. ''Therefore, I say, we send you from our fire
laden with gifts, but hungry; though with hope you will
return in triumph.''

"And therefore,'' shouted all four at once, as they
raised their hands above their heads, ''we bid you good
fortune, and bid you—''

"—*BE GONE!*''

Or those were the words Calvin thought he caught the
beginning of before four bolts of lightning sent them first
into brightness, then into blindness, deafness, and pain,
and then oblivion.

The sun was setting when they awoke, sprawled on
the ground now, but once more facing the outcrop behind David Sullivan's barn. All still wore the garments
of Galunlati, and the boys still clutched their new weapons.

Their mundane clothing was with them, too, down to Sandy's watch and Alec's earring.

Of the effigy of David that had strode from the rock face the only sign was a pile of pebbles mixed with sand.

"I'm . . . hungry," Alec gasped nervously as he found his way to his feet. "I wonder if there's anything left from the reception?"

"I wonder if Darrell's sober yet?" a very pale David added.

"And I wonder how long we've been gone," Liz inserted with a shiver.

"A couple of hours, looks like," Sandy managed, glancing at the sun. "And me . . . well, I just wonder."

Calvin was silent, but thoughtful, as he fingered his uktena scale.

They changed clothes in the barn.

They ate very well that night.

And a year passed marked by nothing stranger than growing up.

# PART TWO

---

# *Shadowed Warrior*

# Chapter IV:
# Divination

*(east of Whidden, Georgia—
Thursday, June 14—11:35 P.M.)*

Don Scott wondered which he was going to run out of first: endurance, nerve, or blood.

The latter, at present, seemed most likely, as he paused in the moonlit forest trail to slap his cheeks and forearms for the third time in as many minutes. He supposed he'd learn one day that the 'skeeters in his neck of the south Georgia woods considered his own special blend of O-positive the equivalent of an inch-thick sirloin from McDevitt's Grille down in Whidden. Or, more accurately, like that grade-A 'shine old man Gilmore ran off in his still out in the swamp—the stuff his latest stepdad, Robert Richards, had let him sample exactly once, the day he'd turned fifteen.

But why in the world did they have to choose him? He was just a skinny burr-haired kid, shorter than most of the guys in the ninth grade at Whidden High, and nothing special any other way except that his little sister's friends said he had great eyelashes.

Make that his *late* little sister, he amended, as a lump

rose in his throat. She'd been dead four days shy of a year now, Allison had, and—

*No!* He couldn't deal with that—not now, not here. Awful though his sister's death had been, horrible as the ensuing week had become, a far worse thing had happened to him that night—something so terrible he refused to even think about it until he had no choice but to think about it, which he wouldn't let himself do until time and place were perfect.

*So* terrible it had made him sneak out of his mom's rural ranch house in the middle of the night to try to set it straight.

If nerves and fatigue didn't get him first.

Actually, he wasn't much worried about the latter. Or wouldn't have been except that for the last month or so he'd been having trouble sleeping, and felt tired and yawny all the time. His mom had noticed it, of course, and had doubled his dose of vitamins and threatened to take him to the doctor if he didn't perk up—which he hadn't. It wasn't that he felt bad, though, more that he simply didn't *feel*. It was as if he was in a fog all the time, and more than once he'd found himself having to concentrate to answer even the simplest questions, as though speaking was no longer pure reflex. Anxiety, one of his mom's friends had opined. Stress. Nerves. Yeah, sure.

Whatever it was, the effect was that a fairly short trek through the woods to Iodine Creek was making him as tired as an all-day Boy Scout hike. He was even *panting*, dammit! (Sweating went without saying, in south Georgia in the summer). And this route had never made him do that.

Maybe it *was* nerves. Maybe it was the fact that if he relaxed control even a fraction he could easily scare himself silly.

God knew the woods were enough to accomplish that

by themselves. Oh, sure he'd lived in them all his life, had trod every deer trail and logging road for five miles roundabout, and camped by every creek and river. But tonight it all seemed different. Perhaps it was the moon: impossibly heavy and yellow, and so bright he could read the Nike logo on his sneakers without bending over, and pick out Dexter Holland on his red Offspring T-shirt without squinting. Or possibly it was the breeze—steady in spite of the tangle of palmettos, deer berries, and thorny wait-a-minute vines that grew so close among the sprawling live oaks they came close to walling in the trail. Certainly that was part of it, because even the slightest stirring of the air made the tendrils of Spanish moss that festooned every limb and twig sway like the ghosts of the Yamasee Indians who'd lived here until they'd walked into the Okefenokee and disappeared, or the Spanish soldiers who'd died at Bloody Marsh a couple of counties over.

Unfortunately, he very much feared that . . . *difference* was because it was close to the anniversary of *that* night, and perhaps because *this* night knew he was going to attempt some magic.

But he wouldn't think about that either—until he got to *that* place. If he thought about it—destination or intention, either—he might chicken out and have to spend another day getting re-psyched, never mind having to sneak out all over again.

Sighing, Don gave his arms and neck a final quick swatting, added his bare legs for good measure, then resettled his backpack and started off once more. Fortunately, the trail was straight here, and wide enough for the moonlight to reach the ground, so he decided to jog. Maybe it'd help burn off his case of nerves; perhaps if he focused on his pulse, his breathing, and the pounding of his feet on the sandy soil, he could forget.

And for five minutes actually managed to. Which, unhappily, only hastened his arrival—and then he *had* to recall.

He paused to catch his breath and steel himself one last time. Iodine Creek lay ahead. He could already smell its brackish, tannin-dark waters, and now caught the faintest glimpse of its surface glittering among the cattails along the farther bank. Between him and the nearer shore was only a thin screen of palmettos and a pair of live oaks that framed the trail like a gateway. He hesitated there, feeling the soil soft as flour beneath his sneaks. Once again a lump rose in his throat, even as a chill danced across his body—for his subconscious had already reacted to what his eyes only then acknowledged.

It was still there—sort of—between the right-hand oak and one of its water-bound kin: the lean-to he and his best friend, Michael Chadwick, had built two summers back so they could camp out all night and not be rained on.

The one where they'd talked about school and parents and sex, where they'd wrestled and had tickle fights and compared hard-ons and drunk stolen beer on the sly, where they'd discussed forestry school and video games and CD's and *Dungeons and Dragons* and which girls of their acquaintance were most likely to relieve them of their troublesome virginity.

The lean-to where Michael had died.

*No!* Don corrected. *Where he'd watched Mike be murdered.*

Almost he bolted at that, for the memory pounced upon him with the stealth of one of the panthers that were supposed to be extinct in Georgia and were not. Shoot, if he squinted a little, he could still see it! That pile of palmetto bayonets could easily be old Mike in his sleeping bag. And that broken branch lodged beside the shelter could almost be *her*: that old witch his friend

Calvin had called Spearfinger, who had lulled him into paralysis with that eerie song of hers, holding him thus immobile while she calmly stuck her preposterously long finger into Mike's side and with casual deliberation slowly picked out his liver a tidbit at a time and ate it raw. Mike had never awakened from that. And though Calvin had killed Spearfinger a day later, Don had never truly awakened from it either.

Not many people his age had had friends die. And fewer yet had *seen* them die. No!—had been forced to *watch* them die. That was the worst thing Don could imagine: having to stand frozen in his tracks and see the person he loved best in the world, even including his mom and sis, be slowly drained of life and not be able to stop it. It wasn't like he saw Mike at school one day, and then that night somebody called and said he was dead. That would have been a clean break, but without the force of finality because he had not witnessed the transition. But to observe the process, and to *know* . . .

He'd even missed the funeral—had still been in shock, the doctor said. And his mom had been so traumatized herself by the death of his sister (whom he'd never much liked because she never liked him, and besides she wasn't a boy and didn't *understand* him, as Mike had done instinctively) that she'd never taken time to talk to him about the loss of his best friend until the wall of his sorrow had grown too thick and high for anyone to breach.

And now, very simply, Don wanted to make his peace with Mike. He wanted to see him, and talk to him, and apologize to him, and tell him that he was sorrier than anybody had ever been or could be that he had not been able to save his life.

Not that he hadn't tried to contact him before, of course. Shoot, he'd paid the fortune-teller at the Willacoochee County Fair a month's allowance for a seance.

He'd asked her to call up his friend, but hadn't told her the name 'cause he didn't trust her. And she'd let him down. Oh, she'd got Mike's name right, but everything else was wrong, so Don knew she was either a fraud or that some other Mike than *his* Mike had come calling in her crystal ball.

Since then . . . Well, one of his buddies had taken him to a witch-woman in the swamp who'd read his tea leaves, but she'd only mumbled about cars and girl-friends, which every guy his age wanted. He'd even bought a deck of tarot cards at a shop in Savannah and by slow degrees puzzled through their intricacies and double-talk. He'd brought them along tonight, too, just in case. But even they had been unable to put him in touch with his bro.

His friends had said he was nuts—but Don knew they were wrong. *He* had witnessed magic, had himself been snared by a paralysis spell and watched a shapechanging ogress devour his best friend's liver. But even more spectacularly, he'd seen his Cherokee friend, Calvin, change into an eagle and assorted other critters! And if the world allowed for spell-songs and shape-shifters, somewhere it surely should admit some art that would let him talk to Michael one last time.

And what better place than here, where Mike had died? And what better time than tonight, when the moon was full and the anniversary of Mike's death but four nights away? He probably should've chosen the day it-self, but he didn't think he was up to that, and his mom would be watching him like a hawk anyway. Besides, and much more practically, the forecast called for show-ers then.

Taking a deep breath, Don swallowed hard, then squared his shoulders and strode into the campsite. He scanned the sliver of open earth atop the riverbank—not much larger than two cars side by side—for a staging area, and finally chose a waist-high stump at the western end. His stomach growled as he plopped down there, reminding him yet again that he hadn't eaten in over a day—doubtless another reason he was tired. That had been some trick, too: fasting without his mom being the wiser. But she was preoccupied with her own sorrows—as usual—and didn't think it odd that he took his meals to his room—and flushed them down the john on the way.

But it was what you were supposed to do, darn it! It was what Calvin had done. And it was what it said to do in the Book.

The Book . . . a worn old pamphlet on Cherokee magic he'd found in the Hinesville library. He had it now, and the other things he needed. He unslung the backpack and drew them out: four sticks as long as his forearm, each stained a different color, but all made of wood from a lightning-blasted tree, which the Book said were strong medicine. Next he produced a string: a two-foot length of cordage twisted from the inner bark of a North Carolina hickory he'd found on the same autumn leaf viewing trip as he'd got the most important object: the stone. The old man at the rock shop up at Asheville had called it *cairngorm*, but he knew it was simply a perfect, finger-long crystal of smoky quartz.

And if he was lucky, it would help him contact Mike. If not . . . well, he had one final ace up his sleeve. But since Mike had been killed by a Cherokee monster, Don figured a Cherokee means of reaching him might succeed where others hadn't and ought to be attempted first.

So it was that a minute later Don had shucked his clothes and stood naked in the center of the clearing. He felt a little silly doing that, and it wasn't specifically called for, but he was a white boy, and he wanted whatever powers he invoked to take him as seriously as possible, and the less that branded him as Caucasian, the

more likely he figured they'd be to pay him heed. Besides, in a sense he was making a blood sacrifice—to
judge by the mosquitoes already homing in, which
seemed to have invited the neighborhood gnats as well.
He'd be itching like hell tomorrow.

In the meantime, he ignored them as he knelt and
inscribed a two-foot circle in the sand with the red stick.
That concluded, he used the blue one to divide it into
quarters oriented north and south, east, and west. The
black stick limned a second circle around the first, and
the white stick drew lines parallel to the enclosed cross.
That concluded, Don stuck the sticks into the ground at
the cardinal points: red to east, blue to north, black to
west, and white to south.

Pausing only to wipe his hands on his well-nibbled
thighs, Don returned to his pack and pulled out three
more sticks. Again the wood was from a lightning-
blasted tree, but this time it was from a red cedar, one
of the plants of vigilance and also one that grew in
graveyards thereabouts. One stick was straight and
roughly two feet long, the others Y-shaped and six
inches shorter. These last he planted on the north/south
axis, then laid the third across them.

Satisfied with his work so far, he fished out two final
objects: a lump of charcoal, and a square of denim from
a pair of jeans Mike had cut off at Don's house. The
former he placed on the cross's western arm, the latter
on the east. An instant only it took to loop the cordage
around the crystal and suspend it from the cross-stick,
and he began. Holding his breath, he knelt at the south
side of the circle, then slowly repeated the formula he
had memorized from the Book. He did it in Cherokee
first—or his version of that tongue, for he had no idea
how to pronounce the odd-looking words, but he hoped
the powers would understand his intent:

*Sge! Ha-nagwa hatunganiga Nunya Watigei, ga-husti tsuts-kadi nigesunna. Ha-nagwa dungihyali. Agiyahusa aginalii, ha-ga tsun-nu iyunta datsiwaktuhi. Tla-ke aya akwatseliga. Donald Larry Scott digwadaita.*

And then, just to be sure, he did it again in English.

*Listen! Ha! Now you have drawn near to hearken, O Brown Rock, you never lie about anything. Ha! Now I am about to seek for it. I have lost a friend and now tell me about where I shall find him. For is he not mine? My name is Donald Larry Scott.*

Eight times Don intoned the formula: twice from each prime direction. And when he had finished, he reached over the pattern he had inscribed and began to swing the crystal in a circle.

Round and round it went, faster and faster—a bit faster than he expected, in fact. But inevitably the pace slackened, and as it did, the circle tightened into an ellipse.

And as the crystal slowed, so did Don's breathing—and so, it seemed, did the wind, until not a limb swayed or twig twitched or leaf shivered. Chills raced across Don's ribs. The dark hairs on his forearms and legs and the nape of his neck prickled, and his skin went rough with goosebumps.

Slower and slower, and as Don's breathing and the sighing of the wind fell silent, so did the rest of the night. Tree frogs ceased their chanting, mosquitoes and gnats their insistent buzz. The gator that had been bellowing in the nearby swamp broke off in midnote. And the crickets and cicadas stopped their contentious chatter. The only sound was the slapping of the creek against its banks and the non-noise of distant wings high above.

Slower and slower, and now the stone swung in a line, due east and west. But though Don had carefully knotted the string exactly over the center of the circle, he could not help but note that the arc tended to stretch a little further on its western transit—enough so that he could actually see the twig rock that way in the forks.

Which meant that Mike was dead.

Which he already knew.

What he did not know and, because of his contact with Calvin, had cause to wonder, was *how* dead.

Sighing, Don removed the charcoal and fabric (had Mike been alive the stone should have pointed toward the latter), moved to the south, and repeated the formula he had used before. Once more, too, he spun the crystal.

And again, after a nerve-wrackingly long time, it tended west.

Which only reinforced what it had told him already. For west, so the Book said, lay Tsusginai, the Ghost Country, the Cherokee land of the dead.

Yet that was not the direction in which Mike's grave lay, for his father had had him cremated and the ashes scattered on the Atlantic, thirty miles to the *east*. Which meant that what remained of him as a conscious entity resided where the sun set.

And so, Don Scott faced that way and called out very softly, ''Mike? I need to talk to you.''

Silence . . .

Silence . . .

Still that unnatural silence, as if all the woods wished and waited with him.

Silence . . . save for the lapping of the creek . . .

And then, abruptly, a splash: a crystalline sound, the perfect noise to focus the night. The ground thrummed softly beneath Don's feet, and the wind resumed. But this time it carried a thread of melody.

Don tensed automatically. The last time he'd heard

music in this place it had been Spearfinger's terrible chant: *Uwelanitsiku. Su sa sai!*

But this time it was the sound of a wooden flute, and the tune one Don recognized. It was Mike's favorite song: Deep Purple's "Smoke On the Water." But somehow, rendered thusly, as a long slow sigh upon the wind, it acquired a plaintive quality, a thin, reedy eeriness fraught with pain and loss.

Tears started in Don's eyes as he rose. But just as he did, the string gave a twitch and suddenly shifted axes: north—toward the creek.

Don gulped, for part of him knew he ought not to be fooling around with such forces as he was. And another part knew he'd expected no result at all and was crazy to think he'd found one now, and a third part told him he was on the edge of some life-changing event and that he'd be well advised to fling the crystal in the river and run like hell and let the harsh light of day burn away whatever had answered his summons there in the Georgia night.

Instead, he eased toward the bank and looked down.

Iodine Creek glittered like a sky of black glass fractured by reflected lightnings, yet showing, in the calmer places, the shadow-sisters of the summer stars.

But he could see nothing more—yet the song persisted, no louder, but somehow clearer for all that, and coming, he was certain, from the water.

Grunting, Don scrambled down the chest-high bank to pause at the bottom, balanced on a root that curved down from the oak above. He squatted there, a pale naked wraith of a white boy, shimmered into silver by the moon, the only darkness the cap of hair on his head, the sketchy triangle at his groin, and his haunted eyes.

When he looked down he saw his own face mirrored. Clear it was: uncannily so. Grasping the root with one hand, he bent forward for a closer look, and when he did, it seemed the music grew louder and the breeze stirred the stream more vigorously, bending the ripples into patterns he could almost recognize.

And then he saw it! Gradually taking form atop his phantom features was another face: squarer of chin, more stubby of nose, and crowned with unkempt blond hair. The eyes were the color of the creek, and yet he knew they were blue. And then that face, which looked up at him through his own reflection, smiled, and the body that floated beneath it raised a hand.

*"Mike!"* Don Scott whispered—and had no choice but to grin back, and extend a hand in turn.

# Chapter V:
# An Hour Almost Struck

*(near Sylva, North Carolina—*
*Friday, June 15—midnight)*

Calvin was doing something he had vowed never to do: he was wishing, very hard, for rain.

Yeah, if a bank of clouds would just come rolling in from over the Smokys to the west, they could blank out the persistent moonbeams slanting in through the new bedroom skylight of Sandy's hillside cabin like ramps laid in place for day. Then—maybe—he could sleep. As it was, the rays found the knotty pine walls far too easily, and awoke strange images there: here a tree, there an eagle or uktena, yonder a leering booger-face like one of the Davy Arch masks that hung, interspersed with handwoven baskets, from the exposed top plate of the opposite wall. And if he loosed his imagination even a little, the rays would conjure a crooked, grinning hag's face—or, incongruously, a badger. Never mind what happened when they touched the coverlet—undisturbed now, on Sandy's side, courtesy of a seminar on Bucky-ball over at Chapel Hill, which would claim her until late tomorrow. That was really bad, because the coverlet bore a black-and-white pattern, pirated from M. C.

Escher, that depicted fish flying into birds, each shifting to the other where they met. And shapeshifting was the last thing he wanted to be reminded of just now.

That was the other reason he wanted rain. If clouds brought welcomed darkness, rain would bring a steady sussuration that, again—if he was lucky—might lull him to sleep. Certainly it would give him some focus besides the things that had been troubling him with increasing frequency lately—and looked set to have him tossing and turning and staring at the irksome wall and equally unpromising ceiling most of this night as well.

*If only he hadn't made the promise.* The Red Man had warned him about such things, damn it!—but that caution had come two days late. Oh, it had seemed like the right thing to do at the time—almost exactly a year ago now, at the close of the Spearfinger Affair—but tonight . . . he wondered.

He'd been in south Georgia, then, recovering from one of his and Dave's Otherworld jaunts. He'd intended to hang out there and get his head straight about shapeshifting and such. But *then* he'd been accused of murdering his dad and discovered that Spearfinger was following him in hopes of getting at Dave. And somewhere in there he'd fallen in with a pair of Florida runaways named Robyn—that was the sister—and Brock. Brock had been just a kid: thirteen and full of attitude and testosterone and curiosity. Unfortunately, he'd also ferreted out the secret Calvin had tried so hard to hide because nobody *could* know such things and view the world the same after.

But Brock had seen him change shape and, like most kids his age, was crazy to know things others didn't. He'd promptly attached himself to Calvin like many lads did to sports heroes and rock stars, and Calvin, unused to being idolized, had enjoyed that adoration. In due time Calvin had literally dissolved Spearfinger—and had a war name and an atasi to prove it (and odd new tattoos on his shoulder blades to mark it: quarter-sized cross-in-circles, surrounded by curving sun's rays). But he'd been unable to dispose of Brock so neatly; and finally, after the dust had settled, Brock had asked him to teach him magic. Calvin hadn't wanted to—even then he knew it was dangerous and had in no wise made him happy—and had told the boy as much: that sure, it *sounded* wonderful, but it was in fact far more a curse and responsibility to be endured than a treat to be enjoyed, and that he suspected Brock wanted it so as to be thought special, when the last thing in the world one ought to do with magic was show off. Still, the kid had looked *so* earnest, and had begged *so* pitifully, that Calvin had promised to meet him back there in Willacoochee County a year from then and teach him one piece of conjury.

And now that year was nearly up, he had a promise to keep, knew he had to keep it—and didn't want to. But, as the Red Man said, promises were not to be taken lightly, especially when they concerned magic, especially when one was an apprentice adewehi.

Not that he'd actually seen Uki in the year since he'd acquired his war name, he hastened to add. Mostly he'd been taking high school equivalency courses at Western Carolina University and learning about the world at large—or the consensus reality most folks assumed was that world, more properly. But he'd been studying other things as well: had read every book on Indians he could find, had started haunting the pow-wow circuit, and had spent what little free time remained learning to identify every single plant and animal in the Appalachian woods, with their real and reputed properties.

That had all been cool. But now rashness had caught up with him, and he was afraid: afraid to fulfill the promise he'd made—and afraid to break it.

Trouble was, Brock showed every sign of holding him

to the very letter of his vow. True, the boy had accompanied his sister to England to escape their abusive step-father and be with her when she delivered the kid the old asshole had got on her. But he'd sent Calvin a series of notes—one per month, like clockwork. The latest had arrived earlier this week: too recently to send a reply. It had been postmarked in York; the message short and to the point:

> *Cal, m'man!*
>
> *Greetings from the motherland—my motherland, anyway. I'm heading out on Saturday for your old home turf—so to speak. I'll see you where I saw you last. Be there or be square! Looking forward to learning lots. Aloha. Make that Siyu!*
> *(I read that in a book!)*
>
> > *Cheers,*
> > *Brock-the-Badger No-Name*

And that was that. Brock assumed he would fulfill his promise and was flying all the way from England to collect.

Calvin therefore had no choice but to oblige.

But if that troublesome lapse of responsibility was giving him grief (and that didn't even count the small matter of what sort of arcana might be *safe* to teach a flaky teen), it was nothing to the other problem that had been deviling him of late.

He had become haunted.

It had been subtle at first, all small signs: a coolness near the winter fire where no drafts could find their way. The scent of tobacco smoke while hunting in the trackless woods. A voice, one ridge over, calling out to Forest.

Unfortunately, Forest was one of his dead father's favorite beagles, now in custody of one of his old man's hunting buddies down in Jackson County, Georgia—not far from where Spearfinger had first appeared, in fact. Which didn't bode well at all.

—Not in light of the sightings. Always at the *between* times they were, sunset or noon, midnight or dawn. A man-shaped shadow on open ground. A deeper darkness among the banks of rhododendron upslope from the cabin. Once, he was certain he'd seen eyes peering from a tree at precisely his dad's height. But whenever he looked closely at any of them, they vanished. Even when he'd squinted through the hole in a water-bored stone, he'd got zip.

And now there were even more tangible signs. He'd leave something lying around—a new-flaked spear point, say, or a handful of porcupine quills. And the next time he looked for them they'd be gone. It was always his stuff, too: things that were part of his Cherokee heritage. He'd always found them—so far. But every time—*every* time—they'd moved west, as if some odd magnet had drawn them that way. And Calvin knew what lay in that direction. Tsusginai, the Ghost Country, in Usunhiyi, the Darkening Land, realm of the Cherokee dead.

And this week, the displacements had grown even more frequent, the spectral images clearer, so that he now found himself loathe to face the setting sun, because that was where the half-shapes always stood, the point from which the bodiless shadows spread.

And Sunday, he realized with a shudder, was the first anniversary of his father's death! Why hadn't he remembered that? Perhaps because he'd been sort of unstuck in time all spring, and not, for a change, thrall to schedules? Or maybe he hadn't *wanted* to recall.

But *something* evidently, did, for the empty orbits of one of the masks on the wall across from him had suddenly acquired open eyes!

*Wolf clan*, he noted with a start: his own clan, though it had taken him most of last summer to chase down anyone at Qualla Boundary who knew enough of such things—and of Calvin's genealogy—to tell him so.

But now something was taking shape below that mask. It could almost have been another shadow—except that it was slightly too dense, and the moonlight reflected off it a tad too unevenly. And it could easily have been Sandy's Driza-Bone that hung on the brass coat stand next to the door directly above Calvin's outdoor boots—except that was half a yard too far to the right.

Whatever it was had now acquired arms, a suggestion of legs, and an odd sort of three-dimensionality, as it continued to stare at him from the mask that was now much less a mask and far more the likeness of his father: fortyish, square-jawed, and prematurely aged, but still handsome beneath longer hair than Calvin recalled.

Chills stomped across him where he lay propped against the headboard, wishing on the one hand that Sandy would walk in right *now* and by some cogent observation about quarks or cosmic string banish it forever, and on the other hand hoping very hard indeed she would stay gone longer so as not to have her peace of mind disturbed by whatever post-trauma stress Calvin might succumb to.

And so he lay and watched, his skin alive with goosebumps, where it wasn't drowned in the sweat breaking out like pustules across his forehead, chest, and shoulders.

The image was almost complete now, though he couldn't tell skin from clothing, nor what form either might have. A lump plugged his throat as a host of memories flooded back—most of them bad.

He hadn't loved his dad.

A half-blood himself, Maurice McIntosh had tried to

seal off his son from his Cherokee heritage, insisting that being different rarely made one happy, and wanting Calvin to be happy at all costs. That had prompted rebellion, which had led to words, and finally, when Calvin was sixteen, a schism. But there'd been moments of closeness, too; and as Calvin grew older, he regretted more and more that there were a whole host of topics he wanted to discuss with the old man and would never be able to.

But the worst thing was that they'd parted in anger. Calvin's last sight of his dad had been of him standing in the doorway of the ranch house down at Stone Mountain two Christmases back, staring at him accusingly, with an awful mixture of pain and anger branded across his face when Calvin had repeated yet again that no, he was *not* going to move back in, because he still hadn't got his head straight about which world was his: white, or Cherokee.

He'd missed the funeral, of course, first because no one had known where to find him, then because they thought he'd precipitated it—though how a guy barely twenty was supposed to scoop out a grown man's liver without a struggle, he had no idea.

But one thing he *did* know was that if he could see that mask-face just a *little* more clearly it would show the same angry/hurt expression he'd seen on that final holiday.

Fortunately, he couldn't quite get it to focus—yet didn't dare look away. Vainly he tried to think of some formula to banish such things, even as his more rational aspect told him that something which had no substance could wreck no physical harm; that *he* was master of his mind, and no other.

And yet those eyes bored into him—accusing, almost pleading—and now, it seemed, beckoning; as though his dad's shade was trying to convince him that if he would only slip out of bed and come closer, they could reconcile all the guilt that lay between them and give them both peace.

But then Calvin saw something that made him shiver so violently he could actually hear the bed frame creak.

His father was not alone! Another shape accompanied him, a smaller one, whose face had begun as knotholes in the paneling. More shadowy than his father it was, and yet clearer. A boy, he thought: blond, early teens, solidly built and intense. The expression—what Calvin could make of it—could only be described as haunted.

Michael Chadwick! It was Mike Chadwick!—one of the three boys he'd met in south Georgia during the Spearfinger Affair. And the one thing this kid had in common with Calvin's dad was that they had both been killed by that monster!

But Spearfinger was dead herself, and Calvin had been absolved of the blame . . .

Or had he?

Assorted law enforcement agencies had backed carefully away (or been backed away) from a situation too outré to bring to hearing, much less trial. And Uki had told him that while he had done wrong by admitting Spearfinger to this World, he'd balanced that by removing her again.

Except that, apparently, two . . . ghosts . . . ? shades . . . ? spirits . . . ? thought otherwise.

Which didn't make sense either, because Spearfinger had killed *four* people. Present company excluded, she'd also done in a redneck housewife in Jackson County and the ten-year-old sister of Chadwick's best friend, Don. Which, beyond the obvious difference in sex, just didn't jive.

Abruptly, a clock chimed in the greatroom, announcing 1:00 A.M. And with that, the visitations faded, in reverse of how they'd formed, with his father's eyes going last. But as the last echo drifted into silence, he heard a voice, faint but clear, whisper, ''Help us, my son, only you can.''

Whereupon reality reclaimed the night.

For a long time Calvin lay there, flat on his back, staring at the ceiling, watching the shadows of the rafters slide as the moon continued its march. More than once he thought of phoning Sandy at her hotel and trusting to her solid good sense to set him a course that was true. And far more than once he considered making a pot of coffee and sitting up the rest of the night. Surely he could find *something* to distract him until daylight and temporal distance dulled his memory to the point where he could dismiss tonight's occurrence as a dream.

But still the words gnawed at him: ''*Help us, my son, only you can!*''

But how could one help the dead? Shoot, what kind of help did the dead *need*? Where did one go? What did one do?

What was Michael Chadwick doing with his father's shade?

And, drat it, what about his promise to Brock, that was rapidly approaching zero hour?

Well, nothing could be resolved here, and at least two problems had to be resolved, one of them quickly.

But waiting until daylight to leave would increase the odds of Sandy catching him at home (she was an early riser and had a tendency to make check-in calls over her morning coffee). And if that happened, he'd have to lie, which he wouldn't do. Or else there'd be discussions, and *more* delays, and explorations of options he'd already explored in his own mind ad nauseam. And of course she'd want to come along, when he didn't even know where *along* was, or how long it might take to get there. None of which was good for a high school physics teacher who had bills and a mortgage and needed to start short-session summer school in a week herself.

Which left one choice.

Calvin eased out of bed, grateful for the sheepskin rug that muffled even the gentlest of thumps—Sandy was a light sleeper, thus nighttime stealth had become a habit. Then, moving with a silence honed equally by habit and hunting in the woods of more than one World, he spent the next quarter-hour dressing—jeans, black Frye Boots, black T-shirt, black leather jacket, stooping falcon ear-stud—and collecting a minimum of food, money, and gear, including most particularly his two war clubs. A good bit of what he needed was already squirreled away in his motorcycle saddlebags—he'd learned long ago not to rely on having only one of anything crucial, and knew from experience that he tended to hit the road on impulse. Besides, if it came to it, he could live off the land—Lord knew he'd done it before. He'd start off civilized and wing it from there.

So where *was* there? What was to be his destination?

He only knew that it lay to the south: Whidden, Georgia, if he was to deal with Brock in a timely manner.

And along the way lay certain other folk he could consult.

Before he left, he scribbled a note for Sandy and set it on the counter by the sink, signing it with his name in the Cherokee syllabary.

*You're fond of saying it's easier to get forgiveness than permission, so I hope you practice what you preach, 'cause I'm gonna need some heavy-duty forgiving! I've got a couple of problems haunting me that I've got to resolve. But never doubt that I'll come back. Love. He-Goes-About.*

RᏃᏌ

Five minutes later, he rolled his BMW R/80 GS out of the garage, cranked it, and let it mumble along at idle until he'd navigated the steep narrow switchbacks of the rocky pig-trail called 'Coon Hound's Despair—which was also Sandy's drive. The moon was still bright when he glided onto pavement, nor was it all that long until dawn and Target One. And for a while Calvin rode down empty mountain highways, almost like a ghost himself.

# Chapter VI:
# Stealth and Bribery

*(Qualla Boundary, North Carolina—
Saturday, June 16—just before dawn)*

If it had been the kind of night Calvin hated—not for any flaw in the entity itself, but because of what it conjured—it was now the kind of morning he loved.

The air had been clear, the sky a jeweler's spill of stars, when he'd left Sandy's cabin—and it had remained that way throughout the ensuing ride. And though the bike had speed aplenty, he'd chosen a slower pace around the well-banked curves that sparkled like gray snow as they ribboned through the forested peaks that reared rough silhouettes of black and blue, veridian and violet around him. It was less than twenty miles to Target One, and he'd split shortly after 1:00 A.M.. But he tripled the distance by taking the long way round: east on wide, smooth US 23 almost to Asheville, where he'd been seduced by a Waffle House's promise of a wee-hours coffee fix, then back west again along Highway 19, which wound its way in tighter curves and steeper grades through far less traveled country. Twice he saw bears, three times deer, and once had to swerve to miss a meandering 'possum. But no falcons. Which was probably just as well, for though peregrines were his totem, they were also diurnal and tended to haunt the coast. A sighting now would therefore be significant—but he didn't *need* such things to make him wary.

Besides, it was hard to dwell on omens when he could watch morning arrive. It began as a wash of pink at the eastern hem of the sky and a piping of red along treetops and ridge lines, followed by a gradual gauzing of the more distant vistas and deeper valleys as fog awakened to dress the *between* time. It was still a few days shy of summer, but the edge of chill cutting the air served to remind him that every joy carried a ghost of intransience that was close-kin to pain.

His shadow was still stretching long before him in the ruddy predawn light when Calvin rolled into the seat of the Eastern Cherokee commonly *called* Cherokee, but more properly termed Qualla Boundary. In spite of his deliberate delays, it was still earlier than he expected; too early, to be honest. Nothing was open yet, at least not along "The Strip," as locals termed the ugly stretch of bogus log cabins, tourist traps, restaurants of assorted qualities, and gift shops that sold more crafts of Taiwanese tribes than Native American.

Fortunately he found an all-night burger joint a block off the main drag and got a booster shot of caffeine there, adding an order to go: double hash browns and breakfast biscuits—two each of sausage, ham, steak, and bacon. Those safely bagged and bundled into his jacket, he kicked the bike awake and rode north past the Museum of the Cherokee toward Smoky Mountain National Park. After a few miles, he turned left to follow a narrow, rutted road that angled sharply up a ridge before leveling after an eighth of a mile to flank it above a steep-sided valley.

A further quarter mile up the hollow he passed an arch of walnut trees, rattled across a wooden bridge, turned left around a laurel hedge—and found himself facing a small but well-maintained ranch house perched between a frown of mountain and an acre of neatly mown lawn. A cinder-block structure to the right disgorged an assortment of cars in various stages of dismantlement—all of them Thunderbirds from the sixties, save a single hawk-nosed '71, which, atypically, looked as if it might actually run. Calvin grinned at that: some things never changed—including a certain person's obsession.

No lights showed in the house, which didn't disturb him, since it wasn't his destination anyway. *That* lay to the left, where a tiny, weathered log cabin snuggled between the laurel, the mountain, a creek, and the yard—rather like a determinedly poor relation. It was roofed with split-wood shingles, and the full-width porch was rough-planed boards. The single door was flanked by two windows, while numerous strings of drying vegetation hung from the rafters and along the walls. It might have been a scene from the last century—except for yet another T-Bird glaring around one side, this one a perfectly restored '66 Town Landau: burgundy, with a black vinyl top. Which meant that Target One was in residence.

Grinning, Calvin cut the engine and walked the bike to within ten feet of the steps. He parked it there, rearranged the still-warm food in his jacket, and crept silent as a shadow across the remaining yard and onto the porch. A beagle stared at him dubiously from the rough boards but didn't lift its head. He raised a finger to his lips. "Shhh! Winford!" he hissed. A scrawny one-eyed raccoon he didn't recognize hissed at him from a river cane basket tucked amid the rafters.

The door was open, which was normal, and dawnlight was plenty to see by as he eased in. A large room reached around him from the left, dominated by a fieldstone fireplace with a raised hearth. The furnishings were rustic—mostly unrestored antiques: solid and comfort-able. A few armchairs lazed about, and long tables lounged before each window. Shelves engulfed the right-hand wall, all full of books—*thousands* of them on every topic, though they tended toward archaeology and anthropology. A curio cabinet by the far end held an assortment of Indian artifacts, including two shell gor-gets and several soapstone carvings.

An open door showed just past it. He tiptoed that way, even so fearing his boots might make the pine floor creak. A smaller room lay beyond, dominated by an old-fashioned iron-framed bed. A figure sprawled diagonally across it: male, mid-twenties, and trimly lanky; copper-skinned and black-haired; facedown and carelessly na-ked upon a patchwork quilt. He was snoring softly.

Calvin's grin widened as he padded the two paces to the bed. Holding his breath, he extended a finger and slowly drew it along the arch of the nearest bare foot.

It twitched. The snoring fumbled.

Another stroke, this time with an S-shaped flourish.

"Wha? Huh . . . ?" Then, like an explosion: "*Jesus Christ! Shit!*"

Calvin caught a blur of long limbs twisting, of bright eyes flashing, and of something much brighter and more deadly-looking flashing as well—and was suddenly crammed between the iron footrail and a very strong and undoubtedly pissed-off Native American holding a Bowie knife to his throat.

The grip tightened, the blade flickered again, before sense returned to those blazing eyes and the pressure lifted.

"Look down—cuz!" Calvin gasped. The face inches from his own—a handsome one, as it happened—tipped just far enough forward to note where Calvin's custom-made Rakestraw poised a finger's width from his balls.

"Fargo, you asshole!" the man growled, as with one

smooth flick of his wrist he flung his weapon past Calvin's head to thunk home in the mantle. Calvin exhaled gratefully. His cousin—for so it was: his father's sister's only boy by a half-Irish father—released him and snatched up a pair of jeans as he staggered to his feet.

"No wonder you sleep with the doors open and your bare ass moonin' the rafters." Calvin laughed, likewise rising.

"Mr. Bowie's *still* less dangerous 'n a woman," his cousin chuckled, now minimally decent. "And he's a helluva lot more reliable."

"I noticed," Calvin observed wryly. "So, how're you doin' . . . *Churchy*?"

"*Watch it!*" the man shot back.

"You prefer Kirkwood, then?" Calvin teased.

"I *prefer* Kirk," the man gritted as he gathered his shoulder-length hair into a stubby tail. "I suffer *los turistas* to call me Thunderbird *when* I'm duded up— that's what's in the program for *Unto These Hills*. The folks that pay me to talk about Native Americans call me Mr. O'Connor. *You* may call me God or Oh-Wise-One, if cuz, or Kirk, or Hey-You won't cut it."

"I brought breakfast." Calvin yawned, patting his jacket. "—The hard parts, anyway. I presume you've got coffee?"

Kirk froze by the door and fixed him with a scornful glare. "I'm an archaeologist, sir. You know the motto: 'Have trowel will travel; have percolator, will travel much further and not be grouchy.' "

"Dug up any good dead Indians lately?"

"No, but I've had some reburied." Kirk snorted as he ambled toward the other room. "But that's business," he added, "and I refuse to talk business before breakfast."

"Prob'ly just as well." Calvin yawned again. He dropped the bags of biscuits on a table and flopped into an armchair. Fatigue found him instantly, and he watched through increasingly heavy lids as his cousin plugged in a hot plate and set a battered aluminum coffee pot to perking. Without intending to, he dozed, rousing with a start as something hot and wonderful-smelling steamed into his nostrils.

"Breakfast is served," Kirk said primly as he waited for Calvin to focus enough to receive the cup. "You take yours black, if I recall."

Calvin sampled it and sighed appreciatively. "Not your basic Maxwell House, is it?"

"Antigua. You like?"

"Passable."

"Sooooo," Kirk continued, backing toward another armchair, "in spite of your calculatedly casual entrance, I doubt you dragged your skinny ass away from your lady's lovin' arms just to feed your impoverished anthropologist kinsman hash browns and ham." He raised an eyebrow and waited.

"You got it." Calvin sighed. "But if I stay here, I'm gonna fade before I get anything told. So how 'bout we go outside and watch the mornin' saunter in?"

"Fine with me," Kirk replied. "I gotta feed Sammy anyway."

"Sammy?"

"Sammy Davis. What else would you call a runty one-eyed 'coon?"

"Tsk," Calvin clucked as he followed his cousin back outside. "I figured you of all people'd be politically correct."

"I am," Kirk countered instantly. "Money's the most P.C. thing there is. I mean, do you s'pose old S.D.J.'d have got rich if he'd been a two-hundred-pound white Baptist?"

"Search me . . . but—"

"That's not why you came."

In reply, Calvin slumped down on the split-log steps, leaning against a porch post. Kirk sat opposite. For a while they busied themselves with biscuits and coffee. The 'coon found its way from the rafters and nuzzled Kirk's greasier hand. He passed it half a biscuit. It trilled.

Eventually Kirk cleared his throat. Calvin saw him watching and cleared his throat in turn. "I want some advice."

"First time in your life!" Kirk snorted.

"Possibly. But I really do need some. I mean, I know I've been kinda distant the last couple of years—pre-occupied, and all. But you've gotta remember that I was hangin' out up here while you were off at college, so it's not like you've exactly been available either."

"So which me do you need?" Kirk asked seriously. "Your cousin, your *Cherokee* cousin, your *mechanic* cousin, or your *anthropologist* cousin?"

"I *need* my shaman cousin, 'cept I don't have one."

Kirk gnawed his lip. "*That* stuff, huh?"

An eyebrow lifted. "You've read Mooney?"

"Does the pope shit in the woods?"

Calvin grimaced and exhaled slowly. "What would you say if I told you that a shitload of the stuff in there's true?"

Kirk puffed his cheeks. "I'd say . . . well, first I'd say you were crazy—if you're talkin' about what I think you are. But then I'd remember that my flaky young cousin's always been a straight shooter, so he must have good reason to believe it's true, whether or not it actually is."

"That's as much as I could hope for, I guess."

"There's more, I take it?"

Calvin nodded. "How 'bout uktena scales, an ulun-suti, and Spearfinger, for starters? Mix in shapechangin' and ghostly visitations. Spice with over-rash promises."

Kirk whistled. "Sounds like heavy stuff."

"You could say that."

"Sooo," Kirk wondered, leaning back, "how long a tale *is* this, anyway? I ask because, unlikely as it may seem, I've actually gotta *do* something this mornin'—and I've gotta run on white man's time."

Calvin looked crestfallen. "It's a . . . long 'un, actually, to tell it right—couple hours, at least."

"Well," Kirk announced, "the way I see it is that you're freaked out over something and dead on your feet on top of it. So I tell you what: you grab some z's now, and tonight we can burn the midnight lamp as long as we have to."

"And until then?"

"Like I said, you crash here this morning, I'll feed you tonight . . . and this afternoon . . ."

"Yeah?"

Kirkwood Thunderbird O'Connor smiled fiendishly. "That's when I exact my consultant's fee."

Calvin regarded him warily from over the rim of his cup.

"You remember how to play stickball, don't you?"

Calvin's eyes narrowed. "You mean *anetsa*?"

Kirk rolled his eyes in turn. "God, cuz, you're a worse purist than *I* am!"

"You know I hate that game!"

"I know you hate rollin' around on the ground and gettin' hurt, which is not the same thing. I also know you're damned good—or *used* to be," he added with a challenging sneer.

"You got sticks?"

"I always got sticks."

"Got a ball?"

"I don't *need* a ball. *I'm* the driver. You're the one who needs a ball—balls, too, if you got 'em."

"I meant to practice with." Then: "*Driver?* What happened to Lloyd Arneach?"

"More money elsewhere."

Calvin merely grunted.

Kirk's face softened. "Hey, if it's that big a deal, I'll get somebody else."

"No." Calvin sighed. "It can wait."

"Good man!"

"So who's playin'?"

"Bunch of the guys up here."

"Pow-wow practice?" Calvin asked, thinking of the big yearly festival on the Fourth of July.

A shrug. "Kinda. Wolftown boys—of whom you, by clan, are one, if I recall—are playin' a bunch of white guys from the University of Georgia."

"*White guys* can't play stickball!"

"These can—well enough to make the Choctaw world champs sweat—and *they* play regularly. As, I might add, do the Na Hollos."

Calvin scowled uncertainly. "Na Hollos?"

"Choctaw for 'White Thing.' "

"Oh."

"I assume you've been abstaining from the company of women like you're supposed to?"

"No more than you've been fasting!"

Kirk smiled lopsidedly. "Well, coffee's close to black drink."

Calvin polished his off and levered himself to his feet, suddenly all weariness. "And if I play, you'll hear me out with an open mind?"

"Promise, cuz. Promise!"

"*Promise*," Calvin muttered to himself as he slumped back inside the cabin. "*That's the whole damned trouble!*"

# Chapter VII:
# Hard Falls and Close Calls

*(early afternoon)*

The big July Fourth pow-wow was still two weeks off, Calvin knew, as he surveyed the mixed-culture crowd ambling about the Qualla Ceremonial Grounds, but you sure couldn't prove it by him. Part of the present press was simply the economics of tourist season, of course: one more opportunity to twist a few extra bucks out of flatlanders who might otherwise have driven straight through to max out their plastic up in Gatlinburg or the Smokys. But with what was at least *apparently* an event taking place—well, folks were just naturally more inclined to stop. He didn't blame the locals for profiting from illusion. Qualla wasn't exactly the richest square mile on earth, even if it didn't look as bad as some other reservations—like Rosebud, South Dakota. Or at least not as bad as it had looked in *Thunderheart*.

But be that as it may, what mattered now was satisfying his cousin's perverse sense of fair trade so that he could, in turn, pick that cousin's mind. Calvin was good at anetsa—almost a natural, some said. But he didn't *like* to play—he supposed because he was at heart a more peaceful soul than the aptly named Little Brother of War required. To be really good at stickball, you had to abandon your higher brain functions and rely on reflex, adrenaline—and killer instinct—at least as much as skill. A high pain threshold helped, too. But Calvin, more so than most, had good reason to fear what might happen if he gave raw emotion free rein.

On the other hand, Kirkwood knew a bloody lot about Native American cosmology, religion, and folklore. And in spite of the fact that Calvin had more ''hands-on'' experience than any Cherokee had acquired in a couple of centuries, his cousin was more likely to have squirreled away the sort of esoterica Calvin had glossed over in his own wide but less disciplined reading. Kirk also had a solid background in logic and ethics, both Native American and import. And he knew Calvin as well as anyone.

Trouble was, while Kirk had been around enough to be open-minded, he was also educated enough to be skeptical; and though Calvin knew he would *try* to accept what he had to say nonjudgmentally, it was a lot to ask *anyone* to swallow.

It also assumed he survived the next two hours.

He checked his watch. It was nigh onto 1:45 P.M., and the game was supposed to start at 2:00. Scowling, he gave the crowd one final scan, noting that a number of local artisans were attracting good business—folks like Eva Bigwitch, Davy Arch, and Eddie Bushyhead, in particular. Good for them. A quick check on tiptoes to locate Kirk found him conferring with a clump of event coordinators. Pausing only to untie the red bandana that bound his *tihlskahlti*—his ballsticks—Calvin trotted that way, which was also toward the ball ground.

It was roughly the size of a football field, but with far less clearly defined boundaries. Indeed, there *was* no out-of-bounds, and more than once Calvin had seen players tumble into the spectators with little regard for

life or limb on either side. Near each end of the long
axis a pair of man-high saplings had been thrust into the
ground an armspan apart. These were the goals—at least
they were in the Cherokee version of the game. The
Mississipi Choctaw—the only tribe that still maintained
official teams and codified rules—used twelve-foot-high
poles stuck in the earth, and other Southeastern tribes
had similar variations.

Just like they used different sticks. Calvin's borrowed
pair were Cherokee-style: yard-long splints of hickory
planed thin with a draw knife, then folded in half and
flared to make a hand-sized loop at the bent end, the
remainder doweled and lashed together, with leather woven through the loop to form a basket.

The crowd thinned as Calvin approached, and he recognized some people—players on his own team, mostly:
the Bauchenbaugh boys and their dad; Casey Cooper,
and the inevitable strutting figure of Rifle Runningbear,
who'd been in a couple of movies—and was presently
flirting with a woman. Most knew Calvin only slightly,
and vice versa. He hadn't grown up in these parts but
*had* spent summers here in the company of his grandfather, who'd been one of the tribal elders, which connection entitled Calvin to a certain amount of respect.
Unfortunately, the old guy had lived *way* back in the
hills, and Calvin hadn't been able to get into town often;
thus, he'd had little contact with tribesmen his own age.
He was accepted partly because he had a B.I.A. card,
but mostly because he had kinfolks thereabouts—and
was a good player; though a certain begrudged quality
came with it: an ongoing tendency to test him.

But all that was in his head. As far as any of the
spectators knew, he was just another Cherokee: taller
than some, and maybe a little slimmer than the stocky,
neckless, wide-shouldered lads that comprised the bulk
of his team. But like the rest he had thick black hair,

tending to long. And like most of them, too, he'd be
playing in cut-off jeans (a pair of Kirk's, since he'd
brought none).

Speaking of which . . . He paused by a scatter of similarly abandoned clothing at the eastern edge of the field
to shuck out of his shoes and shirt, as the rules required.
His watch joined them, but only then did he realize that
this really *wasn't* a good idea, because it meant exposing
his uktena scale necklace, which he wasn't *about* to
leave in Fortune's care, seeing as how it still contained
an indeterminate number of shape-shifts and only
needed to taste blood to stir up trouble. Too, going shirtless revealed the sun-circles Uki and the Red Man had
branded into his back. They looked like tattoos, but a
sharp eye would realize they were *other*.

Oh well, there was no help for it—not if he was going
to get anything useful out of Churchy.

The Wolftown boys were warming up now: using
their sticks to scoop up the ball (like a lopsided golfball
made of hand-stitched buckskin around a rock core),
then flinging it at each other—sometimes with appalling
force. A really good throw made an audible whistle.
They were also laughing a great deal—and tossing good-
natured insults at their opponents.

The visitors, he observed, as he intercepted a wayward
shot and flung it back, showed more variation than the
hometown team, ranging in apparent age from late teens
to early forties—(*that* was a mistake!). Most were leaner
than the Cherokee norm, some even downright skinny,
with a couple of really small lads, but also with a fair
number taller than the tallest Wolftowner—at five ten,
Calvin was himself a touch above average. A few were
blond, a couple red-headed. Some wore ponytails, many
sported earrings, and one had a thick, waist-long braid
that was bound to tempt *someone* past endurance. There
were even two women: a thin, curly-haired blonde, and

a buxom redhead. Calvin wondered if they'd be required to go topless, too. As it was, their whole team wore white T-shirts emblazoned with a pissed-off-looking bat grasping tihlskahlti.

Calvin even recognized a couple of them. One was a middle-sized auburn-haired guy whose intense expression rode raptor-handsome features. Calvin couldn't remember his name, but knew he'd been dancing pow-wows since he was a kid and had lately started a small Drum. A couple of others danced or sang, too: a ballsy thing to do, for white boys.

"Everybody come on out and line up!" Kirk yelled abruptly. And anetsa was underway.

As the teams began to face off in midfield, Calvin finally got a look at the Na Hollo captain: a short, stocky, strong-looking man in his early thirties. His black hair was caught up in a bun and a tattooed Mayan glyph showed on one shoulder, while two more, in a different style, decorated his burly torso. That which bracketed his right nipple looked like an insignia from the first *Star Trek*, but was in fact a Southeastern Indian motif. "That's John Gregory," Richie Bauchenbaugh confided. "Part Choctaw. Better watch 'im; he's better'n he looks."

Calvin only half heard him, though he dutifully laid his sticks on the ground before him as the rest of the Wolftown boys fell in on either side. *That tattoo!*—it represented the eye markings of a peregrine falcon—which was *his* totem. What it meant on a member of an opposing team, he had no idea—save that falcons had a habit of impinging on his reality at crucial junctures, often as not in warning. Which was all he needed, seeing how he already had half a dozen crises about to boil.

Oh, well . . .

Kirk, who was Driver, a.k.a. referee, stood at the far end of the facing ranks, a willow withe held whiplike in his hand. He studied the teams for a moment (there were roughly twenty on either side), and frowned. Then, striding down the line, he made adjustments, matching each person against someone of similar bulk or build. When play began, everyone would be charged with keeping his opposite number out of commission. The guy currently facing Calvin was a wiry fellow in his mid-twenties, a few inches shorter than he, with slightly receding brown hair and wire-framed glasses that would last about five seconds: not a good match. Kirk noted that as well and substituted the red-haired dancer. Calvin probably had him by a pound or two; on the other hand, Red-hair was taller and might have reach.

"Okay, you guys know the rules," Kirk was saying, probably for the Na Hollos' benefit. "You *have* to use the sticks to get the ball off the ground, but after it's knee high, hands are okay. You have to take it *through* your opponent's goal, and you—or someone from your team—has to bring it around the goal and onto the field again. Remember, stay with your man. You can take him out at any time, but I don't want to see any unnecessary roughness. That *clear*, Rifle? I'm gonna give you guys one minute to get your heads straight and look pretty for the cameras, and then it's war—until one team scores twelve points."

"How many breaks?" someone asked.

"None—'cept the ones in your bones!"

A general nervous chuckle.

Calvin took a deep breath and reclaimed his sticks, looking past the Na Hollos to survey the crowd at large. Most were typical tourists: white folks in bright colors, shades, and baseball caps. There were also a fair number of locals, most clumped together to one side. One was not, however, and Calvin found his attention drawn to him like a moth to a flame.

If not clearly Cherokee, the man was nevertheless so

determinedly Native American as to be almost a cari-
cature. Likely in his early thirties, he stood half a head
taller than the surrounding crowd: easily six three or
four. His jet black hair hung in thick braids like twisted
tar, and he wore tight jeans, western boots, and a skin-
tight black T-shirt emblazoned with a cobra's head *af-
fronte* picked out in scarlet, save for poison green eyes.
Even at this distance Calvin could see that he was leanly,
if powerfully, built.

And his eyes . . .

Calvin shouldn't be able to discern any detail at
this distance, yet somehow he knew that man's eyes
were . . . wrong. In spite of the glare, they were wide
open, not squinted to slits; and they had a cold quality
to them, like a reptile's. He felt a sudden chill and wondered, half seriously, if the lids might not flick in from
the side or bottom.

Nor could he resist following that troubling gaze, for
the man was glaring at someone in the encircling
crowd—and glaring hard.

It was then that Calvin saw the girl.

Though reasonably tall, she was slim and lithe. Native
American, too—probably—but with her inky hair growing to a point on her forehead and cut short enough on
the neck and sides to show her ears. She had a small,
pointed chin and enormous dark eyes that, together with
wide cheekbones, gave her a feral cast. She too wore
black—jeans and riding boots—but a green T-shirt depicted a grinning Indian boy: Nathan Chasing-His-Horse
from *Dances With Wolves*, if Calvin could trust his
memory.

And then, cat-quick, the woman's head snapped
around. Her eyes darted about, then stabilized—fixed,
Calvin was certain, on him. The tall man's face swiveled
his way, too—and his eyes narrowed, his lips curved in

an odd, surprised smile. The hair on Calvin's neck prickled.

"*Hweeee!*" a voice cried.

Calvin jerked himself back to the business at hand *just* in time to see Kirk fling the ball high in the air. The sky was slashed by upraised sticks, by arms fair and bronzed, as the teams surged together. He was jostled from the right as he forced himself toward the huddle of legs and backsides that were vainly trying to recover the ball from the ground. A hard impact from the left was Red-hair checking him—and not doing badly. The air filled with grunts and half-heard curses. He was already sweating.

All at once the seething mass of bodies broke asunder. Part of it boiled his way. The ball exploded from between dark hairy legs, caromed off a foot—and bounced toward him. He snapped his sticks toward it, simultaneously bracing for the impact old Red-hair ought to deliver—assuming he knew that much.

Closer . . . One stick brushed the ball. He flipped it upward, even as he dropped his other stick to grab it.

And felt all the breath burst out of him as someone slammed hard into his ribcage. The ground scooted out from under him; strong hard arms clamped around him; and he was borne to earth. The ball shot into the sky— he saw it there, along with his other stick and a flash of dark red hair.

And couldn't move!

He'd been pinned by a college boy!

Grunting, he dug his elbows into the ground and twisted—hard. Red-hair flipped off him. Half-dazed and panting, Calvin struggled to his feet, snatching up his sticks as he rose.

Following the shouting showed him that the Na Hollo captain had caught the ball on the fly and was dashing toward the goal, short legs pumping like pistons. Rifle

Runningbear was closing on him, though. Gregory wasn't going to make it. . . .

But he did!—was through the goal. Rifle caught him there and slammed him to the ground. Which meant the Na Hollo either had to escape or get the ball to a teammate to bring it out again. Neither seemed likely, as body after body flung themselves into the fray. The saplings shuddered, bent beneath the press of flesh. The Na Hollo with the long braid dropped his sticks and hauled on a Bauchenbaugh in hopes of freeing his captain. One of the Wolftown boys jogged around and was probing somewhere near the Na Hollo captain's head.

Suddenly he stepped back, raised his sticks—and threw—just as a small blond guy laid him low.

And the ball was coming straight toward Calvin, who was—almost—alone in midfield.

Out of the corner of his eye, he saw Red-hair on an intercept course with either himself or the ball. Calvin was closer, ran faster. He grabbed at the ball and missed, saw it roll along the ground toward the crowd. He chased it. Red-hair was right behind, with members of both teams charging up fast. Calvin made a grab, barely touched it, but accidentally spun it even closer to the crowd. He grimaced, steeled himself for impact, yelled "Look out!" mostly from reflex.

He had it then, prisoned in his sticks. But there were too many people around for him to escape. Desperate, he spun in place and flung the ball back toward midfield—just as Red-hair piled into him again. He toppled backward, felt his shoulders scrape the ground. Saw sky, then feet, then mostly stars. "Sorry," Red-hair panted, scrambling off him—primarily for the sake of the startled tourists, he imagined.

Calvin found himself lying on his back surrounded by spectators. He remained where he was for a moment, gasping, regaining both breath and equilibrium, as he heard the tide of play surge away once more.

Abruptly, a face swung into view above him—a familiar face. He squinted at it, puzzled—then had a chill. *It was the weird-looking guy he'd seen before!* The one with the disturbing eyes. And those eyes were staring—not at him, but at the uktena scale plainly visible on his bare chest!

The man's mouth opened, as though he were on the verge of speaking, but something clicked in Calvin, and he sprang up again. Red-hair was waiting on him at the margin of the crowd, looking concerned. If Calvin went out, so did he.

A point had been scored, apparently; probably by Casey Cooper. The teams were regrouping in midfield—raggedly, though. Not everyone had to be present. Calvin jogged that way, and for the third time in as many minutes saw the ball rise, fall, then sail directly his way.

He batted it to the ground, ran toward it, with Red-hair right behind, racing a middle-sized blond in a buckskin breechclout—Frank, he thought his name was.

Calvin reached it first, extended a stick. Flipped the ball up, felt it thump into his hand. His fingers closed on it. He ran . . .

And was lifted from the ground. . . .

For an instant he floated there, oblivious to gravity. And then he fell—hard—aided perhaps by Blondie's arms. He'd been bodyslammed.

*But he still had the ball!* He tried to fling it away, but someone was kneeling on his arm. He twisted, felt pain in his back and shoulders, knew a muscle had pulled, but managed to roll over just as a heavy body piled onto his back. More joined it quickly: half a ton of young male muscle grinding around on top of him. It was hard to breathe. If they didn't get off soon . . .

Something was digging into his chest, too: something hard and sharp. He felt it slice into his sternum, knew by the gush of warmth that he was bleeding. And the world was getting dim, as the pressure on his chest grew too great.

*Dammit!* This wasn't right! You weren't supposed to pile on this hard and this long! Where was Kirk? He was supposed to stop stuff like this!

But he couldn't escape. . . . Not as *man,* he couldn't.

But if he were smaller . . .

Another body hit somewhere above. The pain bit into his chest. Calvin's awareness narrowed. *Out,* he wanted *out!* And to do that . . .

*'Possum? Squirrel? 'Coon?*

Pain wracked him; his body spasmed. Something very far away remembered and screamed *No!* His arms felt odd, especially the one with something hard in it. It drew back. The thing rolled free.

And the weight diminished. Shouts filled the air. The weight was . . . gone.

Air hit Calvin's lungs.

He dragged in breath after breath. Felt his cutoffs oddly loose.

And almost screamed—for he had glimpsed his arm: shorter than it should be and covered with thick dark fur. "Jesus!" he gasped—and flung himself back to the ground, grinding the uktena scale into his flesh once more, feeding it on his blood as he thought desperately, *Man, man, man!*

Pain again, and a stretching—and then darkness. . . .

The next thing he knew, hands were easing into his armpits, and he was being moved.

He opened his eyes, saw Kirkwood looking at him with an odd mix of concern, curiosity, and—almost— fear. "Cut up chest and maybe cracked ribs, cuz," he said shortly. "You're not playin' anymore today. Sorry."

"Tonight . . . ?" Calvin was desperate enough to counter.

Kirk's face went even grimmer. "Very definitely yes," he muttered. "After what I just saw—or thought I did—no way I'm lettin' you escape now!"

"What'd you see?" Calvin managed, as blackness once more hovered near.

"Something I hope nobody *else* saw!"

But as a pair of unknown Cherokee carried him from the field toward a waiting van, Calvin glimpsed one particular face among the nameless crowd: the guy with the odd eyes, staring at him—speculatively.

Unconsciousness, he concluded, was better.

# Chapter VIII:
# Recompense and Revelation

*(north of Qualla Boundary—*
*Sunday, June 17—2:00 A.M.)*

"Sorry to be such a pill," Calvin grunted as he eased into a more comfortable position in the armchair Kirk had dragged onto the porch for him hours earlier. As the last set of taillights winked out behind the walnut trees, the yard faded to a plain of moonlit dimness surrounded by mountains of laurel, with the banked embers of a bonfire still glimmering and smoking out past the steps like a baleful red eye—which was *not* a comforting image. In the ranch house up the hill a single light still shone in a bedroom. He resented it: it upset the ambience, like a chaperone at a party—which in a sense it had been. But he was damned grateful for it, too, because it was in Kirkwood's parents' place, and therefore belonged to Calvin's own aunt and uncle. The ones who suffered their crazy college-educated son to live in a handbuilt cabin on the lawn and who gave him no grief when—like tonight—he hosted the forty-nine: the postball game party.

"Huh?" Kirkwood asked with a start.

"I said I was sorry to be such a pill."

"I'm the one who oughta be sorry." Kirk sighed as he nudged Winford the beagle aside in order to clear a phalanx of beer bottles from the path to the door. More ranked around it—everywhere Calvin looked, in fact; unopened and empty, both. A couple even camped behind his chair, though not of his consuming. Tempting though it might have been, especially tonight, Calvin still abstained.

"I'm the one who thought he could wind this thing up at a reasonable hour," Kirk continued. He sighed again, gave up on the bottles, and slumped down in the rocker next to Calvin's. "I should've known better. God knows I've been around enough Indians *and* anthropologists to know what kind of partiers they are! And put the two together—*wow!*"

"Those guys were *anthropologists*? The Na Hollos?"

Kirk nodded and sipped absently from a bottle of Corona. "Most of 'em were. Couple of art majors, some microbiologists, of all things. Forestry, journalism—grown-ups. You name it."

Calvin chuckled—then winced and grunted again. That had hurt!

Kirk noticed it and scowled. "So . . . how are you? You got back from gettin' poked and prodded just as the party kicked in. I kinda missed the full report."

"The full report was that I'm shaken, cut up, and cracked, but not concussed or broken—and have a torso mummified with Ace bandages to prove it. Specifically, I've got two cracked ribs and a pair of oddly healed gashes in my chest—which I shouldn't have! Other than that, I'm healthy as an ox, 'cept that I've got some symptoms of stress—which I knew."

"Well, gee, man," Kirk said contritely, "I really am sorry about all that. I shouldn't have made you play."

Calvin shrugged, then realized that his kinsman had probably interpreted his comment as an accusation—

which it wasn't. "It was the right thing to do," he replied. "Favor for favor, and all that."

"At least you gave the team a rallyin' point. Shoot, those Georgia boys were out for blood!"

"Girls, too. There were girls, too."

"We beat 'em, though. Boys and girls. Barely."

A pause. Then, from Calvin: "That's not what I meant, though."

"About what?"

"About how I shouldn't have been hurt like that."

Kirk regarded him curiously through tired eyes. "So is this, like, *it*, then? Are we on the edge of the big 'un?"

"If you're up for it. *I* had a nap; you didn't."

"Gimme a sec to whip up some coffee?"

"Any munchies left?"

"Oughta be." And with that, Kirk polished off the beer he'd been nursing and disappeared inside.

Calvin leaned back in his chair and closed his eyes, trying to muster his thoughts. Before he'd even begun, though, Kirk was back—with a bag of Ruffles and an enormous mug of what proved to be very black and strong coffee. Calvin sampled it. "Jesus, man; this'd dissolve a friggin' spoon!"

Kirk laughed softly. "So maybe it'll keep a . . . *wizard* awake?"

A wary chuckle—and another wince. "If that's what I am."

"You tell me."

Calvin shook his head. "Why don't you tell me what you saw—or thought you did—first."

Kirk rolled his eyes and sipped his coffee. He didn't look at Calvin, rather gazed out at the lawn. "I'm . . . not *sure*," he began carefully. "But what I *thought* I saw when I finally whipped that bunch of guys off you, was . . . Well, it looked like your whole body was startin' to shrink, and your arm—which was all I got a good look at—was all drawn up and . . . and gettin' *furry*!''

"And then?"

A shrug. "I blinked, you groaned, and were back to normal.''

Calvin fished down the front of his T-shirt and dragged out the uktena scale on its thong. Even in the half-light it gleamed: the size of his palm and roughly triangular, milky-clear save at the tips of two of the three points, which were red as blood. Carefully, and with more than a bit of trepidation, he slipped it over his head and passed it to his cousin. "Know what this is?"

Kirk took it, held it in the light streaming out from the window. "Can't say for sure, but if I had to make a stab in the dark, I'd say it was . . . some kinda fish scale.''

Calvin smiled. "Half right.''

"Which half?''

"It's a scale—but *not* from a fish.''

Kirk eyed him skeptically. "You're not sayin' . . .''

Calvin nodded. " 'Fraid so, cuz. That little bit of vitreous protein you're holdin' is probably one of the three or four most valuable things on this planet.''

"I think I'll let *you* explain why.''

" 'Cause at one extreme it represents a challenge to physics as we know it, 'specially the law of conservation of matter and energy.''

"And *a la otra mano*?''

"It's proof that what most folks call the supernatural really exists.''

"You're *shittin'* me!''

"I wouldn't even be *tellin'* you, 'cept that it's part of a larger problem I can't resolve on my own—which is why I'm here. Oh, there're a couple other folks I can talk to, sure—and I'm goin' to. But you're the only one who knows enough about *our* people to help me do what's right from that point of view.''

"Some folks'd say it's the *only* point of view."

"And some folks'd say there's no such thing as magic."

"What do you say?"

Calvin's reply was a sip of coffee. Then: "I say that I'd like to know what *you'd* say if I was to take that scale, and cut myself with it hard enough to draw blood, *and* wished to be an animal—it has to be something I've eaten, so that I can absorb the genetic imprint; and I have to have in some sense hunted it, which I think has something to do with adrenaline either priming or fixing the pattern—and then turned into that animal."

"Sounds like fun," Kirk replied nervously, but his eyes were dead serious.

"Not hardly!" Calvin snorted as he retrieved the scale. "It hurts like hell for one thing; and you have to concentrate all the time to remind your *self* you're human. See, the animal instincts kinda have to kick in to ensure survival. But they want to override—which you have to let 'em do if you're gonna fly, say—assuming you're a bird, which I have been. Never mind that the smaller you go and the further from primate, or especially mammal, the less space there is in the brain for *you*, simply 'cause there're fewer brain cells available— which means you run a higher risk of forgettin' who you are and bein' trapped in that shape forever."

"Ah," Kirk mused, "I see. It scares you to turn, never mind those bigger issues you were talkin' about— and when you get down to it, most folks ere on the side of self-preservation."

"Right."

"So how does this relate to your wounds not healing?"

Another shrug. "Normally when I get hurt and then shift, the injuries vanish when I change back. I guess the reason they didn't this time is 'cause I didn't shift entirely.''

Kirk exhaled heavily. ''My cuz, the coverboy for the *National Enquirer!*''

''Better make that *National Wildlife!*''

''*Field and Stream*?''

''And prob'ly *Playgirl* as well!''

''*Playgirl*?''

''Your clothes don't shift with you—nothin' that's not in your genes does. Which means you tend to wind up naked in odd places.''

Kirk laughed out loud. ''I'll bet you do!''

Calvin looked glum. ''It also means my tattoo's fadin'—the old one, anyway—and that something that was . . . ahem . . . snipped off when I was a wee lad's growin' back.''

''I won't even ask.''

''Aw shucks, I was hopin' I'd get to show you.''

Another sip of coffee. ''Okay, then. So why don't you tell me the whole thing? I get a sense I'm gettin' ahead of the game.''

Calvin sighed, took a long swallow of coffee. ''Okay, man, well, it's like this . . .''

For the next hour Calvin told his cousin the whole tale of his magical adventures, from the time he'd first met David Sullivan and his Faery friend, Fionchadd, two summers back, through his journey to Galunlati, his fight with the uktena, and Uki's taking him on as apprentice. Nor did did he neglect the war in Faerie which had affected the sun in Galunlati, and how he'd inadvertently let Spearfinger into this world. He continued with a detailed account of Spearfinger's tracking of him, which had allowed her to kill four people, including his father. And concluded with his promise to Brock, Gary Hudson's wedding, and the subsequent war-naming ceremony.

Kirk remained quiet throughout, listening intently, and only speaking to ask clarifying questions.

Eventually Calvin fell silent. "That's about it." He sighed. "Except for the stuff I actually came here to ask about."

Kirk's eyes were huge. "Like, what you told me already's not enough?"

Calvin shook his head. " 'Fraid not—and I have to ask you to keep that under your hat."

"And if I don't?"

"I know where you live, I can shapeshift, and if I chase you down and sample your blood, I can *steal* your shape, so who'd even know?"

"You'd *do* that?"

"I devoutly hope not. But I could. I suppose I would if I had to . . . for the good of the world."

"*Shit!*"

"A crock of which this is!"

"So what about the statue of your buddy that Spearfinger made and sent to get him? What became of that?"

"It . . . collapsed. Just fell away to its component parts. As best I can tell, Uki used the magic in it to breach the World Walls when he zapped us off to Galunlati. But that's *not* why I came, cuz. This has all been to give you background on the thing that's buggin' me. Two things, actually."

"So shoot."

"More coffee?"

"Fine."

Two minutes later, Calvin dived in again. "Okay, then," he said. "I told you about that kid, Brock, right? The one I promised to teach one piece of magic? Well, I've got about two days before that comes due, and I don't know what to do!"

"What do you *want* to do?"

"I knew you'd ask that!"

"Then why'd you come?"

"To absolve myself of guilt, I reckon. But to answer your question: my head tells me to stand the kid up and write off that friendship as too risky."

"And your heart?"

"It says I've gotta go through with it. It says magic carries an obligation to use it right. But along with that comes the responsibility to do *everything* right. Never to fuck up, in other words. To *always* do the right thing, 'cause if you don't, you're liable to find yourself in a bad situation, and if that happens, you're more likely to use magic—which always causes trouble."

"So you're sayin' one should only use magic for good?" Kirk countered, gnawing a finger. "That's not Cherokee. We say that you can't separate magic from the rest of reality, as I'm sure you know. That the whole world's suffused with magic, that you can't get away from it, and that everybody uses it, just like any other art or skill—including stuff that might be good for one person but not another. See, every hunter used huntin' songs and such as that. And the myths are full of shape-shifters. *Traditionally*, you wouldn't be that special."

"Maybe. But *I've* never seen anything good come of it; it only complicates your life and makes you unhappy. And unhappiness *can't* be good—not intrinsically."

"Hmmm. I'll have to think about that 'un."

"What about my promise to Brock?"

Kirk leaned back in his chair and puffed his cheeks. "Well, as I see it, you've gotta go through with it. Number one, you'll guilt-trip yourself crazy if you don't, so you might as well at least meet the kid. Do that, state your position clearly and concisely. Tell him exactly what you think, and explain *all* the risks and ramifications. And if that doesn't work . . . you show him something that scares the livin' pants off him, but that he can't get the gear to duplicate solo."

Calvin scowled. "It's a thought."

"Otherwise you break your promise. And if you break your promise . . . well, you *have* to honor promises, or you yourself have no honor. You'd be no better than a—'scuse me while I stereotype my fellow humans—white man."

"I was afraid you'd say that."

"And the other problem?"

Calvin told him about the ghosts.

"Man, oh *man*," Kirk groaned when he had finished. "Remind me to head for the high timber next time I see you comin'!"

"I'd just turn into an eagle and find you."

Kirk stared at him for a long moment. "Yeah, you probably would. Okay then . . . only I'm not sure *what* to tell you, man. I'm an ethnohistorian; myth's not my thing. In fact, you should've probably talked to that John Gregory guy who was here earlier, that's his bag. All I can do is offer a couple of points. And the main one is to remind you of what you probably already know about ghosts. The first thing is that, according to *our* traditional worldview, a person who dies without all his parts is denied full admission to the Ghost Country."

"And since Dad and that kid are missin' their livers—"

"Right. They can't rest."

"What about the women?"

A shrug. "Search me. Maybe the gods are sexist."

"And the other thing?"

"Ghosts get lonely—so they tend to try to lure their loved ones to the Ghost Country so they can be with 'em."

Calvin struck himself on the forehead. "Oh, my God!"

"Sorry," Kirk told him helplessly.

"Any idea how to placate one?"

Kirk shook his head. "Not a clue. Maybe if the missin' parts were reunited and given proper burial?"

"The missin' parts were in the stomach of a monster that dissolved in a south Georgia river!"

"Which gives you one *more* reason to return to the scene of the crime—beyond keepin' your promise."

Calvin yawned. Kirk saw him. "Yeah, me too."

"Sorry."

"Anything else before we crash?—not that either of us is likely to sleep."

"One thing—make that two things."

Kirk grimaced, finished his second cup. "Shoot."

"That guy at the game: tall, lanky—weird eyes. Who is he?"

Kirk looked troubled. "He's a *problem*, is what he is. And actually you hit pretty close when you commented on his eyes."

"In what way?"

"Well, his name's James Rainbow—or that's what he calls himself, how he signs checks, and all. But folks around here have taken to callin' him Snakeeyes, for obvious reasons."

"Very obvious."

"He's from Oklahoma—supposedly: fresh off the boat. He's also a witch—so folks say."

Calvin frowned. "Not good, that."

"Not when you know what witches really are—that in a culture that believes magic is everywhere, a witch is somebody who uses it specifically for harm."

"Shit!" Calvin spat, pounding the arm of his chair with his fist. The coffee sloshed onto the porch beside him, narrowly missing Winford. "Fucking *shit*!"

"What?"

"Oh, nothing—except that the bastard saw my uktena scale."

"Probably thought it was just a fish scale, like I did."

"Yeah, but what if he didn't? I mean *something* in that guy really put the wind up me. And he sure was lookin' at it mighty hard when I was lyin' there. And if he saw what you saw . . ."

"Shit!"

"And the girl?"

"What girl?"

"You *have* to have seen her! Good-lookin', short hair, wild-lookin' face—big eyes, and all. Had on one of Nathan's T-shirts."

"Oh, right; I know who you mean. She's pretty sharp, isn't she?"

"You know her?"

"I wish!"

"Okay . . . *Churchy!*"

"Uh . . . well, actually, I don't know her name, though believe me, I've asked. She showed up the same time old Snakeeyes did, which is to say about a week ago. She hangs out with him a lot, only she doesn't actually seem to like him. You never see her without him being around—but you never see them really close together, either."

"Not like lovers?"

"Hard to say. Not in public, anyway. She doesn't seem very happy, and less so the closer Snakeeyes gets."

"More mystery."

"Yeah," Kirk sighed. "And I'm afraid I've had enough for one day—and night. So what d' you say we sleep on all this, and maybe some new insight'll be waitin' for us tomorrow."

"Except that I can't *wait* till tomorrow—not past breakfast, anyway. If I'm gonna fulfill my promise, *and* check with the other folks I wanta check with, I've gotta head out at oh-bright-thirty."

"It's already oh-bright-thirty."

"Before noon, then."

"You sure you're up for it? I mean with your ribs and all?"

"The bod'll heal. But if I stand up Brock he might not—emotionally. 'Course on the *other* hand—"

"*Fargo!*"

"Okay, okay. Need some help cleanin' up?"

"Yeah, but not from you. You're gonna sleep. You can have the sofa if you want. Or the bed's plenty big for two; I'm easy."

"So I hear."

"Asshole."

Calvin bit his lip. "Actually . . . if it wouldn't bug you too much, I think I might take you up on that. We'd probably both sleep better if we knew somebody else was close by."

Kirk grinned wickedly as he rose. "I don't suppose you could turn into a really pretty girl, could you? Long legs, big—"

"No, but I could turn *you* into a eunuch real easy!" Calvin cried—whereupon he leapt from his chair and chased his cousin into the cabin—until his ribs reminded him why he oughtn't to do such things.

Blessedly, Calvin was asleep as soon as he hit the covers—as if sleep itself reached up to engulf him. For a long time fatigue kept any dreams away, but shortly past dawn one found him.

Not a dream actually, not in the sense of actions and images. Only a soft male voice murmuring insidiously, *"Change, change, change, change, change . . . beasts have no worries, no responsibilities, and are not bound by promises . . . change, change, change . . ."*

Somewhere, too, children were crying.

# Chapter IX:
# Sneak Attack

*(north of Qualla Boundary, North Carolina—*
*Sunday, June 17—morning)*

Calvin felt as though a take-no-prisoners game of anetsa had been played on his body when he awoke the next morning. He'd assumed he was in pretty good shape— Lord knew he jogged, did heavy chores around Sandy's place, and generally kept himself busy outside. His muscles were hard, his stomach flat, his endurance dandy. But that evidently wasn't enough to see him through even five minutes of a stickball game. And if *he* felt this bad after so little play, how must the other guys be feeling? Never mind that most were probably hung over.

On the other hand, as a too-abrupt stab at dragging the pillow over his head to shut out the morning light reminded him, *they* didn't have cracked ribs and lacerated chests. Well, some of 'em probably did, but that was neither here nor there.

It was then that he remembered the dream.

He'd had a disturbing dream about wanting to change shape. *No!* About someone *urging* him to change shape! Which meant it was some kind of sending! Which was even worse, because nobody was supposed to know he

109

could do that except his friends. Only . . . who would send him dreams like that? Not Uki, surely; not something so . . . negative. But not Dave or any of that crowd either. First because it was totally unlike them—even if one of 'em could do such a thing, which he doubted. And secondly because they all knew enough about mojo to realize it produced more problems than solutions. Never mind that none of them knew about his visitations. Or at least *he* hadn't told 'em.

His eyes popped full open at that, as adrenaline gave his system a jolt somewhere between a shock and a shiver. That made his chest hurt more, but was also enough to convince him that the low-level pain oozing through his arms and legs was mostly muscle soreness, which would disperse as he kicked about. Not bothering to suppress a groan, he flung off the pillow and dragged himself upright to sit on the edge of the bed and collect his bearings. Kirkwood's side was empty, and to judge by the minimal wrinkles in the quilt on his half, he'd pretty much died when he hit the hay.

But not so far he couldn't dream.

Jesus, but that bugged him! Shoot, maybe *Kirk* had sent it. They'd shared the bed—and had both crashed with their minds musing on the arcane. Maybe his cousin's subconscious had conjured up the concept of permanent escape as an option, and he'd picked up on it.

Maybe, maybe, maybe. Well, he wouldn't learn anything sitting here in his drawers.

Yawning, he reached for his jeans—

—and couldn't find them!

But . . . hadn't he left them on the trunk beneath the front window when he'd cashed in? Of course he *had* been preoccupied then. Still . . .

Scowling fiercely, he rose, his gaze stumbling about in quest of, minimally, his pants. Unfortunately, the movement also put his eyes in line with a shaft of sun-

light and set him squinting into a glare that was not that
of early morning. A glance at his watch confirmed his
suspicion. It was nearly eleven!

He'd wanted to be on the road by now!

Swearing softly, he padded around the foot of the bed
and headed for the door. And caught himself up short.
*There* the little sons-of-bitches were: his clothes *and*
boots, all clumped up against the wall below Kirk's window, along with his backpack. Which didn't make sense.
Preoccupied he might have been, but not so much he'd
have shucked his duds there—or pushed them up like
that. Of course it could have been one of Churchy's
jokes, but he didn't think so; it wasn't nearly subtle
enough, for one thing. And then he realized something
even more troubling. The morning light had been lancing in the window on his side, which meant that was
east. Which made this *west*, which meant—

*No way!* No way his entire wardrobe could have me-
andered off westward like that. Small stuff, yes: quills,
and arrowheads, and such like. But not a couple of
pounds of cotton, denim, and leather.

Yet there they were—mundane stuff, too, which was
a change.

"Shit!" he muttered, as he fished out his Levis and
slipped them on. "I don't need this!" But as he approached the door, he caught a strong whiff of new-
perked coffee and fresh-fried bacon, and decided that
cousin Kirkwood *might* get to live another day after all.
And come to it, that his kinsman had plenty of reasons
to lie abed late, given that he'd pretty much been up for
twenty-four hours and had imbibed a fair bit of brew,
which Calvin hadn't. No sleep plus hangover was doubtless as uncool as a battered bod and bad dreams.

He'd made it to the other room by then, and leaned
against the curio cabinet, surveying it. A breeze wafted
in from the open front door to the left, to ease out its

backporch twin close on Calvin's right. His cousin was nowhere to be seen, but he could hear someone rattling and thumping around in the yard. Yawning again, Calvin sauntered to a small table in what served as the kitchen corner. It was set for two, with a percolator steaming on a hot plate and a platter of bacon still fresh enough to be warm covered by a grease-soaked paper towel. There was also a carafe of orange juice and a round of cornbread—probably baked in the fireplace, if the residual heat and coals were any indication. He poured himself a half-cup of java (Antigua, rather) and broke off an edge of the bread, into which he inserted a strip of bacon. That done, he wandered to the back door, which opened onto a small and very cluttered back porch. An instant later, he stumped stiffly down the steps in quest of his kinsman.

It wasn't difficult—if one had functional hearing. Or at least *something* was making an ungodly racket behind that head-high screen of laurel halfway between the porch and the creek. Partly it sounded like a tiny but intense rainstorm on a plastic roof, and partly it sounded like a very irate bobcat roused suddenly from a three-day bender and forced to sing "Down By the River." Calvin grinned as he stepped into the yard. Some things never changed, and one of them was his cousin's . . . singing.

A glance around showed it a fine morning indeed: the sky clear, the air still cool and dry enough to be comfortable. But halfway to the screen, a darkness passed overhead, even as, for the briefest instant, a shadow flicked across the ground. A skyward glance showed something occluding the sun, but it took a moment's squinting to determine that a large bird was circling up there. Buzzard he assumed at first, only it didn't look quite right. But a closer inspection, aided by a shading hand, showed it to be an . . . an *owl*. Which was damned unusual in daylight. The glare and distance kept him from identifying the species, but the mere fact of it gave him chills—especially in light of his dream.

Owls were often witches! Or witches were often owls. And though Calvin was not one to jump to conclusions, neither was he one to ignore facts. Maybe there was no connection between the odd dream, atypical conduct from the wildlife, his over-obvious uktena scale, and a weird guy over at the Boundary whom gossip said was a witch. Then again . . .

Pausing to polish off the coffee, he continued around the hedge toward the source of the caterwauling. It came, as he expected, from a complex maze of chest-high wooden panels covered with rice matting on the outside and lined with plastic sheeting. A pulsating snake of clear plastic tubing coiled up a sapling at one side, to empty into a bucket full of holes suspended from a branch, from which appliance water poured with force enough to comprise a make-do shower. Kirk was underneath, happily soaping his hairless chest, while a bubbly puddle slowly formed around the flat piece of slate on which he stood.

"Ahem!" Calvin called. "You're pickin' up a lot of static on your radio—oh, was that *you*? Sorry!"

Kirkwood blinked out from under his flag of sodden hair as he rinsed off his torso. "You don't like my singin'?"

"Is *that* what that was? I thought somebody was stranglin' cats. But I guess I like it better than some things."

Kirk squatted down and did something obscure to the hose near his feet, at which point the bucket's arcing streams fizzled down to drips. He grabbed a large red towel from a nearby post and applied it to his face as he joined Calvin. "Like what?" he asked with an innocent grin.

"Like the company that hangs around here, for one thing," Calvin replied seriously, pointing to the sky, where the owl still circled. "Like you not wakin' me up when you were supposed to, for another."

Kirk was squinting into the glaring heavens. "Why're you in such a hurry?"

" 'Cause I've gotta be in south Georgia tomorrow night—like I told you."

"Yeah, but where were you so hot to get to this mornin'?"

"Athens, mostly. There's somebody I need to talk to down there."

"This somebody have a name?"

"Dave Sullivan—if it's any of your business."

Kirk's face turned serious as he looked back down at his cousin. "If that's what I think it is circling around up there—or who—it may very well be my business."

"You're thinkin' what I'm thinkin'?"

"Maybe."

"I've still gotta go to Athens."

"No, you don't."

"The *hell* I don't!"

"I've *got* a telephone, Cal. You can accomplish the same thing that way and lots faster. Besides, I've got breakfast ready—brunch, I guess it is now—and *you* look like you could use a shower. Better strike while the pressure's good."

Calvin eyed the apparatus dubiously. He *was* feeling pretty fried. And there was something pleasantly primal about cleaning up *and* looking at landscape at the same time.

Except—

His face clouded. Once more he glanced skyward, but the owl—if that's what it had been, for he was no longer certain—had disappeared.

Kirk wrapped the towel around his waist and indicated the maze. "Be my guest."

"Maybe it'll wake me up," Calvin agreed sullenly, unwinding his Ace bandage before shucking his jeans and boxers.

Kirk flopped up against one of the posts that supported the screen, just out of the range of spray. He looked troubled, Calvin realized, as he stepped under the bucket and found the tap that turned on the water. It was cold, bracing, and straight from the ground, courtesy of Kirkwood's well. He stood there for a long appreciative moment, close to gasping at the cold, and let the water soak him all over, then felt for the soap. When he blinked his eyes clear again, it was to see his cousin still present, gazing a discreet few degrees off direct, but still sort of halfway looking at him. And he still looked troubled. In fact, Calvin realized, he looked old and weary. And his mouth kept twitching, as if he was about to say something and kept changing his mind.

"Something buggin' you?" Calvin asked finally.

Kirk's gaze shifted toward him, hard and piercing—and suspicious. "Why do you ask?"

" 'Cause you look like hell."

"It's not deliberate."

"Was that an excuse or an evasion?"

Kirk moved his gaze to the ground and folded his arms across his chest, gnawing his lip.

"You . . . sleep okay?" Calvin asked carefully.

"Did you?"

"Mostly. Had some uncool dreams, though."

"What kind?"

Calvin told him.

Kirk listened, brow wrinkled, his mouth a thin line. "I didn't dream anything—I don't think. Certainly nothin' like that, so you couldn't have been pickin' me up. But . . ." He paused, puffed his cheeks. "Oh, hell,

Cal . . . I didn't dream, but I . . . I heard something, and maybe—*maybe* saw something, too.''

Calvin stepped far enough out to hear clearly and let the water pound his back. It was lessening in force. He'd have to finish soon. ''What kind of something?''

Kirk shrugged, rolled his eyes. ''I . . . don't know. Maybe nothin'—I, uh—that is, this is gonna sound really stupid, but don't laugh, okay? But . . . where'd you take your clothes off last night?''

Calvin regarded him seriously. ''I *thought* I did that on my side and left 'em on that big trunk under the front window. Only when I looked for 'em just now they were under *your* window. I assumed you'd put 'em there as a joke, or something.''

''No joke.''

Calvin knew by his face he was telling the truth. ''No.''

Silence. Then, from Kirk: ''I saw your dad last night, Cal—I think I did. I woke up just before light and had to whizz, and I got up, and tripped on your boot—I guess it was migratin' or something—and . . . and then I went out on the back porch, and while I was lettin' fly, I got this feelin' of something not right out there in the yard, and I finally saw this sorta half-assed shape over by the trees.''

''What kinda shape?''

''Hard to tell. Man-sized, though. And to tell the truth, I sorta thought it was maybe that Snakeeyes asshole snoopin' around, 'cept that it wasn't tall enough for him, and it . . . it had a smaller shape with it like—''

''Like a kid?'' Calvin finished for him. He retrieved the soap again to give his hair a go. A minute or so of that, a rinse, and he'd be done.

''Like . . . a kid. Actually, there might even have been *two* of 'em, but one was real hazy like. And—''

''*Two!*'' Calvin broke in. ''Boy or girl?''

"Boy, I think. Both of them. I—*Dammit!*"

"What?" As Kirk started toward the house.

"Telephone."

"Ignore it."

"Can't. Guy at the game promised to call me about a survey job this mornin'. I can't let him hang. Sorry."

"You're gettin' too corporate," Calvin called to his cousin's departing back, as his kinsman's amble broke into a jog, then a run. He made the back door on the fifth ring. The towel didn't.

And Calvin was alone with his thoughts, cold water, and a pretty mountain morning.

Closing his eyes, he stepped back into the shower, soaked his hair thoroughly, then stuck his head out again and commenced lathering it. Inevitably, some ran into his eyes, making them sting. He blinked, squeezed his lids shut, as he tried to rinse his eyes clear.

Then . . .

"*Goddamn!*" as something slammed into his shoulder—something soft and warm and sticklike. And with it came the heavy thump of wings, and air fanned against his flesh, and then another hit, and this time a thin-edged pain tore into the flesh of his clavical. Calvin flung himself out of the shower, ducked below the level of the screen. Some kind of large bird was flogging the hell out of him! But even as he tried to get his bearings, wings smacked his face. Claws scraped his back, missed, then grabbed again and hung on. Half blinded by soap, he could only beat at whatever had latched onto him, but to little avail. Sharpness slashed into the hand he tried to work under the gripping talons; a beak snapped at him as he scrabbled vainly for the neck in hopes of throttling whatever it was. Something clutched at his throat . . . pulled. A beak stabbed at his eyes. He flung himself flat on the ground, rolled onto his stomach, then had an idea and half-staggered, half-crawled back under the bucket. With one hand on the bird, the other found the faucet and turned it up full. Water beat down, but the bird would not let go. His vision was marginally clearer now—except that he had to keep his eyes closed lest that beak find them. But the little he could see showed that the water pooling about his knees swirled with red.

More claws, more wings, more impacts, more shrieks, more yells and curses. Again something tore at his throat, yanked, tore, then yanked harder.

*It was going for the scale!* It was the owl, and it was after the uktena scale!

"Get the hell away from me, Snakeeyes!" he gritted, beating at the bird.

"Fucking *hell!*" another voice broke in, distantly. "*Hang on!*" Already much closer.

And with that, the owl—or whatever—that had been assailing him ceased its attack. Venting a frustrated cry, it released him and flapped noisily into the air.

Calvin was crouched panting beneath the shower, absently watching blood draw deltas down his legs on their way to the sea around his feet, when Kirk pounded up to him. "What the hell was *that* all about?" his cousin demanded.

"I was attacked."

"I could see that much, stooge."

"Well *I* couldn't see anything. What was it anyway?"

"Owl, I think—probably the one we saw earlier. You know, *that* owl."

"If that was an owl, I'm Mickey Mouse," Calvin grunted as he turned off the faucet and accepted the towel Kirk had brought him. He didn't wait around to use it, though. One final quick scan of the sky—innocently clear now—and he wrapped the towel around his waist, retrieved his bandage and clothes, and started toward the cabin. His ribs hurt like hell. "If you don't mind," he gasped, "I think I'll finish up inside—it's safer that way."

"Sorry!"

"I was the one dumb enough to stand naked and blind with my mojo hangin' out in full view of something that evidently wants it."

"Maybe."

Calvin stood on the porch, applying the towel to his hair, as Kirk paused in the door and waited. "No *maybe*—except possibly to the last, except that there're too many coincidences."

"So what gives?"

Calvin donned his jeans and followed Kirk inside. Kirk had made a beeline for the coffeepot. "There's still the small matter of breakfast. I mean I'd *like* to pretend I'm leadin' a normal life, like I was a day ago."

Calvin grimaced sourly—both from frustration and a whole new assortment of pains—but eased down at the table, only then realizing that he was still bleeding in trickles and his hands were in tatters. Fortunately, Kirk seemed nonplussed, though he passed him a wad of paper napkins. "Yeah, well, it's like that, magic is," Calvin told him apologetically as he commenced dabbing. "Once you start foolin' around with it—or it with you—it won't ever leave you alone."

Kirk sank down opposite and filled his plate mechanically. His face was grim. "I repeat," he said finally, "what gives?"

"Well," Calvin sighed, "after we eat, I guess I'd better split. In fact," he added with more conviction, "I'm *gonna* split. Things have already gotten too risky for you up here. If I stay, they'll only get worse."

Kirk eyed him steadily. "I'm goin' with you."

"You can't."

"Why the hell not? Asshole or not, you're still the

closest thing to a brother I've got. I'm not lettin' you—''

"*No*," Calvin interrupted. "You *can't*. Don't you see? It's me they're after—two *different* thems, best I can tell. One wants my scale—that's pretty obvious. If I leave, you'll be cool."

"And you'll be in deep shit."

"Maybe—but it'll be deep shit I know how to prepare for, now that I know kind of what kind of threat I'm up against." He wondered, though, if he felt as confident as he was talking, but soldiered on. "And furthermore, if that was Dad's ghost you saw last night, I really oughta hit the high timber."

"Why? It's obviously gonna follow you."

"Right! Which means it won't follow you, 'cause even a ghost can't be in two places at once—I hope."

"But . . ."

"No, think, man! Ghosts seek out their closest kin for company, right? That's what you said last night. So I'm Dad's closest kinsman, given that his parents are dead, as is Mom—unless you count his older sister—your mom. But that's all according to the *white* system. But by *our* system—our *traditional* system—his closest kin would be your mom; that hasn't changed. But you, as sister's son, would actually be closer kin to him than I am. And since this ghost business seem's to be following traditional lines, at least in part, it means I'd better stay as far away from the rest of my kin as possible—especially since you and your mom are more vulnerable than I am. And while I'm pretty darned sure it wants me, I'd hate to tempt it otherwise!"

"But—"

"No buts. Breakfast, packing, and I'm outta here, and I hope like hell nothin' happens to you before I get back."

"Anything you can do, uh . . . otherwise?"

Calvin shrugged. "I might be able to ward the place. But it's awfully big—and you do a lot of comin' and goin'."

"How 'bout if you just ward me?"

Calvin looked thoughtful, then strode to the front door. His cycle was still in the yard—though it likewise looked as though it might have moved a foot or two to the west—which made him shiver all over again. Steeling himself, he stepped onto the porch, then checked the sky. It was clear, save for a few specks very high up indeed. A pause for breath, and he ran for it. He unlocked the BMW's saddlebags, fished inside one for the war clubs he'd wedged in there. And wondered, briefly, why he'd not shown them to Kirk last night. He supposed because he'd forgotten them. Lord knew he tried to, most times, though he'd practiced with them a bit. Still . . .

A pause to relock the compartments, and he returned to the house. Kirk was still at the table, looking puzzled. Calvin strode over to him, handed him an atasi. "Here," he said. "Whatever else this is, it's also a weapon. Presumably it'll bust heads, whether human, bear, or raptor. It, uh, came from somewhere else, and maybe it's got some power for good in it. I'd suggest you keep it with you always. Sleep with it, if you have to. And make damned sure you've got it with you if you go outside, even if it's just to take a piss. Okay?"

Kirk looked solemn. "Fine."

"And *don't* let Snakeeyes see it!"

A troubled scowl, touched with irritation.

"Sorry to freak you, man! Shoot, I'm sorry I've fucked up your life, when all I wanted was a little advice."

"No problem. It's been a pain, somewhat, but God knows you've left me with plenty to ponder."

"I hope that's all you have to do."

"Me too."

The next fifteen minutes were a flurry of activity, last-minute questions, speculations, and instructions. Calvin finished dressing, repacked his knapsack, and added most of the leftover breakfast including the coffee in a thermos and the orange juice in a canteen. They neatly filled the space the atasi had vacated.

Calvin paused on the porch to give his cousin a hearty hug. "Sorry again," he murmured.

Kirk held him close. "No big deal, kid. You be careful. And me . . . well, I always *wanted* to be a warrior."

"I hope you never have to be," Calvin told him as they broke apart. A moment later, he was astride the bike, vaguely aware that once again Kirk's phone was ringing. He did not drive slowly this time, but was grateful for the cover—for every time he hit clear terrain, he saw the shadow from overhead. Often enough, in fact, that shadow lay right atop his: the outstretched wings of an . . . owl.

# Chapter X:
# Mojo in Milledge Hall

*(Athens, Georgia—*
*Sunday, June 17—midafternoon)*

According to the map tucked inside Calvin's black leather jacket, it was slightly more than a hundred miles from cousin Kirkwood's place north of Qualla Boundary to the traffic light that had just caught him at the juncture of Thomas Street and Broad on the fringe of downtown Athens, Georgia. A hundred-odd miles as the road curved, he corrected; less than that as the crow flew. Or the owl.

Fortunately, the owl wasn't flying anymore—or else was maintaining a very discreet distance indeed. Certainly he hadn't seen its shadow overlying his own for nearly two hours, and he'd been on the road less than three. Which *didn't* mean he'd dropped his guard, only that, as best he could determine, there were three possible causes for the critter's absence.

The first was that it really had been an ordinary owl which had simply followed him a ways, then lost interest. Not likely, granted, but conceivable.

The second and far more reasonable possibility was that it had *not* been an ordinary owl, but was still subject to natural laws to the extent that it had either become tired or had realized that Calvin could maintain sixty miles per hour a lot more easily than it could, and longer.

The third was that the damned thing didn't like cedar.

Witches didn't like cedar. That was . . . not quite a fact, maybe—and it wasn't a topic he'd ever raised with Uki—but his medicine-man grandfather had claimed as much, and Mooney had recorded essentially the same. Experience seemed to bear out the theory, too, because a few miles south of Qualla he'd entered a stretch of road so overhung by trees they veiled all view of the sky for seconds at a time—and conveniently enough, a lot of them had been cedars. Once he'd realized that, it had taken but an instant to zip off the road, trim a few sprigs, and affix them to the bike—and inside his jacket, his pockets, and the bandana he wore inside his crash helmet. The shadow had been waiting for him when he'd emerged, of course, but the instant it had tried to superimpose itself upon his analog again, it had missed a couple of beats and fallen back, at which point he'd lost sight of it.

Now if he were only rid of it for good. . . .

A honk from behind informed him that the light had changed. He blinked, gazed down the hill toward the University of Georgia campus, and gunned the bike. Thomas Street became East Campus Road without altering otherwise, and Calvin zipped along until forced to slow by the railroad tracks beside Tanner Lumber Company (where Dave had brought him in quest of material for the loft he and Alec had constructed in their dorm room during Calvin's one previous visit to the Classic City). Just past that, to the right, he glimpsed the terrace behind the art department, then Friedman Hall's ground level and the back of Baldwin Hall: the anthropology building.

Another light, up a hill, right turn into a parking lot, and he was zeroing in on Target Two. He parked the cycle in a slot designated for same and climbed stiffly off, then activated the theft alarm and pocketed the key. A pause to stretch, unhook his helmet, and retrieve his backpack—*Lord*, but his ribs were sore, never mind his shredded collarbone and hands—and he strode across a scrap of walkway to the side door of Milledge Hall: the westernmost of a pair of Williamsburgesque dormitories that bracketed a small courtyard on one side while facing the larger one of Reed Quad on the other. A corridor stretched straight ahead, stairs went up to the right. He took them, turned right at the top, then right again, to gain the opposite end of the U. Second door from the end, to his left, and he knocked four times, a certain pattern Target Two should have recognized.

*If* it/they was/were home, the alternative to which was only then occurring to him. He *hadn't* called from Kirkwood's, though he'd intended to and probably should have. The main thing he remembered from his previous conversation, more than a week ago, was that finals began next week.

Another knock, and then—

"Calvin, m'man!" David Sullivan cried, whisking into the hallway to snare Calvin by the less-damaged shoulder and yank him inside. "I *figured* that was you!"

Calvin shot him a reproachful glare as he stumbled into the small room. "Then why'd you leave me standin' on the doorstep?"

" 'Cause it's good for you to suffer."

Calvin couldn't resist a derisive snort as he helped himself to a seat in the very secondhand armchair squeezed below the single window and between two institutional-style desks. The loft above housed massive speakers with storage space between. "I've suffered enough in the last two days,'' Calvin continued, holding up his bandaged hands for emphasis.

David flopped down on the lower of the bunk beds opposite and turned down the stereo: REM's latest, appropriately enough. In token of the heat that permeated the cramped room despite a box fan and open windows, he was wearing gym shorts but no shirt or shoes. "Jesus, man, what happened?"

"The owls are not what they seem," Calvin replied cryptically, leaning forward to shuck out of his jacket though retaining his black T-shirt. "You, uh, don't act surprised to see me," he added.

A mysterious chuckle. "Maybe I'm *not*."

An eyebrow lifted. "Oh?"

A shrug countered. "I've got a girlfriend who can scry, remember? And a roomie with an oracular stone."

Calvin leaned forward abruptly, his face an even mix of relief and concern. "He's got it *here*?"

"Where else would it be?" David replied with a touch of sarcasm. "The damned thing has to be fed blood once a month or it'll go crazy. You think he'd leave it a hundred miles away, where his mom could find it?"

Calvin shrugged expressively and flopped back into the chair again. "Well, I'd hoped he had more sense than that, but you never know, with McLean."

"He's got more sense than I have," David replied flatly. "And more caution. It's just that he likes to believe that the world works in a certain way. He likes things predictable."

"He's got the wrong friends, then."

"Tell me about it."

"Speaking of which," Calvin said, "uh, where's Liz?"

David checked his watch, did a fast mental calculation. "Prob'ly gettin' down with Toad the Wet Sprocket, if she got to Atlanta in time."

Calvin smacked himself on the forehead. "Oh yeah, right! That all-day concert she won *one* ticket to."

"You got it!"

"Leavin' you and McLean to slave over finals—the bitch."

David's reply was a mute, resigned shrug. In the lull, Calvin scanned the room, noting piles of books and CDs; the quarter-scale poster of the new Bugatti EB 110; a wooden nail-keg full of umbrellas and swords, both metal and rattan, as well as a bokken. "So, what *about* the big Mach-One, anyway?"

"Huh? Oh—he went on a pizza run with—Oops! Never mind."

Calvin's eyes narrowed suspiciously. "Who?"

"*Never mind.*"

"*Dave!*"

"You'll find out soon enough."

"Gimme a break, Sullivan, I don't have time for this shit!"

David checked his watch and smiled smugly. "*Au contraire*, Red-Man, if you're here for the reason I think you are, you're on your way to south Georgia to fulfill a certain bargain you were fretting about on the phone last week. Only you're not actually supposed to meet the kid until tomorrow. And since ground zero's less than five hours away, you've got plenty of time. Therefore—"

He did not finish—or if he did Calvin couldn't hear him because his ears were suddenly full of fabric, as David launched himself across the room and stuffed a pillow into his face. Calvin pushed it back immediately, but by then, David had hauled him off the chair and was sitting astride his belly, pinning him to the floor. Calvin writhed and twisted, but could not escape nor protest, for his mouth was still half-clogged. David promptly dived in, tickling him unmercifully. Eventually, however, Calvin got a hand free, but that only left his side more unprotected. David tickled harder, Calvin kicked and giggled—and swore. Once he managed to reach David's side and got in a counterattack, but David twitched away. Calvin grabbed his leg and yanked hair—hard.

"Jesus Christ, Fargo!" David yipped, as his start allowed Calvin to get his other arm free.

"Get off me, you asshole," Calvin gasped. "Dammit, man, I've got three cracked ribs!"

"You're kiddin'!"

Calvin yanked up his T-shirt, exposing the Ace bandage. "Not hardly."

David scooted backward to lean against the bank, looking very contrite. "Oops! I, uh, *thought* you felt funny down there. But Jesus, guy . . . what happened?"

"Got ambushed by a bunch of white boys."

"Accidentally? Or—"

"Anetsa."

David nodded sagely. "I . . . see."

"Well *I* don't!" came a deliberately deep voice from behind him. Definitely male, but disguised. There was also an obvious aroma of oregano, tomato sauce, and cheese. But before Calvin could twist around to investigate, he found his ribs assailed again.

"*No!*" David shrieked.

Which was all the opening Calvin needed. As whoever it was hauled him back, simultaneously digging into his armpits, David shot past him. And then, with a flip and a thump, it was Calvin's turn to find himself sitting athwart someone's thighs, while David knelt on the would-be assailant's upper arms and the two of them tucked up his shirt and attacked both ribs and belly.

Alec—for so it was: David's longtime best friend and

much-suffering roommate—was mortified.

The smell of pizza grew stronger—and then, abruptly, another face swung into view behind Alec's: female, pretty, framed by blond hair—

"Sandy!" Calvin managed between grunts, gasps, and guffaws, as he sought to disentangle himself and rise. She held, he could hardly help but notice, two boxes from Domino's Pizza.

"Do I know you?" she inquired distantly.

"I hope you—" (embarrassed giggle) "—know *somebody*—'cause otherwise these two assholes here are gonna be mighty pissed."

" 'Cause a good-lookin' woman brought pizza?" David interrupted, releasing their victim. "Not hardly!"

Alec simply rose, dusted himself off, secured his shirttail in his cut-off cammos, and looked put-upon. "There's beer, too," he muttered.

Calvin could only grimace helplessly. "Christ, gal, what're *you* doin' here?"

Sandy deposited the pizza on the nearer desk and eased around to look him square in the eye. "Maybe I *do* know you . . . or would if you told me what *you're* doing here. Or possibly explained why you think it's cool to head off into the wild blue with no more than a *very* cryptic note of explanation." She propped herself against the bunk, looking at Calvin with a mixture of amusement, irritation, and perplexity. Khaki hiking shorts and a sleeveless black T-shirt added to her air of determined competency. David, obviously familiar with most of what was happening, tactfully investigated the pizza.

"Sorry," Calvin sighed as he sank back into the chair from which he had been so gracelessly evicted. "I guess things just reached a head, and . . . I didn't want to tell you 'cause I knew you'd want to come along, and I— Well, mostly I just thought it was too risky."

"Well, you'd better think again!" But Sandy's expression, though still dangerous, held a note of humor. She'd won so far—or at least established parity. Now came the bargaining.

"Mind tellin' me how you found me?" Calvin asked. "I mean even with educated guesses, you were playin' pretty high-stakes odds."

Sandy grinned like a Cheshire cat. "I don't mind telling you if you don't mind telling me what's going on with you—besides this business with Brock, I mean."

"What makes you think there's business besides Brock?"

"Your cousin."

Calvin's mouth dropped open. "You talked to Churchy?"

Sandy nodded, sparing a smile for David, as he passed her a slice of pizza. "Actually, he called me—I think it was right after you left. He told me some stuff, but wouldn't be real precise—except he let something slip about you going to Athens."

Calvin rolled his eyes. "But how'd you get here ahead of me?"

"I hadn't finished unpacking from my trip—or that camping trip we took week before last, for one thing. I live closer to here than your cousin does, for another."

A sidelong glance. "How long've you been here, anyway?"

Sandy grinned. "Long enough to get these lazy asses out of bed and make one of 'em point me to a pizza place. Would you believe they were still sacked out at *noon*?"

"Late night partyin', huh?" Calvin wondered, lifting an eyebrow at David.

David shook his head sadly. "Late night at the science library readin' 'bout plate tectonics."

"Punctuated by a trip to the 40 Watt," Alec added, with a grin.

"That was research, too."

"It was?"

"The La Brea Stompers were playing, which were named for a set of tar pits out in California. And plate tectonics is responsible for those tar pits—sort of."

It was Alec's turn to roll his eyes.

"Okay," Sandy said primly. "You've had my explanation, short form. I want yours."

"I'm goin' to see Brock. I don't have any choice."

"And what're you doing here?"

"Visiting friends."

"And?"

"Solicitin' advice from friends who know more about mojo than I do."

"And?"

"What?"

"Any other problem?"

Calvin sighed. "You're not gonna take no, are you?"

Sandy shook her head.

Another sigh. "Okay, folks, let's eat, and then . . . I guess it's time I told you about the ghosties. . . . "

The ground-beef-and-onion pizza was gone, and the supreme-with-extra-cheese seriously depleted, along with five-sixths of the six pack of Dos Equis Sandy had brought, when Calvin finished. He'd told it all, too—as much as he could remember—as much as seemed relevant. Not that he'd wanted to, exactly, but once he began—trying to gloss over as much as possible—first Sandy, then Alec, and finally even David had seemed compelled to stop him every two sentences for an elaboration or clarification. Eventually he'd given up and laid out the long version—there *was* time for it after all, much as he hated to admit it. And somehow the more deeply into it he got, the easier it became to explain. It was catharsis, he realized, when, after nearly an hour, he paused for a sip of the orange juice Sandy had thoughtfully provided. And catharsis, much as it hurt to undergo, in the end felt mighty good.

"So," David said when Calvin fell silent, "I guess the next question is what can *we* do about it?"

"By which you mean . . . ?" Alec asked, looking startled. "I mean, *which* we?"

David glared at him. "You and me, of course."

Sandy raised an eyebrow in challenge.

"And Sandy," he added, blushing. "Uh, sorry, it's just that me and Alec are *used* to this sort of thing, and sometimes we get hidebound about thinking other people might either be involved or want to be involved."

"I don't *want* to be involved," Sandy broke in quickly. "But it doesn't look like I have a choice. It involves Cal, therefore I have no choice."

"Sure you do," Calvin muttered. "You could stay home like I wanted you to."

"Like a good little housewife? Which I'm not!"

"Like a brilliant physics teacher who could get in over her head—and who would be missed if she went AWOL."

Sandy stared at Calvin incredulously, conflicting emotions chasing each other across her face. "You mean to tell me," she said with an effort, "that you think *you* wouldn't be missed?"

"Not by as many people as you," Calvin shot back. "I've kept my name out of paperwork deliberately."

"As is your right," Sandy replied. "But are you even *listening* to yourself, Cal? The way you're talking, it sounds like you're afraid you might not . . . come back."

Calvin shrugged helplessly, feeling outnumbered. "That *is* a possibility—and more so now. Back when it was just me gettin' together with Brock—"

"And you'd actually have put yourself in a situation you might not return from with no more word to me than one cryptic note?" Sandy interrupted, close to shouting.

Calvin had never seen her so angry. Her earlier good humor—which he'd thought a bit forced—was obviously shredded completely. "I . . . honestly didn't think of that," he said at last. "I mean, I knew it was dangerous—or that once I saw the ghosts it was. And I knew that I didn't want you mixed up in it—'cause whatever else you say, two people dead or vanished or crazy is worse than one. But I guess I never really thought not comin' back was a possibility."

"You wouldn't," Sandy muttered, her eyes misting. "Cocky son-of-a-bitch."

Calvin looked at her helplessly. "Okay, okay, I'm *sorry*! I played the whole thing wrong by tryin' to play it right and spare as many people as possible."

"Which you haven't done, if what you said about what happened up at your cousin's place is true."

"Which I concede," Calvin sighed. "But remember, he's better equipped to deal with that kind of thing than you are."

"Barely."

"So what do you want me to do?"

"Let me go with you, of course. No, let me rephrase that. I want you to try and stop me from going with you! You thought Spearfinger was bad? You ain't seen nothin', baby."

Calvin shifted his gaze toward his friends, seeking silently for support. "Dave . . . ?"

"Don't look at *me*, man," David said, wide-eyed. "I already volunteered."

Alec looked uncomfortable. "And me, of course."

Calvin shook his head. "No, folks, look: it's not that

bad—not yet, I don't think. Besides, don't you guys have finals?''

Alec shot David a knowing look. "There . . . is that.''

"Which could screw up your whole future if you miss.''

David shrugged. "There's always incompletes.''

Again Calvin shook his head. "No guys, I can't let you. One, it really is my problem. Remember what Uki said? That I have to be responsible for my actions? Well, that's what I'm doin'. *I* brought Spearfinger into this world, remember? *I'm* the reason my dad and those kids got killed. *I'm* the one who made that stupid, rash, conceited promise to Brock. *I'm* the one who played in a stupid ball game with my shirt off, so that the whole friggin' world could see what the world doesn't need to know exists!''

"All of which you did for completely altruistic reasons,'' Sandy countered, her former anger dispersed as quickly as it had erupted.

"All of which involved me showin' off,'' Calvin shot back. "I mean, if I'd been really good at what I was fakin'—good at woodcraft, and all—I could've shot a real deer, without havin' to conjure up Awi Usdi, and none of the rest of this would've happened.''

"But it *has* happened.''

"Right! And *I'm* the one who has to set it straight!''

"Which is not to say you can't have help,'' David noted.

"Which *is* to say that nobody's gonna risk anything important to them for my sake—not that can't be fixed.''

David gnawed his lip. "Still, we don't have any tests until Thursday, which gives us three days. I mean, what's the difference between an A and a B, really?''

"Dean's list,'' Sandy replied instantly. "*Magna cum laude* versus *summa cum laude*, maybe. Possibly scholarships.''

"Which, in the larger scheme of things, hardly seem important."

"Speak for yourself!" Alec snorted.

"No," Calvin said finally. "You guys aren't goin', and that's that! And if I wasn't afraid of messin' up the best thing in my life, I wouldn't let even Sandy go, no matter what she says. But if you guys really do wanta help out . . . well, it *would* be nice if Alec could fire up the old ulunsuti." He cocked a brow at Alec hopefully.

Alec, in turn, looked troubled, his face shadowed, his expression firm. "Well, gee," he began in a quiet voice, "this . . . seems to be a day for honesty, so I guess I'd better be. I wish you hadn't asked me that, Cal. I *hate* using that thing, not from fear, but because—well, just because it really freaks me. It can't exist and do the things it does, and yet it does. And I'm into science and logic and rationality, and it circumvents those things. I mean . . . jeeze . . . I'd walk through hell with you, man, bear any kind of physical hardship or discomfort. But that thing fucks with your *mind*! And I'd like to at least keep that under *my* control."

"Which means you won't do it?"

"Which means I want you to know what I'm risking when I do."

"*When?*"

"Oh, I'll do it, of course. I just wanted to lay out the facts first. Except—"

"What?"

Alec looked exceedingly uncomfortable. "Could I ask, like one favor?"

"Sure—I guess."

"That we ask it just one question. I mean, this thing freaks me enough as is, and . . . well, frankly, I don't even know what would happen if we tried to ask more than one question at a hit."

"That sounds fair," Calvin agreed, after a pause.

"Right," from David. "So . . . what do we ask?"

Calvin scratched his chin. "Well, there's no point in askin' it about Brock. That's the least of my worries and could be solved in a positive way—like by showin' him how to ward, or find things, or something. The only thing to ask there would be to see if the ulunsuti predicts any unforeseen negative effects from whatever I teach the kid—and I don't think it works that way. You have to be specific, don't you?"

Alec frowned, followed by a long sigh, then a nod. "It won't work to ask it what to do about a situation because it mostly shows places and . . . events."

Calvin gnawed his lip. "Well, that certainly narrows the field. I can't ask it about what to do about the ghosts—or about what kind of threat this Snakeeyes guy is—if he even is one."

"Could you maybe ask what the most immediate threat is, though?" Sandy suggested.

"Even that might be stretching it," Alec replied hesitantly. "I mean, I'm not trying to hedge or anything, but that's kind of a multiple-choice question."

"Would it help if *I* did the asking?" Calvin wondered.

Alec shook his head. "Not really. It was given to me, and I think it's kinda bonded with me now—I guess 'cause I . . . feed it and all. And yeah, I know we've all linked together and used it, but *I* used it so much back during the war in Faerie that I can kinda—I dunno—tell what it *likes*, I guess. And I don't think it likes anybody to use it except me and Liz—and she's not available."

A shrug. "Whatever."

Silence.

Then, from Alec: "Actually . . . it works best if you just sort of *worry* at it, and let it show you what it wants."

Calvin exchanged glances with Sandy. "Not what I wanted, exactly, but worth a try, I guess."

"It's your call," she told him.

"So," David said brightly, reaching for the penultimate slice of pizza, even as he eyed the remaining beer speculatively, "when do we begin?"

"Twilight'd be best," Calvin replied. "That's the next *between* time."

"Besides which, it'd give us time to crash for a spell," Sandy yawned. "Which I, at least, need to do."

"And would give these fine lads a chance to study some," Calvin added.

"As if we could," Alec muttered.

But that settled it. Calvin and Sandy shed their boots (Calvin also his shirt and jeans) and slid into the lower bunk together. David and Alec claimed opposite corners and went through the motions of reading. To Calvin's surprise, he slept.

"I guess I can't put this off any longer, can I?" Alec asked from the open door roughly five hours later. The sun, visible through windows at the end of the hall, had just touched the horizon. The shadows were long on Reed Quad. Somewhere a stereo was playing Jesus and Mary Chain.

"No time like the present," David told him, in mid-fidget.

Alec grunted, padded barefoot to his closet, and rummaged around inside. Eventually he produced a hiking boot, from which he withdrew a small clay jar, tightly stoppered with bark. Pausing to lock the door on his return, he studied the group for a moment. "I guess you guys remember the ritual we've used with this thing before." He sighed. "You're *bound* to, Cal, seein' as how you came up with it. Anyway, it seems to work, so I reckon we oughta stick with it. But there's also the—

uh—small matter of priming it with blood. . . . "

Calvin pulled out his Rakestraw and studied it meaningfully. "Mine oughta do just dandy."

"Probably the best choice," David agreed. "Best I understand these things."

"I'm open to suggestions, Cal," Alec went on, "concerning ritual, and all."

"Well," Calvin said, puffing his cheeks. "Every other time we've sat in a circle with our knees touchin', held hands, and you or Liz did the rest. I'd say we do that again. Oldest to the west, I guess, 'cause it's closer to Death—that'd be you, Sandy—sorry, old gal. Youngest to the east—Alec, I suppose. Dave, you and me'll have to flip for the others."

"Or I could take north," David countered. "This *is* Cherokee mojo we're talkin' about here. And my main adventure in that World was in the north—just like you fought Spearfinger in the south."

"Good point. Okay, so are we ready?"

Alec sighed again. "I reckon."

The next few moments were spent arranging themselves on the floor. A round rag rug filled the space between the bunks and desks—a dorm-warming present from Sandy, as it happened. It was exactly the right size to encompass the four of them sitting cross-legged with their knees touching—*bare* knees, as was preferred, and which was the case anyway, since everyone except Calvin was in shorts, and he'd never put his jeans back on after awakening.

Alec set the pot containing the ulunsuti in the center. Before continuing, though—and unlike the earlier times they had used the oracular stone—Calvin reached into his backpack and drew out a wooden pipe ornamented with hawk feathers and as long as his forearm. With it came sprigs of herbs and a small turtle shell he inverted into a bowl.

"Best to clear the air first," he said in a low voice, whereupon he proceeded to fill the pipe with one of the herbs—*Nicotiana rustica*, he informed them: sacred tobacco—and once it was lit, to blow its smoke to the four quarters, plus up and down. That accomplished, he censed them all with a smoldering bundle of the cedar he had cut, and as an afterthought, handed a bit of that same cedar to the other three. Finally, he set the remnant to smolder in the bowl, which he placed to the west. When he had finished, Alec took the pot in one hand, unstoppered it, and carefully tipped its contents into the other.

A white leather bag slipped out. He took it, and with a frown furrowing his brow, opened the drawstring and let something fall onto his palm.

The ulunsuti—the jewel from the head of the uktena—looked somewhere between a fist-sized raw diamond and a blob of melted glass. It was transparent, but not so much that one could see through it without distortion. And it was split by a darker septum of red.

"Ready when you are," Alec murmured breathlessly. "To prime the pump, I mean."

Calvin set his mouth, took the knife, and in one swift motion drew it across the palm of his left hand. Before the blood could more than well to the surface, he clamped it atop the stone Alec still held. It didn't hurt, really, but Calvin felt an uncomfortable sucking sensation, as if the stone fed not so much on the blood, as on the life essence of which it was a part. He didn't remove it, however, until the feeling had subsided, at which point he slowly eased back his hand.

The stone shone as clear as ever, but the cut was only a thin pink line. His other gashes seemed likewise to have shrunk. Even his ribs felt better.

All but Alec clasped hands and stared at the stone, as Alec fixed it with a look of intense concentration. Not a trance, like Liz did, nor like he sometimes managed, or like Sandy's meditations occasionally precipitated. This was more a focusing, a contest of wills played out invisibly.

No one breathed. No one *dared*.

Then, very slowly, the room receded. For an instant Calvin saw the septum of the ulunsuti glowing like fire. And then, abruptly, it was gone, replaced with . . .

. . . *a forest . . . night . . . streamers of Spanish moss above a too-familiar stream identifying the location as south Georgia . . . a Power Wheel scribed into sandy soil . . .*

. . . *eyes: green eyes: a sensation of cold . . .*

. . . *a blasted plain, dark sanded, the sky like sunset . . . a range of mountains lit with sunset fire glimmering far off . . .*

. . . and then a—a *face*—or a mask, it was hard to tell which. Not human, though, but a cat's: mountain lion, it looked like, but darker, more silvery. And as Calvin stared, fascinated, its lips curled back. But instead of the expected snarl, there came words. "Trust the woman," it demanded, its voice between a growl and a hiss. "Trust the woman—or be damned."

Its eyes met Calvin's then: yellow and slitted—though he knew big cats had round pupils. But as he stared, the colors shifted, the yellow grew paler, the dark pupil eased toward red. And all at once Calvin was once more staring at the ulunsuti.

No one spoke, as if all feared to shatter a moment which had obviously passed yet was in a more subtle way omnipresent.

Finally Calvin risked a heavy sigh. "That wasn't very comforting."

"Not if you saw what I did," David replied with a gulp.

"What . . . did you see?" Alec wondered shakily.

"I'm feeling brave," Sandy managed. "I'll go first."

"Well, gee," Calvin grumbled a quarter hour later, when David had finished recounting his version, "this is a real pisser. I mean we obviously all saw the same thing. Only . . . it was so damned inconclusive! I mean, I don't know a thing more than I did! Like, I don't know if that was the present, the past, or the future—or whether all that was happenin' all at once, or sequentially, or what."

"I got a sense of sequential," David supplied hopefully, but his expression betrayed doubt.

"It looked," Alec said carefully, "as if you were gonna have to make some kinda choice. But then along came Mr. Thundercat—and I don't have a clue what that's supposed to mean."

" 'Trust the woman?' " Sandy supplied.

"You got it," Alec replied. "Only who was he? And . . . which woman?"

David lifted an eyebrow. "Cal? You're the expert."

Calvin could only shrug. "Who he—*it*—was, I don't know—unless it was one of the Ancients—the Ancient of Panthers, I assume. But what he was doing responding to *your* ulunsuti, I have no idea."

"And the woman?"

"It could mean me," Sandy replied instantly. "In which case it means you have to trust me to come along."

"Assumin' one's to believe the first panther that meanders through a vision," Calvin countered.

"*Assuming*." From Alec.

"So what now?" David yawned—surprisingly unperturbed for someone who'd just had his consciousness zapped half a dozen places, plus seen an animal speak.

Calvin checked his watch. "Well, whatever else gets

done, there's still the small matter of my promise to Brock, which *has* to be dealt with. After that . . . maybe the thing to do is to straighten that out, then check back with you guys tomorrow. How 'bout that?''

David eyed him warily. "It sounds logical, which means I don't trust it. What's to keep you from goin' off on some other tangent soon as you finish with Brock?"

"Nothing," Calvin told him. "Except that while there *was* a clear reference to night in a place in south Georgia I've seen, there was nothing else in the vision that indicated any time frame at all."

"Good point," Alec agreed. "And one we hadn't considered."

"So . . . ?" From Calvin.

Sandy took his hand. "So I guess we decide first of all whether we drive another five hours tonight and try to find a place to crash at three in the morning, or deprive these lads of the last of their study time by spending the night here and heading out in the wee hours."

Calvin rolled his eyes. "Uh, the last time I counted on that, Kirk let me oversleep by three hours."

"Fine," Sandy countered instantly. "So you sleep, I'll drive."

"What about us?" David wondered. "I mean, I know you don't want us to go with you, but we'd—that is, I'd—really like to help."

Calvin laid a hand on his shoulder. "You can help. You stay here, stay out of trouble, and run interference for us—which there may very well be. And if you guys don't hear from us by tomorrow night, contact my cousin Kirkwood. And if you haven't heard anything a week after that, try to get hold of Uki."

As if in response, thunder rumbled from a sky grown suddenly dark and grim.

"The sooner we leave, the less rain we have to drive in," Sandy sighed, and rose.

Once again, and closer, came the thunder.

# *Chapter XI:*
# *Scene of the Crime*

*(east of Whidden, Georgia—*
*Monday, June 18—mid-morning)*

"Are you *sure* you can still find the place?" Sandy
yawned as Calvin braked her Bronco to a halt at the end
of an almost-overgrown logging road—one of the hun-
dreds that threaded the pine forests of Willacoochee
County like fracture lines in a slab of green glass. The
look she fixed on him was his least favorite: the subtly
doubtful/delicately superior one she affected in lieu of
reminding him outright that she *was* older and more educated than he—and that, just possibly, she saw his
back-to-nature/live-off-the-land resourcefulness more as
testosterone-enhanced, ego-surfaced adolescent male
braggadocio than true, gut-level competence. Granted,
he hadn't suffered that look in a while; but what on earth
had awakened it now? God knew they'd lived together
for nearly two years, never mind the camping trips, the
hikes in the woods, even that one foray into Galunlati.
Surely she should trust his woodcraft after all that.

And if not . . . well, he'd just have to live with it. He
could bitch, or he could prove her wrong. And in any
event, the last thing he needed on a day when he wanted

to play things calm and careful was an argument. Still, he couldn't suppress a scowl as he flicked off the lights and wipers, turned off the ignition, and opened his door.

Sandy saw it, bit her lip. "Sorry," she murmured. "I oughta know better, oughtn't I? It's just that—well, I guess your stress is rubbing off on me, or something."

Calvin shrugged with deliberate nonchalance and hopped to the ground. Heat bit at him, and blood-warm stickiness that wove through the remnants of morning drizzle, all legacy of the storm that had escorted them from Athens less than twelve hours before. "No big deal," he muttered, wiping his forehead.

Sandy shut her door and joined him at the back of the vehicle, hunched over, as was he. The sky was gray-white, the trees silvered, the air still, save for the soft rattle of rain on pine needles and palmetto fronds. They were already sweating.

Calvin grinned ruefully as he commenced off-loading a pair of backpacks. (He'd reluctantly left the cycle in David's custody.) "Well, gee, I guess I oughta be glad *something's* rubbin' off," he said, "seein' as how I really need to abstain until this is over."

Sandy retrieved the smaller of the two packs and hoisted it onto her shoulders. "Now *that* might make an interesting experiment!"

He secured the other pack and slammed the door. "What?"

"To attempt a precisely controlled ritual or bit of magic at different intervals after sex."

"I'll keep that in mind." He laughed, with another grin, as he joined her on the damp ground beside the road. "It'll give me something to look forward to."

Sandy yawned again. Calvin did, too. They caught each other, snickered. Tension was disarmed. "Told you you should've let me drive," she said—and yawned once more.

"I was too wired. 'Sides, I've had more sleep than you the last day."

"And you've pushed yourself a lot harder."

"Any coffee left?"

"I'll check."

Whereupon Sandy returned to the driver's side of the Bronco, opened the door, and rummaged around on the console. An instant later she returned with a thermos, the cup already unscrewed from the lid. Calvin held it while she poured, took a long, grateful sip. It was good stuff: the last of the batch they'd brewed in the motel room up in Hinesville where they'd spent the night—morning, better say—after their five-hour, rain-plagued sprint from Athens. The four hours of sleep they'd grabbed there at Sandy's insistence had helped a lot, too (she'd suggested, rightly, that whatever he was about was better served with him fresh than stiff and sore from sleeping in the truck or the woods, and that she'd be better company that way as well). But he still felt like he was hitting about a cylinder shy of all eight. It wouldn't do to let that show, though; wouldn't be cool to let Sandy know he was less than perfectly confident.

One final pause to toss back the now-lukewarm coffee and to pull the hood of his army surplus raincoat over his head, and he caught her eye. "Well, old lady, I reckon we'd better get goin'."

"Well, old man," she echoed, "I reckon we had." And followed him into the woods.

"At least it's stopped rainin'," Calvin noted absently a quarter of an hour later, as he paused to divest himself of his raincoat. Sandy mirrored him, set her pack on a fallen cypress log, and shucked out of her top layer of clothing, to stand sweating in jeans, hiking boots, and Black Crowes T-shirt. Calvin was identically clad save that he wore Frye boots and a black T-shirt emblazoned with a diving falcon.

"How much farther?" Sandy wondered.

Calvin studied the sky, then the surrounding land-scape. The clouds were scudding away to the east—rapidly, though the forecast was for more and harder rain that night. Meanwhile, the air had a new-washed feel to it, with the sun lancing hot and clear on leaf and trunk alike. He could almost hear the woods steaming—God knew *he* was: his bandana was soaked through, and not with rain. The pines had shifted to a mix of hardwoods, mostly oaks and poplars; there were fewer palmettos, and more dogwoods, oleander, and wild black cherry. The breeze brought two dominant odors: the sickly sul-fur-sweetness of a pulp mill somewhere to the north, and the more subtle scent of coastal marshes not far east-ward.

"We're close, I think. I didn't see this part in daylight much, but it looks pretty familiar. There were some sites I wanted to . . . avoid, 'cause of their vibes, so I've kinda taken a roundabout way. But unless I miss my guess, we oughta be no more than a quarter mile west of Iodine Creek, which is where I camped. Once I hit that, I can scout both ways until I find my old campsite."

"Or we could *each* take a direction, which would be quicker."

"Have it your way," Calvin said, and soldiered on.


Fifteen minutes later, Calvin eased between a partic-ularly large mass of palmetto fronds and the glossy leaves of a wild magnolia, and breathed a sigh of relief. "How's *that* for dead reckoning?" he asked Sandy as she panted up behind him. "Spot-on, first time out."

Sandy squeezed around him, and together they sur-veyed the location.

Yep, this was it, all right: the secluded creek bank,

screened by palmetto and oleander to the west, with a
low bank to the north giving way to a gentler slope here
on their end. The creek itself was maybe ten yards across
and head-deep (he knew from experience) at center; the
opposite shore overhung by red cedar and live oaks, the
latter bearded with Spanish moss. Marsh began a short
way beyond them.

And right there was the huge live oak beside which
he'd made camp when he'd stopped here a year ago,
hoping to get his head straight about magic, never imagining that Spearfinger was already in his world, tracking
him and leaving corpses in her wake. He'd slept *there*,
built his *asi*—his sweat lodge—*yonder*— Were those
bare sticks lodged in that palmetto what remained of it?
Probably not, given that the area had caught at least one
hurricane last season.

But where was Brock? The kid had been very specific:
they were to meet at this place (because it had power),
today (because it was the anniversary of their first en-
counter), this time (ditto). So where *was* he? Nowhere
in sight, that was for sure. Calvin hunkered down, scan-
ning the earth beneath the tree in search of the footprints
he was certain the boy would not have thought to hide.

Nothing.

Sandy joined him.

Still nothing.

"How long do we wait?"

"I'll give him till dark," Calvin replied. "Then I'll
ask you to stay here while I go back to the Bronco for
the rest of the gear. We'll camp here for two days—or
I will. After that, I'll leave him a note and split, obligation fulfilled. Then I'll—*Shit!*"

Calvin slapped a hand automatically atop his head,
where something hard and sharp had smacked it from
above with sufficient force he half-expected to find
blood. But even as he touched his hair, an object

bounced to the ground. He laughed ruefully when he saw it: an acorn. "Damned squirrel!" he gritted.

Another hit. A very precise one.

He looked up, squinting into the green gloom of the leaves.

And saw the elf.

Or that was his first impression of the slim boy he could just make out lounging along a nearly horizontal limb fifteen feet above his head. Certainly there was a definite feralness about the white skin, the jet black hair, the full and very merry red lips. Nor was the effect lessened by the lad being barefoot and shirtless.

"Took you long enough," a clear adolescent voice called, with a hint of British lilt overlying a southern drawl.

"Brock, you asshole, get down here!" Calvin snapped, feigning anger.

"Yes*sir*, sir," the boy replied promptly—and rather than climb down, simply slid off his limb and dropped the whole distance. He landed in a springy, bent-kneed crouch an arm's length in front of Calvin. Calvin reached out to steady him, even as he hopped back reflexively.

"Well, you've sure changed," Calvin observed as Brock rose, grinning.

He had, too. Though still small for fourteen—he barely came up to Calvin's collarbones—Brock had grown inches in the year since Calvin had seen him, and was now less a skinny kid than a wirily graceful young man. Nicely made, too, as his shirtlessness revealed. But what had changed most was his . . . style. His "look" when they had first met had been pseudo-punk: lots of clothing, most of it black; lots of layers, lots of pockets and zippers and tabs; spiky hair, earring. All that was gone. Oh, he was fashionably pale—doubtless a side effect of British weather—but the thick hair that *had* been sunburn-blond was now jet black and sprawled unbound to his shoulder blades like a tattered black silk flag. As for the minimal rest, he wore low-slung tight black leather pants that had probably cost a fortune and would have looked more at home on a concert stage than in the Georgia woods—and nothing else. The pants had been torn into artful tatters about the calves, and the whole effect truly was otherworldly. Totally inappropriate for the locale, of course, but otherworldly.

"You look . . . different," Calvin told him.

"You don't—much."

"I assume you have other clothes?"

"You don't like these?"

"Not for here."

"I shucked the rest when it started raining. They're in my pack. It's behind the tree. You didn't look there for prints. And I didn't come out here to leave any."

Calvin tried not to smirk. "Am I supposed to be impressed?"

Brock raised a black eyebrow into an inky forelock. "I kinda hoped you would be."

Calvin grimaced resignedly and reached out to give the boy a brief but firm hug, then backed away to lean against the tree, arms folded. Brock beamed, full of himself as always. Sandy looked bemused. Calvin introduced them, noting appreciation and possessive resentfulness flit across the boy's face in quick succession as he bowed rather than shook hands. Calvin shrugged at her where Brock couldn't see. "So," he said, to save Sandy having to make small talk, "is that what the well-dressed young wizard is wearin' in Britain these days?"

Brock's face brightened, as if the sun had lit on it. "Does that mean you're gonna *do* it? Gonna live up to your promise?"

Calvin gnawed his upper lip. Might as well get it over

with. "I made it, therefore I have to . . . but I'd really like to talk to you about some stuff first."

Brock shook back his hair, revealing small ears Calvin half expected to be pointed. "I got time."

"And I've got an expensive vehicle parked by the side of the road two miles away," Sandy inserted, with a knowing glance at Calvin. "What say we pick it up and go into town for lunch?"

"You go," Calvin told her. "What me and Brock-the-Badger No-name need to talk about's better done right here."

Sandy puffed her cheeks in frustration. "Okay then, you guys build a fire. I'll bring lunch—but I *hope* we can sleep in town."

"Cool," Brock cried, grinning like a fool.

Calvin cuffed him on the shoulder. Sandy rolled her eyes and pushed back into the woods. Calvin wished he'd remembered to remind her to be on guard against owls.

"Fire," Calvin said, as he rose to pace out an area midway between the tree and the river. "We need a fire."

Brock looked apprehensive and shifted his weight, but made no other move. His expression all but screamed, *Yeah sure! In* this *heat?*

"To cook on," Calvin prompted. "And to discourage other influences"—he aimed a reflexive look at the still-blue sky—"and to cheer up the day if the rain comes back, which it's supposed to."

Still Brock did not move, seemed lost in hero worship.

Calvin straightened. "That was a *hint*, kid! For a fire, you need firewood, and it's been rainin' a lot, so why don't you see what you can find under some of these brushpiles?" He indicated a size and length. "An armful that big if you can manage it. *And watch out for snakes!*"

Brock's mouth opened as if he were going to smart off, but thought better of it—wisely. It wasn't too soon for the kid to learn patience, nor to discover that most things worth having required preparation and planning, of which magic was not the least. And while Calvin waited, he cleared a section of ground of leaves and the sparse undergrowth, then scooped a circle a yard in diameter in its center. A pair of thigh-thick branches dragged in from either side made seats. And while he was prowling, he found a bit of kindling himself, mostly dry, perhaps indicative of the fact that the rain here had been light. A search through his pack brought out charcloth, thistledown, and the inner bark of cedar: all good tinder. Paper and match would have done, of course, but this time . . . well, the kid had crossed an ocean to be here, and foolish or not, he deserved some content for his trouble.

*If he'd just get his fuzzy butt back!*

Calvin checked the sky again, wondering why he was so jumpy. And just then Brock returned: arms full to overflowing with a staggering weight of exactly what Calvin had ordered. The boy's face was smudged, his chest, arms, and belly begrimed and plastered with leaves and splinters of bark.

"Over there," Calvin grunted, pointing.

Brock nodded sullenly, dumped the mess, then ambled over to lounge beside Calvin. "Okay," Calvin began with a sigh, "most times when I need a fire, I just build a fire. Matches or a lighter, paper, and so forth. But one of the underlying tenets of magic is that you have to have the proper reverence for both the *act* and the *preparation*—in fact, you really shouldn't separate 'em. I honestly don't know how a lot of it works, and I suspect some of it's simply a matter of mental discipline. But a lot of it involves fire. But if you just strike a match and dive in from there, you've taken fire for granted, and Cherokee never took fire for granted. They called it Sacred White and Sacred Red, and there were priests whose only job was to keep Sacred Fire burnin' from year to year. But you had to treat any fire with reverence. You didn't put it out with water, because fire and water were enemies and fire might not work for you then. And to piss on a fire or something like that was an insult and could bring bad luck. Therefore if to make a really proper fire you first have to find just the right tinder—gather thistledown when the thistle's ready, not when *you* are, and stuff like that—and then make cordage and find poplar wood and cedar and make a bow-drill, and put forth all your skill and coordination—and patience and endurance—until you've got an ember, and then take care of it like it was a baby—*then* you appreciate that fire and won't use it for anything frivolous. You get my drift?''

Brock nodded skeptically.

''You can relax,'' Calvin told him, as he held out flint, steel, and charcloth. ''I'm not gonna make you do any of that, but I'll show you how sometime—this is only slightly more modern. Besides, I'm not gonna teach you anything *yet*—but I wanted to impress on you how serious this stuff can be, that it's not a toy to be used to impress your friends and make 'em think you're cool.''

Again Brock nodded.

And Calvin bent himself to making fire. Flint struck steel, sparks flew into charcloth, went out. Again sparks flew, caught this time. Calvin held the down close, blew into it—gently: ever so gently. Flame flared, caught scraps of cedar bark. More fire. He set it under twigs, and blessedly they too caught.

''Cool,'' Brock cried, bending close.

''Hot, actually.'' Calvin chuckled, leaning back. ''Now that that's over, how've you been? When'd you get here? Shoot, *how'd* you get here, and all?''

"Been here 'bout an hour longer than you," Brock told him. "Flew into Atlanta yesterday morning, picked up some stuff, and took the bus down to Hinesville, then hitched the rest of the way."

Calvin started to say something about that being both stupid and dangerous, then remembered that he'd done pretty much the same thing, eschewing the flying, when he'd been Brock's age. "Good enough," he said finally. "So, were you plannin' to camp here, or what?"

A shrug. "I've got a one-man tent I rented, got food, got some cash my sis gave me."

Calvin perked up at that. "How *is* Robyn, anyway? And the kid?"

"She's fine. Got a new boyfriend who's in a band. The kid's a kid: loud, smelly, wet frequently. Cute, though."

"Who's he look like?"

"Mr. Potato Head, mostly. Folks say he looks like me. Hard to tell, without hair."

Calvin studied him for a long moment. "And what're you doin'? That doesn't seem to figure in your notes much."

Another shrug. "Goin' to school, which is pretty neat. Got a part-time job in Robyn's guy's folks' store. I get by, and Mom sends me money."

"How d' you like London?"

"Awesome, man! So much to see, so much to do! All the museums and churches and stuff, and all of it so old; and all the neat folks and stores and things. Everything you want's there, man!"

Calvin gestured at the surrounding woods. "Everything?"

"Well, not this, but the countryside's not bad, 'cept that it rains all the time, and you can't get a tan." He looked down at his flat white belly. "The guys back in

Jacksonville'd laugh me off the beach now. Shoot, I don't even have a tan line anymore.''

"Got any friends? A girlfriend maybe?"

"Couple of guys I hang with. A chick or two, nothin' serious.''

"You're a bit young.''

"I'm *fourteen*!''

"I'm not talkin' about your hormones or your plumbin', kid, I'm talkin' about your head: responsibility, and all that unpleasant stuff.''

"They've got condoms in England, man!''

"And I hope you *use* 'em, if you're doin' anything that suggests one—but that's not what I was talkin' about.''

Brock cocked his head.

They spent the ensuing half hour catching up on a year, the only caveat seeming to be the one subject they had come there to confront. Calvin spoke a lot about finally starting college, of his studies of his own people, of what living with Sandy was like, of her place in North Carolina and their friends. And Brock talked more of his older sister, Robyn, whom Calvin could have loved had he let himself, and of life in England, and how his mom was putting her life back together after the revelation that her second husband had raped her own daughter and left her pregnant, prompting her and Brock to run away from home the previous summer, on which occasion they'd met Calvin—and been exposed to magic.

Eventually Calvin shifted his position to avoid a knob on the branch that was poking his butt. He added a twig to the fire. It burned almost smokelessly, the heat rising straight up, keeping the campsite—relatively—cool. "It really is good to see you, Brock,'' he said at last. "You look like you're doin' pretty good; sounds like you're doin' okay, too.''

Brock looked wary. "Sounds like you're leading up to something."

Calvin sighed. "I am. I didn't want Sandy to come down here at all, and I wasn't sure I was coming, except that you seemed to want it so bad, and I *had* promised, and . . . Well, I really do like you, and you did me a bunch of favors back a year ago when all that Spearfinger stuff was goin' down . . ."

"I sense a *but* approaching."

Calvin nodded. "*But*, Brock, I can't stress enough to you that magic's a responsibility—and I've debated long and hard about what I could teach you and still be safe. Something that would be real to you and obviously not a trick, 'cause I owe you the real thing. But not something you could get in trouble with even if you misused it—and that's been a lot harder than you think. See, I don't know *that* much, and so much of what I do know's mixed up with folk wisdom and folk medicine, or else it's just not relevant to your reality. Like, I know some huntin' charms: ones to make you shoot true. But you don't hunt, unless you've changed in the last year; and you shouldn't use 'em for any other purpose except for that purpose, and only then if you intend to use as much of what you kill as you can. Am I makin' sense?"

"More or less."

"And there's also the question of most of what I know bein' Cherokee magic, except that even that's a bad way of puttin' it, 'cause properly experienced the whole world's magic to a Cherokee. There's an intricate play of forces and cause and effect between—I was gonna say the natural world and man's world, but really there's only the one, and men are a part *of* it, not apart *from* it, but they can still manipulate it in some senses. But anyway, I'm not sure how appropriate it even is for me to teach you Cherokee magic if you're not of that blood—you're not, are you?"

Brock shook his head.

"Seminole? Creek? You got the hair."

"Comes in a bottle."

"Oh, yeah, I forgot."

"No big deal."

Another pause to tend the fire and check the sky. "Anyway, like I was sayin', I'm not even sure it's cool to teach you Cherokee magic 'cause you're not of that blood, so it might not work for you—that is, you haven't grown up soakin' in it, even unconsciously, for years. Nor am I sure what'd happen if you tried it over in England, say, given that it's a place with its own kind of magic. I'm not sure how the different kinds would get along."

Brock's eyes narrowed. "You sure there's even magic *in* England?"

"The place is supposed to be eaten up with it," Calvin replied, thinking that he knew rather too much about the assorted magical Otherworlds that lay about this World. "There's magic—or what we call magic—everywhere."

Brock's eyes were wide, earnest, and far too hopeful. "But you're still gonna teach me something, aren't you?"

"I promised, therefore I will. But I want you to think about it for awhile, first, okay? I want you to go off somewhere by yourself and think. I want you to think about what you could use magic for that would enable you to do good things for people—and you can forget about shapechangin'; *that's* right out. What I've in mind isn't anything major, so we don't have to do any preparation, or anything, elsewise I'd make you fast and sweat and purge and go-to-water—and I may anyway, just so you'll know how to center yourself properly. But for now, just go off and think. Try to get centered, get serious, and . . . just think."

Brock rose, his face indeed very solemn. He glanced down at his dirt-stained chest. "Can I clean up first?"

"Be my guest. Just be back before noon."

"Why noon?"

"One of the *between* times, therefore a good time to do magic."

"Oh."

Calvin checked his watch again, then the sky. Brock paused halfway to the stream. "Why do you keep doing that?"

"What?"

"Looking at the sky. It's like you're watching for something."

"I am," Calvin said softly.

"What?"

"Better you don't know. Better we conclude our business and go our separate ways."

Brock stood unmoving, looking hurt.

"Not 'cause I don't like you," Calvin told him, motioning him on to the creek. "But 'cause I like you too much."

Brock's reply was a stiffening of his shoulders as he turned and wandered down to the waterside five yards away. He squatted there, scooped up water and splashed it along his face, arms, and chest, sluicing away the grime his load of kindling had smeared across him. He rose then, stood shimmering and dripping in the morning light: black and white and golden like a young god—then put on socks and sneakers and marched up the bank toward the woods.

Calvin caught him by the forearm as he passed and pressed something into his damp fingers: a sprig of cedar. "Hang onto that," he said, and let go. He did not see which way Brock went, nor did he hear, for the lad moved with the silence of the dead.

Calvin stared at the fire, watching the wood slowly

blaze up then turn to coals. Glory and decay—like a man's life, if a man was lucky enough to even have glory. Most merely lived, then rotted. Brock wasn't one of those; neither was he, nor Dave, nor Sandy, nor Cousin Kirkwood. They all had their edges, their madnesses, their contacts that could lead them to glory—but perhaps too soon thereafter to ash and ruin.

At least he was close to solving one problem: a few hours from now it would be one down, two to go. *If* he was lucky. If Brock kept his head on straight. If Sandy didn't interfere. If there was no owl.

Speaking of which, he should've warded this place before now. Sighing, he wandered to the nearest cedar tree, cut a number of dark-needled twigs from it, and marked four with pigment from his pack. He had just started to plant the red one on the east side of the campsite when he heard footfalls in the undergrowth to the southwest.

Probably Brock returning.

It was Sandy though, red-faced, sweaty, and breathless, her backpack bulging with supplies, along with plastic bags slung from both arms. Calvin started to say something about it not being *that* urgent, but then he caught the expression on her face.

''Something's wrong?'' he asked, as he took the parcels from her.

She nodded, even as she unslung her pack. ''Check the paper—it's in that bag there.''

Calvin stared at her quizzically, then did as instructed, rummaging among cartons of juice until he found a folded copy of the local weekly rag: the *Willacoochee Witness*.

He could not avoid the headline:

LOCAL BOY MISSING, FEARED DROWNED

And below it was a picture of a chipmunk-cheeked teenager about Brock's age. A boy Calvin had seen all too much of the previous summer, a boy who'd lost a sister to Spearfinger, who'd seen his lifelong best friend leisurely slain by that same monster. A boy who'd helped him kill her at last, maybe at the cost of his peace of mind.

Don Larry Scott.

"Let me see that," Calvin groaned, even as he once again checked the sky.

# Chapter XII:
## Okacha

"*Brock!*" Calvin bellowed into the suddenly nervous quiet. "*Get back here!*"

The campsite rang with the sound, as if the entire landscape sensed the urgency in his voice and hushed to let him have his say. A breeze ventured through, hopefully accidental, in which case it might well be the vanguard of the threatened rain. Or it might be something else. For Calvin suddenly felt as if, already knee-deep in arcana he wanted no part of, he had stepped into a hole and was now in up to—at least his waist, if not over his head. "Have you read this?" he asked Sandy, indicating the newspaper still clutched in his hand.

She nodded, even as she straightened from unpacking the first grocery bag.

"You know who this kid is, don't you?"

Again she nodded, but just as she was about to speak, a commotion to the northwest heralded Brock's return. He fairly stumbled into the clearing, his cacophonous arrival markedly in contrast to the stealth with which he had departed. His pale face was flushed and sweaty, his hair wild. Scratches showed vivid red along his sides where he'd evidently encountered a patch of wait-a-minute vines. "What's the deal?" he gasped, then fixed Calvin with a scowl. "What's wrong?"

Once again Calvin indicated the paper. Brock padded over to peer around his arm, while Sandy stared over his opposite shoulder, wiping her brow. "Recognize him?" Calvin asked for the second time in a minute.

Brock squinted—the light was bright, as the sun neared the zenith. "I dunno, he looks *kinda* familiar . . ." Then: "Oh, yeah, sure! It's that guy we met last summer, back when we were messed up with that Spearfinger sh—I mean crap."

"That's him," Calvin affirmed. "And he's missing."

"A little too coincidentally," Sandy added.

Calvin looked at her intently, then back at the paper. The *Willacoochee Witness* was a weekly rag, published on Saturdays, thus the information they confronted was already two days old at minimum. But this way, at least, they could get a sense of the whole tale, not frustrating fragments acquired piecemeal.

"Read on," Sandy urged.

Calvin did—aloud, mostly for Brock's benefit—and so that he wouldn't get in a hurry and miss something important himself.

## LOCAL BOY MISSING, FEARED DROWNED

### By Raymond Bryan Stepp

Whidden—The Whidden Police announced yesterday morning that they had launched an intensive search throughout the entire tri-county area for fifteen-year-old Donald Lawrence Scott, called Don or Don Larry by his friends. According to police, the boy's mother, Liza-Bet Scott-Richards, missed him when she attempted to call him to breakfast Friday morning. Since then, investigators have little to go on, the main item of note be-

ing the discovery of ritual paraphernalia near
one of the boy's favorite campsites on Iodine
Creek roughly a mile northeast of his mother's rural home. Analysis of this material in-
dicates that the boy had practiced some sort
of divining ritual of probable Native American origin, a fact borne out by evidence found
at the scene, notably the presence of several
volumes on Native American religion. Mrs.
Richards confirmed that her son had become
interested in the occult in the year since the
death of his longtime friend, Michael Chadwick, and of his sister, Allison Scott, adding
that Scott had recently learned that Chadwick's grandfather had been a full-blooded
Cherokee.

Police now believe the boy drowned while
pursuing some aspect of this ritual, possibly
the rite known as "going-to-water," a suppo-
sition borne out by the discovery of his clothing, and of his footprints leading down to the
edge of Iodine Creek but not returning. There
was no sign of a struggle, police say, and they
have all but ruled out suicide. Divers have
checked Iodine Creek for almost half a mile
downstream, and have dragged it, to no avail.

Scott, a rising sophomore at Whidden High
School, is described by his classmates as a
quiet boy, friendly, but withdrawn and moody
after the death of his friend.

He is fifteen years old, five feet three inches
tall, and weighs one hundred fourteen
pounds. He has short, dark brown hair, gray-
green eyes, and a crescent-shaped birthmark
on his left side just below the ribs. He also has
an appendicitis scar, and is presumed to be
wearing borrowed or stolen clothing, perhaps
not fitting him well. Anyone having information is encouraged to contact the Willacoochee
County Sheriff's department or dial 911.

"Jesus," Brock breathed, his face, if possible, even whiter than normal.

Calvin crumpled the paper and flung it to the ground, then kicked at the nearest log savagely. "*Dammit!*" he spat. "*Goddammit!* Why'd he do it? Why couldn't the little son-of-a-bitch be more careful?"

"Cal—" Brock began tentatively.

Calvin spun on him. "*You!*" he snapped, pointing first at the boy, then at the paper. "Yeah, you! Brock! That could've been you so easy, boy. That could have goddamned been you! See what comes of foolin' around with magic? That kid did—and look where it got him!"

A puzzled look crossed Brock's features. Then: "But how do you know it was magic?"

"Because I know!" Calvin gritted. "I know that kid, and I know what he was into: weird stuff, just like you. Shoot, if nothin' else this oughta teach you once and for all how dangerous this business is."

"But how—?"

"Because my cousin saw his ghost two nights after he vanished!" Calvin told them wearily. "I'd been seein' my dad's ghost for a while, Brock. And then I started seein' him with another shape, which I finally figured out was the ghost of that Michael Chadwick boy Spearfinger killed. Only that didn't quite make sense, 'cause as far as I knew he wasn't an Indian. 'Cept now we find out that he was part Cherokee. And then . . ." He paused, gulped. "Night before last my cousin saw my dad's ghost—I'd told him about it, and he's open-minded—and he saw another, too, just not very well. But he also *thought* he saw a third, which makes sense if Don Scott was in the Ghost Country himself."

Brock looked incredulous, even as Sandy looked troubled. "The Ghost Country?"

Calvin nodded. "Tsusginai, in Ununhiyi, the Darkening Land. The Cherokee dead go there, apparently—

maybe until they're reincarnated, or something. And evidently those of mixed blood do too, sometimes. The
problem is that . . . my cousin says that somebody who
dies without all their parts—like my dad and Michael
and Allison did—can't be granted admission to the
Ghostland, so they become uneasy and start hauntin'
folks. Plus, ghosts get lonely and start wantin' their
loved ones with 'em.''

Sandy looked thoughtful. ''And the paper said Don
had gotten into divination. I bet . . . he was trying to contact Michael's spirit, and—''

''And *got* him!'' Calvin finished for her. ''I bet Don
found some kind of ritual for that in one of those books
that article mentioned, and tried it—and Michael came:
poor, lonely Michael without his liver or his best friend.
And Don, half crazy and probably half in shock, went
with him.''

''But Michael was *dead*!'' Brock protested. ''Why
would Don look for him?''

''Maybe . . . to make peace with him?'' Sandy suggested slowly, looking at Calvin. ''From what you said,
those guys were real close. If one died, and the other
had to watch but couldn't help him—''

''He'd feel guilty as hell,'' Calvin groaned. ''I
should've thought of that! I should've come down here
and seen how the kid was actually doin', instead of re-
lyin' on reports.''

''Don't start that,'' Sandy warned. ''You start guilt-
tripping yourself, you'll wind up like he did—'cause I
bet that's what he did: guilt-tripped himself.''

Calvin felt suddenly very old. ''Yeah, and I can just
guess that the closer to the one-year anniversary it got,
the worse Don felt. Shoot, he had to have been goin'
crazy. He might even have been seein' ghosts, same as
I was. Only I was wary and strong and suspicious. He
saw what he wanted and . . .''

"You mean Don's . . . dead, too?" Brock gulped.

Calvin shrugged. "Hard to say. If he is, it's not in any conventional way, unless he actually . . . died, if that makes any sense. But it sounds to me more like he was just physically transported to wherever Mike is. He's . . . stuck, I guess, can't go on 'cause he's not dead, can't come back 'cause they won't let him—or he doesn't want to return."

"Awful," Sandy muttered under her breath.

"Yeah," Calvin agreed. "And I bet I know how he did it, too! Except—Jesus, but I wish I knew what books he used. I've got some ideas, but who knows what weird little local libraries like the one down here might have?"

"You *could* check," Sandy observed matter-of-factly.

Calvin glared at her. "Sure, and have people conveniently remember all those murders last summer, just about the time that weird Indian boy started hangin' round! No way I'm gonna attract that kind of attention again."

"But I could," Sandy countered practically. "Or Brock."

"Maybe," Calvin grunted.

"But," Brock said in a small voice, "what about . . . you and me?"

Calvin rounded on him. "You *still* wanta do that, after this?"

The boy scowled darkly. "After what? A newspaper article and a bunch of wild guesses? What's that got to do with anything?"

Calvin was practically speechless with frustration. "You're really gonna hold me to it, huh?"

Brock shrugged, but his eyes were fearless. "I guess I am."

Calvin could only grimace helplessly.

"So what do we do?" Sandy asked carefully.

"What we do," Calvin replied, thumping down on the ground—which reminded him a little too pointedly of the state of his ribs, ''is first of all confirm my suspicion. In the meantime''—he looked at Brock—''put on some clothes. The 'skeeters'll eat you alive if you give 'em half a chance.''

Brock was pacing about the clearing, his face a mix of emotions: concern and anxiety and real fear, blended with anger and frustration. Calvin glared at him. ''Cool it!'' he snapped. ''I'm gonna go through with it. In fact''—he levered himself upright— ''what I was gonna teach you may actually prove useful, so come on, snap to. You're fixin' to get some hands-on experience.''

Brock froze with his shirt in hand, suddenly all intense interest. ''I am?''

Calvin nodded. ''I'd intended to teach you the finding ritual anyway—even though it now looks more dangerous than I thought it was. But you can still use it. Besides, it'll take you a while to assemble the equipment to do it yourself, and I'm not gonna give you mine, nor lend it. Maybe by then some of this will have sunk in, and you'll have learned some sense.''

''You sound like an old man!'' Brock muttered, disgusted.

''I *feel* like an old man, right now,'' Calvin told him. ''Now, do you wanta learn, or not? As soon as it's noon, I'm gonna try to confirm where Don is. You're free to watch—you both are, though Sandy's seen it done enough it should bore her silly. But if you're *interested*, Brock, I'll explain as I go along.''

''Sure,'' Brock said, after a pause. ''Sorry I was a jerk.''

Calvin shrugged. ''We all are, sometimes.'' That said, he picked up a twig and sketched a cross-in-circle in the earth by the fire. ''Okay then: you know what that design there is?''

''You called it a Power Wheel. I've seen you use 'em before.''

"And will again, probably. But do you know what they represent?"

"I give."

"The world, and the four directions which define the world, and the four powers that control those directions, and about a zillion other things. It's a common image in most mythologies."

"That why you've got one tattooed on your butt?"

In spite of himself, Calvin blushed. "I've got one on my butt 'cause I was young and stupid and irreverent one time. I wanted a tattoo, so folks would think I was cool, and I wanted it hidden, so they'd think I was mysterious, and I wanted it weird so I could feel smarter'n everybody else. But then I found out what it really meant, and came to *believe* that, and—well, I'm just as glad it's fadin' now."

Brock looked as if he would like to ask a question, but didn't.

"Now as I was sayin'," Calvin continued, "most rituals are properly begun with an invocation to the quarters, each of which has a ruling color and about a zillion gods and/or animals in corresponding colors, each of which has sovereignty over something or other—it's too complex to go into here and not relevant to what we're doin' anyway. East is red, for instance, probably 'cause of the sunrise. North is blue, which makes no sense to me 'cause south is white, and you'd think north would be 'cause of snow, and—"

"And north *used* to be black," a voice interrupted from the undergrowth behind them. "It changed."

Calvin looked up, startled. For an instant he thought Sandy had spoken, since the voice had been female. But a check showed her as perplexed as he. Abruptly, he was on his feet—just as a woman walked calmly into the campsite.

Calvin blinked—they all did—but he . . . *recognized*

her! It was—he didn't know her name, but it was the woman from the anetsa game, the one who'd hung around with ... *Snakeeyes*! Already wired, Calvin felt his pulse rate shoot up another few notches. "You—!"

"Hello's a more common greeting," the woman said calmly. "Or hi there, or perhaps ... *siyu*!"

Calvin did not reply, but his concentration widened enough for him to note that she was wearing jeans, somewhat torn and muddy, boots not unlike his own, and a red cambric shirt under a multicolored vest. She also sported a knife at her waist and a small backpack. Her eyes looked tired, as if she hadn't slept in a while.

"I'm not your enemy—*Edahi*," the woman went on with a weariness that both matched her expression and suggested she had already resigned herself to the opposite assumption.

"A name's a dangerous thing," Calvin replied carefully. "Yours might be good to know right now."

The woman smiled. "How 'bout Okacha?"

Calvin puzzled over it for a moment. "Okacha?"

"Creek for 'wildcat.' "

Well, *that* certainly hit her dead on, Calvin acknowledged, what with that short-cut hair, those enormous dark eyes, and the way she moved. Sandy, he noted, was watching him at least as closely as she was the newcomer. He expected Brock's brows to collide any second.

Okacha was ignoring them. She paced to where the Power Wheel lay scratched into the sand and inspected it for a moment. "You won't find him that way," she sighed. "He's not in this World, and we *both* know which way the Ghost Country lies. But if you'll help me, maybe I'll help you."

Calvin could only stare as the woman stood waiting for an answer.

# Chapter XIII:
# Coosa, and More Imminent Legends

"Excuse me," Sandy inserted, her voice low, cool, and perfectly controlled but full of implicit threat. "I hate to be rude—but who, exactly, *are* you?"

The female stranger—Okacha—stared at her speculatively: an odd expression, combining recognition of comradeship and acknowledgment of potential rival. "Sorry," she replied wearily. "I'm *really* tired—and when I get like that I kinda tend to forget that just 'cause *I* know who somebody is, that person doesn't automatically know who *I* am. I'm Okacha—like I said." She extended her right hand.

Sandy took it warily, shook it perfunctorily—and did not break eye contact. "But that's not *who* you are."

Calvin and Brock exchanged resigned glances. At least *their* pecking order was unambiguous.

Okacha studied Sandy for a long moment, her small, full lips drawn to a thin, grim line. "No," she sighed at last, "that's definitely *not* who I am."

"I saw you at the game," Calvin broke in, mostly for Sandy's benefit, since Brock, by his expression, was more concerned with the arrival of yet another interruption of his quest for magic. "You were with that . . . tall guy," Calvin continued, so Okacha would know he was at least partly onto her.

"Not *with* him," she shot back firmly but without hostility. "I was in his presence, but definitely not *with* him."

Calvin raised an eyebrow. "Sorry."

"You'll understand when I tell . . . what I have to tell."

"So shoot," Calvin replied, trying to mask major-league edginess with a veneer of cool. "Grab a log and make yourself at home." He left her to it and resumed his familiar place between the roots of the live oak, leaning against the trunk. He found Sandy's hand surreptitiously. Brock thumped down to the right, nearer the creek, and commenced drawing designs in the sand with a stick.

Okacha folded her legs under her and sat opposite; her back very straight, her face still and composed. "Do you remember the Legend of Coosa?" she asked carefully.

Calvin's interest level immediately kicked up another notch. "That's the one about the girl who goes down to the river for water—or to bathe, or whatever—right? And while she's there, she meets a mysterious man, or else one of the underwater panthers, and—"

"*Hang on!*" Brock interrupted pointedly, looking up. "What the hell is an underwater panther?"

Calvin hesitated, waiting for their visitor to reply. This was, after all, supposed to be her story.

Okacha gnawed her lip thoughtfully. Then: "Lots of folks say they're monsters," she began. "But that's 'cause they live underwater—in deep rivers and lakes. And since those are traditionally gates to the Underworld, *some* folks"—she glanced at Calvin— "just automatically assume that anything that comes from such a place is by default a creature of the Underworld itself and therefore chaotic or crazy, if not actually evil. Actually . . . well, they're just themselves, good and bad by turns, like other people. As to what they look like . . . well, my people—the Creeks—were wrong in thinking of them as being monsters. Actually, the Tunica hit 'em a lot closer: think of 'em as like werewolves, sort of— were-panthers, rather. They can look like men—and usually do when they're on land. But in the water they're like big cougars or panther or mountain lions, except that their paws are larger—and webbed. All of which is gettin' away from the story—which I'll take over, if you don't mind.''

Calvin shrugged expansively. ''Be my guest.''

''Thanks,'' she murmured, then continued. ''Like you said, a woman used to go to the river all the time, and eventually met this underwater panther—in which shape doesn't matter—and as often happens under those circumstances she got pregnant. Well, as you might expect, there were some . . . odd things about the child, and the people in her village figured out what had happened, and a lot of 'em were afraid, 'cause they didn't want a child in their town who was half monster, as they thought. So they tried to drive the woman away. Well, naturally she complained to her lover, and he told her to ask everybody who was on her side to leave and go with her. And she did, and they all went over a mountain. But a few days later, they came back and found the town drowned, and a lake where it used to be, and no sign of the people who'd given her grief. But you can still hear their drumming under the lake, sometimes.''

''Oh, neat,'' Brock cried. ''Hey, and there's a story in England kinda like that, only it was a whole country that sunk. It was called Ys, and you can hear the bells, and—''

''Right,'' Sandy acknowledged. ''I've heard that, too.''

''But what about the girl?'' Brock wondered. ''What happened to her? And her kid?''

Calvin remained silent, not liking where this was heading.

And he liked it even less when, instead of a verbal reply Okacha simply stretched her hand into the space between them. Her skin was tawny rather than ruddy or tanned, he noted. And her hands were long, smooth, and graceful, though her fingers themselves were oddly stubby. But then she spread them, and Calvin could not suppress a chill, even as he heard Brock yip and Sandy gasp.

Okacha's fingers were webbed! Thin skin connected the joints closest to the hand on all five fingers. And then he *really* got a start, as, without warning, tendons flexed in the palm, and her oddly thick and pointed nails elongated further—and became hooked claws.

Calvin stared at them for a moment, then back at her face. No wonder she looked so feline. No wonder she had such huge dark eyes, such uncanny grace.

''That answer your question?'' Okacha asked Brock, smiling at him sadly. Calvin half-expected her teeth to be pointed. They weren't—though she had especially prominent canines.

In spite of her apparent sincerity, the boy paled. ''M-made a damned good st-start,'' he stammered.

Okacha withdrew the hand and folded it under her other arm, then leaned back against her log, looking more weary by the minute. ''I'm the last,'' she murmured. ''That is, I hope I am. And if I'm really lucky, I won't pass on the curse.''

Sandy could only shake her head in awed perplexity. She glanced sideways at Calvin. ''And to think that you deal with this kind of stuff as a matter of course.''

''Not hardly!'' he snorted, squeezing her hand. ''Not in the last year, anyway.''

"Did you say *curse*?" Brock inquired abruptly, all alertness, eyes narrowed attentively. "Are we talkin', like, for real badness, here?"

"Not like you mean, probably," Okacha told him with an ironic laugh. "But in the sense that it's something you live with and endure without desiring, yet can never escape—then yeah, it's definitely a curse."

"Could you, uh, be more specific?" Calvin ventured politely, though with an edge on his voice. "I've kinda got the feelin' you didn't just *happen* to be passin' through here."

She gnawed her thumbnail thoughtfully, then nodded, as if she had come to some decision. "It's the curse of otherness, first off; the curse of knowin' everyday you're not like anyone else. Of havin' to watch every tiny little thing you do for fear you'll let something slip and betray yourself, and therefore leave yourself open to ridicule—or worse. And yeah, you're right, I'm *not* here by accident. But I'd rather wait on that, since old Brock here asked a good question."

Whereupon Brock grinned smugly, looking inordinately pleased with himself.

"What I am," she confessed in a sad, resigned voice, "is a magical creature in a nonmagical world. No, don't freak," she continued. "I saw how y'all reacted to my hand and what I've already said. You believe me, and you've all seen enough other things to accept the possibility that some pretty off-the-wall stuff can be true. But why am I trustin' you with this stuff? you may reasonably ask. Or maybe, why am I buggin' *you* with my problems? Because I've seen enough and heard enough and know enough to know I can. But before I get into that, you folks need to know a couple of things. First of all, whatever I tell you, I need to tell fast. And whatever we do needs to be done in a hurry. We've got a little time, but not much."

Calvin frowned suspiciously. "What's the rush?"

"Snakeeyes," Okacha replied flatly. "He'll be here sooner or later—probably sooner. I only barely escaped him, and he's bound to come after me—and you, too, now; because you're with me, and because of what you are and what you . . . have and know."

Calvin puffed his cheeks. "So what, exactly, is the deal with you two?"

Okacha grimaced, "Okay, I'll lay it on the line. First of all, it's pretty obvious that I'm part water-panther: descendant of the woman who caused the drowning of Coosa, to be precise. But what that means in the real world, besides some neat little biological aberrations I have to work to hide, is that when I'm immersed in water, I change into a panther—or have to work *very* hard not to. In that form, the dark side of my personality becomes dominant: the instinctive side, you could say— it's sort of like that movie *Cat People*. Oh, I can overrule it, to some degree, but I'm extremely susceptible to violence—and to suggestions of violence. My—call it my medicine—increases, too, and I can be used as a source of it for certain purposes, most of which I don't approve of, but which, in panther shape, I can't avoid."

Calvin's scowl deepened. "What do you mean you can't avoid?"

Okacha sighed. "That brings us back to Snakeeyes. He's a witch—you've probably heard that from your cousin Kirkwood—who's a neat guy, by the way. And if you've heard that, you also know Snakeeyes has got a lot of people freaked up at Qualla, 'cause callin' somebody a witch is a pretty basic insult, since it means accusin' them of usin' the powers of the world for impure purposes—which makes them impure. And you *know* how important purity is to traditional Cherokee. But be that as it may, I don't have time now to explain how I fell under his influence, but suffice to say, he caught me at a vulnerable moment, and though I've *looked* free, he's had me on a pretty short rein. Fortunately, I was able to escape about the same time you left Qualla—I was *goin'* to ask you for help at the game, but then you got hurt and I couldn't.''

"But how did you *know* about me?" Calvin demanded, utterly confounded.

"I saw the scale—among other things. It's obvious, if you're like me."

"Yeah." Calvin groaned. "And he saw it too, didn't he? And recognized it."

Okacha nodded regretfully.

"And he'd like to get it, wouldn't he? Just like he got you: get it, and use it for his own ends!"

Again Okacha nodded.

"But being . . . what you are," Sandy broke in carefully, "aren't you stronger than he is?"

A shrug. "Not in human form, except for my claws and my reflexes, a little. But all he has to do is get me wet when I'm not expectin' it, and I'm in trouble. And I haven't told you the worst part, either. See . . . I'm like a cat in more ways than one, and one of 'em is that I . . ." She paused, blushing. "I come into season. And when that happens, I get *really* irrational—and *very* indiscriminate. So what Snakeeyes wants to do is to wait until I'm in that condition and get a child on me, and then kill me and manipulate that child, which he could do in a way that would never work on an adult—the available power's about the same, and all."

"But why would he kill you?" Sandy asked, grimfaced.

" 'Cause he's afraid of me, and he can't control me—not always. Oh, a lot of the time he keeps me kinda doped up—and he's got a mental bond on me I can't really break—it's like he lets me go and then reels me back in.''

Calvin's eyes narrowed. "But what about now?"

Okacha regarded him seriously. "When he shifts shape, his hold on me weakens."

"And the further away Snakeeyes goes in animal shape, the less his hold on you, right?"

"Right. And when you beat him off when he was in owl shape, it addled him for a while, and he lost all hold on me for the first time since he caught me. It only lasted a few minutes, but I had a plan in place in case that happened. And the minute I felt Snakeeyes's hold on me relax, I hopped in his car and drove as fast as I could away from him. And between the distance and the fact that he was in another shape, I managed to elude him long enough to get here. Not that it did any good," she added bitterly, looking apprehensively at the sky.

Calvin's eyes narrowed. "But that stuff at my cousin's place: how'd you know about that? And how'd you find us, for that matter?"

"Snakeeyes told me—in a sense. Whenever he does that—changes shape, or any other major magic—well, it's like a resonance. The same way a fire can make your face hot, his magic makes mine . . . resonate—even when he's not actually drawin' on it. And when that happens, it's easy for me to see what he's up to, and know what he knows, to some extent—like your destination, which he probably overheard. He can't hide anything magical he does from me, nor I from him, not at close range. The more distance, the less that works, though."

Sandy looked thoughtful—and worried. "So that's how you know he's approaching?"

"As long as he's usin' magic during his approach, yeah—if he's shifted shape, or something like that. And like I said, he *is* comin'. He knows what Calvin's got on a thong around his neck, and he wants it, if for no other reason than 'cause it'll decrease his dependence on rebellious, unreliable me.''

Calvin did not speak for a long moment, then: ''So what was all that stuff you were goin' on about when you arrived? All that about us helpin' each other, and all? Seems to me we've both got a bunch of problems.''

Okacha gnawed her lip, as if trying to regain patience. ''Very well,'' she said. ''I mentioned a bargain earlier. Here it is. *You* are haunted: this I know from what I've sensed, what I've heard, and what I've seen. Your father's ghost roams restlessly on the fringe of the Ghost Country, free neither to continue on nor to return, and he'll stay that way as long as his body's incomplete. But if you went there, I think I know a way his spirit could be put to rest. And of course there're those *other* spirits, too: that boy Spearfinger killed, for one. You could probably help him also. But even more importantly, there's Don Scott—yeah, I saw the paper, and I guessed the rest.''

''We were right about him then?'' From Calvin.

''Pretty much,'' Okacha replied. ''I've talked to the bobcats hereabout, and they told me how it was: basically the boy missed his friend and called his ghost and couldn't resist the ghost's complaints of loneliness, and so the boy reached into the water and went with him.''

''And you think you can help us bring him back?'' Sandy asked.

Okacha nodded. ''I think so. He doesn't belong there; he can't stay.''

''Okay,'' Calvin said, ''you've told us you *might* be able to help us—and I'll be frank: if you *can* do all that, I'd be mighty grateful. But you've also said you need something from us as well. I think it's about time you told us.''

Okacha took a deep breath. ''I . . . know how to get to the Ghost Country—I've already told you that. It's a thing passed down through my family, from my water-panther ancestor. He told his human wife how to get there and explained some of the mysteries of the place and made her memorize them. She told her daughters, and so on. I've never been there, but I think if I were to go I could hide there long enough to figure out some way to escape Snakeeyes. If nothing else, he won't be able to follow me.''

''Which leaves us to deal with him,'' Calvin noted.

''Which is where the rest of the bargain comes in,'' Okacha countered. ''Without me here for him to draw on, you're stronger than he is. He should be afraid of you, and even if he's not, you should be able to defeat him—when he comes after you.''

''Now wait a *minute*!'' Calvin shot back instantly.

Okacha looked at him frankly. ''I don't know of anybody else who *could* beat him, Calvin—and he *is* a threat to your clan and kin at Qualla, and probably elsewhere as well. If I were to walk out of here right now and never be seen again, he'd still exist—and be evil—and do evil. I don't think you're the kind of man to allow that. Not when he can kill your family and friends and thus add all the years they would have lived to his own sorry life.''

Calvin took a deep breath. ''Maybe, maybe not. But I won't kill him. That's flat. I've got enough deaths on my conscience.''

Okacha did not reply. No one did.

''Can we even trust her?'' Sandy asked at last, not looking at their visitor.

More silence. Then, from Brock: '' 'Trust the woman,' '' he whispered. '' 'Trust the woman—or be damned.' ''

''Where'd you hear that?'' Calvin snapped, a sick feeling in his gut.

Brock's eyes were huge. ''I—I don't *know*! It—it just

came to me, like someone whispering in my head!''

"Someone who *could* be Snakeeyes," Calvin pointed out.

"Shit!" Sandy murmured.

Okacha simply stared at him, her eyes keen as daggers. "Not Snakeeyes. He can't do that—not to an ordinary person, not when they're awake."

"Unless you're lying," Calvin growled.

"You've got more to lose than I do if I'm not," Okacha said simply, but her voice was tight with despair.

Sandy gnawed her lip. "I think . . . we ought to trust her," she said at last. "I can't say how I believe that, but I do. Cal . . . ?"

Calvin puffed his cheeks. "I dunno, folks," he sighed at last. "Some of it sounds reasonable, in a sense—and even fair, given that we're talkin' high stakes and big risks here: a trip to one World to save a lot of folks in another, and a good deed done both ways. But there's a lot to be considered. Like, who's goin'? What do the others do while we're gone? What kind of time frame are we talkin' about? What're the risks?"

"Yeah, and how do we *get* to the Ghost Country?" Brock chimed in.

Calvin had been so intent on sorting through the ramifications of Okacha's revelation he had frankly forgotten the boy. Now he glared at him. "What's this *we* bullshit?"

A confident shrug. "I assumed I was goin'."

"Like hell!"

"But *Cal*!"

"*No!*"

Brock stood up, furious, hands on hips. "No, *hell*! Who the fuck do you think you *are*, man? I *know* you've gotta go, 'cause that's what you do . . .'cause there's not many people in the world that *can* do what you've gotta do. But you can't do *everything* by yourself. You've gotta have help. That's where I come in—me and Sandy, 'cause I bet she wants to go too, and I bet you'll tell her the same bullshitty thing!''

"No, Brock.''

"Just a word, man," Brock snorted, turning away. "Just a goddamned *word*!'' He spun around again, face red with fury. "Look, man; I'm not dumb enough to think you'd actually hurt me. But if you conk me on the head, I'll come to eventually and follow; and if you lock me up, I'll escape eventually and follow; and if you just up and run off, I'll just bloody well follow! And we both know what'll happen if I try to do that on my own: why, I'm really liable to wind up in trouble. So your choice isn't whether I go, it's whether you've got me where you can keep an eye on me or not!''

Calvin gaped incredulously.

Brock was still wound up. "Besides,'' he half-sobbed. "Besides—you *owe* me, man! You owe me a goddam piece of magic.''

"What if I was to teach you that now?''

"I wouldn't listen!''

Sandy was smirking in spite of herself. "He's got you there.''

"Seems to me like he's got you every way,'' Okacha observed. "And he's right. He's just the kind who *would* try to follow. And I'll bet he's resourceful enough to find a way. Besides, he's heard everything, which means that if he stays and Snakeeyes finds him, we could all be in trouble. I—''

Okacha froze, her face a mask of alarm. Her muscles tensed; the tendons in her neck stood out like cables. She closed her eyes, and Calvin saw her jaws clamp hard, as if she resisted something by main will alone.

"Okacha?'' he called softly, then much more force-fully as, oblivious to the pain in his ribs, he leapt to his feet and crossed the small space between them. "Oka-

cha!'' He grabbed her shoulders, shook her. *"Okacha!"*
Finally, desperately, he drew back a hand and slapped
her face—once, twice—but as he attempted a third,
Sandy was there restraining him. He blinked back to
himself, wondering what had gotten into him—but
equally unclear what was to be done about their companion. She was still under whatever control had been
affecting her, whether of her own creation or of Snakeeyes's conjuring, he couldn't tell.

But what could he do, short of injuring her? And then
he noticed something: one of the sprigs of cedar with
which he'd intended to ward the site before Sandy's return with the paper had distracted him. He snatched it
up, swept it across Okacha's body like a feather duster,
then held the fresh-cut spray directly beneath her nostrils
so that she had no choice but to inhale the resinous
fumes.

It worked! Scarcely had Calvin brought the sprig to
her nose the second time when the tension flowed out
of her neck and jaw. An instant later, her breathing deepened, her lids flickered, and she blinked at him. Her gaze
was wide and terrified. "Th-thanks," she gasped shakily, "that happened so fast I couldn't resist. But . . . but
we have to hurry! It's Snakeeyes! He's here, in these
woods. We've gotta go!"

"But where?" Sandy cried, looking around frantically—wildly off center and out of her depth, Calvin
knew. "Wherever we go, he'll find us. What—"

"I thought we were goin' to the Ghost Country,"
Brock insisted.

Okacha looked distraught. "Yeah, well, there's no
time for that now." She pounded her fist into her thigh.
"*Dammit*, why couldn't I have been quicker? Why did
I think I had time to waste talkin'?"

"Are you sure there's no way?" Sandy asked edgily.

Okacha's brow furrowed. "There may be one." She

paused, thought a moment longer, then: "Yeah, maybe there is . . . if Calvin's got any more of that cedar . . . ?"

"Bunches and bunches."

"Ward this area as best you can," she told him. "I need time to think." Whereupon she folded herself into a lotus position and closed her eyes.

Calvin scowled, having been interrupted at warding once already, but reached for the small pile of cedar branches he'd cut earlier. He quickly located the twigs he'd marked with color, thought for a moment, and retrieved his atasi as well. It wasn't magical, in particular—not that he could tell. But it came from a magical place, and since the function of clubs was to protect as well as assail, perhaps that virtue could be called into service here. Scowling, he set the red-marked sprig at the eastern edge of the campsite, then began inscribing an arc in the sand with the pointed end of the club. Brock watched, fascinated. "Why cedar?" he whispered.

Calvin ignored him as he inserted a second sprig beside the white stick in the south. Then, tersely: " 'Cause it's protection against witches, for one thing."

The line reached the western quadrant. Another sprig stabbed into the ground.

"But *why*?" Brock persisted.

Another arc. Another sprig, joining the blue stick in the north. A fourth arc closed the circle.

"Why?" Brock repeated.

Calvin glanced at Okacha. Her eyes were still shut, her breathing slow and measured. She was obviously in some sort of trance. He stared at her for a moment, then drew Brock aside. "This isn't exactly the time for it, kid, but if it'll make you hush, it's like this. In *hilahiyu*, in Ancient Times, when the World was new-made, the plants and animals were all sentient, all with humanlike intelligence and emotions, and such. Anyway, the sun—

I think it was—told them they all had to stay awake for seven days, but one by one they all dropped off to sleep. The only animals awake at the end of the seven days were the ones that can see in the dark. And the only plants were the pine, the spruce, the laurel, the holly . . . and the cedar. And they became the plants that don't shed their leaves—the plants of vigilance against evil.''

Brock looked at him solemnly, but Calvin read fear in his eyes: real uncertainty, which was good for him, if not good in its own right. Sandy was doing as little as possible, though she was standing inside the circle Calvin had inscribed. At least she had the sense not to ask questions that could destroy Okacha's concentration; knew when to ask or protest and when to let be. She couldn't avoid a start, though, when Okacha's eyes suddenly popped open. The panther-woman's face was grim.

"Maybe this'll work," she breathed. *"Maybe."*

"Whatever," Calvin told her. "You call it, I'll do it. Everybody else is on their own."

Okacha nodded. She crossed to her backpack, rummaged within, then pulled out a six-foot length of what was obviously hand-braided cordage. "We don't dare get separated," she said quickly. "So anybody who's with me, stick your left hands this way—yeah, right Brock, right over that Power Wheel Calvin was tellin' you about." Brock looked uncertain for a moment, then shrugged and extended his arm as instructed. Okacha promptly looped the cordage around it and drew it tight, then, with Brock in front, she inserted her left hand beneath the boy's and whipped the cord around it twice, binding them together. "Calvin, you're next," she called over her shoulder. "Stand behind me and put your hand under mine."

Calvin struggled into his jacket and knapsack—a move made awkward by the pain in his ribs—then stuffed the atasi into his belt and did as asked; felt the loop draw just tight enough to feel the rough texture.

"Sandy?" Okacha prompted, lifting an eyebrow in inquiry. "You don't have to . . . I mean, you're not part of this, except as you're involved with Calvin. If you come along, I can't say what'll happen to you, but you'll probably never be the same again. If you stay here, though—well, I can't vouch for what Snakeeyes might do to you. That's not a threat; it's a simple fact. But it's your call."

Sandy gnawed her lip wretchedly, then nodded. "Damned if I do, and damned if I don't, I guess." She sighed. "The devil I know versus the devil I don't, and all that." Whereupon she hoisted her pack and placed her hand under Calvin's. As Okacha twisted the end of the cord around her wrist, binding her into the linkage, Calvin met his lady's gaze above the conjoined hands. He could think of nothing comforting to say, but his helpless shrug conveyed both his approval and his apprehension. Sandy simply looked very, very uneasy.

Okacha finished her work by tucking the free end of the cord back in her own hand. "Just follow me," she murmured. "Do as I do, and sing as I sing. Even if you can't follow the words, try your best."

And with no further notice, she began to chant: softly at first, then more loudly. Though the words were utterly incomprehensible to Calvin, they *sounded* vaguely like what little of the Creek Indian language he had heard. The rhythm was familiar, though, as were the pitch and cadence. And then he recognized them! It had the same form and structure as the chant he'd used to summon the fog that time down in Jackson County when he'd tried for Awi Usdi and got Spearfinger in the bargain. Perhaps this was a version of that same gate-opening song. It made sense. But though he tried his best to follow the unfamiliar syllables, he was filled with dread.

Meanwhile, Okacha reached into a pocket and pulled out a small rattle made of box turtle shell. This she proceeded to shake in time to her chant, as she commenced a slow shuffling dance in the center of the warded circle. Nothing complicated, it was merely what was called a stomp dance: a placement of the feet and a keeping of the beat with the body in time with the chant and rattle, all while following the leader in a circle. Yet, as always happened when Calvin joined one, the whole seemed larger than the sum of the parts. From the outside it looked slow, laborious, and hideously dull. But as a participant . . . something happened. A person became one with the tune and the rhythm, and through them with the other dancers, and through the words in the air and the touch of feet upon the ground, likewise one with the earth itself. It was hypnotic—which was doubtless the intent.

They had made four circuits now and were meshing more as a team. Calvin had already picked up enough of the chant to follow, and sang louder. Brock was managing, and Sandy was doing what she could, her voice low and strained.

And something *was* happening. For as their feet shook the earth, the sandy soil around them began to bounce in time, raising low dusty clouds barely an inch above the ground. But every round took it higher, and then Calvin noticed that on the side toward the creek, a mist was slowly writhing their way.

More singing, more stomping, and the mist reached the dust, and when it did, it merged, thickened, moved faster, as if it thereby gained strength. Two more rounds, and the mixture was lapping about their feet. It carried a chill with it, too, of cold water and sunless places. Sandy evidently didn't like it either, for Calvin heard her singing falter as it rose above her shoe tops, but he sang louder in response.

Brock looked intent, was singing what he could, but keeping step very well indeed. His eyes were closed, though, and in that maybe he was lucky—for the mist had reached their knees.

Louder still, and Calvin was certain they could be heard a long way off—which was not conducive to avoiding notice. But another round found the mist lapping his waist.

Another brought it chest high, and then his head was swallowed. He gasped, as if he had fallen into deep water, but other than the cold and dampness, there was no change save that the song seemed more distant, as if the fog stifled its volume. Calvin strained to sing louder in compensation, but the fog siphoned off the sound as soon as it left his lips. Nor could he see much—Okacha was but a vague shape before him, Brock an even dimmer one to his left. Sandy, who was behind him, he couldn't see at all, but he felt her hand beneath his, an island of warmth in all that cold. He closed his eyes and danced on . . . danced, and sang.

Abruptly, Okacha's hand, that lay atop his own, spasmed, was suddenly warmer and . . . different. His eyes popped open, and by straining his vision, he could just make out her shape less than an arm's length before him. But something was wrong! Her ears were shifting higher on her head, while her brow compressed and the lower part of her face lengthened!

He swallowed hard, flinched—and felt the cord bite into his wrist. Okacha was shifting shape! Which made sense, given what she'd said about water instigating that—for what was fog but water?

But she'd also said it made her dangerous!

And the last thing he needed was for either himself or two people he cared about to be caught so, with a witch coming their way fast on the one hand, while they were bound to a shape-shifting monster he suddenly realized he had very tenuous reasons to trust.

But before he could reconcile himself to action, the rattling ceased, then sounded again, briefly, a muffled noise as Okacha dropped it. The fog swirled and eddied around her—just enough for Calvin to glimpse the oddly proportioned shape ahead of him reach around with her right hand. Claws gleamed there, and though she still sang, that did not stop her from reaching in to rip the flesh of her left hand with her right.

He gasped as the bright blood flashed, visible even through the fog. And gasped again as the blood reached his own hand. It was burning hot! Hot as acid! Hot as fire!

He heard Sandy's sharp intake of breath when it oozed around Calvin's hand to touch hers. She jerked, tried to pull away, but could not. A strangled grunt was Brock.

But all that mattered was the pain in his hand—that awful agony that roiled and hissed around his flesh, as if their joined limbs had been plunged into boiling water. It was the worst pain he had ever felt—far worse than that which accompanied transference to Galunlati, if for no other reason than because, by being localized, it was also more intense.

Hotter and hotter, and Calvin closed his eyes, as if by that action he could shut out the agony.

But he could not. Indeed, it made the pain greater for it removed one less distraction. Reluctantly, he opened his eyes again—and saw to his dismay that the mist had drawn back a yard all around them. Below was still sand, Brock was still to his left, eyes closed, his jaw clamped hard as he strove not to cry out.

But Okacha . . . was completely changed now—or those parts he could see of her through her suddenly ill-fitting clothes were. No longer did a woman stand there, but a panther: a cougar rearing on its hind legs, with its tawny, whiskery muzzle on a level with Calvin's head. And the worst thing—beyond the pain, which suddenly became one degree more distant—was that *it* was still singing; that human words still issued from mouth and lips and tongue in nowise designed to shape them.

For an instant he caught the panther's eyes, saw wildness there—or madness. And then one of the long syllables in the chant began to stretch, to shift itself into a shrill feline scream that filled the world.

And as the scream grew louder and longer and more agonized, more blood pumped from the panther's paw onto his hand—and the agony redoubled. Calvin screamed, too—he couldn't help it. And Sandy did— and Brock, as if each had borne as much as he or she could stand.

Calvin closed his eyes again, wanted out, wanted an end to it all, would do anything, he realized, to stop the agony.

"*Open your eyes!*" came an inhuman growl.

Calvin did—exactly in time to see the gleam of bright claws and the flash of tawny fur as Okacha drew back her free right hand and, with one clean, arcing swoop, slashed those dreadful claws across Brock's neck.

"No!" he screamed. "N—"

But the sound was cut off as the claws continued around to strike Sandy and then himself. The last coherent image he caught was of Okacha's claws tearing at her own neck.

And then the whole world turned to red and pain as boiling hot blood went everywhere. He felt it splatter his face, smelled its acrid copper stench, even tasted it, as some flew into his gaping mouth.

The final thing he knew was that something was tugging against his wrist, dragging him toward . . .

. . . the river.

. . . falling, then, and impact; and cold replaced heat, and darkness light. And Calvin *knew* he was dead.

# PART THREE

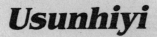

*Usunhiyi*

# Chapter XIV:
# What the Cat Dragged In

## *(Usunhiyi—night)*

. . . black . . .

   . . . white . . .

   . . . *black* again, and then more black; and Calvin concluded that black must be the color of cold, even as white was of heat—which made vague sense if one recalled how metal behaved in a furnace: red-hot, then orange, yellow, blue, white-hot . . .

   . . . *heat* . . . fire . . . his hand was on fire—no, had *been* on fire . . . had been flayed and boiled and fried all at once; had been cooked beet red . . .

   . . . *red* . . . the color of fire, of pain, of . . . blood . . .

   . . . *blood* . . . the taste in his mouth, the warm salty copper tinge . . .

   . . . and then back to black, but this time he realized that he *was* realizing; that he was noticing things and linking notions, which meant he either *wasn't* dead or that the afterlife wasn't at all what he'd expected.

He blinked and caught the black shifting: lighter, and darker . . .

Another blink—eyes full open now—and he saw the paler black.

No! It was *white*—had been for a fractioned second: white as summer lightning . . .

*Lightning* . . .

That had been a sky! A sky of cold turned hot, then cold again.

A third blink, and *up* arrived. A horizon defined itself: a ragged edge of utter dark against a background that, though scarcely lighter, was dimly sprinkled with colors: red and yellow, orange and blue-white—lots of that.

Stars!

He was seeing stars!

White—far off, as it had always been: sheet lightning bleaching a *night* sky, when the last one he had seen was noon day; sheet lightning cutting out the peaks of distant mountains like pyramids of torn paper . . .

He blinked again, noticed that he was breathing— and that his throat and nose and lungs felt clogged and burny.

A cough brought up water that tasted like sand and tannin and south Georgia. He rolled to his side, coughed again, felt pain stab into his chest and twist. He thought something grated.

Which reminded him that he had a body. He moved again—and felt no new pain save the familiar ones in his ribs and hands, though now he thought of it, the cold was a lot *like* pain. Still, that was okay: it meant he was alive. He had eyes, an up, a down; lungs, a tongue— ribs. And now he had a cold heavy weight that pressed down upon something at once rock-hard and yielding. His fingers slid into it as he explored it gingerly.

It moved back, shifted at that touch.

Sand.

Calvin sat up and, when the world stopped whirling, discovered he was hunched over on a broad beach of gritty black sand, where a cold black glitter hissed to itself a yard to the left: a body of water—probably a very wide river. And there were mountains.

He analyzed the surroundings. The beach—or whatever—was easily fifty yards wide on his side and lay at the foot of a ravine whose fractured, black stone walls rose two to three times higher than he was tall. Before, behind, it twisted along the water, a study in black on black. But now that his eyes were adjusting, he could make out other, paler shapes: fantastic forms, gnarled and grotesque. Some were small—the size of his arm or leg; others were as large as horses or cars or houses, and the bigger they were, the more fantastically they whorled and bent.

A word came to him: driftwood. He was seeing driftwood: wrack tossed up by that vast black river.

He stood carefully, feeling his ribs catch and try to bind pain inside, even as his clothes pulled and grasped at his outer form. He was soaked through! And standing waterlogged in a stiff cold wind was certainly one reason he was suddenly shivering uncontrollably. For a breeze was blowing: a strong one from . . . well, from whatever direction was away from the water. And when it struck his skin, it made him shake ánd cringe and want to hug himself . . . but when it had played with him a while, he felt warmer.

Without really thinking about it, he shucked the heavy object—his backpack—that was weighing down his shoulders and cutting into his collarbones, then skinned stiffly out of his jacket, T-shirt, and bandage. His boots and white tube socks followed, but he hesitated at his jeans. And what was this odd thing stuck in his belt? This arm-long length of pale, polished wood, bladed at the end like a double-headed axe?

War club. It was a war club. Good! He'd carry it while he explored, and explore while he dried off and tried to figure out where he was and what had become of . . . the others!

With a jolt like a bolt of the pervasive lightning, a whole set of memories awoke. One instant he'd been completely self-absorbed, intent solely on taking inventory of himself and his place in the cosmos. The next—

*Sandy!* His mouth shaped her name, even as his eyes strained into the darkness. *Brock!* And . . . He frowned. What was her name? The weird chick—the panther-woman who had brought them here?

*Okacha?* Yeah, that was it! Okacha!

But where were they? They should've all been here, for their wrists had been bound together. But strain his eyes though he would, nowhere could he see any sign of them.

On the other hand, this dark, cramped landscape was scarcely all-revealing. The black sand showed dips and ridges galore, as well as curves and twists of shoreline. Never mind the often head-high driftwood that could conceal any number of secrets.

Well, one direction was as good as another. And with that, he wrung out his clothing as well as he could, then, with the club in his hand and his pack on his back, set out shirtless and barefoot down the beach, having concluded that as heaviest of the group, he should have been spat up first; therefore, following the current would sooner or later bring him to the others.

*Or he could simply call them!*

Why hadn't he *thought* of that, dammit? His mind was still a major muddle. "*Sandy!*" he shouted. "*Sandy!*" Then: "*Brock . . . Okacha!*"

Again and again, until his throat went raw.

No answer returned, and so he walked.

But not far, for no more than two hundred paces down the beach (it was hard to estimate distance in the dim light), he rounded a particularly large clump of driftwood—and found himself staring into the wide green eyes of a panther. The beast was sprawled languidly along what had once been a yard-thick limb from a truly gigantic tree before some ancient flood had claimed both trunk and branches. The beast was also wet; its fur glistened darkly, like a seal's. And the eyes . . . he couldn't tell if the light flickering there marked recognition, violence—or insanity.

"Okacha?" he murmured tentatively, fighting an urge to bolt.

From deep in its throat a growl rolled forth.

"Is that you, 'Kacha?"

The growl became a deep rumble. She was purring! Calvin cautiously extended a hand and stroked the slick wet fur between those troubling eyes.

They closed; the purring deepened.

"Welcome to the Darkening Land, huh? Well, it's sure dark enough. Wish you'd had time to brief us, though." He shivered again.

The panther growled. The wind twitched a hank of its fur free. It dried instantly.

"*Come!*" he commanded it, slapping his thighs as he backed to a spot where the wind would have clearer access.

It blinked lazily and drew back its lips just far enough to reveal the tips of its canines, but acquiesced, bounding heavily down from the branch to pad across the sand. It shook itself, growled—or maybe sang. And as it did, the wind picked up, blew harder, warmer . . .

And then the world turned to white and heat as a bolt of lightning flashed down from the starlit sky and struck the limb the beast had abdicated. Apparently tinder-dry, the driftwood burst into flames and burned steadily. *Great!* Just the thing to cheer a cheerless place—especially when Calvin hadn't time to build one himself, what with the need to find his friends to whom it would hopefully serve as beacon. Not that he intended to wait around. He was, however, practical enough to spread his wet garments on the sand sufficently close to the blaze for them to derive some benefit from the heat. That accomplished, he returned to the still-soaked panther. "You comin'?"

It cocked its head, but instead of moving toward him, sank down on its haunches and began methodically licking its fur, abruptly all feline. Calvin merely snorted and continued south.

He had jogged for barely five minutes, when he saw a figure stagger from behind a house-high tangle of river wrack a few hundred paces further on. His heart leapt— then sank a small degree when it proved to be shorter and darker than he had dared hope—but leapt again in gratitude that a third member of their party had survived.

"Brock!" he yelled. "Hey, buddy, up here!"

The boy evidently saw him at the same time, because the next thing Calvin knew the kid was careening toward him.

"Brock!" he yelled again, feeling oddly uneasy about making so much noise in the eerily solemn darkness.

"Calvin!"

"Brock, m'man!"

"Hey, Cal!"

An instant later they embraced soggily; Brock for once having forgotten to maintain attitude. Calvin's ribs twinged, but he ignored them.

"I—I h-heard you c-c-call b-before," the boy gasped into Calvin's chest. "But I was k-kinda z-zoned an' c-couldn't answer."

"Well, I'm glad to see you," Calvin replied inanely. Then: "Sandy: did you see any sign of her?"

The boy shook his head, but when Calvin tried to ease free of his grip, Brock resisted, trembling uncontrollably.

"Brock? What's wrong?"

"C-cold," the boy mumbled. "Kinda . . . dizzy." He

swayed on his feet, and Calvin had to shift his grip to keep him from falling. "Easy, kid," he murmured. "Take it easy; you may be on the edge of goin' into shock. But try to hold on just a little bit longer. There's a fire right up the way. We'll get you there, get you warm."

"W-warm?"

"Yeah, kid, warm."

Brock did not reply, simply stood shivering as chill after chill wracked his small, soaked body. Calvin studied him for an instant, then scooped him up, grunting when he discovered how surprisingly heavy he was for such a little guy. His ribs hurt abominably. But it was only pain. And pain he could endure.

"Keep talkin'," Calvin panted, as he half walked half staggered back toward the fire he could barely see to what he had taken to thinking of as the north.

" 'Bout what?"

"Anything. Recite poetry, or something."

" *'Twas brillig, and the slithy toves* . . . " the boy began.

" . . . *Oh frabjous day!*" he concluded a short while later, when Calvin lowered him down by the fire. Fortunately, it was still blazing, though the panther was nowhere in sight. He glanced about, concerned, but trying not to show it as he helped Brock to a seat on a smaller limb near the flaming one. The boy shuddered again, but seemed to draw strength from the heat. His clothing steamed. "I f-feel better now," he managed—and sounded it.

Calvin stared at him uncertainly. "You need to get out of those wet clothes. They'll dry faster, and you'll get warm a lot quicker, both."

Brock blinked dumbly, and Calvin guessed that in spite of his posturing, he was still pretty out of it. "C'mon, kid, shuck 'em. I'll spread 'em out here by mine, and they'll be dry before you know it.''

The boy nodded sullenly and proceeded to strip, though Calvin had to help him with his shoelaces. Brock hesitated, scowling, when he reached his briefs. "Use your good sense," Calvin told him, trying not to smirk—from sympathy, not ridicule.

Brock grimaced, but turned his back, dropped his drawers, and flung them over his shoulder to Calvin, then squatted by the fire, legs close together, hands draped between.

"I doubt you've got anything to be ashamed of," Calvin observed wryly. "Now, you just stay there and get warm. I've *gotta* look for Sandy. Oh, and if a panther shows up, don't freak."

Brock's expression flickered between embarrassment, alarm, confusion, and indignation so quickly Calvin had to bite his lip to keep from laughing. The kid was recovering *very* quickly.

Brock dipped his head in the direction from which Calvin had first come. "Sh-she's thataway, I think. I . . . felt her break loose from the ties before you did, so I guess that'd make s-sense, anyway."

"Thanks," Calvin told him, and jogged off the way the boy indicated.

So had the panther, by the prints left in the dark sand. But he couldn't follow them far, because maybe three hundred yards north of the burning tree, they suddenly veered left, onto a shelf of smooth stone that suffered no trace of passage to remain on it. The shelf rose into a small headland that jutted into the river. Calvin guessed the panther had chosen the straightest path to whatever it sought, thereby cutting off a loop of meander. And if its senses were as sharp as he suspected, there was at least an even chance it might have scented something he couldn't. And if not . . . well, he wasn't out that much and could take the longer route later if need be.

Increasing his pace to a steady, uphill trot that had him sweating in spite of the chill, he soon reached the crest of the ridge. He was right, too: the height revealed a convolution of river meanders, a large one of which had been circumvented by his shortcut.

It also showed him two figures trudging up the slope from the opposite side.

One was low-slung, sinuous, and feline; the other bi-pedal, and obviously a woman.

"Sandy!" he cried joyfully, and for the second time in less than half an hour found himself running toward one of his companions.

"Cal!"

They met, hugged, kissed impulsively, and Calvin was relieved to note that though she was as cold and wet as Brock had been, Sandy showed no signs of either chill or shock.

"You okay?" he asked when they drew apart.

"As well as I can be, given I don't have a clue where we are or how we got here—and would prob'ly be out of a job if I did," she replied, but then her face clouded. "Where's Brock?"

"Dryin' out and warmin' up half a mile over the hill," Calvin told her, drawing her close with an arm around her waist. "We'll be there in no time." They started up the slope.

But a low growl from the panther made them turn again. It wasn't following, but was frozen where it stood. Calvin eased away from Sandy, walked slowly toward it, knelt, rubbed between its ears. The fur was almost dry—*almost*. Would have been if it had stayed beside the fire instead of coming to find Sandy. "Thanks, Oka-cha," he whispered.

The beast did not move, but made a sound deep in its

throat that was somewhere between a growl and a groan. A wind sprang up, first cousin to that which had earlier presaged the lightning. It played around them, warm and insistent.

And as it did, the panther's fur dried; and as each tuft lost its moisture, skin showed beneath: *human* skin, writhing and changing as the wind blew Okacha's humanity back to her.

She turned her face into it. Already mostly human, she rose onto her hind legs. Her mouth opened whiskered and jowly, but closed again with small red lips. "I would've done this before, but I needed my nose to find Sandy," she gasped, her voice still with an odd timbre, but becoming more recognizable by the second.

And then the wind subsided, and Okacha stood there, fully human.

She was also naked—sleekly so. And very beautiful, Calvin couldn't help but notice. He felt his cheeks warm, knew he was blushing. She laughed, oblivious to her nudity.

Calvin's face grew hot—not from embarrassment, but from a surge of bitter anger that welled up in him so fast it made him choke. *What had this crazy bitch done to them, anyway?* In her desperation to escape Snakeeyes, where had she brought them? And at what cost? Shoot, Brock had almost gone into shock! And here she stood, stark naked and laughing at him, when he'd risked everything on the slimmest of explanations.

"You!" he spat. "You—" Rage made him inarticulate.

"To get us here as quickly as we did, you had to wish yourself dead *and* think yourself dead," she said simply. "I gave you a pain that made you want to die to escape it. And I slashed your throats to make you believe you were dying. The river healed you."

"Bitch!"

"*Cal!*" Sandy snapped. "Stop it!"

"No!" Okacha shot back. "He's gotta get it out. Balance has to be maintained. I had to release the human in the beast to return to myself, but to balance that, he has to release the beast in him—his anger. There's no room for deception here."

Sandy scowled uncertainly, and Calvin was on the verge of venting yet more ire. Except, he realized, it was gone. It had flared, even as Okacha's change had flared. Now it had vanished, burned away, as the beast was burned away in her. "That's gonna take some gettin' used to." He gulped. "It is if we have to watch every emotion."

Okacha shrugged. "My magic awoke your magic. Or it awoke whatever fuels your magic, anyway."

Calvin shrugged and turned again. "We need to get back to Brock."

Sandy was fumbling with her pack. She dragged out a wad of sodden fabric and handed it to Okacha. "Here."

"Thanks," Okacha murmured. "But if it's okay with you, I think I'll stay like I am until I can put on something dry."

Silence, a little strained. Then, from Sandy: "Where are we, anyway?"

"Nowhere near the Land of the Dead, that's for sure," Okacha replied easily. "From the way my mother described it, I'd say we were just on the fringe of the Darkening Land."

Calvin frowned, then frowned more when another thought fought its way through the muddle of his mind to reach the surface. "Snakeeyes . . ."

"What about him?"

"Can he follow us here?"

"No."

"Why not?"

" 'Cause he doesn't know the way—and 'cause he has no business here.''

His eyes narrowed. "And we *do*?"

"So it seems."

"But—"

"Hush, Cal," Sandy interrupted. "I don't wanta hear about that kinda stuff right now."

"Maybe you're right." He sighed. "Maybe we need to get centered."

"I *need* to get warm," Sandy replied tartly, and drew closer.

"I can see the fire," Okacha noted as they topped the ridge.

Two minutes later they were in sight of the tree, on a far-side limb of which the fire blazed. And a minute after that, had rounded it. Calvin, intent on briefing Sandy on his doings since regaining consciousness, and on fleshing out the details of her story, had temporarily forgotten about Brock.

But there he was: all curled up fetus-style between the fire and a limb, bare as the day he was born, and evidently fast asleep. The fire gave his pale skin a healthy golden glow. Calvin couldn't resist a chuckle.

"Cute kid," Sandy observed. "Even cuter without his . . . attitude."

"Cute little butt, too," Okacha noted in turn, elbowing Sandy in the ribs. Calvin found his face warming again, embarrassed for Brock's sake. "Uh, maybe you ladies oughta boogie for a second, while—"

But he'd evidently spoken too loudly—or someone had. Brock's eyes suddenly popped open. He sat up abruptly, and had exactly time to assess the situation— that he was bare-assed in front of two women, one of whom was also blatantly sky-clad—before he leapt with amazing speed and dexterity behind the trunk. Calvin caught a flash of very white buttocks, which were quickly replaced by an indignant stare of blue eyes beneath soggy black hair as Brock peered across the weathered wood.

Calvin guffawed. "Lose your cool?" he called through his laughter. If the kid had regained his modesty, he was obviously fine.

"Pants," came an irate mumble.

"Pants?" Calvin teased. "You mean, like, *your* pants?"

"Traitor," Brock gritted, his eyes flashing with adolescent fury. Then: "Jesus *shit!* What th' fucking *hell*?"

Whereupon he leapt back over the trunk—snagging a foot in the process, which tumbled him into an untidy and *very* revealing sprawl—with a toe perilously near the fire, which made him flop and curse inelegantly as he scrambled to his feet.

"What th—?" Calvin echoed, eyes wide with bemusement.

"Something fucking *tickled* me," Brock spat, grappling unsuccessfully with his jockey shorts as he bounced about on one foot.

"Tickled you?" from Okacha.

"Fucking yeah!" Brock growled, having just realized he had started his skivvies on backward.

"*Tickled* you?" Sandy chimed in.

"Tickled you?" came a third, deeper voice.

Calvin froze, abruptly all seriousness. Where had *that* come from?

More laughter. From beyond the log.

Calvin crept that way at a wary crouch, atasi in hand, but before he'd gone two paces, a shape reared above the driftwood.

As large as a Shetland sheepdog it was, and as furry. But it also had long ears and dark, nervous eyes. And as Calvin gaped in surprise, it hopped atop the tree trunk and squatted there, wrinkling its small pink nose. Calvin blinked. He'd thought it was gray, but now it seemed more tan. But one thing was clear: it was a rabbit—albeit a very *large* one.

The bunny surveyed them solemnly, displaying no fear. It seemed especially interested in Okacha and in Brock, who was minimizing his problem by turning away from the women—and toward the animal. His briefs hung limp in his hand.

"Now I know why you wear so many clothes," the rabbit observed, with what sounded suspiciously like a chuckle. "If I looked like that without my fur, I'd cover my skin, too!" And with that it bounded to the sand before them. "Mind if I join you? Oh, but I've forgotten my manners! It's nice to see you again, Edahi. I'm *sure* you remember me: your old friend, *Tsistu*?"

Sandy stared, Brock alternately blushed and gaped. Calvin looked troubled. And Okacha looked strangely . . . hungry.

# Chapter XV:
# Hide and Seek

"Tsistu," Calvin groaned, his hand lingering by the war club at his belt. "Shit!"

From its place behind the driftwood log, the rabbit stared at him with eyes as dark brown and moist as the leaves blanketing the bed of a mountain stream. Its nose twitched. Its right ear kinked downward. Somehow it was larger. The tawny fur became ticked with gray. It hopped onto a nearer limb—and was instantly the size of a common Georgia cottontail.

Calvin scowled and puffed his cheeks.

A long furry ear cocked his way. "What was that . . . *Utlunta-dehi*?" Tsistu demanded, abruptly twice his previous size. "The word has not been whispered in Galunlati, or the Lying World, or Usunhiyi, the Darkening Land, either, that eludes me! If you *think* too loud I hear it! I can hear the anger in your blood as it flees your brain and seeks your limbs through veins drawn tight to speed its flow. I can hear each metal spike click into its fellow on the odd thing that boy uses to close his leggings. I can hear the hiss as Ancient Red chases the Long Man's spit from that fair-haired woman's clothing to seek the open air. I can hear—"

"Can you hear me tellin' you to stop this chatter, or

you'll be *dead*?'' Okacha broke in sharply, her voice dripping with implicit menace.

Again an ear tilted. ''Can you hear *me* telling you that if I am, you will lose the only guide you have in this place, O long-gone child of the Underworld and the Middle?''

Okacha's eyes flashed fire, looking at least as feral as they had when she was entirely feline. ''Cool it,'' Calvin gritted; then, to the rabbit, ''What did you say about bein' a guide?''

The creature shrugged—or that was how it registered. ''I showed you the way once, Edahi,'' it sighed. ''I thought perhaps you might want me to again.''

Calvin's eyes narrowed suspiciously, liking neither the situation itself, nor the way Tsistu kept invoking his secret names. ''Yeah, you showed us the way, all right: when me and my friends first went to Galunlati. But then you tricked us into killin' an eagle and almost got *us* killed for our pains!'' His fingers closed around the shaft of the club.

''Or you *could* say I brought you to the attention of those you sought more effectively than would have occurred otherwise. Do you suppose Uki would have given you a *second* of his time had you simply come to his door? Poor witless weaklings that you were? I made it so that he *had* to notice you.''

Calvin merely snorted and folded his arms—but kept his fingers near the club. Sandy grimaced uncertainly, clearly out of her depth and willing to let more experienced heads prevail. Okacha was gnawing her lip. And Brock, who had finally managed to contrive a minimum of modesty, flicked his belt home and turned. ''You still haven't told us what you meant about being a guide,'' the boy noted.

The rabbit blinked at him. ''So those tiny ears *do* work.'' He chuckled. ''Well, apparently those of your

elders do not. But you are correct. I will be your guide—
if you will have me.''

''Guide to what?'' Calvin asked carefully.

''Why, to Tsusginai, the Ghost Country,'' Tsistu shot
back. ''That *is* what you seek, is it not?''

''Maybe.''

''Suppose I told you a man called Snakeeyes has sent
many of my kin in the Lying World there? More than
he ought, for he kills them for sport and leaves them to
rot without thanks or apology, using neither their meat
nor their skins?''

''I would say that's true,'' Okacha replied sadly,
'' 'cause I've seen him at it. He kills for the love of
killin' but doesn't use the bodies. Once I saw him run
over a nest of baby rabbits with a lawn mower. He spent
an hour lookin' at what was left. Another time he tied
one alive to the exhaust of his car and drove a hundred
miles with it there. *Another* time—''

''That's fine,'' Sandy interrupted. ''We get the picture.''

''You get very *little* of it,'' Tsistu snapped bitterly.
''But you are correct. I owe him nothing, and I owe you
something, and so I will be your guide.''

Calvin glanced at Okacha uncertainly. ''You know
more about this than I do,'' he murmured. ''What d'you
think?''

She shrugged wearily. ''I don't know much more
about this World than you do,'' she countered. ''I know
two ways to get here. I know a little about what to expect. And I know that what we're lookin' for lies to the
west. That's about it.''

''Ah, but how *far* to the west?'' Tsistu chided. ''Have
you thought of *that*?''

''It doesn't matter,'' Calvin sighed, his voice so heavy
it almost choked him.

''It might,'' Tsistu countered. ''You have left friends

in the Lying World, at least one of whom possesses a talisman of strong medicine. Sooner or later Snakeeyes will discover this. Would it not be best if you were there to protect him?''

Calvin thought of Alec and the ulunsuti. And then considered what might happen should Snakeeyes come into possession of that oracular stone. He shuddered. ''Okay, so what's the deal?''

''Merely this,'' the rabbit said. ''As you know, it is my lot in eternity to die and be reborn—which I do with regrettable regularity. In fact, I do it so often I frequently meet myself returning from the Ghost Country on my way there again—which of course means that I now know all the fastest routes 'twixt your World and the one you seek.''

''So Okacha's right: this isn't the Ghost Country?'' Sandy inserted.

Tsistu shook his head. ''Think of how many have died—then tell me if you see any of them here.''

Calvin gazed around in spite of himself. ''I see none.''

''It would therefore seem you have a way to go.''

''We're tired'' Sandy sighed, sitting down to fiddle with her backpack. ''When would we have to leave? Assuming we decide to trust you.''

''The sooner the better, for time runs strange when one hops between Worlds,'' Tsistu told them. ''But there *may* be time enough to dry those odd skins with which you wrap yourselves.

Calvin looked helplessly at his companions, then back at the rabbit. ''How 'bout if we all grab some shut-eye, then; and you wake us when we can't wait any longer?''

''That seems reasonable,'' the rabbit agreed. ''One can only enter Tsusginai at certain times anyway. An hour wasted now might save two later on.''

''*Might,*'' Calvin grunted under his breath, but he

squatted stiffly beside Sandy and drew her close—then realized her clothes were still cold and wet and jerked away, which made his ribs twinge. "Yuk! You're soaked!"

"I just spent . . . I don't know how long in the water, Calvin!"

Calvin merely sighed. Fortunately his T-shirt, which had been lying on the sand near the fire, was almost dry. He handed it to her, while she dug more clothes from her backpack—likely for Okacha. "Better dry what you can while you can," he told her. "Better do whatever you need time for now. God knows there won't be any later."

"Food?" she wondered.

"Whatever's in the pack." He eyed Okacha, then quickly whisked his gaze away from her casual nudity. "It *is* okay to eat, isn't it?"

"Here, but not elsewhere," the panther-woman replied as she took the clothing Sandy passed her and began to spread it out. "Not until we accomplish our mission," she added. "The Dead can't eat, yet they remember it. And it's not wise to make the Dead remember."

Calvin nodded silently. He wondered what might happen in the next little while *he* would not wish to recall.

But in spite of all that, the heat of the fire reached him. And when Sandy returned from shedding all but her panties and his T-shirt, and snuggled against his side where he lay against the driftwood trunk, he slept.

Breakfast, Brock discovered to his dismay when Calvin toed him awake, was stale, soggy, and hard to eat by firelight. Which seemed to him a waste of a good campfire. Not that they'd been planning to come here— at least not so precipitously, he hastened to add. Still, somebody should've thought to bring along the food

Sandy had picked up in town. Make that any *cookable*
food. As it was, all they had were a couple of cans of
Coke Sandy had stuffed into her pack, and two peanut
butter-and-jelly sandwiches he'd brought along in his,
which the water hadn't got at too badly. Calvin had con-
tributed a Butterfinger (which didn't go far divided into
fourths), a can of tuna (which he'd opened with his
Swiss army knife), and an assortment of cellophane-
wrapped saltines that had likely accompanied a salad
somewhere along the way.

But none of 'em were filling! At best, they reduced
the gnawing in his tummy to a disgruntled growl. Probably the only good thing, he considered, as he polished
off his portion of Butterfinger (fortunately, he'd gotten
an end), was that the rabbit-thing hadn't wanted any.

Brock glanced at it edgily from where he leaned (fully
clothed, thankfully, and nearly dry) against the trunk of
the cast-up tree, the steadily burning limb of which had
been providing heat and light for hours. This was tough.
Oh, he'd seen some magic, sure, had even watched old
Cal shapeshift more than once—shoot, had *met* him
when he was in deer form a year ago. And he'd *read* a
lot about magic—the theory of it, anyway. But that
didn't prepare a guy for doing weird dances and putting
up with pain like he had, never mind getting your throat
slashed and zapping off to other Worlds.

Or for talking rabbits that shifted size and configura-
tion as fast as Brock changed channels on his sister's
TV when he got antsy. Yeah, *that* was a bit much. And
not just any talking rabbit, either, but an archetypal animal: The Ancient of Rabbits, in fact, so Calvin had
informed him under his breath, when he'd asked between clothes-drying sessions.

Yeah, sure.

Brock nursed his bit of candy a long time, knowing
it would be the last familiar taste for a while. And while

he chewed, he studied both his situation and his comrades.

It was still mostly dark, here on the black sand of this odd beach, but the sky was definitely growing paler to what Cal had told him was probably east. It was doing so in a disquieting way, however; and it took a while to determine that it was because the heavens seemed to be, in some strange way, *shaded*: as if the sun's light affected a sky different in shape (if something as diffuse as the sky could be said to *have* a shape—he thought of it as a hemisphere) from that of the World he knew. The stars were fading too, leaving only a few bright sentinels that didn't fit any constellation he recognized.

As for his companions . . . well, Cal had stashed a couple of staves of driftwood in his pack, and set aside a pottery bowl full of embers "just in case," then collected the detritus of their make-do repast: retrieving even the tiniest scraps of paper and plastic. He'd even washed out the tuna can in the river and stowed it away. Now he was carefully trickling sand onto the fire, extinguishing it by slow degrees while he sang softly under his breath.

*Fire and water are enemies:* was that what Cal had said? *Water was of the Underworld.* But if that was so, what about Okacha?

What indeed?

He tried *not* to look at the woman, who, still naked, had wandered down to the waterside and was studying it speculatively. He wished she'd turn around. Well, actually he didn't, 'cause then he'd be bound to blush again, which embarrassed the hell out of him when he was trying to be cool. On the other hand . . . He studied the ground deliberately, noting a whole mess of rabbit tracks, though Tsistu was nowhere in sight. Scouting ahead, he'd said. Yeah, sure.

But—oh, Jesus!—Okacha *was* turning! Was walking

toward them up the beach! Brock suddenly wished she'd put on some clothes, so he wouldn't be having a certain . . . problem centered a hand's length below his navel. Shoot, Sandy had even offered her spares, but Okacha had demurred until they were dry.

Brock supposed it was just another function of skin-changing. You changed, but nothing that wasn't part of you did—like clothes. Which, he concluded, forced you to be pretty laid back about casual nudity—Cal certainly was. He wondered, though, how shapeshifting affected things like braces—or fillings—or pacemakers—or contact lenses.

He didn't get to ask, however, for Okacha had sauntered up by then. "Ready?" she inquired, finally reaching for Sandy's spare jeans. Calvin, he noted, was trying not to look directly at her either, but did look relieved. "Soon as Tsistu gets back," he grunted.

"Ah, but I *am* here!" came a voice as a familiar shape bounded over the massive log and into their campsite.

"Anytime," Calvin told him shortly.

"None like now," Tsistu replied. And with that he hopped away down the beach. Calvin gave the fire one final check, shouldered his pack, secured his atasi, and followed, his face tight with what Brock supposed was pain from his damaged ribs. Okacha joined him—barefoot, but in jeans and T-shirt. And Sandy jogged up quickly to claim a loose hold on Calvin's arm. Brock rose wearily and fell in at the end—then quickly moved up by Calvin so he wouldn't have to look at Okacha's denim-clad backside and . . . remember.

"This is south," Calvin noted a few moments later, when the driftwood tree they'd camped beside had at last been swallowed by the swelling dunes of the beach. "We need to go west."

"And so we shall," Tsistu told him, pausing ahead. "In fact, we start that way . . . now."

And with that, he turned right—and vanished. Before anyone could so much as cry out, however, he was back. "No, not *that* way," he corrected when Calvin started to angle to meet him. "Follow my prints, then turn where I did ... exactly."

Calvin did, and Sandy, then Okacha. Brock did likewise. It wasn't hard, not with the prints all of them left. Even Tsistu's were clear, though at present, as a pygmy rabbit of some sort, he was almost weightless.

But when Brock joined the others, he got a surprise. The black sand was marked. Well, not exactly marked, but *altered*. Where before it had been the dead, flat black of soot, now it bore a yellow tinge, as if the black grains were mixed with powdered gold—but only in a strip maybe two yards wide that ran dead straight from west to east.

Or the other way around. He stepped on it experimentally when he saw his older companions do the same—and felt a tingle buzz up through the soles of his feet.

"Good God! This is a *Track*," Calvin exclaimed. "I should've known!"

"What's a Track?" Brock asked.

Calvin exhaled tiredly and rolled his eyes. "A Straight Track, actually. Some folks call 'em ley lines, but what they are is lines of ... force that connect— Well, Dave says they exist in all Worlds—that they *connect* all Worlds, in fact. But that they're not always the same themselves. They're invisible in our World, for instance, unless they're activated, which almost nobody there knows how to do. But they're like glimmering golden roads. In Galunlati, the grass changes color. Here—"

"Sand," Tsistu interrupted irritably. "Now, shall we be going, or do you want to take the long way?"

"How long's *your* way?" Sandy snapped, sounding just as irate.

"Shorter than if you turned anywhere but here and went west," Tsistu snorted. "Shorter than if you hopped for twenty days west from where you stand."

"In other words, this is the way to go." Brock sighed.

"That," Tsistu told him solemnly, "it is."


There was something screwy about this whole place, Sandy had decided, when, with more reluctance than she hoped she'd shown, she'd stepped onto that line of goldly glimmering sand Calvin had said was a Straight Track. Herself . . . well, she'd heard him talk about them before and thought they had something to do with cosmic strings: dense threads of compressed matter rather like the substance that comprised neutron stars, except that these formed at the juncture of what some physicists called bubbles. Which in turn had something to do with the residue of contraction after the Big Bang, or such like. It was at that point that, high IQ or no, her chosen subject became as incomprehensible as the math behind fractal geometry or chaos theory.

But then she had little time for reflection because that rabbit-thing—Tsistu, she corrected herself: she had to start thinking to fit this new environment—set a fearful pace indeed, one that had them all moving along at what she suspected was the absolute limit of their endurance. And, regrettably, she probably bore it least well. Calvin jogged, moving efficiently in spite of his injured ribs and panting, but rarely changing pace except as Tsistu did. Okacha seemed to be entirely in her element and loped along like a sleek animal, either beside Calvin or just ahead of him—which pissed Sandy a little, though she tried not to let it show.

Herself, she found more and more matched up with Brock. He was shorter than she and had lived a somewhat sedentary lifestyle while in England, but he was also twelve years younger, and that pretty well evened them out. He was panting heavily, so was she. Sweat sheened all four of them (like Okacha, she'd retained a shirt: a long-tailed one, though she wondered why she bothered). But everytime someone's breathing became labored, Tsistu, who kept ahead—mostly in the shape of a jack rabbit now—slowed just enough to compensate, but never stopped.

So Sandy had little choice but to try to distract herself from her legs and her lungs and from thinking about what in the world she was *doing* here by the expedient of examining the landscape.

It was worth examining. Once they'd climbed out of the wide, stone-walled gorge, they'd found themselves on a plain. Or desert, actually; the sand was still the same grainy black that had lain beside the river, though here and there it bore swirls of gray or silver. And purple: there was a *lot* of that, though whether it was the sand itself or some substance stirred through it that reflected the sky, she didn't know.

The sky . . .

It really *was* purple—mostly; woven with burgundy and indigo. It was like a permanent twilight, an ongoing sunset. Except that there *was* a sun—or at least a definite brightness that glided across the sky in the prescribed manner, a brightness that was too dazzling to look upon with unshielded eyes. But there was also a certain haziness, as if the air was full of smoke or silt.

She supposed that was possible, for the mountains yonder looked as if they could be volcanic. They were pointed enough, ragged enough, almost seemed to glisten like basalt. Except that she didn't think that worked because, according to Calvin, places like this were island universes that floated (in a loose sense) upon the primary World she knew as Earth. They depended on Earth for

the gravity that leaked through the World Walls to sus-
tain them. Which meant that they had (or many of them
did) finite limits. You *could* step off the end of the
World here. And the sky might *be* a vault, held to its
island World by that World's gravity, which in turn depended in part on the gravity of its primary.

"Why not just enjoy it?" Brock asked her suddenly.

"Why'd you say that?" she replied between measured breaths.

"Because you were frowning. And people don't
frown when they're havin' fun."

"Should I be?"

"Given that you can't do much about it until Cal and
'Kacha finish whatever they're doing, you might as
well."

Sandy didn't reply. But if she did not smile, at least
she scowled no longer.

For a long time they traveled, and Sandy discovered
to her surprise that though she was pushed to the absolute limit, her plateau of fatigue did not seem to be de-
creasing. Indeed, it was as if each step—each contact
with that odd golden sand—sent a tiny jolt of energy
shooting up her legs which by slow degrees became a
knot of sustaining comfort centered in her chest.

Trouble was, the mountains seemed to grow no
closer, and they were the only goal she could fix on.
Not that the plain was barren, she hastened to add. For
the last . . . *while* . . . the pervasive flatness had been relieved by strange shapes of twisted stone. Black or
mauve or purple, most of them were; knee-high or
towering tree-tall. Single, sometimes, or in groups like
groping fingers. None passed truly close, but she got
conflicting impressions from them. On the one hand
they had sharp edges, jagged points, and scalloped de-
pressions, as if they had been struck or fractured or

broken, like obsidian blades. But at the same time they seemed to have grown there: to have stood there weathering (for there was a constant wind, accompanied by a wailing that was probably the sound it made blowing between grains of sand) for countless ages.

And if nothing else they at least provided some sense of progress.

Abruptly, Tsistu stopped.

They stumbled to a halt behind him, all panting and gasping, as the shift shook them from the half-dream of their progress.

"R-rest?" Brock managed hopefully.

"Change," Tsistu corrected. "This way."

And with that, he turned ninety degrees, hopped once—and vanished.

Calvin followed, then Okacha—and likewise disappeared.

Except that when Sandy stood where Calvin had been instants before and gazed the same way, she could see him again, jogging along another vague glimmer of golden sand as if nothing had happened.

A pause to exchange tired glances with Brock, and she did the same.

And found herself forced to focus purely on running, because Tsistu all but doubled the pace. No time to look at the landscape now; time only to think about breathing.

Breathing, and running, and the pain in her legs.

And then, all at once, their path dived into another watercourse; they shifted directions again at the bottom . . .

—And the mountains were closer.

*Very* close, in fact, filling a quarter of what world Sandy could make out at all, with the steep walls of the defile rising twice her height on either side.

More running—though not so much as ought to have

been the case, and the mountains filled *half* the sky ahead.

More running—and they were there . . .

It was jarring. For though she had traveled a bit, Sandy was from North Carolina, where mountains bubbled up from the earth in low hills and ridges and humps, so that one came into them gradually. This was much more like the West, where the Rockies rose with startling precision from the Great Plains. Shoot, you could practically put your finger at the point where the plain (for the bottom of the defile was as flat as the surrounding desert had been) ended and the mountain commenced.

Or that would have been possible had the way ahead consisted of stone instead of a cave, the mouth of which arched overhead to curve down again at the top of the defile.

One instant they were at the edge of the mountain, the next, they were under it.

Calvin made two torches from the sticks of driftwood he'd brought along and lit them with the coals he'd kept alive in the bowl. Those, together with a surprising amount of light that followed them in from outside—Sandy thought it was due to the high reflective quality of the vitreous rock around them—allowed them to make decent progress.

No more jogging, though; now it was a steady trek, still following a narrow stream along a yard-wide beach of black sand, while the cave walls rose tubelike around them. The only sound was the chanting of the water and their own breathing, both of which echoed and reechoed into a sort of white noise that was oddly soothing.

Slower and slower, and now they walked. Sandy felt the sweat drying on her body, her heart assuming a more reasonable throb. She was utterly burned out, yet not tired, at once drained and energized, as if all resistance and stiffness and strain had boiled away, leaving only that reservoir of inner strength that was always hers to command.

Yet she had no urge to speak; none of them did. All seemed content to amble along while torches painted alien landscapes in red and gold along the shiny, black-purple walls, and Tsistu's tail (cotton white) continued to mark the way.

Until, abruptly, it vanished, leaving them alone in a high-domed room the size of her cabin, at the far end of which the stream plunged under an arch the height of her knee. Beside it, she could barely make out a glimmer, as if daylight filtered in from a matching arch to the left on their beach.

Calvin staggered to a stop ahead of her. She eased up to join him, grasped his hand unobtrusively.

"He's . . . gone!" Calvin groaned, glancing around at Okacha. "Where—?"

The panther-woman scowled. "I'm not sure. I—"

"What are you waiting on?" came an irritatingly familiar voice from somewhere beyond that low arch. It expanded, filled the chamber with echoes. Sandy didn't want to think about a rabbit that big.

"Where are you?" she called back, unable to stop herself.

"Here, of course: on the other side."

"Other side of what?" Brock chimed in.

"Of the gate!"

"Gate . . . ?" From Calvin.

"Gate! Do you not see it, fools? There, a hop from your kneecaps."

Calvin knelt to peer beneath the arch. Sandy followed suit—and got a shock that sent shivers up her spine. What she saw was hard to describe. Light, yes: a yard-wide span of it below the stone wall beside the stream. But that light was . . . *full*. It was as if the air itself was

a sort of semisolid in which dust floated and gleamed
and glimmered as though supersaturating it. She couldn't
tell how thick it was, how far it persisted; only that the
glare beyond was stronger than the dim flickering which
surrounded them. But what *really* got to her was that
even as she watched, a darkness settled onto the arch of
light from above, as if—there was no other phrase for
it—a gate descended. Down it went, at an ever-
increasing pace, until no light showed at all—whereupon
it slowly rose again. Twice she observed that process:
that rise and fall, which lasted maybe a minute from
cycle to cycle. Yet at no time did the light extend higher
than her knee.

"What is keeping you?" Tsistu called again.

"Good sense," Calvin growled. "So, what d' you
think, Okacha?"

The panther-woman frowned. "I think we've gotta go
through. I don't *know*—I *can't* know, but I really think
we do. Everything I've known so far's been based on
what I've been told, on what I feel. But here—I only
know what the legends say."

"And what *do* they say?" Sandy inquired wearily.

"That to the west the sky vault comes down to the
earth, so that one must run beneath it to reach the Ghost
Country."

Sandy rolled her eyes. "Gimme a break, woman."

Okacha's eyes flashed fire, but her words were calm
when she spoke. "I'd suggest *you* keep an open mind,"
she whispered. "See what you see and draw your own
conclusions."

"I see quite *wonderful* things out here," came Tsistu's voice from the slit. "But all I hear is the cackling
of fools. Come or stay, but the gate will soon close for
the last time this day, regardless. Then you will have to
await sunrise. And Snakeeyes will have twelve more
hours in which to prowl your World."

Calvin grimaced worriedly. Sandy wondered how much he hurt. "How far is it?"

"Not so far I cannot run through before the gate falls. Maybe further than that for slow ones such as you!"

"Shit!" Calvin spat. "You mean you brought us here, and now we can't get through?"

"I wouldn't have wasted my time so foolishly if what I propose were not possible," Tsistu shot back. "You can pass—but you have to be fast."

"How fast?"

"Fast as me."

Again Calvin sighed. "But . . . we'd have to crawl. And nobody can crawl fast."

"No*body* . . ." Tsistu let the word fade off suggestively.

"Nobody *human*," Okacha breathed at last. Sandy gazed at her quizzically, wondering what the hell *that* meant.

Calvin too stared at her, his expression a mix of doubt and dread.

"A panther can move that fast," Okacha said quietly. "And there's water right beside us."

"Ah, so *your* brain works," Tsistu's voice rumbled.

"That's fine for you," Brock grumbled, kicking at a chip of glassy stone. "But what about the rest of us?"

Calvin gnawed his lip. "It's possible," he said at last. "But I don't even want to think about actually doin' it."

"Doing what?" Sandy inquired, though she feared she already knew.

Calvin's face was grim. "Usin' the scale," he murmured, his hand moving to the thong at his throat. "I can use it to change shape into something fast."

"So, do it!" Brock told him flatly.

"Easy for you to say," Calvin replied with a frown. "You don't know the whole story. See, I *can* use the scale to change—but Uki told me last year at my naming ceremony that it can only empower an indefinite number of changes—and I don't know how many I've got left."

"Which means we could get stuck in animal form and not be able to change back," Sandy finished for him.

Calvin glared at her. "There's that *we* again!"

"The gate closes for the day in five more cycles," Tsistu announced from beyond.

"I'm goin'." Okacha sighed, tugging at her shirttail. "Maybe I can do some good, even if you guys can't."

"I have to go too," Calvin agreed solemnly. "Sorry, Sandy, Brock, but you guys have to stay here."

"The cave is sometimes occupied at night," Tsistu informed them helpfully. "More than once I have seen an uktena come here."

"There's only *one* uktena at a time," Calvin called back.

"Only one *great* uktena. Who is to say he does not have offspring? For certainly there is more than one ulunsuti! Or perhaps it is the one you slew, passing time here before it returns to Galunlati. Doubtless it will remember you. . . ."

Calvin slapped the rock wall with his bandaged hand, obviously having trouble restraining his anger in such an impossible situation. Sandy understood. She knew how he was about things like this: hating responsibility, yet constantly taking it on himself; willing to risk anything for a friend, but reluctant to suffer a friend to risk anything at all for him. And above all, hating to be manipulated, hating to have his options limited by things he could not control.

Okacha looked at him thoughtfully, then at them all. Sandy would not meet her eyes. "If anyone stays here, there's a good chance they'll die. If we all go . . . somebody may make it back."

"But he only said an uktena *might* come here," Sandy protested.

"And if it does, you'll die," Calvin told her dully. "Trust me on that one!"

Brock had said nothing recently—surprisingly. Sandy turned to him.

"I think we *all* oughta go," the boy mumbled, as if he had heard her thought. " 'Kacha doesn't need a scale to change, but the rest of us do. So what I say is that since the main thing is that Cal gets through, he change first, but leave the scale behind when he goes. Then me and Sandy'll use it and follow—with the scale, of course."

"And if somebody gets stuck and can't change back?" Calvin challenged.

Brock shrugged. "Bein' an animal beats bein' dead."

Sandy rolled her eyes but did not reply. The kid was right, dammit. There were only unpleasant options. To remain here was one kind of risk, to go on was another.

"Four more cycles," Tsistu called impatiently.

Calvin looked at her, shrugged helplessly. "I don't see that we've got a choice."

"You change first," Brock repeated, "when you go through, and then when we shift back to human again, both. That way you've got the best chance of making it."

"And you?" Calvin asked him icily. "What about you? And Sandy?"

"I've got a sister and a mom and some mates," Brock replied. "But none of 'em cares about me as much as they do about somebody else. I'm *nobody's* number one, therefore I'm expendable."

"Bullshit!" Calvin snapped. Then, more softly: "Sandy?"

Sandy felt a bolt of cold strike her heart. "I . . . don't want to go," she said. "But you and Okacha kinda have to. And if you go—and leave your scale—Brock'll go— might anyway, given how small and quick he is. And if he goes . . . well, I don't want to be left behind here, uktena or no.''

Calvin vented a long exasperated breath. "Damned if we do and damned if we don't, huh?"

"I'm ready," Okacha announced abruptly. "Anybody that wants clothes on the other side better shuck 'em here and put 'em in a pack. I'll carry one pack, 'cause I'm probably gonna be the strongest."

"Yeah, I guess you're right," Calvin conceded wearily, sitting to tug at his boots. "Which brings up the next problem: what shapes do we use?"

"It has to be something we've eaten, right?" Brock asked.

Calvin nodded. "And in some sense hunted, or at least chased—preferably something mammalian and of roughly your own size."

"What're *you* goin' as?"

"I'd prefer a deer," Calvin told him, already at work on his second boot. "They're fastest. But they can't go through an opening that low. The only other thing I can think of is to be another panther—I made it a point to eat some last year. That way I can also carry the other pack."

Brock's brow wrinkled, while Sandy did quick inventory of what she'd eaten that might be useful. She'd hunted a bit, and tried lots of game, including venison. But she hadn't sampled any of the big predators. Which left . . . what?

"Rabbit," Brock said. "That's all I've eaten that's small and quick—and I did shoot one once."

"Sounds good," Sandy agreed. "What do you think, Cal?"

"I think you should hurry," Tsistu called. "Only three more times will the gate rise now."

Calvin had finished stripping, and Brock was on his way. Sandy followed suit. As she reached for the zipper to her jeans, she saw Okacha plunge into the stream at their side. When she resurfaced an instant later, it was as a panther. A very sleek, very wet panther.

Brock was down to skivvies by then, and Calvin scooped up his and Okacha's clothes and stuffed them into one of the packs. Okacha took it in her teeth, growled once—and leapt toward the low arch of light.

"Two more times," came Tsistu's voice.

Sandy was wearing only her long-tailed shirt now, having crammed everything else into the other pack. And she intended to retain it as long as she could. Calvin had removed the scale from his neck and was holding it in his palm. "You know how to do this, don't you?"

"*I* do," Brock volunteered, snatching at it.

Calvin ignored him. "You cut yourself with it—it's very sharp, and I tend to just make a fist over it—and when you feel yourself start to bleed, you think very hard about the animal you'd like to be: what it would be like to have that shape. It hurts like hell. And for God's sake, whoever goes last, remember to bring the scale! Hold it in your mouth if you have to, but *bring* it."

"Hurry!" From Tsistu.

Calvin grimaced again, closed his eyes, and folded his hand upon the scale. His lips twitched, and his brow furrowed, but Sandy could not bear to watch the change occur. Instead, she heard Brock's startled "Oh, gross!" and then the groans and grunts of whatever was happening to Calvin. Not until Brock muttered, "It's cool," did she turn around again.

Calvin was gone, but in his stead a panther crouched. It blinked up at her, switched its tail nervously, then eased aside to slide the scale from under its left front paw.

"Go!" she told it, kicking at it in the direction of the gate. "We've no time to waste on chivalry."

An instant only it paused, and that to retrieve the second pack, into which Sandy had reluctantly wadded her shirt, and then it too dived for the gate and was gone.

"Ladies first." Brock laughed edgily, passing her the scale.

"Children first," she countered.

"More folks depend on you than on me," Brock told her solemnly. "Now do it! We don't have time to waste."

"I—" But then she realized the truth of what he'd said. Wordlessly she took the scale, folded it in her hand, and closed her eyes.

*Rabbit,* she thought desperately, even as she clenched her fist around the scale and felt the edges bite—an unexpected pain. She knew the warm gush of blood, and then a . . . drawing, rather as she had experienced when they'd empowered Alec's ulunsuti only two days before.

*Rabbit,* she thought again, and tried to think the pain away, to focus only on rabbit: small, hunched over (and did she hunch over at that, or was it only her imagination?), furred, clawed—long ears (how must it be to feel them grow?), small mouth, small eyes, small . . . everything.

*Rabbit, rabbit, rabbit . . .*

And then all she thought of was how she was going to stand the pain, as her whole body warped and twisted and realigned.

And then it was over. When she opened her eyes again, it was to gaze at short range on Brock's bare ankle, and beyond it at the comfortably high arch of the gate. She was instantly afraid. That was a *human* here. Humans were the enemy, and this place was full of the odor of snakes and cats and other things that hunted. She had to escape—toward the light: that's where she had to go; toward that sliver of light that even now was growing lower.

Something moved under her paw as she leapt that way, something vitreous she slid out of her grip, even as the boy's hand swooped toward her. She moved quickly then—toward the light.

—Ran.

Faster, as the light brightened, and the gate began its slow decent. But . . . something was wrong! The air was too thick! It was like running in water—water she could breathe.

But behind was the snake-place and the boy and the smell of cats. Here was no odor save burning and something she only knew as death. All she had to hope for was light.

And with light ahead and growing brighter, she ran faster.

# Chapter XVI:
# Beyond the Sky

Air!

Cold, sweet air!

Sandy couldn't believe how great it felt just to be able to breathe again. For a long time she simply lay where she was: sprawled on all fours on what looked like a mix of sand and gravel, and smelled like a million things besides. Her sides heaved, her half-starved lungs dragged in breath after blessed breath. Unfortunately, each inhalation also brought more scents—and they were but part of the stimuli that besieged her, that insisted she ought to *run*, that it was folly to lie thus exposed, that a thousand predators were waiting to—

*No!* She was human—*human!* What *mattered* was regaining her own form, getting her bearings, and reconnecting with Cal—wherever he'd got off to. At present, half-dazed as she was, she wasn't certain.

Still, it wouldn't hurt to rest a *little* longer: rest, and pant, and drink in air that though cold and thin *was* air, not that . . . stuff back in the gate. *That* had felt at first like a very heavy dust storm—only the solid quotient had increased geometrically the further into it she'd pressed, eventually becoming so great she'd actually held her breath to *avoid* breathing because it choked her,

even as the thick air slowed her, like in one of those bad
dreams when she tried to run and couldn't. But then the
resistance had waned, the dust had thinned—and she'd
been able to lope along to end up here.

Here?

She raised her head from her paws and had just begun
to peer around when a scuffling thump from behind startled her so much her rabbit reflexes made her hop half
a dozen yards before she knew it. She turned warily,
ears sifting the bitter wind in alarm.

Smell told her as soon as sight: it was another rab—

*No*, she corrected, it was Brock! In bunny shape, true,
but the boy himself. She *had* to think that way, had to
remember what she really was. Steeling herself against
instincts that demanded flight, she scurried back toward
him.

He looked none the worse for wear, save for the heavy
panting obvious along his snow-white flanks. And,
thankfully, the thong that held the scale was looped
around his neck, with the talisman itself clenched awkwardly between his chisellike teeth. She wondered how
he'd run like that, breathed that way.

He blinked at her: ruby eyes full of fear. The scale
dropped from his mouth as he twitched from within its
tether. She nudged it with her nose, then scooted it between her front paws and pushed inward hard enough
to slice her foot pads and bring forth blood. She stared
at the red trickle dumbly, felt the rabbit-mind swoop
back and threaten to overwhelm her. She fought it,
closed her eyes, pressed harder—thought *Human, human, human* . . .

Pain engulfed her, making her flinch and gasp and
almost flip away the scale, but she held firm, tried to
focus on it alone, as agony that was only slightly more
tolerable now that it was familiar warped her body.

A gasp became a scream—and she was herself

again—still crouched on all fours, but now blinking down at what looked suspiciously like a very alarmed farm-raised rabbit. Which was reasonable, given Brock's background; it was unlikely he'd have eaten much wild game, even if he had shot some. She swallowed hard, shivered—as much from shock as from the sudden cold—then blinked again as her senses realigned, with smell vanishing almost completely, and vision flooding her brain with sensations, chiefmost of which was that she was on a sandy shelf facing a smooth vertical cliff the color and texture of charcoal gray velvet, and that the prevailing light was dusky. A glance around showed her one of the packs a few yards away: right where it ought to be if something large had dropped it upon emerging from the gate. She retrieved it gratefully, hurried it open—

And then realization struck her so hard she had to sit down in the middle of struggling into her shirt.

*Where was Calvin?*

*Where was Okacha?*

*And where was Tsistu?*

"Christ, no!" she groaned aloud. "Don't tell me . . ."

A muffled crunch interrupted her, and she turned to see Brock-the-Bunny hopping toward her. He paused just inside the limit of her reach and wrinkled his nose. She picked him up, though it took all her will to keep from screaming—or retching—so awful did she suddenly feel to find herself alone here in this place. Even so, her gut spasmed, cramped. Nausea hovered near. She almost cried out. Something wet and red trickled onto her foot. *Great! That was* all *she needed!*

Brock, however, obviously had other priorities, which he conveyed first by wriggling violently, then by nipping her hand. She slapped at him, then nodded dully. "Oh, yeah, guess you *would* like to be a boy again, huh?" Her comment segued into a nervous laugh that was per-

ilously close to hysteria. Brock twitched his ears, which
seemed to mean yes. She set him down and slid him the
scale. He took it awkwardly—rabbit paws weren't made
for fine manipulation—and hopped away. She didn't
watch any longer than it took to see his eyes close and
blood well out onto the white fur from between the
paws. There was no noise, save the grating of coarse
sand.

And then the scrabbling stopped, to be replaced by a
distinct intake of air and—thankfully—Brock's voice
gasping shakily, "God*almighty*, it's cold!"

"You noticed," she snorted, glancing his way only
long enough to catch a flash of him bare, goosebumped,
and crouching, before averting her eyes and thrusting the
pack toward him. "Here! I think your clothes are—"

"Thanks," Brock broke in, scrambling toward it on
all fours. The sounds of fabric being fumbled out and
sorted through followed. Then, abruptly: "*Uh-oh!* Uh,
where's Cal? and Okacha . . . ? And whazzit's name?
Tsistu?"

Sandy twisted around to face him, saw concern war
with self-conscious embarrassment on his face. "Those,
my lad, are damned fine questions."

Brock hastily pulled up his pants. "You didn't see
'em at all?"

Sandy shook her head, in marginally more control.
" 'Fraid not."

"Tracks?"

"No time to check."

Brock skinned on his T-shirt, then sat to work on
shoes and socks. "So, what *is* this place, anyway, d'
you reckon?"

"Gimme a minute to get my head straight," she replied, as she paused to tear her spare T-shirt into strips
to help alleviate her "problem." That accomplished
(very discreetly—Brock didn't notice a thing), she lo-

cated the rest of her clothes and finished dressing, then
took closer stock of their surroundings.

The main thing—the most pervasive thing—was the
presence of a vast cliff behind them and extending in a
gradual curve as far as she could see to either side. It
was impossibly smooth, too, though perhaps that was a
function of it being composed of more of the purple-
black-gray sand that was ubiquitous on . . . the inside,
she supposed it was. Impulsively, she poked it and
brought her hand away covered with dark powder—and
got a sense that the cliff face was *not* precisely solid,
but rather grew more compacted the deeper one pushed,
exactly as the air in the gate had done.

A glance up the escarpment showed nothing but its
own surface merging with a sky that was such a disturbing mix of purple, gray, and black with what she
could only describe as a *non color*—or the color of nothingness, or of absolute clarity—that it made her sick to
gaze upon.

Which forced her attention back to the ground.

Where she got another shock, for as best she could
tell, she and Brock were marooned on a ledge averaging
forty yards wide that followed the cliff in a ragged line
to both left and right horizons. What really freaked her,
though, was that even this far back she could tell that
the shelf did not so much break off into empty space as
simply . . . dissolve, like tatters of rusty metal. She could
see fragments of it out there, with sections of that not-
color showing through.

"The World ends here," she murmured, as Brock finished with his shoelaces and shivered up to join her, his
face as perplexed as her own as he returned the scale.

"Ends?"

"Looks to me like we're on the fringe of one of
those island Worlds Cal talked about. It overlies our
World, but . . . not continuously, I guess. Something

makes the fabric of matter go thin here. And beyond, there's just . . . *nothing.*''

''Then what's that yonder?'' Brock countered, pointing to his right, away from the cliff.

Sandy strained her eyes—she had to in the purple twilight gloom that was the prevailing illumination. Perfect for the Darkening Land, she supposed. ''I'm not sure,'' she told him at last, then took a few steps closer and tried again. And this time she could make out, right at the edge of one of the more distant parts of the shelf, where it began to filigree away to nothing, what looked like a vast stone archway. More specifically, it resembled one of the trilithons at Stonehenge, except that it was more trapezoidal and the space between the uprights was far wider—maybe thirty feet. Nothing showed beyond save a vague brightening of the air—and a golden glitter low down that might mark a continuation of the Track.

''It's another gate, I think,'' she told Brock. ''Probably the Track we were following continues through there. Or that makes sense, anyway: Cal said the Worlds were all connected by Tracks, but sometimes all that exists *are* the Tracks, along with what little matter they can attract to themselves. I guess it's like . . . I dunno— think of a globe that you throw bits of wet tissue on. Those are the Worlds. And then take some thread and glue down one end so that it won't move, and then wrap the rest around the globe so that it connects all the tissue. Those are the Tracks. They're straight, because they join two points directly; yet not, because they follow the curve of the earth. And they're little roads of matter connecting larger hunks of it: little morsels of compressed space-time, maybe. God, but I wish I had time to prowl around.''

''Well, you don't, '' Brock replied flatly from where he was retrieving a small glassy stone from near the gate they'd entered by. "I think I know what happened to Cal, though." Whereupon the boy pointed to the ground, where footprints were plainly visible in the grit: rabbit prints in a variety of sizes, all arrowing toward the trilithon—and evidently, to judge by the spacing, at a rapid clip indeed. And superimposed atop them were the tracks of two panthers, one slightly larger than the other. "I think," Brock whispered, "that when our friends came out, they saw old Tsistu, and . . . well, they just couldn't resist. Their animal instincts took over, and they chased 'im."

"Damn!" Sandy spat. "I bet you're right! It'd be just like him, too—Tsistu, I mean. 'Cause according to what Cal says, he's a trickster. And he probably thought it'd be real cool to con a couple of us into shifting shape and then lead us off on a snipe hunt somewhere."

Brock's face was even paler than normal. "Yeah, but . . ." He paused, swallowed. "But, what if Tsistu hadn't *been* here? Suppose we'd come out of there as rabbits and met Cal and 'Kacha as panthers, and—"

Sandy exhaled sharply. "Oh, Christ, yeah! We could've been *eaten*. I bet old Tsistu'd have enjoyed that!"

"Or else he expected it and drew 'em off deliberately."

"Whose side're you on, anyway?"

Brock ignored her. "We have to find 'em. We have to keep on heading west."

"If we can even tell which way that is, given that there's no sun here."

Again Brock looked startled. "There's not?"

"Look up and tell me what *you* see."

He did. "It . . . makes me sick."

"And the cliff?"

"Not much better."

"I bet I know what it is, too," Sandy said—thinking up explanations helped keep the impossibility of their situation from sneaking too close. "I bet it really is the dome of the sky—sort of. It's the limit to the matter that can be attracted to that World back there. It's like an . . . an accretion disk, with just a bit more air on the outside where we are. But Cal said the sun and stars and all are sort of semi-immune to some of this stuff; that is, they exist in all Worlds simultaneously. So I bet vagaries in the gravity between the earth—*our* earth—and the sun and moon come into play here and make the. . . . what Cal calls the sky vault, rise and fall. It really is like the myths, in other words."

"Cool," Brock replied. Then: "Hey, isn't that the other pack out there toward that gate-thing? What say we pick it up and boogie? It's on the Track anyway."

Sandy's reply, after a pause to catch her breath through another cramp, was to join him.

A moment later they reached it. She unslung her lighter pack and passed it to the boy before claiming the heavier alternative.

"Good idea," a voice cackled into the thin, cold air.

Sandy shivered, even as she jumped. The sound had come from the trilithon, still a hundred yards away, right where the *something* of the ledge met the *nothingness* beyond. A long way for speech to travel, that was. Yet she had heard it.

She exchanged troubled glances with Brock and stopped to retrieve the war club from Calvin's pack. Small comfort, maybe, since she had only the vaguest idea how to use it, but better than nothing. "Get behind me," she hissed, backhanding the boy, when he would have strode brazenly forward. "This isn't our World. Folks here might kill you fast as look at you."

"Yes, we might!" came that voice again, even as Sandy began to walk closer. She swallowed, shivered again, finding it nearly impossible to keep everything in mind she needed to. Like searching for the speaker, like testing every step lest the ground dissolve and precipitate her into . . . Never mind!

"Oh, yes, we might certainly kill you," that voice repeated. And now Sandy was certain it belonged to a woman—an *old* woman. She still hadn't seen her, however.

"We might kill you," the voice continued, "except that those who come here are already dead, so that would be foolish, wouldn't it? To kill those who are already dead?"

"Who are you?" Sandy called, and immediately felt like an idiot, for the question betrayed a whole host of weaknesses in her and Brock's position that could easily prove fatal. Nevertheless she advanced a pair of steps. Brock followed, standing very straight, but his eyes were wary.

"If you were closer, you could *see* who I am," came that cackling again. And this time Sandy listened carefully and realized that the sounds she heard and the language that formed in her head did not align. Oh, she heard speech all right, but it wasn't English—or Cherokee.

"But if you were closer, I could see who you are as well, could I not?" the voice went on. "And if I could do that, perhaps I would see things I do not like."

Sandy swallowed hard. "May . . . we approach?"

"Nothing forbids you. The forbidding comes later."

"Let's go," Brock muttered. "We're in deep either way."

Sandy nodded and took a slow step forward. Others followed. Brock fell in behind.

The gate grew in size—faster than it should have, as if some trick of perspective was at work. She could feel the subtle energy pulse of the Track with every step.

Finally, when the trilithon arched five times her height above her head, revealing little beyond except a murky darkness through which the Track shot like a dirty neon ribbon, she saw the speaker.

It *was* a woman: the oldest one Sandy had ever seen, and so bent and humped and crusted with dust she had first mistaken her for one of the boulders that clumped around the base of the uprights. The crone was sitting crosslegged and had gray hair that flowed unbound down her shoulders, confined only by a twist of dull-colored leather around her head. Her hawk-nosed face was lined and seamed like a relief map of the Dakota Badlands. And her clothes—well, all Sandy could tell for certain was that they were buckskin: worn, beaten, and scoured by the winds of centuries. The only ornaments were ear-spools made of what looked like vertebrae, incised with skulls.

"Greetings . . . grandmother," Sandy began, trying vainly to recall the formalities traditional among Calvin's people. She had actually met very few of them, so such courtesies were *not* second nature to her.

The old woman nodded slowly, like one half-asleep and remembering. "Greetings, daughter. Greetings, son."

"H-hi!" Brock said, slipping around to stand beside Sandy. She could practically feel him wishing he was taller.

"Do you have business here?"

"Perhaps," Sandy replied carefully. "Have you been here long?"

"Long enough to see some things."

"Have you seen a rabbit pass this way in the last little while?"

"What *kind* of rabbit?"

Sandy hesitated. "Difficult to say," she sighed at last. "His appearance seems to . . . alter."

"Ah, *that* rabbit!" the crone chuckled, and Sandy noted for the first time that her hands were busy with something in her lap she couldn't quite make out. "That rabbit: he comes here often. So often I tire of him. Perhaps I will make a pouch of his hide one day and put a stop to him."

"He'd deserve it, too," Sandy agreed. "But have you seen him recently?"

Again the old woman nodded. "He ran fast. But then, he was pursued. It seemed a merry chase. I did not stop it, though I should have."

"Why?" From Brock.

"Because those who pursued him were not dead. And only the dead are allowed here. Only because they sought to bring death with them did I permit them to pass."

Sandy puffed her cheeks. "So only the dead can go through this gate?"

Another nod. "Beyond lies the Narrow Road. At the end of the Narrow Road lies Tsusginai, the Ghost Country. Those who would go there must pass by me."

Brock looked startled, but Sandy could tell his brain was working ninety miles an hour. "*Everybody?* Everybody who ever died?"

The crone cackled. "There is not room here for everyone who ever died! They come here whose soul-blood compels them here. Here they may remain or return—eventually—as pleases them. Or as pleases those who rule the Worlds and the souls of men alike."

"There's more than one . . . place like this, then?" Sandy ventured, unable to resist.

"As many as there are nations. Perhaps as many as there are souls of men, if you hoe to the center."

"What was that about blood compelling?"

"All men come from the earth," the crone replied. "The earth calls them all, though most choose not to hear. Yet the call is there: the oft-unheeded desire for a center that speaks to the soul, for the earth from which the ancestors came.''

''But we're all out of Africa,'' Brock pointed out.

''Not in your souls,'' the woman countered. ''A soul, once incarnate, links to that land in which it first experienced life. And there are more souls all the time, born in all manner of places. Or maybe there is only one, and I am a fool.''

Brock looked confused. Then: ''Oh, I see. Everybody who comes here is somebody who first incarnated in, like, Indian places. Like Calvin's dad: he was part Cherokee. And Don's friend, Michael—didn't he have Indian blood, too?''

''Cherokee,'' Sandy affirmed, surveying the darkness beyond the gate speculatively. ''What must one do to pass?'' she added.

''Be dead.''

Brock was still scowling. ''But . . . what about Don? He wasn't dead—but he came here anyway—I think.''

The old woman frowned. ''He was dead in his soul. And he came with one of the dead.''

''And . . . what about us?'' Brock blurted out, and Sandy could have—not killed him, but maybe flayed him alive.

''What about you?''

''We . . . have business in Tsusginai,'' Sandy admitted. ''May we pass for a little while?''

''Are you dead?''

''No.''

''Do you bear the blood of those whose place this is?''

''Not that I know of.''

''Do you come in the company of one of the dead?''

Sandy shook her head.

''Then you may not pass.''

Brock's eyes narrowed. "What if we just ran by you?"

"I would unmake the Road."

"The *whole* road?" Brock burst out incredulously.

"Enough that you could not follow it."

Brock shrugged at Sandy. "Looks like we're stuck."

Sandy grimaced and began backing away. "So it seems." She inclined her head toward the old woman. "Thank you, grandmother, for your wise and honest counsel."

"Peace go with you until the end of all days," the woman replied.

"So what do we do?" Brock muttered as they headed back to the edge of the sky vault.

"I'm not sure." Sandy sighed. "But if you're up for a risk, I may have an idea."

"I'm all ears," Brock told her.

"Good," she whispered back. " 'Cause you may have to be."


. . . the buck was still ahead, but she was closing. She saw the white flicker of its tail as it fled; observed by instinct the tense and flex of muscles in its narrow legs as it ran; smelled as much as saw the sand kicked into clouds in its wake. She could hear, too, the heavy panting as it strove to outdistance her, the muffled click of hooves on whatever solidity underlay the drifting sand. And she could smell its fear, mingling with the oddly smoky odor of earth, and, more distantly, the scent of humans. But the bitter smell of panic was most pervasive, was what sent her loping onward: a lean cat-shape, muscular, poised, and capable.

She was bloodlust, hunger, and drive—and hot desire to fall upon her quarry, to feel her fangs in its throat, its steaming blood in her belly.

She was also Sandy Fairfax, and this was a mask she

wore, for a specified time, for a particular reason. And while she wore it, she had to balance, to grant the beast its freedom, yet retain control. It took finesse—perhaps more than she could muster—to both summon and suppress the urge to kill.

She was closer now: maybe *too* close. Close enough for the final lunge, but not yet near enough for the other.

But she saw it—clearly, where had been haze and the tunnel vision of pursuit. It reared before her, suddenly huge: a dark arch of stone above purple-gray-black sand, down which a body-wide ribbon of gold lay gauzed by drifting black dust.

. . . reared before her, and the deer passed under . . .

. . . reared above her and she too dived beneath.

Movement stung the corner of her eye, then: the crone, abruptly all alertness. Her head snapped up fast as a striking rattler. Her fingers drew lightning in the air.

The buck coursed faster, misstepped, staggered, as if the Track had turned to mud where a foot touched down, then gathered itself and leapt across something she could not see. Its flight arched long and high.

She followed, felt the sand go soft as she too flung all her strength into forward motion. The heavy muscles in her hips and legs bunched and strained as she released them, pushing out with feet and claws to maintain what purchase she could on what was becoming *gone*.

The sand dissolved beneath her belly. But the deer was straight before her and she forgot *human* and let base instinct carry her on.

. . . on . . .

For an instant, fear beyond anything she had ever dreamed filled both sets of reflexes as the ground evaporated, so that for far too long she hung suspended above a colorless, shapeless void. Only the Track remained, no more than a glimmer of dust.

But ahead was the buck and clear ground.

And after an eternal instant, her front paws struck . . .
. . . sand. She had found solidity.

But kept running, as did the deer, though its pace had
slowed, even as she strove vainly to restrain that which
she had freed too fully there at the last. It had saved her,
then; she dared not let it damn her now.

But at least the earth was solid. Not until she had run
a hundred paces more, however, did she finally pause to
glance back. The Track was still there, glimmering beneath its film of black sand, while around her sand
curved up into layered striations of many-colored stone
like the sides of a canyon. Above, a gray-purple haze
passed for sky but clearly wasn't.

Fortunately, those images distracted her enough to
banish the worst of the beast. She slowed automatically,
the better to examine it, then noticed something else and
bent to shake a forgotten encumbrance from her neck.
It plopped to the sand, where it glittered. Behind her she
heard the muffled click of uncertain hooves approaching.

Her nose told her *buck*, and the beast awoke again.

She closed her eyes, looked down, saw salvation spar-
kling on the sand. She slapped it between her paws,
pushed, felt pain and the gush of blood that stirred the
beast once more.

Closed her eyes . . . felt far more pain . . . and opened
them again as human.

The deer was looking at her hopefully, but clearly
afraid; as if instincts likewise warred behind those huge
dark eyes. She stepped toward it, then hesitated, abruptly
sick at heart. *It had no hands!* Therefore, it could not
regain its shape as she had done.

But before she could determine an alternative, it
reached out and licked her, wrapping its tongue around
the hand that held the scale. She stared at it incompre-

hensibly. Then: "Oh, *I* see!" Whereupon she relinquished her hold.

The deer took the scale in its mouth. She looked away discreetly, busying herself with once again digging her clothes from the pack. "You can stay that way a little longer," Brock called shakily a moment later. "Gotta get my britches on."

She nodded, busy restoring her own modesty. "That was a close one," she called back—and almost jumped, so startled was she at the sound of her own voice. "Jesus—that thing almost had me. Which means *I* almost had you."

"Nah," Brock snorted. "I'd have outrun you. Deer are made for distance, panthers are sprinters."

"Yeah," Sandy grunted, finishing up and resecuring the pack, but retaining the war club. "But what about *underwater* panthers?" The sound of a zipper told her it was okay to turn around. She did.

Brock shrugged in the midst of putting on his shirt. "Who knows? All I know is that was a brilliant idea."

"Crazy guess, more likely," Sandy gave back. "I didn't know if I got enough of 'Kacha's blood in my mouth back when we transferred to matter; nor that having to look for her a couple of times since then was enough of an adrenaline jolt to bind her pattern—*nor* that I'd turn into a panther instead of . . . her. For that matter, suppose I'd pulled a Calvin and gone off chasing Tsistu? Where would you be then?"

Brock started, looking for a moment genuinely afraid, but then all his youthful bravado came flooding back. "It was a risk. So's life."

"Too big a risk, though," Sandy replied. "Definitely too big, and one we don't dare run again."

Brock only shrugged again.

Sandy glared at him. "Don't give me that!" she snapped, feeling two days' worth of tension suddenly rise to a boil—or was it (as recent evidence indicated) a much more predictable, if no less annoying "complaint" arriving atypically early?—probably as a result of too much shapeshifting, she suspected. "That . . . *thing* there's only got a finite number of charges, don't forget."

"I'm not *likely* to," Brock shot back as he retrieved the scale and its thong from where he'd laid them on the ground. "Seeing as how you remind me about every two minutes!"

"Better than getting stuck in animal shape and not being able to get back—which could happen at any time, kid! And it's *Cal's* scale. I'm not sure we have the right to use his resources the way we have, given that we just did what we did for a pretty selfish reason."

"To save our skins was selfish?"

"To keep from waiting," Sandy countered. "We could've stayed where we were."

" 'Cept that we don't know for sure Cal'd even come back that way—or 'Kacha. Or how long we'd have had to wait there—*with* no food."

Sandy merely glared at him. "The old woman has to eat something."

"Don't count on it," Brock snorted, finishing his last shoelace. "But I tell you what: seeing as how we can't go back now—or that it'd be stupid to, anyway—what say we call a truce? I mean, we don't really have any choice but to go ahead, do we?"

Sandy grimaced sourly. "Not really. But one thing: no more shapeshifting unless it's a matter of life or death. And you give me the scale until we reconnect with Cal."

"That's two things," Brock grumbled, even as he complied. "And that presupposes we *do* reconnect."

* * *

"Well, hell," Brock sighed an indeterminate time later as he slumped to a halt. Sandy trudged up beside him and tried to mask a gasp as a particularly virulent cramp caught her. They'd been traveling single file—not because it was necessary; the Track was wide enough for two to walk abreast, though not with a lot of room to either side—but because of the psychology of the place: the subconscious desire to stay as close to the center of the only marker they had, yet likewise as far away from the walls, which, though they looked like striated stone might not be—and beyond which, she suspected, based on a couple of things Cal had told her, lurked nothing.

"Hell," Brock spat again, under his breath.

"An apt choice of words, unfortunately," Sandy agreed, surveying the landscape before them. It wasn't the rough-walled but arrow-straight tube canyon they'd had no choice but to follow, lo, those many . . . miles, if that word had relevance here. But that was as much good as she could think about their current situation.

Nope, it sure wasn't the canyon anymore—only because they had suddenly found themselves on the edge of a widening of the Track into a roughly circular depression maybe a hundred yards across. But at least it had the feel of *somewhere* to it, as opposed to the nowhere of the Tracks, and Sandy was pretty sure they'd reached the edge of another island World. Granted, it was hard to tell in the perpetual twilight, but there seemed to be a difference in the sky—though a check back showed nothing more certain than the pervasive gray-purple haze.

The problem was threefold.

First, as best she could make out, both by sight and the cessation of the subtle energizing that had been pulsing up through her feet, the Track had ended. Or if it continued straight, it was into a wall of solid stone.

Second, with straight ahead no longer an option, they

still had too many choices, for easily a dozen arroyos opened off the perimeter of this place, some narrow, some wide, but all equally promising—or threatening.

The third problem was that the whole surrounding area, including what she could see of those canyons that fed off of it, was paved not with dust and sand, but with stones. Which meant no prints to follow.

"You thinking what I'm thinking?" Brock asked helplessly, already starting to prowl around the perimeter.

"I'm thinking that we're in deep shit," Sandy told him frankly. "*Very* deep."

"I'm thinking that Cal and 'Kacha are in deep shit, too," Brock replied in a low voice. "I'm thinking that if Tsistu was just playing with them, he'd have dropped the chase by now and sent 'em back."

Sandy nodded grimly. "I was thinking the exact same thing."

"And we can't track 'em through here," Brock added. "Or I can't—not on stone."

Sandy shook her head. "I can't either."

"So what do we do, then?"

"What we do," she told him, "is think."

"Great!" Brock spat sourly.

"Could be worse."

"It could?"

She shot him a thoughtful, speculative smile. "Brock, my lad, it's time you learned some magic."

# Chapter XVII:
# Thunders, Black and Red

*It's time you learned some magic.*

Brock gaped stupidly. *Sandy* had said that. Not Calvin, who was supposed to be the hot-shot shaman, but his buddy's practical, no-nonsense girlfriend! Shoot, she was a high school physics teacher, for Chrissakes, which ought to put her headspace about as far from mojo as anyone could get. Learn some magic, huh? Yeah, sure.

On the other hand, that's what he'd come stateside for. And though part of him wanted to concede that what he'd experienced already in the way of shapeshifting and Worldwalking absolved Calvin of his obligation by any reasonable standard, one could also argue that his sometime master hadn't *taught* him any magic at all; that he'd *experienced* it, but not *learned* it. And if Sandy agreed to lay some on him, too, why that still left Cal down one promise—technically. And two of a good thing was better than one any day of the week.

On the *other* other hand . . .

"What . . . kind of magic?" he asked carefully.

Sandy started to speak, then winced as if in pain. "Something . . . you can do better than I can at the moment, if what I know about Cherokee magic's reliable," she replied finally. "I suspect it's something you'd do

better than me anyway," she added. "Besides, it's what
Cal had decided to teach you."

Brock shifted his weight and lifted an eyebrow,
prompting, yet trying not to seem too impatient. Behind
her—all around—irregular breaks in the striated stone
sides of the depression marked the entrances of numerous small arroyos. He could scarcely resist the tempta-
tions to explore them—prowl them all and see to what
new wonders they led.

Or—he shuddered, then blushed because Sandy had
seen him—what those canyons might lead to them. "So
what's the deal, then?" he wondered with calculated
nonchalance.

"The Finding Ritual," she replied. "Cal told me he
was pretty sure that's what Don used to locate Michael—except that he thinks it worked too well and
summoned Mike himself, instead of just showing in
what direction he was. But *I* think that, either way, we
oughta try it now. If we're lucky, it'll have the same
effect it had then and draw Cal to us. At worst—well,
hopefully it'll at least show us which of these blessed
canyons to try."

Brock nodded, still trying hard to keep his cool,
though he could already feel a restless anticipation well-
ing up inside. "I'm waiting."

Sandy had squatted and was rummaging in the pack
that held Calvin's clothes. "Ah-ha!" she cried a moment
later. "I *thought* he took it off."

"What?"

She held out a leather bag half the size of her hand,
fringed at the bottom, and with a length of leather thong
making a loop at the top, rather like the one that held
the uktena scale. "His medicine pouch"—as she carefully loosened the opening, then proceeded to peer inside. Brock noticed that she touched as little of the actual
bag as possible. "I don't know as much about this stuff

as I ought to," she continued. "I'm not like you; one reality's enough for me, preferably one that makes sense. But that doesn't mean I haven't picked up some things— or read some stuff."

Brock crouched beside her. She wasn't touching the contents either, he observed. But she did seem to have located what she wanted, for she was obviously manipulating something toward the opening by the expedient of squeezing the outside of the bag with the barest pressure of fingertips. "Hold out your hand," she told him abruptly.

He did—and felt a tiny jolt as something heavier than expected plopped into his palm: a red-brown stone, roughly the size of his little finger, with a length of twisted cord knotted around the middle.

"Why'd you do that?" he ventured. "Not touch it, I mean?"

Sandy colored unexpectedly. "Because, as of those two rounds of shapeshifting, it's got to be . . . that time of month a week early. And according to the traditional Cherokee worldview, which at the moment I feel inclined to respect, women in that condition are supposed to avoid contact with men and with ceremonies or objects that involve male power. I think it's cause our natures are so fundamentally . . . different, probably 'cause of the procreative thing. Or else it's the old purity thing: men are men, women are women, and ne'er the twain shall meet."

"But Cal—"

"Cal's male, and this stone is part of his power. You're another male, therefore if we're gonna be able to use it at all, you're the lucky boy. Don't worry, I'll coach."

Brock nodded warily. "I'm listening."

And did, as Sandy explained what sounded like a fairly simple ritual involving spinning the stone in a circle until its line of arch tended in one direction.

"The only problem," she concluded, "is that I don't know the words of the formula that's supposed to activate it. I've only heard it in Cherokee—and I only know a word or two of that."

Brock's brow furrowed.

"I think I know a way around that, though."

His brows shot up. "Oh?"

She nodded. "I know the sense behind a lot of the formulas, if not the actual language. And I know enough about the theory of magic to know that formulas exist in part as a focus of will. Which I guess means that if you try to do the right thing, it may happen—especially here, in what's already a magical place."

Brock regarded her uncertainly and sat back on his haunches, fingering the cord but not touching the stone. He thought the shadows had shifted on the fractured walls around them, but couldn't be certain.

"What you do," Sandy began, "is address the stone and ask it to do what you want, like find something— or somebody. That's the basic idea. But what you have to remember is that even though you seem to be talking to a dumb rock, the Cherokee thought everything had a life force—a kind of sentience. Therefore, you sometimes have to trick things, because nothing likes being ordered around. Like, you turn away a storm by calling to it, then pointing out that its wife is doing something she shouldn't somewhere else. Yeah, I know, it doesn't sound logical by our rules, but we've both seen firsthand that our rules don't always apply." She paused for breath, then went on: "Also, you sort of assume an antipathy between opposites. If you want something to happen in the west, you invoke the powers of the east; if you want something to affect a squirrel, you invoke animals that prey on them. And there's the color thing. See—"

"I know the color thing," Brock broke in impatiently. "And I more or less get the rest. So give me a sec and let me think. I don't suppose you've got anything to write with, do you? Or paper?"

"Actually, I may," Sandy gave back, already fumbling in her pack. A moment later she handed him a stub of pencil and a checkbook. "Use the deposit slips. Sorry, but they're all I've got."

"They'll do," Brock grunted. "Now, 'scuse me while I go off and try to figure something out."

Ten minutes and one consultation with Sandy later, Brock had produced something he thought would do. He scanned it one final time, then returned to where Sandy was sitting with her back to a boulder the size of a Galapagos turtle. "What d' you think?" he ventured.

She took the scrap of paper and scanned the crabbed script. "I think it's fine."

He exhaled tension and shrugged. "I hope so. I'd read a couple of those formulas and all, so I sorta knew what they were supposed to sound like."

A sigh. "No time like the present."

Without further discussion, Brock made his way along the Track to what, as best he could tell, was the center of the depression. A final pause for breath, and he began.

He let the stone slip through his fingers, then the cord, until he held the knot at the end. As he flicked his fingers to start it twirling, he began to sing, trying to mimic the way Calvin did such things:

*"Hark to me! Hark to me! I call you, most excellent*
    *Brown Stone!*
*The Red Stone and the Black Stone are nothing*
    *compared to you! Nor are the White nor the Blue!*
*The rocks of this place stand silent when you speak,*
    *and I know you always speak true!*

*Therefore, speak truly now; speak and show me which*
*way my friend Calvin McIntosh lies!*
*This I humbly crave of you, I who am called Brock.''*

And while he sang, he tried to focus on three things:
on the memory of Cal's face as he had last seen it, on
his desire to *find* Cal, and on the string. At first he neither felt nor saw anything except a brown blur describ-
ing a circle that was gradually narrowing into an ellipse.
But then he *did* feel something: a subtle, but discernible
tug in one direction. He kept on chanting but closed his
eyes, hoping thereby to lessen his conscious influence
on the pendulum. Not until the tugs became insistent did
he raise his lids again.

"Seems pretty clear," Sandy observed, staring at the
stone. "It's pointing toward the wide one over there."

"Then that's the way we go," Brock declared flatly,
and rose. Sandy handed him the medicine bag. He
stowed the stone in it, stuffed it in his pocket, and re-
shouldered his pack. "I guess we oughta be off," he
continued, and started walking.

Brock never knew how far they wandered, for time
and distance, which already acted oddly in this Otherworld, seemed to redouble their efforts at perversity in
this place of twisting arroyos and convoluted canyons.
Nor did it help that there was no obvious sun by which
to chart the day (though there *were* shadows, of a sort,
visible even in the pervasive gray-purple gloom). At
least, by slow degrees, it had grown warmer.

But one thing he did know for sure was that he was
wildly relieved when he led the way around one final
outcrop and found the canyon emptying into a narrow
rocky valley, its harsh, dim bareness fuzzed here and
there with a few low bushes and scraggly trees—and, at
its opposite end, a building.

Buildings, actually: a series of stone-walled structures set under the face of a gray and mauve cliff several hundred yards opposite the canyon by which they had entered. It reminded him of pictures he'd seen of the cliff-dwellings out west—except that the architecture was not quite the same, being more horizontal and somewhat more ornate. In fact, now that he studied them, the strongest similarity was that the structures seemed to have been secreted beneath the cliffs.

And then he heard the thunder.

A slow grumble, it was, as if the sunrise had been awakened too early and was voicing its displeasure. He glanced skyward automatically, but saw nothing save the familiar swirls of purple, gray, and black that, if they were clouds, were like none he'd ever seen. The air felt odd, too: tense and nervous, like it did before a storm. Which didn't jibe with the near-lifeless landscape at all. Fortunately, there were breezes, in lieu of the stale air that had characterized the arroyo.

Brock shook his head. It was all too strange.

"There's . . . a wall up ahead," Sandy panted beside him, pointing to a long rocky ridge twenty yards further on. Brock had thought it a natural feature. "Guess we oughta check it, then," he grumbled, already trudging toward it.

No gate showed in the head-high piled stone barrier, but there *was* an opening where one wall ended and another passed by an armspan further back, as if it were the entrance to an open-roofed spiral—which in fact it proved to be. They looped twice, as best he could tell, while the walls either rose or the floor descended. The air also grew damper as they progressed, until it was almost like invisible fog. Its clamminess made Brock shiver.

And then he turned a corner—and staggered back involuntarily, nearly colliding with Sandy until he got his bearings.

The spiral had spat them out at one side of a circular, open-roofed ''arena'' maybe a hundred feet across. The pavement was hard gray sand, the walls blank save for subtle patterns formed by the irregular stones. A pair of trees faced each other halfway around, one with black bark and red leaves, the other exactly the opposite. In spite of their unlikely coloration, Brock thought they were honey locusts.

But he had little time for dendrology just then, for directly across from him and Sandy, lounging on a series of woven mats beneath an awning made of a complex webwork of furs and feathers, were two boys. Or that's how they looked: two Native American-types, roughly Brock's own age, so he judged, and no more heavily built than he, but maybe taller (it was hard to tell at this distance, in this light, with them reclining). One had long black hair secured into a forelock with a large white bead and seemed to be wearing no more than a loincloth made of what looked like black leather. He also had uncannily ruddy skin.

The other was harder to assess in the gloom, possibly because his skin appeared to be dead black. Only his orange-red hair, shaved on the sides and greased up into something like a Mohawk, his scarlet loincloth, and discs of some shiny metal at his ears and on his chest made him visible at all.

But Brock observed all that unconsciously, for bare instants after he saw the boys, he saw what occupied their attention. ''Oh, crap,'' he said, and gulped, nudging Sandy—unnecessarily, probably, given how rigid she had suddenly become. ''*Oh Jesus!*''

For, sprawled between the boys, having their ears scratched like household pets, were two panthers—one larger and darker, the other smaller and more tawny, its fur still (though not surprisingly, given the unlikely humidity) slightly sheened with damp.

"Looks like we've found 'em," Brock muttered.

"And more than we wanted," Sandy added with a sigh. Then, as she took a deep breath and squared her shoulders: "Well, we can let 'em have the initiative or take it ourselves." And with that, she retrieved Calvin's atasi, wrapped the handle in what was left of her T-shirt (to avoid pollution, Brock assumed), and strode across the arena, straight toward the boys.

Brock had never liked staring contests—mostly because he always lost them. And he liked the present one no better. Sandy was older than he, dammit; they ought to be looking at her! Instead, utterly silent, they were gazing intently at him with storm-dark eyes that were so damnably piercing they looked as if lightning flashed there: bright spots in a thunderous gloom.

And he didn't know what to do! Precedent in his own World said visitors should wait to be acknowledged, that to speak out of turn could be rude, even fatal. But suppose these lean healthy lads had some other worldview? Suppose they held to a system that said higher life forms did not address lower ones?

And so they remained, locked in impass four yards apart, as Brock became ever more nervous and impatient, which made it harder to think clearly by the second. But then, finally, the larger panther shook itself from the loose grip of the ruddy boy and padded over to rub itself against Sandy's legs. She reached down automatically and scratched behind its ears. A sideways glance showed a gleam of tears.

The abandoned lad lifted an eyebrow at his companion, then looked back at Brock. "It is the way of Fatchasigo and I to speak only to warriors," he said at last, his voice light but authoritive. "Is one of you a warrior? Or both? Or neither?"

"Actually, we speak to everyone *but* warriors," the darker one corrected with a sly smirk. "Yet no one of faint heart could reach here, in which case my twin should not have spoken at all. And in either event, we could not tell which of you *was* the warrior. One of you is almost a man. Certainly he is old enough to know the arts of war. Yet—"

"Yet the atasi is in the hands of the woman," the ruddy boy interrupted. "And a beast of great medicine chooses to stand beside her, and so we are confounded."

"And more so because those to whom we speak most commonly are dead, and you are not," the dark twin added.

"Are you then magicians?"

Brock exchanged wary glances with Sandy and nodded for her to speak. She grimaced, cleared her throat, and began. "*Siyu*, warriors—and if you are worthy of more exhalted titles, forgive me their omission, but I am unfamiliar with the customs of this place."

"The dead come from many quarters," the red twin replied. "Ignorance, though undesirable, is not unknown, in both the dead and the living."

Sandy paused to allow the other his say, but he remained silent. "Greetings, then. My name is Sandy Fairfax, and in my own place I am esteemed . . . if not a wisewoman, at least one wise in certain ways of the world."

"Wisdom is *always* to be respected," the dark boy acknowledged, with another smirk.

"But are you also a *warrior*?" his brother persisted.

Sandy gnawed her lip. "I am skilled at certain forms of combat."

"Can you use that weapon?"

Sandy glanced down automatically. "I never have."

"But it seems a fine one!" the red twin exclaimed. "Indeed, the workmanship looks familiar. Let me see it."

She hesitated, then extended the weapon, handle first, toward him.

He studied it for a moment, then passed it to his companion, who did likewise before handing it back. "It is the work of our father's brother," the red twin acknowledged. "How did you come by it?"

Again Sandy exchanged glances with Brock. "He gave it to a friend of ours, who . . . left it in my keeping."

The dark twin's eyes narrowed. "And when was this?"

"Before . . . we passed the edge of the sky vault."

Both sets of eyes widened abruptly.

"You came *that* way . . . in *those* bodies? Only the dead are fleet enough for that—or beasts."

The panther that was Calvin growled.

"You have never told us whether or not you are magicians," the red twin noted. "Again I ask: are you?"

Sandy scowled uncomfortably. "We know something of the ways of magic—a very little."

"Do you know how to change shape?"

"Not . . . *how*, precisely, but we have . . . means to do that."

"And was that fine beast beside you always a beast?"

She shook her head. "He was a man—a warrior of the Ani-Yunwiya. He was learning to be an . . . *adewehi*, I think the word is."

"And this other creature?"

"A . . . woman born of both worlds but truly part of neither."

Both twins looked troubled. "Why came you here, then?" the dark one demanded.

"Here?" Sandy echoed. "We came *here* to find our

friends who were tricked into shifting shape and led astray by . . . someone who proved unreliable. I would rather not speak of what brought us to Usunhiyi until our friends return to their proper bodies.''

Again dark eyes narrowed. ''Ah, so you would cheat us of our pets! But they are such fine creatures, of rare and marvelous kind.''

''They're people,'' Sandy shot back furiously. ''You can't make pets out of people!''

''I see no people!'' the dark twin snapped.

Sandy's face was set. ''Nevertheless, they are.''

''Will you fight for them, then?'' the red twin inquired.

''If I have to.''

''She cannot!'' a third voice inserted, so close to a growl it was almost incomprehensible. Brock started, so did Sandy. But theirs was nothing to the reaction of the twins, each of whom flung himself a body length away from what was no longer—entirely—a tawny panther. Okacha was drying—finally. And as she did, her human form was returning.

The twins recovered their composure quickly—probably so as not to lose face. ''Who are *you*?'' the dark one spat at the uncertain shape between him and his brother.

''I am called Okacha,'' came the growl, though the face was now more human than feline. ''My grandmother many mothers back was the child of a woman of the Muscogee and a *Wikatcha*.''

''And why should this woman not fight us?'' asked the dark boy.

''Because my nose tells me that she is in that condition which renders her unfit for the company of men.''

The twins exchanged troubled grimaces. ''Well, we are not polluted yet, though that atasi may be, if it not be purified. But that is for its owner to decide.''

"And he cannot decide in that shape," Okacha noted from where she was dragging clothes out of the pack Sandy had passed to her.

"Therefore—"

"The boy must fight one of us."

Brock looked first at Sandy, then at Okacha, as a cold, sick dread awoke in him. "H-how do you *mean* fight?" he stammered.

"Ah, so you *do* have a tongue," the dark twin chuckled. "I was wondering if you intended to let these women speak for you all day. But to answer your question, the best fights are between those who are most equal. Therefore, we will fight you in whatever form you choose. Ourselves, we are good at all."

"Does this have to be a . . . *fight* fight?" Brock managed.

"Are you a coward?"

Brock took a deep breath and shifted his weight. "No! But . . . Well, I mean, could it be a game? Or gambling?"

"It could be a *ball* game," the red twin admitted.

Brock felt his heart flip-flop. Why hadn't he kept his mouth shut? Board games he was decent at; he won more than he lost at poker, and was hell on wheels in a video arcade. But the rest . . . well, he was in decent shape, but hardly an athlete. And from everything he'd read, southeastern Indian ball games were definitely designed for those in A-1 condition. Shoot, the only ball games *he'd* ever played were grammar school softball and the bit of cricket he'd picked up in self-defense during the year he'd just spent in England.

"You don't seem eager to accept our challenge," the dark twin noted with a wicked grin. "Perhaps you *are* a coward."

Brock tried to keep his shoulders straight and his face calm, though his nerves were in tatters. "I don't know *how* to play your kind of ball game," he gritted. "Besides, isn't it usually played with big teams?"

"It is," the red twin acknowledged. "So what I had thought was that you could take turns shooting at the goal, while the other tries to prevent it—and the one who hits it most out of, say, ten tries is the winner."

"Or five in a row," the dark twin added.

Brock scowled. "Yeah, but that gives you all the advantage, seeing as how I've never played before."

"True," the red twin admitted. "Is there a ball game *you* know that we do not? If you were to play our game and then yours—"

"And a third to break any tie," the dark twin broke in.

"Then that would be fair all the way around."

Brock's scowl deepened. "The only ball games I know involve someone throwing a ball and the other trying to hit it."

"Which works perfectly!" Red cried. "In ours, you try to hit a stick with a ball; in yours, a ball with a stick!"

Brock stared at the war club dubiously, noting that it was roughly the right length and width, and flat on one side. "I suppose I *could* use that for a cricket bat."

"Well," the dark twin announced with a malicious smile, pointedly ignoring the women, "I think we should get to it. Do you want to begin, brother? Or shall I?"


*Tattoos.*

For some stupid reason, all Brock could think of, as he faced the dark twin in the center of the sand-paved arena, was tattoos.

Even at the relatively short distance that had separated them during the audience that had led to this godforsaken duel, the boy's skin had seemed black. Here, though, without the sheltering awning and at no more than an arm's length separation, he could see that what he had taken for inborn pigmentation was in fact an intricacy of angular black tattoos that covered every visible surface of the boy's body, including even his eyelids and the complex curves in his ears. What skin showed through, in hair-thin spaces behind the patterns, would have looked copper-red—had it not also had a tendency, very faintly, to glow like metal hot from a forge. Otherwise, save for his loincloth, the boy was bare.

Excepting his jeans, and much against his will, Brock was too—and not happy about it, partly because of the cool damp air, and partly because it only emphasized his opponent's superior condition. The dark boy's spare muscles were clean-cut and firm; his soft-edged and a touch flabby. On the plus side, they were close to a height, and not that far off weight-wise, except that the dark boy, being more muscular, was undoubtedly stronger.

And there was the grin. That damned, wicked, secretive grin that, along with the sly twinkle in the boy's eyes, told Brock he could trust him about as far as he could throw him.

Speaking of which, he supposed it was time he did some throwing. Sparing his opponent his best cocky glare, he turned to face the target pole that centered the arena. And shuddered involuntarily. It hadn't been there when first he and Sandy had passed that way, but then, when he'd turned from agreeing to this stupid contest, there it was: twenty feet high, and with a skull on top that might, from its fangs and length of muzzle, be bear. He was beginning to understand Sandy and Cal's aversion to magic.

Squaring his shoulders, he gave his sticks (similar to those he had seen in *Last of the Mohicans*) an experimental swing, then clicked the cups at the ends together like salad tongs. Red (he'd heard no name for his opponent's brother) had given them to him, saying they were his own and to use them well. Yeah, sure, like he was supposed to play a game he'd never played before for impossibly high stakes and win!

"I will grant you five practice throws," Fatty (so Brock had christened the dark twin, being unable to remember his real name beyond Fat-something-or-other) laughed, and without further comment, flipped a small object in Brock's direction. He grabbed at it with his sticks but, as he'd expected, missed. Blushing furiously, he bent over and clumsily picked it up with the wooden cups. Roughly the size of an unhulled walnut, it was made of two pieces of buckskin not unlike those that covered baseballs, laced together with rawhide over a lightly padded stone core that probably made it hurt like hell if it hit you—which he suspected Fatty would be sure to arrange.

As if he had heard that thought, Fatty cleared his throat and backed off a way to give him room. Brock gnawed his lip, rearranged the ball in the basket of his sticks and, aping the single example Red had given him, drew both hands back over his right shoulder and threw, releasing the ball at what he hoped was the optimum instant.

It wasn't. The sphere shot straight up in the air, then plummeted to earth at Brock's feet. Fatty snickered.

A second shot fell short of the pole by two yards.

The third sent the ball backward.

Number four was closer. And number five almost hit.

*Maybe if I tried ten more times I might make it once,* Brock thought gloomily. His opponent merely grinned again, retrieved the ball from where it lay by the pole, backed up ten paces, threw—and smacked the skull so hard a fragment of the cheekbone broke off and fell to earth.

"You get first throw," Fatty told him with another grin. "Since this is war, I will not wish you luck."

Brock nodded, then wandered up to where the ball still lay at the base of the pole and picked it up with his sticks.

Only his reflexes saved him.

He heard the soft thud of feet rushing toward him and had just time for a glance from the corner of his eye to show Fatty charging straight at him, before his opponent was practically atop him. *Dammit! he'd forgotten that the rules let his adversary try to stop his shots—which apparently included stopping him!* Desperately, he dashed away, striving to put the pole between him and the onrushing boy, hopefully thereby delaying him long enough to get in a shot.

And succeeded well enough to spin on the fly and throw. He was reasonably on target, too—until Fatty simply flung one of his sticks into the air and knocked the ball back toward him. Brock scrambled for it, realizing suddenly there weren't nearly as many rules as he'd thought, and that what remained didn't necessarily favor him. Still, he was agile if not strong or long-winded, so he managed to snatch the ball before Fatty could interfere further.

Or so he thought. He had held the ball in his sticks for maybe two seconds before he felt himself hit by something heavy, strong, and purposeful, and carried backward at least ten feet. His skin flinched from that contact, as if he had received an electric shock. The air smelled strongly of ozone.

And then the ground slapped him and showed him stars.

When his vision cleared again, it was to see Fatty's bare back filling most of the horizon, and to feel the weight of his body across his chest as Fatty calmly snapped off a shot while sitting atop him.

Brock jerked and twisted but could not escape. And of course the shot hit dead on.

And what made it even worse was the fact that not only was it a clear hit, but it bounced back so precisely that, even allowing for Brock's writhing, Fatty was able to catch it in his sticks. Which gave him a second clear shot.

By number three, Brock had recovered enough to try to block the ball's return—which he did by striking at Fatty's stick with his own. Fatty, however, only chuckled, clamped his thighs closer around Brock's body (it was getting hard to breathe!), and threw again.

He almost missed; indeed, barely grazed the skull's forehead, but it was enough. Another hit and he'd have won round one. Brock doubted he was good enough at quasi-cricket to manage so decisive a victory in the second. Meanwhile, he put all his strength into bucking as the ball arched back toward them, simultaneously thumping his opponent on the head with his sticks—if Fatty could cheat, so could he.

"Now, you're getting the hang of it," Fatty laughed as Brock indeed managed almost to dislodge him. Nor did his opponent catch the ball. Instead, it zipped past him, rolling to a stop near where a grim-faced Sandy was standing beside Okacha beneath the black-trunked tree. Fatty was off him in a second and running. Brock dived after. Closer he came . . . closer. But it was too late, for even as he put all his frustration into one final burst of speed, Fatty snatched the ball and threw.

And of course hit home, thereby assuring his victory in the first round.

Brock was disgusted. He did not meet Sandy's eyes— nor Okacha's, never mind the dark boy's or his twin's, as he dropped the ballsticks where he stood and reluctantly claimed Calvin's war club from the panther-woman.

"I thought you were a warrior," Fatty taunted as he strolled calmly up.

Sudden anger welled up in Brock. It wasn't fair, dammit! Fatty had cheated—and cheated—and cheated! But he didn't dare let himself get riled; that'd give the twins a moral victory as well as a technical one. But he had to burn off his anger, *had* to. Without really thinking about it, he slammed the war club into the black bark of the honey locust tree.

The world turned white! Sound that was beyond noise overwhelmed Brock's senses, even as it snatched him from his feet and slammed him to the ground. A hard, crisp sound it had been, like ripping paper amplified a million times.

Or like lightning!

When he could see again, it was to gaze upon Fatty's face looking shocked and stricken. He had dropped his sticks and his mouth was a perfect *O*. His cocky Mohawk was singed. "If you promise not to do that again, I will concede victory." He sighed.

"And if you promise not to do the same to the other tree, I will likewise," said his ruddy brother, trotting up to join them.

Brock stared at them stupidly, then sought Sandy for explanation. From where she had likewise been knocked to the ground, she merely shrugged dazedly and looked pained. Okacha, however, showed a secret smile. "If you won't tell them, I will," she whispered to the twins.

The boys looked at each other, as if each wished the other to go first. Finally Red spoke. "The trees are sacred," he said. "They grew from the water that gushed from our mother's womb before we were born. Our father gave them to us to remind us that trees are our brothers, too. Also, the roots fill all the land here, and bring knowledge to the trees and tell us things, so that we do not have to go about ourselves. But when he gave them to us, our father told us to protect them with our lives. That we allowed you close enough to strike one made him angry. We dare not allow that again—for he will be watching us now!''

Brock blinked at his opponent, still half-dazed himself, both from the brief, if intense, exertion of the contest and from the vast sense of relief that flooded him. *He had won!* Against all odds he, Stanley Arthur Bridges (here he admitted the name he had told no-one present) had triumphed against a boy who surely was not a boy; who—if what he suspected was true—was probably some sort of demigod. Not that it mattered. What mattered was the victory. Now Calvin could go free; now they could proceed on their way and . . . And put an end to all this foolishness, he realized, at that moment acknowledging once and for all how sick he was of magic, how much he longed for the ordinary.

''A fine game.'' Fatty grinned, seeming none the worse for the wear, either physically or mentally, now that he'd regained his composure. Without further ado, he turned and strode back toward the shelter, leaving Brock and his friends no choice but to follow. An instant later, the dark twin flopped down beneath the awning, motioning Brock, Sandy, and Okacha to join him. Calvin did likewise, curled up between Brock and Sandy. The red twin reached behind him and dragged forward a pottery jug, which he passed to Brock. Brock sniffed it, smelled water tinged with something spicy and earthy— and was instantly thirsty beyond belief. An exchange of gestures with his hosts seemed to indicate that drinking was called for, so he took a long swallow—and was immediately refreshed. When he had chugged his fill, he passed the pitcher back to his adversary, but the boy shook his head and gestured that Brock should distribute it among his friends.

Sandy took it gratefully, Okacha almost as eagerly,

and when they poured some into a bowl and set it before Calvin, he lapped at it with vigor.

"You can stay as long as you like," Brock's former opponent said. "But I ought to warn you that we can be rather unpredictable hosts. We are not always as you see us now."

"We need to be traveling anyway, don't we, Sandy? Okacha?" Brock replied, making a move to rise.

"What about your friend?" the red boy wondered. "You evaded my question before. But how did he come to be in that shape? And how do you propose to change him back?"

Once again Brock shot Sandy a wary glance. "Show him, Brock," she sighed.

Brock hesitated, then reached into his pocket and pulled out the uktena scale necklace. He extended it in the palm of his hand, ready to snatch it away should the need arise.

Instead, both boys vented gasps of surprise, though neither moved otherwise. When he thought they'd had time enough to recognize what he held, he closed his fingers over it and drew it back. A glance at the boys showed their faces to be masks of chagrin. "Only one thing in all the Worlds looks like that," Fatty observed.

"The scale of the great uktena!" his twin agreed.

"Had we known you bore such a talisman," Red continued, "we would not have challenged you. For surely the fact that you carry such a thing marks you as a very great warrior indeed. At the very least, it marks you as a *friend* of a very great warrior."

"It . . . belongs to Cal here," Brock replied anxiously. "He used it to change shape so he could come here, but left it with us so we could change as well. But then Tsistu tricked us, and—"

"*Tsistu!*" Red spat. "That one is the plague of half

this Land, with his tricks and his jokes and his deceptions.''

Brock shrugged. ''He was our guide. He said he owed us—that is, Cal—a favor. He did fine until right at the edge of the . . . World, I guess you could say, before this one.''

''That would be his way,'' Red agreed. ''But had we known he was involved in this, we would have had yet another reason not to test you. It is enough that Tsistu does, without us lowering ourselves to his level.''

''I—'' Sandy began.

A growl from Calvin interrupted them. Brock glanced down to see the sleek beast looking powerfully unhappy. Even as he watched, it raised a paw, and reached toward the scale Brock still clutched in his fist.

He relinquished it, but felt a chill as the panther closed a heavy paw around it and brought it against his opposite footpad. Brock felt his heart skip a beat. Surely Cal wasn't going to *change* here. He'd seen the process before, and it wasn't pretty. To do so here seemed . . . well, it just seemed rude!

But it was too late. For scarcely had he caught the bright flash of blood between the panther's paws, when, with a flood of heat, Calvin lay crouching between him and Sandy. Brock jumped back reflexively, saw her do the same. Unlike before, it had taken almost no time at all. He had caught only a twisting of the air.

''God bless—*that* was fast!'' Calvin gasped, as he blinked, stretched, and found a more comfortable—and modest—way to sit.

''You're not kiddin'!'' Sandy breathed, reaching over to enfold him in an awkward hug that segued into a lengthy kiss. *So much for pollution,* Brock thought. Or maybe that didn't matter now that combat was over and nobody was doing magic.

"The drink hastened the process," Fatty supplied helpfully.

Calvin eventually let go of Sandy, whereupon he looped the scale back around his neck. He did not speak.

The twins looked uncomfortable. "It occurs to me," Red mused, "that we have heard of you. For are you not the one once called Edahi, and later Nunda-unali'i, and other things? We are sorry we did not recognize you, though truly we did not expect such a one as you to come here, at least not yet. Still, that does not excuse us. And in compensation, we would offer you a favor."

Calvin still looked somewhat shell-shocked—not without reason, Brock conceded. But then he took a deep breath, sat up very straight, and announced in an odd clear voice, "I, Nunda-unali'i, thank you for your courtesy, and I tell you now that there is only one thing I want, and if I am allowed that, my friends and I will leave this place as quickly as we can."

"And what might that thing be?" Fatty replied.

"I have come here to Usunhiyi in search of my father's ghost, so that he can proceed in peace to whatever awaits him here and may trouble me no more in my World."

"But what about—" Brock whispered into the ensuing pause.

"And further," Calvin continued, ignoring him, "if I can make one request into two, I'd like to know where another unhappy spirit is. This one's a boy, but there may also be another boy from our World with him. That is all I ask; all I have to say."

The brothers scowled at each other, then seemed to reach some unspoken accord and nodded. Red pointed to the escarpment behind the shelter, the one that overhung the stone buildings. "Follow that cliff left to where there is a crevice in the stone wide enough for one person to pass through at a time. Beyond it, you will find a plain wherein lies a river. This plain is called *Uyo-husv'i-sisekayi*: the Place of the Waiting Dead. Go there, and when those you seek become restless, they will find you.''

"You have my thanks," Calvin replied formally. "*Wado.*"

"May your quest be successful, Nunda-unali'i," Fatty replied, and rose. His brother joined him. "You may take the water jug if it pleases you," he added. "And you may leave when you choose, though I would suggest you do it quickly. For now, my brother and I must be about our own business."

"And the first thing we should be about," his twin chimed in, "is to have a word with a certain rabbit."

"Tell him I will taste his blood yet," laughed Okacha.

Calvin, however, was silent until their hosts had stridden from sight behind the high stone wall. And then he only said, "Get me some pants and my boots, and let's travel."

# Chapter XVIII:
# Ghost of a Chance

*"Damn!"* Calvin growled under his breath, as he pressed his shoulder blades hard up against the stone of the crevasse. "It wouldn't do for somebody *fat* to try to get through here!" And with that he sucked in his gut and pushed on to the right. But even so the stones of the opposite wall scraped his chest and thighs like dull knives as he continued down the defile toward the slit of dull-toned light gleaming tantalizingly five yards further on. Rock was inches from his nose, too: he could smell it here in the stuffy half-dark. But the scent of striated sandstone was now mingling with the odor of cedar and woodsmoke. He wondered what that portended.

"I'd presume that those who usually come this way are the dead," Okacha noted from his left, sounding about as unhappy as a live person could. "I guess it's not a problem for them." He didn't look back to check on her—probably couldn't have seen her anyway: Sandy's head was in the way, with Brock next in line.

"Fat people die, too," Sandy muttered. Then: "Ouch! *Hell!*" as a breast snagged on a sharp knob of stone Calvin had felt drag across his ribs seconds before.

"Just go *on*!" Brock grumbled. "I'm gettin' claustrophobia here in the middle."

"Be glad you're small," Sandy told him smartly.

"Cool it, guys," Calvin sighed an instant later, "we're through." Sparing but the briefest glance over his shoulder, he led his companions once more into open air.

Behind him and ranking to the horizon on either side rose cliffs similar to the ones back at the arena, if a good bit taller, though still not impossibly high ones such as he half remembered from when he'd been a panther. These towered maybe a thousand feet, every inch fissured and striated and blasted into strange, linear sculptures by wind and sand.

And beyond, stretching flat and almost featureless as far as the oddly murky light allowed, lay a plain. The effect was desert, but while there was sand and what he assumed were rock outcrops, no dunes were evident, nor was there any sign of life, either animal or vegetable, save where a dark line parallel to the horizon roughly a half mile away might mark the skimpy vegetation along a riverbed. Across it, almost at the limits of vision— west, he assumed—he could dimly make out a range of mountains, visible most clearly when they were cut into relief by bright flashes of sheet lightning. Pinpricks of light dotting the space between might be fires. Thunder rolled in the distance, too; or perhaps that was drums. The wind was warm without being sticky and tight with the threat of rain.

Yet if it had ever rained here, Calvin doubted it, for beneath the glaze of sand that shrouded the ground lay what seemed to be a solid sheet of rock. No bare patches or swirl lines showed in either, nothing to indicate water had ever run there; indeed, nothing gave any hint nature had ever disturbed it.

—Except the footprints: millions upon millions of

footprints. The majority were human, mostly bare. But there were animal tracks as well: panther, squirrel, deer—rabbit. He scowled at that last, and scowled harder when he followed a fresh set half a dozen paces and found them shifting size just in that small distance.

"Tsistu!" Okacha spat beside him. "Shit!"

Calvin did not reply. Instead, completely on impulse, he folded himself down where he stood and commenced removing his boots and socks. Somehow it didn't seem right that rubber and the designs of men should leave their mark on this place. His companions seemed to sense that, too, and followed his example.

Brock finished first and stood, gazing around. "Are those . . . buildings, or what?" he ventured in a whisper, which seemed the only appropriate form of vocalization in this land of perpetual gloom.

Calvin followed the boy's pointing finger along the line of the escarpment to where, maybe thirty yards to their right, the first of a series of buttresses flared out from the cliff base to comprise what looked like a row of roofless, open-fronted rooms, rather like, though he hated the simile, a ruined motel. Whether the partitions were natural or the work of hands, he couldn't tell.

Absently, he started that way—until a tug reined him back. "Hang on!" Sandy urged through a sudden yawn. "*You* got to rest back there with the boys; Brock and I haven't stopped since we got up."

"Yeah, but *we* had to run after Tsistu!" Okacha growled back, though her face showed immediate regret at her sudden anger. "Sorry, 'bout that: I'm just real jumpy, I guess."

Brock giggled. "Jumpy! Yeah, sure. Ha-ha!"

"Hush," Calvin snapped, then yawned, too, feeling unaccountably tired. "Yeah, maybe we'd *better* cool our heels a spell."

"The boys *said* the dead would find us anyway,"

Brock reminded them, shuffling the short distance back to the cliff.

"Good point," Calvin acknowledged. "I have to say it really is kinda peaceful here."

Okacha yawned and stretched and, even human, looked very catlike. Calvin suppressed an urge to scratch behind her ears. At least she was wearing clothes again, even if, being Sandy's, they were a bit snug in places he didn't want to notice—or be seen noticing.

A second yawn found him. "Jesus," he groaned as he joined Brock against the rockface and drew Sandy down beside him. "I really *am* gettin' droopy-eyed."

"It's the air and the warmth and the hiss of the wind so low you can't really hear it," Sandy replied. "The wind probably ionizes the air, and—"

"Hush," Calvin murmured into her hair.

And did not resist when his eyelids drifted closed.

*No!* he told himself as he jerked them open again. He couldn't sleep now! Not when he was on the verge of solving the major problem that had brought him here in the first place. On the other hand, it sure was nice just to lie here and rest and enjoy the simple comfort of friends and decent weather and a stomach that wasn't complaining.

*NO!* he told himself again, and this time he sat up and blinked. And realized what was bugging him.

He had to take a leak.

Grimacing irritably, he eased Sandy's hand to the ground, rose as quietly as he could, and padded silently toward the nearest stone buttress, not so much for modesty as to mask any noise that might disturb his friends. He had already unzipped his fly when he stepped around it—

—And found himself in a forest! A tiny wooded glade, to be precise, scarcely larger than the open area around Sandy's cabin; walled on three sides by oaks so gnarled and twisted they looked like illustrations from one of Brian Froud's picture books, never mind the moss and shelf fungi and ferns with which they were encrusted. Around them frothed more ferns, waist-high at least, but those petered out in the open area he'd blundered into. There a stream wandered down from some unseen source higher up to tinkle and splash among boulders that were themselves half-hidden beneath a shawl of moss. The very air felt damp. Nor was there any sign of the desert, either before, around, or behind him.

He blinked.

When he blinked again, he saw the man.

He had stepped from behind the largest tree—so Calvin thought, already feeling his heart rate increase as he came on guard. He wished he'd brought the atasi, but it was back with the others. Oh, well, it was probably too late anyway, for the mist that had shrouded the man had floated away and Calvin could see him clearly.

Clad only in a buckskin loincloth, he was perhaps an inch taller than Calvin and more powerfully built, though a looseness softening those muscles and a trace of fat around that still mostly flat belly hinted at middle age and a dissipated life-style. His coppery skin was dark, but whether that was a function of Native blood or white suntan, he couldn't tell. The hair was shoulder long and black, however, which favored the former.

It hid his face, too, for the man was looking down as he calmly picked his way among the rocks and across the stream. But as he drew nearer, he twisted just enough for Calvin to note a thin dark line on his right side just below his ribs: a line from which a steady trickle of red blood oozed.

And then the man looked up, and Calvin saw his face: Native American for sure; Cherokee, quite possibly. In fact, it looked like . . .

''Dad!'' Calvin burst out before he could stop himself.

''*Calvin?*'' Brown eyes brightened hopefully.

Calvin was at once dumfounded, relieved, and scared out of his skin. The result manifested as inarticulate nervousness. ''Uh, jeez, well . . . uh, how're you doin'?'' he managed finally, serving up the first reasonable phrase that fought its way to his tongue. A lump formed in his throat, all unbidden. His eyes misted—or perhaps that was the humidity. He was briefly dizzy.

''I'm fine—as fine as I can be,'' his father replied easily. ''*You* look like you oughta sit down, though.''

Calvin nodded, wide-eyed. ''I prob'ly look like I've just seen a ghost—or am seein' one,'' he gulped, and felt immediately like a fool.

''Just think of me as your dad,'' the man told him. ''Think of me as plain old Maurice McIntosh dressed up in funny clothes—or dressed down, I guess you oughta say.''

Calvin chuckled nervously, but managed to grope his way to find a stone of the proper height. The moss prickled beneath his palms as he braced against it. His father chose one opposite. ''It's a lot easier here to think of folks as themselves than as *what* they are. I mean, how often do you think of somebody alive as a human bein' 'stead of Joe or Jane or Jeffrey?''

Calvin couldn't help but smile. ''You've turned into a poet—or a philosopher.''

''I've turned into nothin' I wasn't before,'' Maurice replied sharply, but with a trace of sadness. ''You just never bothered to find out what I was. You were too busy tryin' to find out what *you* were to check. All you knew was that I wasn't what you wanted me to be. You never looked beyond that to see what I was.''

Calvin swallowed hard and had to force himself to meet his father's gaze. ''I—I'm sorry. I never thought of it that way. But I didn't come here to argue.''

"Statin' facts ain't arguin'.''

"No, I guess it's not.''

"I've missed you . . . son.''

Another swallow. "So I gathered.''

Maurcie stared at him intently. "I'm sorry I deviled you like I did, boy—but I just felt like I had to. I'm stuck here, see; I'm stuck and can't go either way. There's ways I could've died and it would've been no problem—a car wreck, or sickness, or something like that. But the *way* I died . . . Well, it's not a matter of the body parts, exactly—I mean they take things out when they embalm you, and all. But *that* part of me was removed in a way that's part of the heart and soul of our people—and *my* soul—my *real* soul—my centerthing—knows it and won't let me go on. It's not really the Black Man doin' it—not his fault anyway. He just knows that I won't be satisfied long as I know I lost part of myself the wrong way. Which is kinda funny, if you think about it.''

Calvin stared at him perplexedly. "How so?''

"'Cause I never *believed* that stuff! Shoot, I never liked any of that stuff, never liked bein' an Indian, which I'm sure you know. But deep down in my center I believed. Deep down in my *center* I wanted Spearfinger to be real. Deep down I wanted to be everything I tried to keep you from bein' 'cause I thought even knowin' it existed would make you want it—only most folks wouldn't understand it, and therefore wouldn't understand you if you wanted it or made yourself part of it, and therefore you'd be unhappy.''

"I . . . understand, I think,'' Calvin whispered.

"I *hope* you do, boy!'' Maurice shot back fiercely. "'Cause I've been tryin' to figure out how to explain it to you ever since you walked out that door when you were sixteen and said you were gonna go find your real self, were gonna *be* your real self or die tryin'. I let you go 'cause I knew I couldn't stop you and have anything good come of it. But ever since then I've spent every day tryin' to think of exactly the right way to explain why I'm like I am and why I raised you like I did, so you'd understand without doubt or distance. Why, I've probably thought enough words to fill a million books if they was all wrote down—and I *still* don't have 'em. But I know you've come far since you left, and have made a man like there ain't been in five hundred years of our people—ever since they got to *be* our people. And I know that you're a much better man than you'd ever've been if you'd done what I wanted you to. I'm proud of you, son—and I know you're the one who can help me.''

"I'll try," Calvin replied helplessly. "I'm not sure that I can. I—"

"One other thing," Maurice broke in. "Two other things, that is."

"What?"

"Like I said, I'm sorry if I bothered you, but you don't know how lonely it is here when there's nobody much to talk to; and you can't go *on* 'cause the Black Man doesn't want your pissin' and moanin' upsettin' the folks he's gotta look out for until they decide to go around again; and you can't really go *back* 'cause you just ain't supposed to. It's the loneliest thing in the world, son—shoot, in the Worlds!''

Calvin simply stared. "You know about *them*?"

A shrug. "Everybody does; they just don't all know they know."

"What was the other thing?"

"I'm sorry I was a bad father. I'm sorry I didn't listen and tried to cut out your heart to save your head."

"It's fine," Calvin murmured. "I'm sorry, too."

"Why?"

Calvin had to blink through tears. "For bein' a bad son. For not listenin', for not respectin' my elders, for payin' too much heed to the message and not to the messenger."

"It worked out okay, though."

A sniff. "Did it? You're here, and that really *is* my fault."

A shrug. "You were tryin' to do good. You had no way of knowin'."

Calvin wiped his eyes. "No, you're wrong there. I *could've* known 'cause I could've thought things out more clearly. I was actin' on impulse, and that'll get you killed. Except that it killed you and a bunch of other folks instead, and that's even worse."

"Folks die, Cal," his father said simply. "I'd rather die like I did than in a car wreck on 285 or by fallin' off a skyscraper down in Atlanta. Shoot, ain't nobody died like *I* did in two hundred years—not since they moved Galunlati away from the Lyin' World."

"Nobody but that woman and those kids."

"Yeah, but I was the first of *our* folks. That's something."

Calvin started. "You just called it the Lying World? Where'd you hear that?"

"Folks talk—not enough to keep me from gettin' lonely, 'cause they don't stay when they cross here, most of 'em. But they talk. The Black Man comes sometimes. Sometimes I talk to Kanati's boys—when they're not makin' thunder."

Calvin looked at him askance. "Red kid and black kid?"

Maurice nodded.

"I thought so."

Silence.

"Am I awake?" Calvin asked suddenly.

His father smiled. "You're too alive for us to meet,

with you awake. Sleep's the closest thing to death anybody alive knows. Figure the rest out for yourself.''

"But you're still here?"

"The only part of me that matters is."

"So, how do we finish you up so you can move on?"

"I've been wonderin' about that myself."

Calvin's mouth dropped open. "You mean you don't
*know*? But you said for me to help you! That I was the
only one who could!"

"And you can! Only . . . I don't know *how*—'cept
that I just know it."

Calvin gnawed his lip. "But didn't you say it was
mostly in your mind? That it doesn't matter to the Black
Man, except that it matters to you?"

A nod. "More or less. But it really *does* matter. It
matters so far down in my *self* I don't even know it
matters. It's like the same way I *know* you can help
me—"

"I'm not sure I understand."

"And I'm not sure I can explain—except, well,
haven't you ever had to act so different from what you
really were you *forgot* what you were and started be-
lievin' your own lies? Like, say you had a girlfriend who
liked cats, but you couldn't stand 'em, only you liked
that girlfriend a whole lot, so you pretended you liked
cats, and pretty soon you got so used to pretendin' you
liked cats you forgot you really didn't. Only the part
deep down still don't like em. Your head thinks you do,
but your heart knows better. Well, my head hated the
myths, but my heart wanted 'em: wanted things like
liver-eatin' shapechangers to be real, just so I'd know
something most folks didn't and be a little bit special in
a world that says it loves special things but really hates
'em."

"But," Calvin began slowly, "how can a . . . ghost
lack a liver when your physical body's somewhere else?

I mean, you *were* buried; your liver's—Well, it was in Spearfinger's gut when she died, so I guess it . . . dissolved when she did.''

Another shrug. ''That's a hard 'un, son.''

''Tell me about it!''

''I can't—unless it's like I was sayin': it's the old head/heart thing. My head—my mind—remembers my body as it was supposed to be: complete and entire. But my soul knows what really happened and remembers it another way.''

Calvin puffed his cheeks. ''I . . . think I see,'' he ventured finally. ''My friend Dave's talked a little about it. He knows these folks called the Sidhe—they're the Irish faeries; we've got folks like 'em in our folklore, only they're not myths, I guess, are they? But anyway, the Sidhe live in a World that touches the one we're from, just like this one does, only somewhere else. And they've got physical existence—real bodies—in both Worlds. Only to stay any length of time in any World but the one they're native to, they have to put on the substance of that World—which I guess means that the soul really is separate from the body and can wear the substance of whatever World it's in—and has to, to stay there.''

''So I'm wearin' the substance of Tsusginai, then?''

Calvin nodded. ''I guess. Your soul built it. But it's as physical in this place as your other one was to our world.''

'' 'Cept that my soul remembers me without a liver, so I don't have one?''

Another nod. ''I—''

''Hang on a minute,'' his father interrupted. Calvin blinked at him, startled, as his father reached forward and with a soft touch of his fingers brushed a lock of Calvin's hair away from his forehead.

''What?'' Calvin wondered, frowning.

''That scar you got playin' anetsa when you was a

kid—the ten-stitch job up at your hairline:—it's gone."

Calvin felt for the tiny ridge that had been there at least ten years. He rarely noticed it because of the way he wore his hair. But now that he probed at it—he couldn't find it.

And then he remembered.

"It's the scale," he blurted out, even as he withdrew the uktena scale from around his throat. "That, or the shapeshifting it lets me do. See, everytime I change back to human and it rebuilds me out of . . . whatever it rebuilds me from, my genes only remember me as the blueprint says I oughta be, so it puts me back that way: no cavities in my teeth, no eyes ruined by readin', and all that. I mean, my foreskin's even growin' back, and I bet I've halfway got an appendix. I had a couple of cracked ribs a day ago, too. And of course it takes care of scars."

His father was staring at him intently. "And I'll bet if I shifted back and forth a few times it could grow me a brand new liver!"

A sick dread sneaked into Calvin's gut: relief and apprehension both. "Maybe," he said carefully, "*if* it's got enough charges left in it. Uki told me to be real careful, that it was runnin' low."

"What happens then?"

"You could get stuck in animal shape and not be able to get back."

"Could be worse."

Calvin eyed him dubiously, then looked back at the scale. "If you wear animal shape too long, you forget you were ever human."

His father's face was calm, but his eyes were on fire. "I'd risk it. It'd beat bein' like I am."

"No!" Calvin cried, rising. "I can't let you. I—" He broke off, for he had noticed something terrible. "This isn't my scale!" he groaned.

# Chapter XIX:
# A Dream Within a Dream

Calvin wasn't certain which *him* it was that gazed down at Brock a moment later. Perhaps it was his dream-self, perhaps the "real" him—did it really matter? The prevailing certainty was that the boy still lay where he'd left him: curled into a tight fetal crescent at Sandy's side, close by the base of the preposterous cliff. He was snoring softly. For her part, Sandy slept in a surprisingly trusting sprawl, looking far more relaxed—and vulnerable—than she had when awake. And Okacha—she was also curled up, but catlike: poised. If she'd sported a tail instead of tight jeans, Calvin suspected it would have twitched. He chuckled at the notion.

*He* wasn't present, however—fortunately. Which mostly meant he was spared one batch of metaphysical conundrums, which in turn made it that much easier to focus on the task at hand.

"Brock," he hissed softly. Then, more sharply: "Brock!"

The boy twitched and moaned and shifted to a more comfortable position.

"*Brock!*"

"Wha—? Huh?" And this time his eyes slitted open.

Calvin squatted beside him and shook him roughly. "My scale."

The boy twisted up on his elbow. "W-what scale?"

Calvin grabbed him by the shoulder and jerked him to his feet, then dragged him toward the impossible glade where he had left his father. The boy gaped, yawned, not having regained full awareness. "*What* scale?" he repeated sleepily, still barely able to stand.

When he thought he was far enough from the women to risk raising his voice, Calvin slammed Brock against the cliff—not hard enough to hurt him, but with sufficient force to get his attention. While the boy stared and blinked, Calvin flourished the uktena scale before his startled eyes. "This isn't mine!" he snapped. "And since it *was* mine when I gave it to Sandy, and she's not the kind to play games, and you were the only one who was actually alone with it, it has to be you that swapped 'em!"

Brock had regained some composure by then, and with it a touch of his old surliness. "It didn't hurt anything."

"Where's *mine*, dammit!"

Brock fished in a pocket. "Here." He passed a second scale—minus wire winding and thong—to Calvin, who couldn't help but compare the replacement with the original. He understood how he'd been beguiled, too; for side by side the two were nearly identical. "Sorry," Brock mumbled. "I was tryin' to help."

Calvin glared at him. "By riskin' us all?"

The boy avoided his gaze. "It was spur of the moment. I didn't think."

"Obviously!"

Blue eyes met Calvin's, then; flashed fire. "Cool it, *okay*? Everything worked out, and we've saved some changes."

Calvin bit his lip, suppressing the urge to slap the crap

out of the lad. "But how?" he managed finally.

Brock shrugged. "It was in the cave. You and 'Kacha had gone; so had Sandy. I was by myself, and I guess I got scared 'cause I know how much you hate doing that; only you're a pretty cool dude, so anything you don't like's bound to be kind of a bitch. And then I saw how much it hurt Sandy, and I got real scared, only I knew I had to do it or look like a wimp. But just as I was getting ready, I looked down and saw this other scale. I'd figured old Tsistu was fooling when he said an uktena lived in that cave, but he must not've been, 'cause there was a scale there on the floor. So I said, 'What the hey?' You were worried about running out of charges, so I thought I'd try another one." He paused to take a breath; shifted his weight. "Anyway . . . it *did* work, but I changed back to me just to be sure, and then . . . I guess I figured I'd do us all a favor without telling anybody—I was afraid you'd get mad—so I swapped mine for the scale on your necklace real fast. It was kinda hard to bring 'em both through together, but I did it. I dropped the old one soon as I got through the gate, and then slipped it in my pocket when Sandy had her back turned while I was getting dressed."

"Smart kid." Calvin snorted. "Smart—but dumb."

"It worked, didn't it? And this way we've got a spare."

Calvin puffed his cheeks thoughtfully, at once pissed and relieved. The kid had a point, damn him!

"So, we cool?" Brock ventured, when Calvin did not continue.

"Maybe," Calvin hedged. "I'm not the one you have to convince."


"I'll try it," Maurice McIntosh announced a short time later. He was sitting peacefully in the verdant, misty glade that had no right to exist around the corner of a stone outcrop in an arid land. "If it works, fine; and if it don't, I'm no worse off than I was."

"Unless you get stuck in another shape," Calvin muttered, shooting a glare at Brock, who stood behind him looking both cocky and contrite.

"That's *my* problem, son."

Calvin gnawed his lip. "Yeah, well, I'm startin' to learn that it's never *just* one person's problem."

"If you've learned that much, you've learned a lot, then."

A shrug.

"I can't try that scale-thing until I have it, boy."

Calvin grimaced, but unwound the scale from the wires that secured it. His father rose to receive it. "I'd suggest you try it at sunset," Calvin advised, "then again at sunrise, and so on. Be warned, though: it hurts like hell."

"I know," Maurice replied quietly. "I've seen you do it. I just never knew that stuff about the scars, an' all."

"What if it *doesn't* work?"

"It's magic of this land, therefore it'll work. I believe that as much as I believed in Spearfinger—more, in fact."

Another shrug.

"You're still not happy?"

Calvin shook his head and slumped against a tree trunk, arms folded across his chest. Both Brock and his father stared at him, their faces dark with concern. "What's the problem, boy?" Maurice asked finally, reaching forward to rest a hand on his son's shoulder. Brock snared the empty nest of wires that had held the scale and began resecuring the original.

"You mean besides the fact that I won't know for hours whether or not I've done you any good?" Calvin replied sullenly.

Maurice's grip tightened. "This ain't the time for games, son. Here you have to say what you mean."

Calvin scowled grimly. "You weren't the only one I came here to see about."

An eyebrow lifted. "You mean them two boys?"

Calvin nodded. "Michael Chadwick—who I guess is in the same boat you are. And Don Scott. Have you, uh, seen 'em?"

"I've seen that *first* boy a lot," Maurice told him. "His soul-blood's of this land. He follows me around some—at a distance. Used to follow me to look at you."

"But he was *with* you . . . !"

Maurice shook his head. "That's how it looked, maybe. But it didn't seem that way from my side. I think he was held back by that other boy."

"Don? Yeah, well, he's not even dead—or wasn't when he called up Michael. Have you seen him?"

"A time or two. He's—"

"He's asleep near here," a new voice interrupted: young, and thick with sadness. Calvin glanced around, startled; saw Brock do the same. A new figure had entered the glade. Like Calvin's dad, he wore no more than a loincloth, but unlike the elder McIntosh, he was a boy—about Brock's age, though blond and a little taller and more filled out. He looked . . . lost.

"M-Michael?" Calvin guessed as the lad wandered forward.

Brock glared at the visitor sharply, even as the lad tried to grin. "Mike," the boy corrected. "I don't look much like I did, do I? It's all clothes, though—and hair. When you live in the real world you see what you expect to see a lot of times. Nobody expected to see me as an Indian 'cause that blood didn't show much. Shoot, *I* didn't even know it until I came here. But my *soul* knew. It brought me to the place I'd be happiest."

"You got a bum deal, then," Calvin snorted. "If this is the best it could do."

The boy shrugged. "I'm a very new soul, so they say. And eternity's a pretty long haul. I—"

"So, how'd you find us?" Brock interrupted. He'd finished restoring the scale and passed it back to Calvin, who promptly replaced it around his neck.

"By thinking about me, you summoned me; that's all it takes. Even in the real world it wouldn't take much more. Trouble is, Don did that little bit extra and got in trouble, poor guy."

Calvin frowned perplexedly. "But I thought you wanted him here!"

Mike shook his head. "Not as much as he wanted to come! Me, I'm like your dad: I want to get to the good place beyond the river, hold up a while, then move on again."

"So where is he?" Brock persisted. "I mean, Cal's dad said he was nearby—but where?"

"I come here a lot, anyway," Mike went on, as if he hadn't heard. "And when I got here, I felt you guys thinkin' about me, and I zipped over. But I've gotta go now; I've gotta check on Don."

Calvin reached out abruptly and took him by the shoulders, firmly, but not in anger. "*Where?* Mike!"

Mike dipped his head to the left over his shoulder. "There, not far."

"Will you show us?"

"If you can help him, I'll take you to the end of the World!" Mike shot back savagely. "Come on!" He was already walking.

Calvin hesitated, gazing uncertainly at his father. "You comin'?"

"I'm better off here."

"I'll be back—I hope," Calvin replied helplessly. "Brock, how 'bout you?"

"Wouldn't miss it," the boy grinned and fell into step behind.

As Mike had said, it wasn't far to where Don Scott's mortal portion lay—not *physically*, not from the point of time passed or exertion expended. But it might as well have been the other side of the world, for all the good reaching it accomplished.

One instant Calvin was following the ghost-boy through a tangle of ferns, the next they had rounded an outthrust finger of stone (which might have been one of those buttresses that knifed out from the cliff)—and were in another place entirely, one Calvin recognized.

It was a campsite beside Iodine Creek. Specifically, it was the place where Spearfinger had found Michael Chadwick asleep and murdered him. But now another slept there, nestled in a lean-to that was no longer fallen to ruin: a dark-haired boy Calvin identified instantly as Don Scott. He lay flat on his back on a mattress of moss, with his wrists crossed on his stomach and a peaceful smile on his face. He was bare-chested, too; but someone had thrown a bearskin across his lower half.

"Our clothes don't last here," Mike explained apologetically. "Nothing synthetic does—an' most sewin' thread's synthetic."

"So, what's wrong with him?" Brock wondered nervously.

Mike's already sad expression clouded further. "He's asleep, just like you are, but in a different way. The living aren't supposed to be here, see, and—Well, they just can't handle it for long, and even so they can only meet the dead in dreams, even when you were as close as Don an' me were."

Calvin's eyes narrowed. "Even when you brought him here?"

Mike nodded, looking absolutely wretched. "That

was a mistake. 'Cept that he kept callin' and callin', and he looked so sad, and I missed him, and I could feel him missin' me even more, and I . . . just had to.''

"Yeah, but what's *wrong* with him?" Brock repeated.

Mike squatted by his sleeping friend's head and stroked his brow in a gesture that was as appropriate here as it would have been incongruous back in Georgia. "He just . . . can't *sleep* much longer," he whispered finally. "His body needs more than it can get here. There's no food, and the water's not the same."

Calvin looked puzzled. "But if you're in a dream, and I'm my dream-self, and so is Brock—I guess—then why isn't Don's dream-self here?"

" 'Cause it's tired," Mike replied. "His body's tired, and so's his soul, now. But he can't go back 'cause he won't wake up. And I can't take him back."

"But I thought you guys were friends!" Brock blurted out.

"We *were*!" Mike cried. "We are! It's just that . . . well, one reason Don wanted to see me one more time was to . . . apologize. He said there was too much unfinished between us; mostly that he couldn't live with the fact that he'd had to just stand there and watch Spearfinger kill me. He kept thinkin' that if he'd just been a little stronger or tried a little harder, he could've done something."

"He couldn't, though," Calvin assured him. "I've been in her mind: I know."

"So do I—now," Mike agreed. "But Don didn't—'cept that he does now, 'cause you can't hide anything from people here—not for long."

"So why doesn't he just wake up and leave?" Brock wondered, fidgeting impatiently.

" 'Cause he's still bummed out about me bein' stuck here," Mike replied. "I think most of him wants to go back, but part of him knows that if he does, he'll start worryin' again. So he's shut himself off. But . . . Oh, gee, guys, I'm glad you're here! 'Cause if he don't get out of here soon—he'll *die*!''

Brock giggled nervously. "In the land of the dead? Big deal!"

"It's not his place!" Mike snapped. " 'Sides, I didn't get to live out my days; he deserves to! I want him to— for both of us."

Calvin swapped resigned gazes with Brock. "So, buddy-boy," he sighed. "I guess our job's to take him back."

"I wish you would," Mike whispered. "Or I'd wish that, 'cept for one thing."

Calvin stared at him. "What?"

"He's pining here—'cause I can't go on. He'll do the same back there. The only difference is that there they'll hook him up to machines to keep him alive. And that's even worse than bein' dead."

"Which means," Calvin continued decisively, "that the only way we can save him is if he knows you've gone on."

"And the only way you can do that," Brock added excitedly, "is if you're complete—have your, uh, liver, and all."

Mike nodded.

Calvin managed a cautious smile. "Well, then, you've come to the right place, my lad—maybe."

"Huh?"

Calvin flopped an arm across his shoulder. "Come on, kid. You need to talk to my father."


Michael Chadwick studied the triangular object in his palm warily, his slim fingers rubbing the vitreous surface as if to polish through the tarnish of doubt to the silver of certainty. But the scale remained as it was: diamond-hard and glossy. It was the new scale, though; Calvin had made sure of that, though he checked the one on the thong around his throat to be sure. "You said sunset would be best?" Mike asked, looking at him expectantly.

"In a perfect world," Calvin replied. "It's a *between* time. And that's the best time for workin' magic—'specially what you might call *between* magic. I mean, what with the uktena bein' a *between* creature—shaped like a snake, but horned like a deer—and with you guys bein' stuck in a *between* place, and all . . ."

He leaned against the boulder he had filed default claim to in his father's enclave and concluded his sentence with a shrug.

Brock surveyed the sky warily. "Uh . . . guys, when exactly *is* sunset? I mean, I haven't *seen* a sun here."

"You won't either," Maurice chuckled. "It's something you feel, not a thing you see. And it's not far off—not if Calvin's gonna move that Scott boy before we try it."

"Right." Calvin sighed, rising. "I'd best be at it. And don't you dare start anything without me."

A moment later he (*one* of him; he was never sure which was which here) had gathered Don Scott's sleeping body into his arms. Though the boy made an awkward bundle, he wasn't as heavy as Calvin had expected. Grimacing as he rose, (and feeling his back tug painfully), Calvin made his way out of the south Georgia idyll Don had dreamed for himself and stumped through Maurice's as well. Sandy and Okacha still slept where he had left them, though both had altered positions. He wondered if they also dreamed, and into what dreamworld they had ventured. Still, Don was too cumbersome to lug around while speculating, and so (with assistance from Brock), Calvin eased him to the ground. Brock restored the boy's cover.

Calvin slumped down beside Sandy, suddenly dog

tired. A westward glance showed the same familiar murkiness, the same half-seen mountains, the same sheet lightning. But a ruddiness tinted the pervasive gloom that had not been present before. Maybe it *was* close to dusk.

*God, but he was tired!* Sleepy too (and something told him he ought to be concerned about that). A glance at Brock showed the boy already zoned out, though he sat bolt upright with his head against the cliff. Good enough: the kid surely needed to catch some z's. Himself, he'd just close his eyes a minute, try to center, and get himself psyched for overseeing the ritual Mike and his dad had worked out. Lord, but he hoped nothing screwed up. He'd had enough of this, enough of adapting to alternate realities. . . .

Maurice McIntosh sat cross-legged in the eastern quarter of the Power Wheel he had scribed in the sand with Calvin's atasi. Calvin wondered how he knew that design—but now was the time for seeing, not speculation. Mike occupied the western equivalent. The two looked more alike than Calvin would ever have suspected, now that both wore their hair long and were dressed the same. A wind from the west stirred that hair, sent it slithering across their shoulders like serpents, black and fair. It bore the scent of rain, too, and the electric tingle that presaged a storm. Thunder boomed obligingly. Or perhaps that was drums. Calvin still wasn't sure, as he sat three paces out and waited.

The elder McIntosh stared west, and finally, at some obscure point he had determined, reached to the hollow he had made in the center of the pattern and withdrew the uktena scale. Mike tensed immediately, gasped, then grew quiet. A hardening of the muscles in Maurice's wrists was the only sign that he had clamped down on the token. His eyes closed, and yet Calvin sensed that his father still saw him. He tried to remain calm—he had no idea what form his father might choose, though he'd given him the standard list of precautions, strongly recommending they both pick something close to their own mass and mammalian.

He was not prepared for what he witnessed, however—for though his father's shape did blur and twist, it did not actually *change* much at all. He did not grow fur, nor feathers, nor scales; he put forth no antlers or tail. Instead, he became a younger version of himself. *No!* He became . . . *Calvin!*

But that meant his father had tasted his blood!

"I was there when you were born," came his own voice in his father's cadence. "When they cut your cord, some of it splashed into my mouth and I swallowed it. And in the years since then, you hurt yourself more than once and I tended you. Wouldn't you guess that somewhere in there your blood got in my mouth again?"

"And you've been huntin' me since I left!" Calvin whispered.

"I have—but that rule don't matter here—nor in the Lyin' World, if you *really* want to change."

Calvin didn't reply for a long moment. Then, simply: "I am honored."

"Mike?" Maurice prompted. And passed the scale to the boy.

Once again Calvin waited breathlessly until he saw Mike's face go hard and intent as he fisted the talisman between his fingers and squeezed. Blood flashed brightly.

Again no fur or feathers. Rather, the shape of a teenage boy, slim and dark-haired.

"We were blood brothers once." Mike sighed softly. "We cut each other's hands and tasted each other's blood. Maybe by usin' Don's shape to save myself, I can save him."

Whereupon he passed the scale back to Maurice.

Calvin didn't watch this time, for he suddenly felt a strange distancing from himself, as if he were stressed-out or drunk. He closed his eyes to fight it.

When he opened them again, it was to see his father in his own shape, and Mike in his. Neither showed any sign of a wound.

. . . and when he opened them *again*—for already he realized it had been his dream-self that had witnessed the ritual, that, perhaps, had dreamed even while he dreamed—it was to see quite another shape glaring down on him.

An ancient, weathered hag.

"I have *found* you!" the crone cackled loudly, capering about in a swirl of gray hair and buckskin that raised clouds of dark dust around her gnarled bare feet. She laughed shrilly—more a scream, really—and certainly loud enough to rouse his companions, who blinked up at her in groggy perplexity. Even Don mumbled and twitched, but did *not* open his eyes. Calvin tried to get to his feet, but an artfully "accidental" blow from the old woman's foot caught him in the ribs and knocked him down again. He staggered, winded, only barely managed to prop himself upright against the cliff. No one else moved, still half in thrall to sleep as they were. Only Okacha looked alert enough to act. He hoped she didn't.

Abruptly the crone ceased her capering, swept forward, and stuck her face in his, nose inches from his own. "They call the place you come from the Lying World," she shrieked. "But it ought to be called the Deceiving World! You've led me a merry chase, boy— and were it not for the rabbit, I might never have found you!"

"Rabbit?" Calvin managed to croak between ragged gasps.

"He has passed by me twice since he tricked your friends," the crone snapped. "But I caught him the third time, oh yes, I did! I caught him, and I told him I was tired of him, that he had made me angry. I threatened to make a pouch from his skin. I even pulled out my knife. But do you know what happened *then*, boy? *Deceiving* boy, from the *Deceiving* World?"

Calvin could only gulp and shake his head dazedly.

"I will *tell* you what he did!" the crone cried. "He told me that if I would spare him he would bring me to you!"

"We're, uh, sorry," Calvin choked out, wondering what was keeping the others from getting the hell out of there, given that he was obviously the target of the old biddy's ire. "Like I said, we're sorry. But . . . uh, well, we're ready to leave anytime now. In fact, if you'd show us the way . . ."

"*Which* way?" the crone spat sharply.

"Uh, the way we came, I guess."

"You cannot go back. Not that way!"

But Calvin had no time to protest, for even as he slapped his hands against the cliff in anticipation of pushing forward, he felt his fingers go . . . *through!* It was as if he had punched through a thin sheet of Styrofoam into . . . nothing.

A thin scream broke from Sandy. A frightened yip was Brock. A growl rolled from an Okacha, who was flailing wildly as the earth itself dissolved beneath her and dragged her down.

Calvin looked around frantically, saw the sand fading like ice dropped into hot water.

And then he was falling . . .

. . . falling . . .

With *nothing* all around.

# PART FOUR

---

# *Tskili*

# *and*

# *Adewehi*

# Chapter XX:
# Nothing to Crow About

*(Jackson County, Georgia—*
*Tuesday, June 19—sunset)*

. . . a twisting, tearing sensation that was not pain because pain was too specific to exist where *nothing* was, where the senses had *no* guides: no sights, no sounds, no smells—no anchors for nerve-endings at all . . .

. . . and then that twisting reversed, and stimuli flooded back so fast Calvin had to close his eyes as he staggered headfirst into heat and noise and color. It was like having his breath knocked out, he thought dimly, even as reflex flung his arms forward to stave off a fall.

He fell anyway, and felt his right hand stab into something soft and crinkly instinct told him was leaves, while the left scraped and slid along a surface rougher and utterly unyielding. It brought more pain—but a kind he understood.

He rolled with the impact, heard the rustling crash of similar encounters nearby, punctuated by grunts, groans, muffled curses, and one angry female voice yelling, "*Shit!*" Eventually his back caught against something superficially soft yet stable enough for his eyes to dare showing him a blur of green and flashing lights. It *oofed*

301

in a young male tenor, then went silent. Perhaps it too had realized it was still alive and was content to savor that fact.

But where?

The woods for certain, to judge by the tree trunks that surrounded them. But beyond that . . . ?

He sat up carefully, brushing twigs off his T-shirt and jeans, noting that he had fetched up against Brock, who was sprawled on his stomach, face crammed into tan-brown humus, one leg athwart a rotten log. Beyond the boy, Okacha was already standing, likewise taking stock. A glance to the left showed a wild-eyed Sandy blinking at him in something between bemusement, confusion, and relief. Leaves cluttered her hair—oak leaves. A dark furry shape just past her was the bearskin-shrouded Don. A sneaker slipped from Calvin's hip as he grunted to a crouch—from which position he finally found sufficient sense to assess the landscape.

They had come to rest—if *rest* was the appropriate word—on a wooded slope maybe ten yards above a narrow creek that threaded the defile between two forested hills. Separating them from the stream lay the piled stones of what, in the last century, might have been a bridge abutment or the foundation of a mill. The slope above them continued until it was lost in a tangle of low summer shrubbery, mostly dogwoods and sweet gum, which, along with the hills themselves, placed this probably in middle Georgia. Which was comforting, because it was at least familiar, but also disconcerting, since it meant they were a couple of hundred miles from where they'd left—and, more importantly, from Sandy's R.V. As for the larger trees thereabouts, most were oaks and maples, though hickories and poplars were also in evidence; all in the same full leaf as had prevailed when they'd left their own World. By the ruddiness of the light and the lengthening shadows arrowing toward them from atop the hill, he judged it near sunset. What sky was visible between branches looked gray-white, but the air smelled of thunder—which linked this to the place from which they'd just been evicted.

He shuddered at that. Brock evidently felt it, too, which prompted the boy to roll onto his side. His face was dirty. "So where are we?" he asked brightly.

Calvin started to shrug, but then something tickled his memory. He scowled at the piled stones again—and knew. "Jackson County," he croaked, his voice still stiff and thin from where he'd been winded. "Jackson County, *Georgia*, that is. And unless I'm even crazier than I think, that oughta be Bloody Creek down there."

"You know this place?" Okacha murmured warily, eyes narrow with suspicion.

Calvin nodded, even as he made his way toward Sandy, who, true to her practical nature, was groping toward the still-unconscious Don. "It belongs to some friends of mine," he continued. " 'Course I've only been here once, and that was a few years ago. But I was close to here last summer. In fact, me and Dave and Alec and Liz camped on a knoll just over this hill. These are the woods where I summoned Awi Usdi."

"And got Spearfinger," Brock grumbled under his breath.

Calvin ignored him, except to note that he was likewise up and functional. Instead, he hunkered down beside Sandy, who had rolled Don onto his back and was checking his pulse. The boy was breathing steadily, which was good. "How's he doin'?" he asked in a low voice. Scramblings behind him were Brock and Okacha joining them.

Sandy shrugged. "I'm not even sure how *I* am right now—besides cramping like mad. But as best I can tell, he's fine. His breathing's okay, he's got good color, and his pulse is calming down. I haven't checked his eyes for dilation yet.''

''That was some trip, if it made a sleeping person's pulse go bonkers,'' Calvin observed.

''Nobody'll argue with that!'' Okacha agreed edgily. After a moment's peering across Calvin's shoulder, she commenced prowling the area, collecting boots, socks, bits of clothing. ''Found the packs,'' she called an instant later.

''Good job,'' Calvin called back. He took Sandy's hand while she smoothed Don's brow with the other. ''So, why here?'' she asked finally, her face tight with discomfort.

It was Calvin's turn to shrug. ''I dunno—unless . . . Well, like Brock said: this is probably where Spearfinger first came through, given that I did the ritual near here, and this is the only concentration of rocks ready to hand—which are what she travels through. So I . . . guess that old woman—whoever she was—just sent us to where the World Walls were thinnest—fortunately.''

''Relatively speaking,'' Sandy muttered. ''I—''

A cough from Don interrupted her. She leaned forward, intent on his face, her hair coppery in the ruddy light. Calvin mirrored her.

Another cough, then two more. A long shudder wracked the boy. His eyelids fluttered, then stilled again. ''Wha' time's it?'' he mumbled. And then his eyes popped open, wide with incredulity. ''*Jesus!*'' he yipped. ''Where am I? Who're you?'' Then, after a further round of coughs and blinks: ''*Calvin?*''

''In the flesh—I think,'' Calvin replied.

''But . . . but where'd . . . you come from? An' . . . where're my clothes?'' He fell back and closed his eyes. ''Jesus! I don't *believe* this!'' he groaned. ''Wha' happened?''

Calvin took him by the arm. "What's the last thing you remember?" he asked carefully. Sandy shot him a warning scowl.

Don's lids slitted open; his brow furrowed with concentration. "I remember lookin' in a mirror an' seein' . . . Mike, an'—No, it wasn't a mirror, it was water! The creek out by my house. And he reached up to me, an'—"

He closed his eyes again.

"Don?" Calvin snapped urgently. "You okay?"

The boy nodded.

"How much of the rest do you recall?"

A pause, then: "A bunch of . . . of really scary stuff. But Mike was there, an' I told him I was sorry, an' he said it was cool. But then I didn't want to leave him, an' I knew he couldn't go on, an'—" He broke off, stared at Calvin with tear-brightened eyes. "He's gone on now, ain't he? I dreamed that. But everything you dream there's true, ain't it?"

Calvin nodded in turn. "I think so. I certainly hope so."

Okacha, who had been rummaging among the packs, padded over, still barefoot. "Maybe these'll do," she said tersely, her face grim and troubled as she thrust a bundle of fabric into Calvin's hands. He sorted through it, determined that it was a mix of Brock's spare skivvies and jeans, with one of his own T-shirts, then passed the wad to the boy, who grabbed it gratefully and proceeded to dress beneath the bearskin, amidst many grunts, groans, and crunchings of leaves. "You'll have to do without shoes, I reckon," Calvin told him. "Nobody brought extras. Sorry."

"No big deal," Don sighed, emerging from the fur to slip on the too-large T-shirt. Then, abruptly: "I've gotta call my *mom*! She's gotta be goin' out of her mind! Uh, what day is it, anyway?"

Calvin checked his watch. "Well, if this thing's not

had a breakdown swapping Worlds, never mind time
zones, it's Tuesday.''

Don's brow wrinkled as he did rapid computations.
"Oh, crap! I've been gone nearly a *week*!" He shot to
his feet, then paled and had to sit again.

"Legs wobbly?" Okacha asked, steadying him.

"You could say that." Then, abruptly, even as he
flinched away: "You're . . . *her*, ain't you? The panther-
woman? You were in my dream."

"Yes, I was," Okacha replied matter-of-factly.
"Wanta try to get up again?"

Don stared at her uncertainly, then shook his head.
"Gimme a minute. Uh, anybody got any food?" he
added. "I'm starved."

Calvin shook his head in turn. " 'Fraid not, unless—
Sandy, you didn't happen to pick up any, did you?"

She likewise shook her head.

"I've got that jug of water the Thunder Boys gave
us," Brock volunteered, scrambling toward the packs.
When he returned with it a moment later, he also held
Calvin's atasi. "Thought you might want this close by,"
he said solemnly. "You know, just in case."

"Thanks," Calvin grunted. He sniffed the jug, noted
nothing suspicious, then took a tentative sip. The water
was cool, sweet, and preposterously refreshing. He
passed it on to Don, with an admonition to drink slowly.

"Okay," he continued, as the others slaked their thirsts,
"we know where we are. The next thing we've gotta
figure out is where we go from here, and who needs
what."

"A telephone would be good," Sandy said instantly.

"I know some folks near here who'd probably let us
use theirs," Calvin told her.

"This is . . . close to Athens?" Okacha asked.

Again Calvin nodded. "Maybe eight miles north.
I—"

"Athens?" Brock broke in excitedly. "You mean like in R.E.M. and the B-52's and the 40 Watt Club?"

"More like in Dave Sullivan, Alec McLean, and an ulunsuti," Calvin shot back. "I figure we'll call Dave first, and get him to come retrieve us. Once we get ourselves straightened out down there, we can work out the rest—obviously we've gotta get hold of Don's mom pronto, and—"

"Anytime," Okacha gritted, looking even tenser than before. "I don't like this place." She shuddered.

"Me neither," Calvin agreed. "So what say we collect our gear and boogie? We can work out details walkin' as easy as sittin' still." He paused, looked at Don. "You up for it?"

Don smiled wanly. "I'm cool."

"You're also barefoot," Calvin noted dryly. "I can carry you if you need me to. The closest road's dirt."

"We'll see."

"Fine," Calvin replied, rising. "Everybody ready?"

"Gotcha!" From Brock.

"First thing," Sandy told Calvin, as they trudged up the hill behind the boys, "we need to get hold of Don's mom as soon as we can, and get him home as soon after that as possible, not only for his sake and hers, but because the police already think something weird's going on, and if they find out you're mixed up in it, they'll really go ballistic. So we have to either be very circumspect or very up-and-up."

"Okay," Calvin panted. "Go on."

"Number two," she went on, with a grin. "I've gotta retrieve my truck, if it's not already been found—and thereby hangs another possibly disastrous tale. On the other hand, given that I have to go south to get it anyway, I might as well take Don with me and save his mom a trip."

Calvin didn't reply immediately. Then: "We'll have

to work out the details on that when we see which way the land lays. Meanwhile . . . Brock, how 'bout you?''

''What about me?''

''You cool? About magic, I mean? Or do you think I still owe you?''

Brock grinned fiendishly. ''Let's just say we'll talk about that when *I* see which way the land lays.''

Calvin could only sigh. ''That leaves the big 'un, doesn't it, Okacha?''

Okacha nodded darkly. ''We did make a bargain,'' she said. ''I've fulfilled my part—I think. But now that I've seen what I have . . . I'm not sure I oughta insist you fulfill yours.''

Calvin started to reply, but Sandy shushed him. ''Bullshit,'' she snapped. ''A bargain's a bargain. I'm not sure I enjoyed what we just went through. But I *am* a physics teacher, and I've seen enough warped physics the last few days to keep me thinking for a lifetime— and that's just the selfish part. Never mind that Cal'll fret himself crazy about you if we don't get you somewhere Snakeeyes can't get at you.''

Calvin stared at her, grinning crookedly. ''Which is the next *big* problem. I mean, we *know* how to get help—shoot, we can hitch if we have to. And there's a half dozen ways to get Don back home, and the same for the Bronco. But neither of 'em carries a threat—not like Okacha's from Snakeeyes.''

''Who'll also be a threat to you,'' Okacha pointed out. ''He knows you've got the scale. He knows you know . . . things. Shoot, he probably knows you've got a friend with an ulunsuti.''

''Which is why we've gotta get you someplace safe pronto,'' Calvin shot back. ''Someplace he can't draw on your power, while I figure out how to defuse him.''

''It's not your fight,'' Okacha replied. ''I thought I

was selfish enough to let you do it on your own, but I'm not so certain now. I—''

"Cool!" Brock interrupted from the head of the line. "Hey, guys! Check this out!"

Calvin jogged the few feet to the boy's side—which also brought him to the edge of a wide meadow he recognized, in spite of its margin having been logged off in the last week or two. The ground was scarred, muddy in places where grass had not reclaimed it. And tree trunks—mostly pines, he was relieved to note—lay scattered here and there like matchsticks. But that was not what had now claimed both boys' attention.

He heard it before he turned to follow their incredulous stares: a beating in the air, a collective concussion that was almost audible. And along with it came a rustling of feathers that *could* be heard, punctuated by harsh, strident cries.

It was birds: a vast flock of dark shapes winging their way into view above the treetops to the east. Grackles, he thought, or starlings. Crows, even—maybe. All those had figured in reports he'd seen on TV of vast flocks of black birds troubling middle Georgia. Athens, David had told him, had been in quite a quandary, what with animal rights folks at odds with the downtown merchants on how to evict the feathered pests from the ginkgo trees there. No satisfactory solution had been devised, but the birds had moved out on their own.

Evidently, in large part, to here.

And gee, but there were a lot of 'em! These woods were flanked by a series of pastures and fields, the closest not a half-mile away across Bloody Creek. But if *this* many birds had sheltered there, little could be left for man or beast to feast on. It really was neat, though; the way they were fanning out across the sky in a patch so wide and dense it looked like a cloud. Calvin didn't think he'd ever seen that many birds at one time, and found himself wondering if this was how the passenger pigeons had looked when they'd passed this way a century back.

Only . . .

"Shit!" Okacha snarled from farther into the meadow. Then, "I don't like this! Not at all!"

Calvin tore his eyes away from the birds to stare at her. "Is there . . . something you're not tellin' us?"

She started to shake her head, then to nod, then tensed, and simply shrugged. "Maybe . . . I don't know. I mean, it could be natural, but . . ."

"Look out!" Sandy yelled. "Christ, here they come!"

Calvin whipped back around to peer at the sky once more. But just in the brief instant since he'd last looked, the cloud had thickened—and was now heading their way in an arrow-shaped formation that was far too regular for comfort. Already the shadow of the vanguard was darkening the eastern edge of the meadow. And even as Calvin looked, birds broke off from the bottom and dived into the trees they had just vacated. They disappeared for a moment, lost within the lush foliage, then reappeared below the canopy, still flying straight at him and his companions—too low to either be natural or to avoid.

"*Run!*" Sandy shrieked. "Try for those trees yonder!" She was already sprinting across the field.

"Don't let yourself be trapped in the open," Okacha added. She paused for a ragged instant, then dived toward the nearest fringe of forest—and was instantly driven back by at least fifteen black shapes—grackles—that shot straight for her face, beaks gleaming wickedly.

Calvin simply ran after Sandy, since Brock and Don were likewise charging that way through the shin-high grass. But the brief delay while he watched Okacha had been too long. And even as he reached the middle of the meadow—bare yards behind Sandy—he knew he wasn't going to make it.

None of them were.

"Out of the frying pan . . ." Okacha growled behind him. Then: "Oh, Christ, no . . . *no!*"

Calvin skidded to a halt and turned to stare at her. She was frozen in place, clutching her temples, the tendons taut in her neck and wrists and brow. "W-ward," she managed. "Ward!"

Calvin snapped his pack off, fumbled frantically inside—and found, blessedly, a few small sprigs of cedar. He waved them under Okacha's nose, saw her sniff, then stuffed them in her hand.

"We're surrounded," came Sandy's despairing voice.

But he didn't need to check to confirm that assessment; the last delay had made the crucial difference, for every visible bit of meadow was already so thick with black birds of every kind that he could barely see the grass. And even as he gaped, more dropped from the sky to join their fellows. But what really freaked him, what sent chills coursing along his spine, was the fact that, as soon as they landed, every one of those birds turned to face them. The only clear space was an area maybe four yards across, in the center of which they stood.

A glance skyward showed even more birds circling there, and a thin stream of them was still trickling in from the east, like beams of black light come to rival the setting sun's red. "Shit!" he growled. "We're fucked."

"I doubt this'll be that much fun," Sandy chuckled grimly.

"This . . . isn't natural, is it?" Don whispered, edging close to Calvin. When he did, the nearest birds moved into the resulting gap. Calvin felt his arm brush Okacha's, even as his hand fumbled for Sandy's.

"I guess running's not an option?" Brock gulped.

"Not if you value your eyes," Calvin hissed back. "Those things'd trip you in a second. And once they got you down, if they didn't get you from the front, they'd just dig through from behind. These suckers mean business!"

"So does somebody else," Okacha groaned. She'd evidently shaken whatever had afflicted her to some degree, though she still looked pale and drawn. "I don't think I need to tell you who—nor would it be wise."

Calvin reached impulsively for the scale, nursing a vague notion of turning into some type of bird that could out-fly these others. Which of course was stupid; no way he'd be able to get back with help in time. Still . . .

But he had no more time for deliberation, for at that moment he noted a larger shape winging its way through the black-feathered ranks. The lesser birds avoided it, too, as if they knew themselves prey, and that they were only absolved from that role for this moment.

Closer and closer that shape came, and lower, gliding on wings dappled white and gray. And then flight feathers flared, the tail fanned, and it leaned back for landing—which it did, inside the acre-square mass of birds, a dozen yards in front of Calvin. Having no other weapon, his hand settled on the war club. It was a good weapon—except that it was all but useless here. Magic it might be, in origin. But so, surely, was what confronted him.

No longer an owl—but the shift was both too subtle and too abrupt to register. It was simply as if the air twitched where the owl was—and then there was a man.

A very *tall* man; lean and muscular, with the black hair and ruddy-tanned skin of a Native American. He was also naked—save for a cloak of gray-and-white feathers that swept in soft folds from his shoulders to brush the tips of the grasses and the tops of black-feathered heads. He flipped it across his hips carelessly and spat out a derisive chuckle.

Calvin didn't want to look at his eyes—but did. And saw once again those eyes that were not the brown of his people, but a shocking yellow-green. Like a snake's.

"My mama said it was 'cause a rattler crawled into her bed while she was carryin' me," Snakeeyes said in a low, mocking voice. And Calvin realized this was the first time he had heard the man speak.

"Myself," Snakeeyes continued, as he ambled forward through the birds (Calvin preferred their thousand beady eyes to his), "I think it's 'cause of something I ate—or maybe 'cause of something that ate *me!*"

Calvin could only glare and try not to look afraid. And pray that Okacha kept her cool; that they all did.

" 'Course it helps that I'm a twin," Snakeeyes went on. "Younger twin, in fact. That is, it helps if you *want* to be a conjurer.

"Or," he concluded, as he eased to a halt no more than a yard from the edge of the open place, "it could just be 'cause I *like* meanness. Actually, I think everybody does, they just don't let themselves admit it. Sure looks that way when you see a car wreck, though, don't it? And don't tell me those folks are there out of concern. Nosiree, they're there wantin' to see some guts, or eyeballs popped out, or something. Thing is with me, I just admit to it. I'm a predator, I guess you could say— and the prey is everybody who don't suspect they *are* prey. And sometimes you eat your prey, and sometimes you toy with it a spell first, and sometimes you just kill it flat out dead and leave it to rot. But I never know, myself. It's like fuckin': you never know if they'll pant and moan and beg for more, or if they'll scratch your back and scream. And you never know if you'll scream with 'em, or just knock the hell out of 'em to make 'em hush."

Still no one spoke, though Calvin heard Okacha drag in a harsh breath.

Snakeeyes narrowed his gaze to stare straight at Calvin, and Calvin felt as if those eyes burned through his clothes and into his soul. ''You think you're a big shot, don't you? Mr. Native American? Mr. Cherokee Indian? Mr. Ani-Yunwiya? You think that 'cause you've got a war name and an atasi and've seen a few things that you're special. But just let me *tell* you how special you are. You're special the way an animal in a zoo's special. You're special exactly as much as everybody lets you be special. You take what this woman gives you, and you're grateful; you learn a few secret things from somebody somewhere else, and you think you're Mr. Cool. Only that one ain't tellin' you no more'n he wants you to know, which ain't much—not against all there is *to* know.

''But take me, now: I *am* special—'cause nobody tells me what to do but me!''

''No,'' Calvin replied coldly, distantly aware that he was surprised at himself for speaking, ''you're just crazy. You're special the way a crazy man's special, and that's all.''

''Yeah,'' Snakeeyes hissed back. ''But I'm also *free*—and you're not! I'm not responsible to anybody, and you wanta be responsible for the whole goddamned world.''

''You're—'' Calvin began, fingering the club, suddenly desperate to break this impasse at any price.

''I'm sick of shootin' the shit with the likes of you,'' Snakeeyes broke in. ''You've got some things I want, boy, and I'd thank you to give 'em to me; and if you do, I *might* let you live.''

''And if we don't?'' Brock piped up.

Snakeeyes grinned at him, showing teeth that were far too sharp. ''I'll get 'em anyway—only *you* won't know about it, not for no longer'n it takes a flock of crows to peck into your brain. 'Course it might hurt a little on the way, but you know something, little boy? Little would-be magician boy? There ain't never been a policeman in Georgia ever arrested a flock of birds for murder. And if there was, there sure ain't no jury would convict 'em—nor no jail to stick 'em in.''

Calvin swallowed, tried to catch his adversary's eyes, to challenge him silently.

"I want them things!"

"You want 'em, you've gotta name 'em!"

Snakeeyes vented something between a giggle, a snort, and a hiss—which probably passed for a laugh. "Okay, then, Little Wizard: I want that fine lookin' club you've got there, 'cause I 'spect there's no more'n one other like it in this world, and once I've got this 'un, I can get that 'un, no problem. I 'spect I could learn some powerful secrets from that thing, yessir. But I want that scale you've got, too: that thing you've got hid there under your shirt. Now that's a right fine thing, only you don't know how fine, and you're scared shitless to learn, 'cause you're afraid it'll hurt—or 'cause it might hurt somebody.

"Oh, yeah, I forgot," Snakeeyes continued. "There's somebody near here's also got something mighty interestin': kind of a rock-stone thing. Shiny like. Some say it come from the head of a monster, but I don't much believe that, don't much believe in monsters at all, now; do you?"

"Only the one I'm lookin' at," Calvin growled.

"The other thing I want's my woman."

"I'm not yours," Okacha spat. Calvin couldn't see her face, but if she looked as furious as she sounded— well, he wondered how even Snakeeyes withstood her.

"You're mine if and when and however I want you,"

Snakeeyes snorted, then shifted his gaze back to Calvin. "Now hand 'em over."

Calvin didn't move, nor speak. None of them did. The sun dipped beneath the horizon. The world went black and gold and crimson.

"I can have them birds take you one at a time," Snakeeyes drawled. "And I can have whoever I start with took a little at a time once they get goin'. I can have 'em start at the eyeballs, or end there. Or maybe start with one and finish with the other."

Silence.

"That black-haired boy's got real pretty eyes."

Silence.

"They'd make a nice set with them blue 'uns that blond gal's got. She's your woman, ain't she, Little Wizard?"

"She's her own woman," Calvin gritted.

"She's my woman if I want her to be!" Snakeeyes shot back. "I could fuck her right here, right in front of you. Shoot, I could fuck all of you, boys and girls both. I might even fuck *you*!"

"Not while I've got the scale, you won't!"

Snakeeyes laughed. "By the time you get anything done with that, I've got your woman—or my woman—or one of them boys. The birds get the rest."

Silence.

"And if I get my woman, you really do lose—if you make me mad. Otherwise, you might still get to live. You might even get to keep all your parts. But the longer you wait, the less likely that is."

Silence, still. But this time broken by a roll of not so distant thunder.

Calvin glanced at the sky. The birds fluffed and strutted and beat the air, as if nervous or agitated. A few rose aloft, then settled again. A soft rumbling thrummed up through Calvin's feet—legacy, probably, of a logging truck on the road a quarter-mile beyond the meadow. Or maybe it too was born of thunder.

"Stop that!" Snakeeyes shrilled.

"It's not me," Calvin told him. "Which you knew. If I could command the weather, you wouldn't be here."

Snakeeyes only stared stonily.

"You can have the scale," Calvin whispered.

"That's not what I asked for!"

Calvin squared his shoulders. " 'Kacha's her own woman, just like Sandy," he said quietly. "I can't make her stay, and I sure can't make her go. But I—I'll give you the scale *and* the club if you'll forget about her, and let her and Sandy and the boys alone."

Snakeeyes's eyes flashed fire. "You deaf or *what*?" he raged. "That *ain't* what I asked for!"

"You don't always *get* what you ask for!" Calvin yelled back, hoping by that sudden shift in demeanor to catch Snakeeyes off guard; but more, hoping against hope that what he suspected was true: that more sounds made that thunder than air covering for lightning's haste.

He hoped rightly—for seconds later, amid a rumble of tires, a swish of grass, and a deep growl of machinery, a vehicle erupted into the clearing from the thread of logging road that had been his destination all along. Its lights were off, but in the cloud-born gloom he could see that it was a black Ford Ranger—and that a camper shell covered the bed.

It was racing straight toward them, too: upsetting the birds as it tore along, bouncing over unseen ruts and bumps and hollows. Crows rose in a blur of wings where it passed; grackles shrieked and swore and swerved aside. Some never made it. They croaked and spat and died.

An instant later, the truck was beside them. Lights came on, from both grille and bumper: a dazzle of glare fixed straight on Snakeeyes. Calvin saw him blink and falter. But then a young male voice yelled, "Get the hell in here, Fargo! You wanta live forever?"

"D-Dave?" But already Calvin was stumbling that way, not caring if he trod on birds, or if they pecked him or flew at his face. He grabbed Brock by a shoulder and shoved him; saw Sandy do the same for Don. Okacha was taking care of herself.

"Jump in the back!" David yelled again, then powered up the window, even as he wheeled the vehicle straight at the still-bedazzled conjurer. The movement brought the back of the pickup even with Calvin. He jerked at the latch on the cover and flipped it up. Brock was over before Calvin could lay hands on him. Okacha followed. Sandy shoved Don up to her, then scrambled in herself. Calvin came last—and had to make a final reckless grab as the pickup spun around and roared back the way it had come. He had no idea where Snakeeyes was. All that mattered now was getting over the tailgate (he succeeded, even as he thought it) and slamming the camper latch closed.

He landed hard on the plastic liner and found himself thrust into gloom full of scooting bodies and flailing limbs, amid which a dozen or so birds still flopped. But he got the latch locked just in time.

A sound like hail engulfed them as the truck bounced and bounded. He knew what it was, too: beaks and feet on metal.

"Sullivan's rescue service, at your service," a voice laughed then—but *not* David's. Calvin looked up to see that the rear window of the cab had been slid aside, and Alec McLean was peering in. David was driving. Liz was on the passenger side, crowding in beside Alec.

"Whose truck?" Calvin asked, inanely.

"Mine," Liz replied. "Brand-new—or was."

"That's the last of 'em," Okacha muttered from her corner. Calvin glanced that way to see her fling a limp, feathered shape into the opposite corner. She had obviously just wrung its neck.

"Damned birds," David gritted from the driver's seat. "Can't half see."

Calvin crawled up to stare through the window over his shoulder. Birds were everywhere: flying into the windshield, almost masking the trees David was threading through mostly on instinct and dead reckoning.

"Just a sec," Liz called, and flicked another switch. The world ahead turned to light—far more dazzling than headlights had a right to be. Birds cried and squawked, but whirled away—or at least enough did for David to see where to lurch onto the road. "Roof-mounted foglights," Liz chuckled. " 'For off-road use only,' so the manual says. I'd say we were off-road, wouldn't you?"

"Yeah," Calvin sighed, as he fell back into Sandy's arms. It was a moment before he realized that the pattering against the aluminum shell was no longer beaks, but rain.

"Saved by the rain," Brock giggled nervously.

"Or damned," Okacha countered. And fell silent.

# Chapter XXI:
## On the Fly

*"How'd you* find *us?"*

Calvin had to yell to make himself heard above the thump of windshield wipers set on HI, the rumble of tires across a road surface somewhere between dirt and gravel, and the low thunder of exhausts that was a counterpoint to the real thing tormenting the sky. At least there were more no birds, the rain having driven them to earth—as it was on the verge of doing to Liz's pickup if conditions didn't improve pronto. What had begun as a summer evening thunder-boomer was now on the ragged edge of hail.

Intent on seeing more than a dozen yards beyond the Ranger's hood, David didn't turn. *"What?"* he called back. "I can't half hear you."

Calvin stuck his head inside the cab, narrowly avoiding braining Alec, who had turned just then. "I said, 'How'd you find us?' How'd you just happen to show up right in the nick of time?"

"Ask Alec," David gritted. "It's takin' all I've got to stay on my side!"

Calvin rotated his head forty-five degrees to the right. "Okay, Mach-One, spill it!"

Alec puffed his cheeks in a sour grimace. "I . . . used the ulunsuti."

Calvin gaped incredulously, then his lips quirked into a tired grin. "Way to go, man! We'll make a wizard outta you yet!"

"No way!" Alec shot back, wide-eyed. "David made me do it—not that I wasn't concerned about you guys, or anything. It's just—Well, you know how much I hate using that thing."

"Which is why I appreciate it," Calvin replied honestly. "So what's the scoop? You still haven't said when or where."

"*When* was every six hours after you guys left," David broke in, having relaxed a tad. The rain had slackened minutely—enough to show that they were approaching the open place among the overhanging trees that marked the intersection with Lebanon Church Road—which was, at least theoretically, paved. "Or sunset, sunrise, noon, and midnight, to be more accurate," he continued. "And sometimes it was Alec, sometimes Alec and me or Liz. Today it's been all three 'cause we could kinda feel things coming to a head."

"Mostly mine," Alec grumbled. "It hurts like a son-of-a-bitch, let me tell you—which is one reason I don't like to use that thing. I much prefer hangovers."

"It saved our asses, though," Calvin assured him. "I gather you checked in at sunset and just happened to spot us?"

"You got it," Liz nodded from the passenger seat. "We saw you pop in, and as soon as you said Jackson County, we hit the ground running. We saw some interesting things, too, all along. You'll have to tell us sometime."

"Preferably *not* in a thunderstorm with a wizard on our butts," David added.

"Witch," Calvin corrected. "There's a difference, at least the way my folk use it."

A scrambling behind him was Okacha crawling forward. Calvin withdrew his head from the cab to check on her. Her face was grim. "Well, there's good news and there's bad news," she announced. "The good news is that Snakeeyes seems to have gone to ground back there—probably until the rain lets up, since he can't fly in it nor shift shape while his feather cloak's wet."

"How do you know?" Sandy wondered.

" 'Cause when he's usin' his power I can feel it drawin' on me, and he's not doin' that now."

Sandy scowled. "Why couldn't you sense it before the attack, then?"

Okacha frowned in turn. "I did—but I really wasn't looking for him here, so I thought it was just me being tired from travel, and world-hoppin', and all. By the time I decided it wasn't, it was too late."

"Okay," Calvin inserted to fend of a confrontation he could sense building. "So what's the bad news?"

Okacha looked as serious as Calvin had ever seen her. "Your friend said he used an ulunsuti to check on you, right?"

Calvin nodded carefully. "Yeah, why?"

"Where is it now?"

Alec stuck his head through the window. "I've got it with me. It's in my backpack."

Okacha's face was a mask of despair. "Christ!"

"I didn't exactly have time to *stash* it!" Alec protested hotly.

"No . . . of course you didn't," Okacha replied more calmly. "It's just that . . . Well, basically that means that all four things that bastard wants are here in one place."

Calvin felt his heart skip a beat. Okacha's eyes were huge. Sandy's hand found its way into Calvin's and squeezed.

Alec merely looked confused. "What d'you mean?"

Calvin told him. David and Liz listened in as best they could. In the back of the bed, Don simply stared. "Uh, who *is* this Snakeeyes guy?" he asked softly.

Calvin explained that, too.

"Shit!" David swore under his breath, when Calvin had finished.

"You know what this means, don't you?" Okacha asked, her voice rising to counter the pounding of the rain on the roof, which had increased in intensity.

"I'll let you tell me," Calvin replied. "But I doubt I'll like it."

"It means," Okacha said wearily, "that as soon as this storm ends where he is, Snakeeyes is gonna be after us with all he's got—and *I* may not be able to resist him."

"Shit!" From Calvin and Sandy together.

"As in deep-type, one each," Brock added from the corner he had wedged himself into.

Okacha nodded. "Which means I've gotta get as far away as I can as fast as I can—preferably before the rain lets off."

"We'd better hope it continues, then." David sighed. He was slowing for a stop sign now. The turn signal was flashing right.

"Yes and no," Okacha murmured wearily.

"Why?" Liz asked, crowding in beside Alec at the cab window.

Okacha sighed in turn. " 'Cause on the one hand, it keeps Snakeeyes off balance, though I'm sure he knows the formula for turning storms—assuming he chooses to use it since it takes energy he may not want to spend. But it also—"

"Oh, gosh," Brock interrupted, scooting up to join them, "it also turns you into a panther!"

"In which form it's easier for Snakeeyes to draw on

me, 'cause I have to use more of my will power to re-member that I'm human.''

Calvin gnawed a finger. "It works that way for you, too? But I thought—''

"I should've said 'the good things about being hu-man.' The intellect stays in full force, but I become more like Snakeeyes: more a creature of will and instinct. It's like I have human wants and needs, but cat reflexes. I get mad easier, things like that.''

"And you don't want to piss off a cat," Sandy chuck-led grimly. "Even a small one.''

David grimaced as he made the turn onto Ga. 129—and got a windshield full of tractor-trailer spray for his trouble. The Ranger hydroplaned on runoff. And the rain came harder, pounding so fiercely conversation ceased. David kept going, but at a crawl.

"We've gotta call Don's mom," Sandy reminded them eventually.

"Soon as we get to town," Calvin agreed, then checked the windshield again. It was a good thing David had Second Sight, 'cause he doubted he could see any-thing with his regular vision. The world, as best *he* could tell through slapping wipers, was silver-white.

And then, very suddenly, it wasn't.

The rain ended, as though cut off with a knife, maybe half a mile south of where they'd last turned. The pave-ment ahead was still wet, still sheened with standing puddles, and the sky was lavender-gray with patches of scudding crimson-edged clouds.

"I hoped it'd do that," David breathed, as he began to pick up speed again. "It usually rains hardest at the edge of a front, and I saw this one on radar earlier to-day.''

"You mean it's not *magic*?" Brock cried. "But it came along so convenient-like, I just figured—''

"Not unless the gods planned well in advance," Alec

inserted. "This time of year you can *usually* count on a boomer late in the day."

David slowed for a dawdling car he didn't dare pass because of a hill. "So what's the agenda now?" he asked. "You guys wanta go back to the dorm, or where? I mean, it'll be tight, but we can hang out there until we get our act together. Or we've got some friends who've got houses."

Calvin surveyed the company huddled in the pickup bed. "Let me check with the crew and get back with you, okay? We've still got a couple minutes, don't we?"

"Food!" Don called abruptly. "Can we please stop for food?"

"Good point," Calvin acknowledged. "I could sure wrap myself around a burger or three. But in the meantime . . . Well basically, what are our options—'Kachawise, I mean? I mean, assumin' we all agree that gettin' her somewhere Snakeeyes can't draw on her oughta be our number one priority."

Sandy stared at him solemnly. "Sounds like you've resigned yourself to fighting him."

Calvin could only shrug. "I don't see how I can avoid it now. Even if we got 'Kacha gone somewhere he can't draw on her, he still wants my scale and the club and the ulunsuti. Shoot, with her gone, he'll probably want 'em more than ever, to make up for what he's lost."

"Which still doesn't tell us what to do about 'Kacha," Sandy observed tersely.

Calvin turned toward the panther-woman. "Okay, so where can we hide you that Snakeeyes can't get at you?"

"She *knows* how to get to the Darkening Land," Brock piped up before Okacha could reply. "And she knows how to get there by herself—so why not that?"

Okacha took a deep breath. "First of all, I only knew

how to get there 'cause my mother told me, and her mother before, and she only knew because her ancestor who was a wikatcha told her how. But I guess I've found out that it's not a place living people are supposed to go—as you well know. Oh, I suppose I could hang out on the fringe for a while—on that beach where we first made landfall, maybe. But you saw that: would you wanta spend any time there? Plus, I don't know how long they'd let me stay.''

"Not long," Don supplied in a low voice. He still hadn't moved from his corner. "I think they let me in 'cause I was with Mike an' he kinda vouched for me an' said I was tryin' to help him, an' then I was asleep. But you saw the old woman: she found you guys an' threw you out. From a few things I heard, she does that other places, too. I bet they wouldn't let you anywhere near Usunhiyi, never mind Tsusginai. And—''

"—And if they caught you too soon and tossed you out before Cal can deal with Snakeeyes, he'd be in deep shit," Brock broke in.

"Which sounds like that's out," Calvin concluded, looking back at Okacha. "Which is too bad, 'cause you can get there on your own.''

"It's a shame we can't access Faerie," Liz called from the cab. "Trouble is, the border seems to be closed again, since we haven't seen hide nor hair of any of the folk from there in over a year. And of course the only way to *get* there's via the Tracks—and we don't know how to activate them.''

"We'll file that for reference, though," Calvin replied, noting absently that they'd now reached the fringe of civilization—if more than one convenience store visible at a time was civilization. Up ahead and to the left a set of silos loomed like a concrete castle.

"So what does that leave?" Sandy wondered.

"It leaves," David volunteered from the cab, "one of

the island Worlds like that one Cal and me rescued Finno from, or like that one our friend Myra Buchanan talks about that overlaps out at Scarboro Faire.''

"Or Galunlati," Alec finished for him. "Which we should've thought of first."

Calvin nodded. "That's a possibility. On the other hand, it's obvious—maybe too obvious." He looked at Okacha. "Is there any way Snakeeyes could get to you in Galunlati?"

She gnawed her lip. Then: "I don't know of one, but I do know he's real interested in that kind of thing— which may be one reason he wants Cal's scale—or the ulunsuti. But I suspect that if he keeps on like he is, he'll get there anyway."

"He'll get more than he bargained for, too," Alec snorted.

"But it's too much of a risk—both for Galunlati, if he gets there, and for everybody else if he gets back."

"Which means it's best not to give him any more reasons for going there than he's already got," Sandy observed dully.

"There's another problem too, folks," Calvin reminded them. "In case you guys don't remember, we were forbidden to return there until a year's elapsed— and that won't be up for a couple of days yet. And if we *do* send 'Kacha there, one of us probably oughta go with her to make introductions, and all. Or at least we oughta check with Uki before we start sendin' folks there."

Sandy nodded sagely. "Yeah, from what I've seen of him, it wouldn't do to dump unexpected visitors on him, plus, we don't want to bring trouble to someone who's not involved."

"On the other hand," Alec broke in, "it's a big place—which means Uki might not find her for a while.

And if she's only looking for a place to hang out temporarily . . ."

"Yeah, but then Usunhiyi would do just as well," Brock countered.

"Except that we could send her there a lot faster," Calvin told him. "All we've gotta do is light a fire and burn an uktena scale—which can be done in a car if we have to. I mean, Dave and me zapped there from one once."

"And got lost, too," David muttered. "Don't remind me."

"Yeah, but it still sounds like our best bet." Calvin sighed. "What d' you think, 'Kacha?"

The panther-woman frowned thoughtfully. "Well, given that I can't stay here, and would probably get thrown out of Usunhiyi before I would Galunlati, I'd have to agree—much as I hate to admit it."

Calvin nodded grimly. "You guys *do* have scales, don't you?" he asked those in the cab. "I'd volunteer mine, but they have to be treated if you're gonna use 'em to world-hop, and mine hasn't been; it's only good for shapeshifting—and I'm not sure how many of them it's got left."

David pounded the steering wheel. "Doesn't matter anyway," he groaned. "We don't have any."

Calvin rolled his eyes and slapped the fiberglass bedliner. "Well that's just dandy!"

"Sorry!" From Alec.

"Hey, but wait!" Calvin cried suddenly. "You guys don't have scales—but we could still open a gate. Remember how we used the ulunsuti to open one back at Stone Mountain? To that place they had Finno? And then again down at Cumberland?"

"And we've *got* the ulunsuti!" Liz added excitedly.

"Yeah," David grunted as he brought the car to a

halt at the first traffic light, still a mile north of Athens, where Jefferson River Road turned off to the left. "But you need the blood of a large animal to prime it."

"True," Calvin admitted. "And that's gonna be hard to get in a hurry—unless we use our own, which I'd rather not do. Trouble is, it's not huntin' season, or anything."

Okacha looked thoughtful. "Does it have to be *one* large animal?"

Calvin shrugged. "I dunno. That's how I learned it. At the very least it has to be warm, and there has to be enough of it to soak the ulunsuti when you put it in a bowl."

"Hmmm," Okacha mused, glancing toward the back of the truck, where a clump of dark-feathered bodies still lay. "Well, those guys are probably still warm—and I bet there's at least a couple of cups of blood in 'em."

"We *could* stop at a grocery store and buy some," Brock suggested, with a touch of sarcasm.

Sandy shook her head. "Most carcasses are drained before they're shipped for butchering, even when it's finished in-house. Plus, it'd be cold too. Plus 'Kacha couldn't go out in the rain—which it's doing again, if you count drizzle. Which means we'd have to split up, which I don't think is a good idea."

"Which blows that," David groaned. "At least in the kind of hurry we're in."

"And it still leaves the small problem of when and where to do this ritual," Okacha noted. "Now that the rain's slackened, Snakeeyes'll be after us pronto."

"I doubt he'd confront us openly on campus, though," David countered.

"Except that I can't *be* open on campus," Okacha shot back, "not while there's this much wetness."

"Good point," Sandy acknowledged. "But, uh, what exactly do you need, anyway?"

Calvin counted on his fingers. "You need the ulun-suti, which we've got. You need a bowl to put it in, and blood to fill it. You need at least a small fire. You need a bunch of herbs, some of which I've got, some of which—"

"What herbs?" David called. "I've seen it done, but I've forgotten."

Calvin told him.

David scowled thoughtfully. "And that's all? You're sure?"

Calvin nodded. "I've got the rest—I think."

"Good." David grinned as he gunned the Ranger across the bypass and onto Prince Avenue, " 'cause I may know just the place. But we'll have to hurry."

"We already are," Brock observed dryly. "Or haven't you noticed?"

"Hush," Calvin told him. "Don't forget that you're a large animal, too!"

# Chapter XXII:
# Lab Test

"Hey, that's *Ilex vomitoria*!" Calvin cried, as David braked Liz's pickup to a halt in the parking lot behind one of the older brick buildings on the University of Georgia's north campus—Baldwin Hall, it was called: seat of the anthropology department. He'd been there once before, on his previous visit. Fortunately, only two cars were in evidence at the moment: a newish red Isuzu pickup and a pristine black '61 DeSoto—the last year. He hoped this wasn't *his* last year.

"*Ilex* what?" Brock asked, scowling—and promptly flopped back on his butt as David shifted into reverse and maneuvered toward a long raised concrete platform which probably served as a loading dock. A metal awning overhung a green steel door there—which choice of destinations showed excellent good sense on David's part, given Okacha's situation and the fact that it was still drizzling.

"*Ilex* what?" Brock repeated, when stability had been restored.

"*Vomitoria*," Calvin replied absently. "It's those bushes along the backside of the building, the ones with the shiny leaves. The Southeastern Indians used it to make white drink—which *you* guys call black drink. It's a kind of holly, and it's pretty potent stuff—'specially if you need to puke. It's also used in rituals, conveniently enough.''

"What is?" David echoed from where he'd just unlatched the camper's back window.

"Those bushes there," Calvin sighed as he climbed out—first, in case the coast wasn't as clear as his friend was assuming. It was, evidently, or at least no one was around and the sky was free of birds, if not sprinkles. Alec and Liz were already on the dock, angling for the door. David was fishing in his pocket even as he helped Sandy and the dazed-looking Don down from the tailgate. Okacha came last, sheltering her head and arms with Calvin's jacket as she leapt the yard or so that was open to drizzle in one fluid motion. Sandy shot out an arm to stabilize her when she landed.

Calvin paused to gaze warily around. It was less than half an hour after sunset, which meant the sky still held light, though not much, because of the clouds. As he'd noted before, the lot was all but empty (it had to be faculty parking, too, this close to the heart of campus, but he doubted many anthropology profs worked late especially during finals). And even more fortuitously, the side away from the building was thoroughly screened from both a bank and the street below by a line of walnut trees. "You're a good man, Sullivan," he grinned as he joined his companions. He clapped David on the back.

"Why?" David wondered, fumbling with a key ring.

Calvin pointed to his right, past the line of *Ilex* toward a low concrete retaining wall beyond which a few straggly conifers marked what remained of the old Jackson Street Cemetery after Friedman Hall had been built. "Cedar—lots of cedar. Lots and *lots* of cedar."

"Protection against witches," Brock supplied helpfully.

"I know!" David growled, and unlocked the door.

"What're you doin' with a key to this place, any-way?" Calvin wondered in a low whisper as he followed his buddy into a large room lit only by the light filtering in through high, grimy windows. Most of the floor was taken up with man-tall piles of boxes alternating with ranges of metal shelving he could tell were dusty, even in the dimness.

David waited until they were all in, tugged the door, and let it click closed, which locked it. He did not turn on the light. "This is the anthropology department, in case any of you missed that," he explained, likewise keeping his voice low. "I'm a work-study student here, cleaning potsherds and stuff. Only this quarter I had a screwy schedule, so I had to work nights. And since the building's locked at night, they had to give me a key."

"Trusting fools," Alec added in something between a snort and a chuckle.

"So . . . is this it?" Calvin wondered, indicating the cluttered room.

David shook his head and indicated a door to his left. "This is the archaeology lab—one of 'em. Mostly it's a holding area, actually. We've gotta go up a level."

"I still think this is a dumb idea," Alec grumbled as David steered them toward the exit.

"It is," David agreed, producing another key. "But not as dumb as doing it outside. Okacha doesn't dare get wet, remember? And we're too easy for Snakeeyes to get at elsewhere. Inside—well, he's less likely to mount an attack here in town simply 'cause he's too likely to attract attention. Plus, doing it inside puts one more level of protection between us and him."

"Yeah, but—"

David glared at him. "Look, Alec, I thought we worked this out: Liz's roomies were home; Myra's hav-ing folks to dinner; our room's too susceptible to un-expected interruptions, and we don't have two hours to spend calling around looking for somebody willing to let us use their place for a ritual without question— *okay*?''

"Cool it, you guys," Liz hissed. "Time spent arguing is time wasted."

"Good point," Calvin acknowledged, then nodded at David. "Lead on."

"Not hardly," David grunted. "Come on: upstairs."

Calvin followed him through the door and into a spartan stairwell. They were exactly halfway between floors, and thus utterly exposed, when a doorknob rattled above them.

"Oh, shit!" Liz gritted.

"Bullshit, more aptly," David whispered back. "Let me do the talkin'."

At that moment the door opened, revealing a ruddy-faced, white-haired man who looked rather like an overgrown leprechaun—or would have, had he not been dressed in a blue Oxford shirt and khaki trousers, and been lugging a briefcase instead of a shillelagh.

"Dr. Hudson!" David cried, dashing up the remaining steps two at time, leaving Calvin to gape stupidly and wonder how scuzzy he looked.

"Mr. Sullivan," the man nodded, peering at David over the tops of his glasses. "This is an odd time for you to be about, isn't it?"

"Well, I've gotta work nights, if you recall," David shot back quickly. "Only I had a buncha friends blow into town outta the clear blue, so I figured I'd kill two birds with one stone and catch up with them while I caught up on my shards."

The man studied David for a moment, then shrugged, muttered, "Long as it gets done," and started to ease past him—and everyone else on the stairs.

"Oh—Dr. Hudson," David called. "I, uh . . . That is, actually you might wanta meet a couple of these folks."

The man paused, waiting.

"You've heard me talk about my friend Calvin? Cherokee guy? The one whose cousin graduated from here a couple of years back?"

"O'Connor, wasn't it?" Hudson asked, frowning. "Kirkwood?"

"Yeah. Well, Cal's his cousin."

Hudson shook Calvin's hand. "Kirk's a good man. Knows his stuff."

"Cal does, too," David replied. "Knows some of it better'n Kirk, actually," he added with a wicked wink at Calvin.

"Does he, now?" Hudson murmured. "Well, I'd stay and chat, but I've gotta run. Gotta piss off another bunch of blue-haired ladies."

"Huh?"

"Gotta break the news to 'em that DeSoto didn't go anywhere near their town square."

"Carry on," David laughed as Hudson moved past. "And don't worry, *we* won't break anything."

Hudson didn't reply, but Calvin held his breath until the door clicked shut below them. David grinned at him as he opened its twin at the top. "Smart man, that was: knows *almost* as much about southeastern mythology as you do, Cal."

Calvin merely scowled and followed David into the room beyond.

Maybe thirty feet long by twenty wide, it proved to be a laboratory of sorts, with long tables in the center and marble-topped lab counters complete with sinks along the window wall. David made for the nearest. "Nice thing about this place is that one of the grad students has been doing some research that involves burning native plants to study their resins—which means the sprinkler's disconnected."

"Good thing," Calvin agreed as he glanced around

the room. "Yeah, I think this'll work fine. Now all we've gotta do is gather the gear. You say you know where to find most of what we need?"

David nodded. "There's an herb collection in here we can raid as long as we don't use all of anything, and as long as it won't matter if the stuff's dried."

Calvin puffed his cheeks, then nodded. "I think I saw enough outside to make up the rest."

"Figured you did."

Calvin stared at Okacha uneasily, noting how tense she was. Sandy seemed to have fallen into the support role she tended to assume when not on her native turf and was keeping Brock and Don in line—not that Don needed much. He was mostly dozing—an odd reaction from one who'd spent most of the last week asleep, but not unreasonable, Sandy said, for one who had undergone the stress he had. His main complaint seemed to be hunger.

"There're vending machines out in the hall," David offered. "I'll show you, if you want."

Sandy nodded. "Don probably needs something. The rest of us—"

"We really oughta fast until this is over," Calvin broke in, snatching the keys from a startled David's hands. "It'll only be a half hour or so, if we don't have any problems."

"*If,*" Alec muttered grimly, busy over the zipper of his backpack—which held the pot that held the pouch that held the ulunsuti.

"If," Calvin echoed, likewise shedding his knapsack, but not the atasi, which he stuffed in his belt. "If I'm not back in fifteen minutes . . . I dunno. Fall back on Plan B or something."

"There *is* no Plan B," Alec noted with a frown.

"Sure there is," Calvin countered from the door. "You just don't know what it is yet!"

\*  \*  \*

"I can't believe I actually found *everything* I needed," Calvin sighed a quarter hour later as a wild-eyed David wrenched open the door before he could even knock. "I—*What the hell?*"

Even as he spoke, he was shouldering past his friend, who, in spite of having quick reflexes himself, barely hopped out of the way in time. He strode straight for the clump of people knotted around Okacha. Sandy shot him a concerned look. Brock simply looked startled.

"I was just goin' to get you," David called to Calvin's back.

Calvin ignored him. " *'Kacha?*" he cried, pausing only long enough to dump the armload of leaves and branches he'd been clutching onto a table, before taking a close look at the panther-woman. Unfortunately, as soon as he saw her, he knew what was wrong. She was standing bolt upright, so tense she looked as if she might shatter like a soap bubble if anyone touched her. She was not trembling, precisely; but he got a sense of low-level vibration, as if every muscle fought with its opposite for control. And her face—Calvin had never seen such an expression, for it mixed fear and pain and a rock-hard determination. Okacha's eyes were open, the pupils dilated, but he doubted she saw much. Or rather, it was as if she gazed upon something none of the rest of them could see.

"How long's she been like this?" he demanded.

"Maybe five seconds," Sandy replied. "David was just going after you."

Calvin bit his lip, then nodded. "*Dave! Cedar! Now!*"

David grabbed a double handful from the sharp-smelling pile Calvin had abandoned and thrust it at him. From there, the procedure was familiar: a brief censing with the stuff, then a larger sprig waved beneath Okacha's nose. She sniffed, coughed, then inhaled more vigorously. An instant later, she blinked. "I'll bet you're gettin' tired of that," she gasped weakly as she slumped into a lab stool.

"Snakeeyes?" Calvin snapped. "He's on his way, right? How soon? Can you tell?"

Okacha shook her head wearily. "I'm not sure. I think it just stopped raining up where he was. And I'm pretty sure what just happened was him drawing on me to shift shape, which is a little odd, 'cause he can usually do that by himself. You may have messed him up with the cedar—which may buy us some time, but also may piss him off even worse."

"Which means we've gotta hurry," Calvin concluded with a frown. He glanced around the room, saw expectant eyes. "Okay," he said decisively. "Some of you have seen what I'm about to do. Shoot, some of you have *helped*: you, Dave, and Alec and Liz. The rest of you—except 'Kacha—I'd say the thing to do's to get as far away from us as you can and still stay in the room. I only say that 'cause I'd like somebody to hand if anything fucks up, but I also want you as far from trouble as is viable. Brock, this means you. And Don. You too, Sandy. Sorry."

Sandy shrugged, her face tight with irritation. "I'd argue if there was time, but there's not any."

"You *can* help," Calvin told her apologetically. "You and Brock—and Don if he's up to it—can stick some of this cedar at the windows and doors. Any other opening you can find, too."

Sandy nodded. "Come on, guys."

David, Liz, and Alec looked on with trepidation. "Same as before?" Alec asked warily.

"Well, there's no time to paint up, or anything," Calvin replied as he laid the war club on a table and skinned out of his T-shirt. "And I don't have any mojo water—

No, wait: I do—I think. Brock, you still got that jug from Usunhiyi?''

"Yep. You need it?''

"Bring it over.''

He did.

"I don't see any point in strippin' 'less you guys just feel like flashin' what you've got,'' Calvin went on as he splashed the contents of the jug on his face, chest, and arms. "Mostly it just helps the focus 'cause it makes you aware of yourself as a part of the natural world, and also 'cause it reminds you that a different set of rules are at work. But I don't think it really affects the ritual much.''

David shrugged and slipped off his shirt. Alec followed. They removed their shoes and socks as well, but went no further. "You guys finish dousin' yourself with that—sorry Okacha, but this doesn't apply to you, though it would, ordinarily.''

The panther-woman merely nodded mutely. Calvin thought she looked as tired as anyone he'd ever seen. Mental battles could be as taxing as physical ones, he supposed.

But he had no time to spare for sympathy now, much less speculation.

Risking one final check on the room, he snared his backpack and the assorted bits of flora he'd just gathered and lugged them to the counter along the outside wall. He chose the centermost section, complete with sink, and set to work.

From a Ziploc bag in the pack he produced the buckskin pouch Sandy had taken to calling his sorcerer's kit. From it he removed a number of smaller bags of the same material. He chose one and opened the rawhide drawstring top. Inside was sand—sand from Uki's Power Wheel in Galunlati, to be precise. Using the top of the pouch as a spout, he sketched a replica on the marble countertop, grateful that it was at least natural material.

A second bag produced shavings from a lightning-blasted tree. He had just heaped them in the center of the Wheel and started to erect a tripod over them—each twig one of the plants of vigilance—when a bird smashed against one of the high-placed windows.

It made a sharp report, almost like a gunshot. Calvin looked up instantly, felt his heart skip a beat. Another bird—a crow, he thought—impacted the glass as he watched. Fortunately, the windows were the sort with wire mesh embedded in them. *Damned* fortunately, in fact, because the next five seconds saw ten impacts. More followed, all up and down the range of windows.

"Sandy, check the stair door," he yelled. "Brock, take the other one. Block 'em both if you have to. Liz, keep an eye on 'Kacha, and if you see her tense up again, hit her with more of that cedar. Better yet, stay there and switch her with it."

Not bothering to see if his orders were obeyed, Calvin turned back to his work. A third bag revealed a pottery bowl the size and shape of a human cranium, which he placed by the Wheel and pile of shavings. A moment later, flint and steel had a tiny fire blazing—brighter than it should have, given the quantity of material, nor was it exhausted as quickly as ought to have been the case.

While he fed the fire, he began to chant in a low voice: a formula Uki had taught him that occurred in none of the books he had ever seen. Not even Swimmer had known it, he who had revealed so much to James Mooney.

Alec and David joined him, unbidden. Liz watched apprehensively, then, when Calvin motioned them forward, came along with Okacha.

More birds beat at the window. A pane shattered, but the glass remained intact. An upward glance showed the window dark with beating wings and darting beaks. A thousand black eyes sparked and flashed and accused him. He shuddered and went on with his chanting.

Fortunately Alec remembered what to do, and did it. Calvin was sorry for him, too, for he knew how much Alec hated magic. It was too irrational, he said; he was a scientist; he preferred things that behaved predictably—cause and effect, and all that. Still, now that the push had come, he showed no sign of faltering as he retrieved the jar that held the ulunsuti, undid the seal and pouch, and tipped the crystal into the bowl. It glittered there, even in the twilight gloom, as if anticipating what was intended.

"Just a couple more minutes," Calvin murmured, at the end of his chant, before starting it up again. "Alec, you know the rest? I'd have you do it, 'cept I don't think there's time."

"Whatever," Alec grunted. "Where's the blood?"

David grimaced and flopped a black plastic garbage bag he'd retrieved earlier onto the counter. Undoing it, Calvin reached in and dragged out a dead starling—one of the dozen or so that had flown into the truck during their escape, which Okacha had subsequently dispatched. A pause to fish a knife from his pocket, and he set to slitting throats.

The results were disappointing. Though the birds were still faintly warm (warm enough, he prayed), they'd nevertheless been dead for nearly an hour. And with no heart to pump it, there was precious little blood to extract. As it was, he was reduced to wringing the limp feathered bodies above the ulunsuti, and then smearing it for good measure.

The crystal took it greedily, drank in every drop and seemed to call for more. He tried, eventually passing his knife to David to speed processing.

And all the while the small fire burned, and all the while he chanted.

The impacts of birds against the windows grew more frequent.

Another pane shattered, directly above them; a sliver of glass the size of his finger tinkled to the counter. He made to brush it aside reflexively—and caught the side of his hand along its razor edge. More reflex brought it to his mouth, but then he had another idea and clamped it atop the ulunsuti. It glowed much brighter at that, and Calvin closed his eyes, tried not to look at the gush of blood, which was actually quite considerable, as the stone drank its fill. It had begun to glow now, and as the glow grew brighter, he motioned Alec, Liz, David, and Okacha closer with his free hand. "This isn't how it's supposed to work," he gritted. "But you guys—you who've been there—visualize Galunlati. Try to think of a place that's as far from Uki as you can."

Liz started to protest, then bit her lip and closed her eyes in turn. Calvin opened his again—and saw the ulunsuti's glow increase steadily. In an instant it was as bright as the fire that burned beside it, and an instant after that, it was expanding into a blinding glare like one of Liz's fog lights. And in the heart of that glare, a landscape was revealed: a place of trees too tall for the world of men, and mountains higher.

"Galunlati!" Okacha breathed. "Hope."

*"Despair!"* another voice howled—and then the room was a glitter of flying glass as a man-sized gray-and-white shape hurtled through a suddenly shattered pane.

Calvin felt himself cut again, a dozen times over, but scarcely noticed, for already he was shielding the ulunsuti, vaguely aware that it was drinking even more blood. "Liz—the gate," he shouted.

"Gate, *hell*!" came that awful voice. And Calvin's

senses finally settled enough to see Snakeeyes rise up from where he'd landed on the floor. *Must've shifted to human right before he impacted the window,* he decided dimly. And had no more time for thought as the witch leapt toward him, feather cloak swirling about him like a blizzard of gray-white snow. The flame on the counter flickered.

*"No!"* David yelled, and launched himself at the man—only to be hurled into a table by a casual sweep of wiry arm. From their places by the doors Sandy and Brock flung themselves forward—but they would be too late. A second from now, Snakeeyes would extinguish the fire, and that would be it. He'd have Okacha to draw on, and with that accomplished, getting the scale and the club and the ulunsuti would be no problem. Calvin felt utterly outclassed.

"Don't tell *me* no, white boy!" Snakeeyes snapped. But Calvin stepped before him, inserting himself between the witch and fire. Alec joined him, so did Liz.

And Okacha . . .

Calvin had never seen a woman move that fast. No, he corrected, never a *human* move that fast. One instant she was beside him tense as a spring, the next she had leapt a quarter way across the room and grabbed something from the table nearest the sink, the one where they'd left their assorted packs.

*What?* he wondered. And then he knew.

Before he could do more than register the idea, however, Okacha acted. With blinding speed, her arm flashed out—the arm that wielded Calvin's war club. A glimpse at her eyes made him shudder, for little of humanity showed there.

"Bitch!" Snakeeyes spat, and whirled around to face her.

Okacha's lips drew back in a snarl. Calvin wondered if her teeth were pointed, or if that was a trick of light.

"Asshole!" she shrieked—and swung again, even as she leapt forward. Snakeeyes dodged, but the club caught a corner of his cloak and tore a hole in it. The witch gasped, eyes bright with hate. Birds began to fly through the broken window. The air was suddenly full of shrieks and caws and flapping wings. But the flame behind Calvin held steady—as did his grip on the ulunsuti.

Okacha swung the club again: a figure-eight pattern in the air between her and her adversary. Snakeeyes backed away, but kept his hands before him—not in defense, however, but to—

—grab! Which he did. He caught the club in midswing, stopped it. He yanked—hard. Okacha did not pull back; instead, she pushed.

Unbalanced, the witch staggered back—and in his effort to catch himself, loosened his grip. Okacha did pull then.

Snakeeyes staggered again and almost fell. And those few seconds of awkwardness were enough. One blow from Okacha struck him square on the shoulder (and would have shattered his skull, had he not flinched to block it). A second impact smashed his forearm. He shrieked in pain as the limb flopped limply to his side.

Okacha wasted not a second. One moment she was facing the witch, the next she had spun around and was leaping forward—straight toward Calvin. He saw her coming and acted as fast as he ever had in his life. Not even sparing time to grit his teeth, he thrust the ulunsuti into the now-wavering fire. Birds flew at him; beaks flashed at his eyes. He beat them off with his free hand and saw through slitted lids the crystal flare bright as it drank blood and fire and pain—and then the landscape of Galunlati, and then Okacha leaping through. "I made it!" she shouted. "Here, you need this worse than I do!" Whereupon she flung the atasi back through the gate.

Somehow, Calvin managed to catch it with his free hand, even as he yanked the other from the fire and tumbled the whole apparatus into the sink. He fumbled at the faucet, but Alec—or someone—was there ahead of him. Water quenched the flames, cooled the blood— and the gate blinked out like a candle.

"You son-of-a-bitch," came an almost bestial growl behind him. Calvin turned wearily, too dazed to think straight. But his head cleared instantly as he came face-to-face with the witch's cold yellow glare.

Snakeeyes glared at him as he rose to his full imposing height and drew the feather cloak around him with a flourish of his functioning hand.

"Be in the woods where we met at sunset tomorrow," he hissed. "Or wonder where I am for the rest of your life."

And with that, he closed his eyes, grimaced for an instant—and was an owl.

Calvin tried to scramble atop the counter to block access to the window, but talons raked his face—perilously close to his eyes. Reflex won. He felt a brush of feathers, and then the witch was gone. The few remaining crows and starlings followed.

David blinked at him wearily as he picked himself up off the floor. A bruise already discolored the angle of his jaw. "Could be worse," he managed, reaching out to right a fallen stool. "You guys help me clean up in here. If I'm real lucky, I can blame the broken windows on the hail."

"And if not?" Calvin sighed as he returned the ulunsuti to Alec.

David giggled nervously. "I'll be in almost as deep shit as you are."

"I'm hungry," Don grumbled, yawning, having evidently slept through the whole brief battle.

Calvin rolled his eyes. "Okay," he told the boy.

"We'll feed you, and anybody else who's hungry. Me, I've gotta fast until tomorrow. And then . . . well, I guess I'll know then, won't I?"

"Deep shit," Alec muttered. "Deep shit indeed."

Sandy's only response was to hug him.

# Chapter XXIII:
# Vigilantes

*(Jackson County, Georgia—midnight)*

Calvin nudged a limb further into the fire with a bare foot and leaned back again, resting bone-tired shoulders against the larger log that built an implicit barrier against the night. Across the low-burning flames, Brock was methodically peeling a twig, his pointy features rendered atypically flat by being bottom-lit. The boy wasn't saying much—*hadn't* said much in the two hours since they'd come here. Rather, he seemed content to gaze at the fire and dream. Calvin wondered if he'd had enough of magic.

Or if he even knew he was up to his eyeballs in it right now!

The fire occupied the center of a Power Wheel Calvin had sketched in a patch of bare ground at the western edge of the meadow where they had encountered Snake-eyes earlier that day—and where he would meet him again in less than twenty-four hours. In fact, the boy straddled the eastern spoke, with a red-painted limb from a lightning-blasted tree stuck in the earth two yards beyond the log that braced his shoulders.

Similar constructs marked the other directions, and the

347

larger circle that connected them beyond the ring of back-rest logs was strewn with cedar boughs. He hoped they'd be sufficient; God knew he only had Snakeeyes's word for the time and place of their confrontation. And how good was the word of a witch?

Neither David to his left, the north, nor Alec in the south to his right, had spoken lately, either. No one seemed to have anything *to* say—or maybe too much. For himself, he was so wired and nervous and scared he was practically numb—which manifested in the real world as a superficial calm that those who knew him well would recognize as cause for concern indeed.

Eventually David mirrored his movement and likewise scooted a limb further into the fire. There were four of them: four staves of four kinds of wood that met in the middle, that followed the spokes of the wheel out to where Calvin and his best friends sat vigil. As the center was consumed, more was eased in. It was a comfort, but a small one: the reliability of ritual.

Calvin's stomach growled, testament to another part of the preparations for his impending trial. David caught his eye and smirked, then tried to suppress it.

"This *isn't* a funeral," Calvin grumbled. "Nor a wake—at least not yet. Talkin' *is* allowed. It's just food we—that is, I—can't have."

David rolled his eyes and patted his belly, then reached to a flat, plate-sized rock placed deliberately close by the fire. An iron pot perched there, heavy with dark, steaming liquid. "Sounds like you need more black drink, Fargo, m'man." Without awaiting reply, he dipped a gourd into the brew and lipped it, wincing at the strong herbal flavor, then passed it on to Calvin. "If this is all you're allowed, you'd best drink deep."

Calvin took the long handle carefully, sipped cautiously—and still nearly scalded his tongue. Which might be just as well, given how the stuff tasted. "Good thing I saw those *Ilex* bushes earlier," he murmured off-handedly.

Alec snorted, almost giggled. "Yeah, and I'd *really* like to be a fly on the wall when young Mr. Sullivan here tries to explain that little bit of impromptu pruning as hail damage!"

Calvin raised an eyebrow—as much good humor as he could muster—then cast his gaze beyond David's increasingly cynical buddy to the woods beyond. The trees were tall here, where the oaks and hickories made a crown around the meadow that balded the knoll. Above them he could see stars and a bit of moon. Cygnus, Corona Borealis. Even the white trail of the Milky Way that his people called *Gili-utsunstanunyi*: Where-the-Dog-Ran. He wondered if he'd ever see them again.

*No!* He wouldn't think about that—or like that. He was who he was: Calvin Fargo McIntosh, a warrior of the Ani-Yunwiya, called in Galunlati Nunda-unali'i, and in this, the Lying World, Utlunta-Dehi. And who else of his people numbered a demigod among his friends? Who else had met the Red Man of the East and the Black Man of the West and the White Man of the South and the Blue Man of the North? Not Snakeeyes, that was for sure. Snakeeyes had power—obviously. And he had the warped strength that meanness wrought. But his powers were all of this world. And though few in the Lying World would have believed in them or used them, Calvin knew that he had a few things on his side Snakeeyes did not have—or so he thought. But he didn't dare let the witch get them, either. And that was the risk. With either his uktena scale or Alec's ulunsuti in a witch's power, who knew what would happen?

Who indeed?

Finally, when the gourd had made the circle and they were all as full of the stimulant as they could stomach for a spell, Calvin spoke.

"I just wanta thank you guys for stickin' by me," he said softly. "We've done it before, for each other, and it's always worked out okay—though we didn't always know it was goin' to. But this time . . . I don't know. I have the terrible feelin' that I'm in *way* over my head. And I'm . . . afraid, I guess. And the trouble is, I know that shouldn't be the case. I mean, Jesus, guys, I've fought Spearfinger, I've helped kill an uktena, I've been to the Darkening Land and returned—and this is just me against another guy—yet I'm freaked as hell about it. Oh sure, I've got some things I can draw on—but so does he. Except that I suspect he knows a shitload more about what my limitations are than I know about his— and no, Alec, I'm not gonna ask you to consult the ulun-suti to find out. I don't think it does things like that."

David reached over clap him on the shoulder. "Hey, guy, what're friends for?"

"Not for riskin' themselves like you guys are," Calvin snorted. "Not for lyin' out in the woods when you've got finals to study for, not for bein' hungry when there's no need. Not for—"

"Not for keeping people they care about from going through trials alone?" Alec interrupted with a vehemence that surprised him. "That's bullshit, man, and you know it. Shoot, when you first met us, you barely knew us—yet you helped us. More than once you did that, even when it put you at risk both for yourself and for what you wanted. Oh, sure, you fucked up some— but so have me and Dave—a lot, in fact, and we're probably gonna do it again. But the point is, we're where we wanta be tonight. School's fun, sometimes; gaming and drinking and going to clubs can be real cool. But what makes 'em cool isn't the fact of 'em, it's who you do 'em with. Stuff's no good without friends, Cal. And experience is pretty flat without someone to share it with—so let's cut the crap about you owing us for this, okay?''

Calvin grinned. ''Thanks, man. I appreciate it.''

Brock blinked up from his staring. He too shifted a limb closer to the center. ''He's trying to psyche you, isn't he? Snakeeyes, I mean.''

Calvin shrugged. ''Part of the game, I guess.''

''Making you wait . . . yeah.''

''I know that's some of it,'' Calvin acknowledged. But he *was* hurt, don't forget. We just don't know how bad, or how long it'll take him to heal. I guess he figures that if he waits too long, we might come up with something major to do against him—I mean, he *knows* we've got supernatural connections! On the other hand, if he strikes too soon, we might beat him, too. So he has to find the point when *he's* strongest. Which is at sunset, which is a *between* time. But also goin' into night, which is when *he'd* have the advantage.''

''Assuming he shifts into owl shape again,'' Brock noted.

''And assuming Cal *doesn't* shift into something that can also see in the dark,'' Alec added.

''Which is assumin' that Cal shifts into anything at all!'' Calvin snapped. ''Which I don't plan on—not if I can help it.''

''That last being the operative phrase,'' David concluded.

Calvin nodded grimly. ''Yeah, but I really don't know how many changes the scale's got left in it . . . and if I shift and get stuck, well, you guys can kiss your warm furry fannies good-bye, 'cause Mr. Eyes'll make lampshades out of 'em by breakfast.''

Brock looked alarmed. ''You really think he'd . . . *kill* us?''

Calvin gnawed his lip. ''Not in a way that's traceable to him. But I think there's a real good chance he would,

yeah. See . . . one of the things about witches—my people's style of witches—is that if they kill somebody they
get the years that person would have lived added to their
lifespan. You play your cards right, you could live forever."

Brock's eyes were huge.

"Believe it, kid," Calvin assured him.

Brock swallowed. "I . . . I do, I think. I wouldn't have
a week ago, maybe not even a day ago . . . but I do
now."

"Good for you." Calvin yawned. "It may keep you
alive."

Brock didn't reply.

Calvin returned his gaze to the fire. He gazed at it a
long time, then eased his branch in another inch.

David looked at him. "You miss Sandy, don't you?"

Calvin shot him a sideways glance, then nodded
sheepishly.

"If it helps any," David said softly, "you know she's
doing the right thing. Somebody has to keep an eye on
Don until they get hold of his mom, after all; she's the
reasonable one to do it. Shoot, she knows you can take
care of yourself, man; but Don's still nine-tenths shell-
shocked. Besides, she's with Liz. The two of them can
handle *anything*—'cause I've seen 'em do it. I mean,
name me two other women you'd rather have on your
side in a fair fight."

"Or an unfair one, either," Alec chuckled.

Calvin shrugged. "Yeah, well, I guess you guys're
right. Except . . . oh, I dunno. I guess it's the old conflict
thing kickin' in: my white side and my Indian side. My
liberal white American side—the one that grew up in
Atlanta watchin' MTV and CNN, and votes democratic
and supports abortion and gay rights and the ERA—says
I'm bein' an arch-reactionary male chauvinist by not *in-
sistin'* Sandy be here tonight; that the simple *fact* that

somebody says that women absolutely should not take part in things like this means I therefore oughta insist on her *takin'* part. But on the other hand, the side of my heritage I've had to *learn*—not be warped from birth to try to fit into—*knows* why they shouldn't, which is 'cause what we're on the eve of here is essentially warfare, which is when we're most completely *men*, and that we're therefore forbidden contact with women for fear of pollution—not 'cause they're inferior, just 'cause they're fundamentally *different*, and different things oughta be kept separate."

"Damned eloquent," Alec observed dryly.

"Damned *true*!" Calvin countered. "It's just that right now I don't know which rules to play by. It's hard, guys, to reconcile a world where you can buy comic books with holograms on the cover and be free to talk about 'em; with one where a man can turn himself into an owl and be considered a raving loon. I mean, *both* are equally incomprehensible—equally magic—to most folks, yet there are rules that govern 'em both, too."

"And being a shapechanging sorcerer who's shacked up with a physics teacher doesn't help, does it?" Alec appended.

Calvin grimaced helplessly. "Good point: I *am* bein' a hypocrite—except that I've tried very hard to see both worlds as part of one, with each havin' things in it that're . . . remote from each other's traditional belief systems. I mean, I don't have a clue how holograms work, even though I've seen the diagrams and read the theory, but I also don't see how recitin' certain words can make you shoot straighter—or open gates between Worlds—but they do."

"Well, the only thing *I* believe right now," Brock yawned out of the ruddy silence of the east, "is that it's good to have mates anytime—and that pizza tomorrow night won't be shabby either."

"I'll buy," Alec volunteered.

Calvin found that he had nothing to say to that. And forced his limb further into the fire.

Dawn found Calvin still awake—as he'd intended—though he'd lapsed into a drifty fugue that was somewhere between a trance, an anxiety attack, and plain old sleep-deprivation fatigue. He'd been gazing at the fire a long time; indeed, had watched its slow collapse into the barely smoking embers that now centered the Power Wheel.

But the sun was kindling those coals with a different sort of crimson now, and it was time to greet the day and get on with the second part of the ritual he was determined to follow preparatory to his . . . duel, he supposed it was, with Snakeeyes. Which he absolutely did not want to contemplate right now. And the best way to prevent that was by occupying his brain otherwise. Yawning, he stood, stretched, felt his vertebrae crack and pop. A glance around the circle of logs showed his companions all asleep—or faking it. Except David. But even that most loyal of friends seemed to be in the last stages of a holding action, to judge by the way he kept jerking his eyes open, then drifting off again. Calvin prodded him in the ribs with a toe. David blinked up at him, then over his shoulder at the sun, and nodded. While Calvin shook Alec and Brock back to consciousness, David prepared one final batch of black drink.

"Actually, we need to build that up higher," Calvin advised. "I need to heat rocks for the last stage."

David obligingly punched up the coals, added more wood, then slid the pot as close to the resulting flames as he dared.

"While that's cookin', we can get on with stage two," Calvin confided.

"Wha's stage two?" Brock mumbled sleepily. "Uh,

sorry, I didn't mean t' wimp out on you," he continued, rubbing his eyes.

"I bet *I* know," Alec yawned. "Hey, like, I may get a feel for this stuff yet!"

Calvin grimaced resignedly, but clapped him on the shoulder. "That way, boys," he yawned in turn, pointing over the hill. "If memory serves, the Middle Oconee's thataway."

"You mean, like to *swim* in?" Brock yipped in alarm.

"No," Calvin chuckled wickedly, grabbing him by the neckband of his T-shirt and propelling him along, "like to go-to-water in—which is not the same thing at all."

"Without a suit, I suppose?" Brock groaned wearily.

"Bare-ass nekkid!" David grinned, sounding even more wicked than Calvin.

Brock rolled his eyes. "Seems like I've spent half the last *week* bare-ass nekkid," he grumbled. "Or hangin' out with folks who are."

"Some of whom are even *worth* hangin' out with, I bet," David sighed. "That Okacha's a fox!"

"So to speak," Alec chuckled wryly.

Calvin aimed a gentle kick at Brock's bottom. "Better get used to it, kid—if you're gonna be a wizard."

It took fifteen minutes of picking their way through underbrush and pine thickets to locate a suitable site for the second part of Calvin's ritual—which is to say, a place where the water was deep enough to submerge oneself, yet shallow enough to stand on the bottom for the chanting-and-marking part. Fortunately, the chant was the familiar one from Mooney, the one for players before a ball game—which meant that David knew enough of it to sing it with some prompting. And since Calvin was the one going to war, it wasn't appropriate for *him* to sing. Thus, David, Alec, and the reluctant

Brock found themselves cast in the role of accolytes.

The ritual itself did not take long—again fortunately, for though the stretch of river they had chosen bordered the two-hundred-odd forested acres Calvin's friends owned, the surrounding territory was fairly populous. Which basically meant that the longer they lingered, the greater their odds of discovery—and potentially awkward questions.

Thus, it was with a considerable sense of relief that Calvin heaved himself out of the water and shinnied up the waist-high bank. David, who had preceded him, gave him an arm up and tossed him the towel. He took it gratefully. "You'd think I'd learn how cold river water is, even in Georgia, even in June," he gasped between shivers.

"Beats England!" Brock shot back from where he was fidgeting embarrassedly while he waited on Alec to finish drying—they hadn't counted on this eventuality, and nobody had thought to bring towels. As it was, they were using a ragged pair they'd found in the trunk of David's Mustang.

Alec flipped Brock the soggy bit of terrycloth and reached for his skivvies. "I guess this brings us to stage three, huh?"

Calvin nodded, already surveying the riverbanks thereabouts. "And if you guys'll give me a hand, I see just what we need."

Twenty minutes later, Calvin led his companions to the top of the slope beyond which the meadow lay. They did not travel unencumbered, though, for besides backpacks, they each bore two lengths of willow saplings roughly nine feet long and as big around as half dollars. Calvin had just paused to untangle his from Brock's when Liz's pickup rolled into view. It parked beside David's Mustang a couple of hundred yards away, and first Liz, then Sandy, climbed out. Calvin wondered where Don was and bent their route that way.

Sandy met them halfway and took over one of the willows. "Sleep okay?" she asked lightly, with a twinkle in her eye that told Calvin she was forcing nonchalance.

He rose to the occasion. "Let's just say that my faithful companions here did just dandy. *I* kinda felt like Jesus did the night he spent in Gethsemane."

" 'Cept none of us had thirty pieces of silver," David broke in. " 'Sides, *I* stayed awake."

"And how was *your* night?" Calvin inquired, as Liz joined them and they trekked toward their camp.

" 'Bout like yours, evidently," Sandy yawned. "We finally got through to Don's mom 'round eleven-thirty. She'd gone to Brunswick for a movie, which is why she didn't answer earlier. Don told her he'd just got real bummed out at home and had run off with the idea of connecting with some friends he knew up here, and then got lost, but was afraid to call for help 'cause he was afraid she'd be pissed. It wasn't much of a lie, actually; he was careful about what he said. And fortunately, his stepdad's a cop—and I *think* knows a thing or two about . . . *you know*. Like, he saw all that stuff last year. But anyway, *he* got on the horn and called in a couple of markers, and the upshot of it is that Don's on his way south in a Clarke County Police car at this very moment. In fact"—she paused to check her watch—"he oughta be rolling in just about now." She glanced up at Calvin. "He said to tell you thanks, by the way. Said he'll be in touch when he gets his act together."

"You think this put the fear of God in his mom?" Calvin asked, with a scowl.

A shrug. "I think it might. I sure think she'll pay more attention to him now."

"Good deal."

"So . . . what're these bushes for?" Liz wondered.

"Sweat lodge," Calvin replied. "You plant 'em in a circle 'bout two yards across, then loop 'em over each other, and—" He paused in midsentence. "You *did* remember to bring blankets, didn't you?" he asked Sandy. "Otherwise I'm up shit creek."

Sandy rolled her eyes. "Of course we did! Jeeze, you'd think I'd never helped you build one of these things before."

"And I hope you never have to again," Calvin replied. "Not under these circumstances."

They had deposited their bundles now, at the western edge of the Power Wheel they'd camped in the night before. Calvin flopped a comradely arm absently across Sandy's shoulders. She started to respond with a hug, then winced and drew away.

"What's the matter?"

"Cramps," she muttered through a pained grimace. "All this shapeshifting and world-hopping's brought on my period."

"It *delays* mine," Liz confided to David.

Alec winked at the wide-eyed Brock. "Take notes, kid. I am."

Calvin, however, felt a sick dread tie knots in his stomach. "Oh Christ, I *forgot* about that! I mean, you're serious, aren't you?"

Sandy nodded grimly. " 'Fraid so."

Calvin puffed his cheeks and gnawed his lip, trying hard not to vent the anger that had just roared to life inside him. *She should've* remembered, *dammit! No, I should've remembered*, he countered. *Calm down, kid; you're tired and stressed out. Don't say anything you'll regret.*

"I'm sorry," Sandy sighed wearily. "I shouldn't have got so close. I just forgot. So did you."

Calvin took a deep breath. "Yeah, well, there was so

much else goin' on we both screwed up. But now . . .
I think you'd better leave.''

Liz glared at him incredulously. "*Calvin!* What the
hell are you saying? Do you have any *idea* how much
Sandy worried about you last night?''

He returned the glare. "Do *you* have any idea what's
goin' on here?''

"It's like this, Liz,'' Sandy interrupted, though Calvin
could tell she was fighting to keep her cool. "According
to tradition—the tradition of Cal's people, which I respect—there're a ton of restrictions on . . . commerce
between men and women. Traditionally, a man's supposed to abstain not only from sex, but from *any* contact
with a woman before important undertakings, like ball
games, or war, or—''

"But that's just *stupid*,'' Liz broke in.

"So is being shy about going topless—to some people,'' Sandy shot back. "And if I'd had my head on
straight, I wouldn't have come here now. Unfortunately,
it gets worse. 'Cause even worse than contact with a
woman is contact with a *mensing* woman. Calvin's
folks—his ancestors—insisted they stay away from everyone during that time. Which makes sense, given how
interdependent everybody was: I mean, having somebody's temper go ballistic when you live as close to the
edge as some of those folks did—well, it just wouldn't
be cool.''

"And there's also the small matter of women's magic
bein' stronger than men's, then,'' Calvin put in, with
more than a touch of sarcasm. "If we're bein' *thorough*
here. In fact, if we're bein' thorough I oughta go get
another willow sapling 'cause Sandy's polluted that one
just by touchin' it.''

Sandy glared at him.

"I won't though,'' he added sullenly.

"You're tired, Cal,'' Sandy gritted.

"Yeah," Calvin nodded, "you got it. I'm tired; I'm half a day away from the most important battle of my life; I don't have a clue how I'm gonna defeat Snake-eyes—and now I'm polluted."

"I'm *sorry*!" Sandy snapped. "How many times do I have to tell you that?"

He did not reply.

Liz gnawed her lip thoughtfully. "So the deal is that a mensing woman—"

"Saps a man's strength to replace the strength she loses through menstral blood," Calvin told her irritably.

"Hmmmmm," Sandy mused, "I never thought about the *why* of it, just the fact. Now that's very interesting."

Calvin simply glared at her and commenced sharpening the first of the saplings prior to sticking it in the ground.

"Calvin, my lad," Sandy announced a moment later. "You're worrying too much. C'mon, we need to talk."

# Chapter XXIV:
# War Among the Shifting Shadows

*(Jackson County, Georgia—
Wednesday, June 20—just before sunset)*

The sky, David decided, looked like war. A study in red, gray, and black, it was; like something out of an Australian film: staged for maximum contrast, maximum effect, with a neon-crimson stain filtering through the thick, layered clouds to the west; light against dark— the eternal symbolic struggle. And even as he watched, the image was reinforced, for the sun suddenly mustered strength enough to send a whole phalanx of beams lancing through the stand of pines just past the opposite crown of the hill. Red and black. Cloud and sun. Sunbeam spears and shields of standing timber.

It was a tad too appropriate, he concluded grimly, given that a far more literal battle was imminent. Still, he preferred to gaze at the heavens, which were distant and remote and untouchable, in lieu of, closer in, the drizzle-damp meadow where the lonely, unlikely hump of Calvin's asi hunched like a turtle shell clad in motley; a street-person's shelter wrought of wishes and refuse and Salvation Army quilts.

But the really troubling thing about war was that when you read about it, it was clean. Battles only raged on sunny days because that's how folks envisioned them. Soldiers died neatly: pierced once through the heart and gone. It never rained; men never slogged through mud, or died slowly, sunk to their armpits in bloody muck while they tried vainly to hold in their own foul-smelling entrails.

In short, one never imagined a duel of wizards being staged in a half-assed drizzle.

Yet that was about to be the case. The pyrotechnics to the west promised either a return of clear skies or the continuation of gloom, depending on how the winds blew. And somewhere between here and there it wasn't raining.

Unfortunately it *was* here—almost. The knee-high grass was wet and had soaked David's jeans halfway to his crotch. And though it was summer, he'd had to slip on a sleeveless khaki vest with a hood just to be able to see.

Not that there was much *to* see, at the moment—which was why he'd become so obsessed with the sky. Yeah, the sunset was definitely preferable to the sweat lodge that presently sheltered Calvin in the last third of his purification rite. Preferable, too, to the faltering fire that only his own determined efforts—and Alec's, Brock's, and Liz's—had kept going into midafternoon, so that the load of field stones it contained could grow hot enough to heat the inside of the *asi* and permeate it with steam when Calvin ladled on river water mixed with the last of that which they had brought from Usunhiyi. And very definitely preferable to the glum expressions his companions wore, where they sat on the tailgate of Liz's pickup, gaining scanty shelter from the half-hearted sprinkles.

Liz checked her watch and snuggled closer to David.

He reached down and patted her arm. "Won't be long now," she murmured.

"Official sundown's at 9:16," Alec supplied from David's opposite shoulder.

"All we can do now is wait," David sighed. "Wait and hope."

"Which are two of the hardest things in the world," Liz shot back grimly.

"Yeah, and if *we're* havin' trouble with it," Brock appended from Alec's left, "think how poor Cal must feel."

"I doubt he's feelin' much of anything, right now," David snorted. "That's one of the points of the ritual: to take oneself out of oneself. To move oneself to a more . . . spiritual plane, so to speak."

"Which isn't cool if it addles your wits and reflexes instead of sharpening 'em," Liz muttered under her breath.

"Poor Cal." Brock sniffed—he'd evidently caught a cold.

"And poor Sandy," Liz countered. "This has to be double hard on her: to have the person she loves best in the world laying his life on the line, and her not allowed to watch."

"In fact, to have maybe made it worse," Alec grumbled.

"Hush, McLean," David hissed. "We don't need to be reminded."

"At least they talked it out." From Liz.

"Reached an accommodation," David corrected. "Cal didn't exactly look like a happy camper when he came back from that walk."

"Yeah, but think how Sandy must look," Liz persisted. "He knows what's happening. She gets to sit by the river and worry."

"That's as close as tradition'd let her be, though,"

David replied. "And if there's anything both Sandy and Cal respect, it's tradition. They don't necessarily like it—but they respect it."

It was Alec's turn to check his watch. "Can't be long now."

David pulled the hood further over his forehead. A raindrop slipped from the rim and splashed on his nose. The bill of Brock's Atlanta Braves cap was beaded with them. Alec wore a wide-brimmed Australian hat, Liz a thrift-store bowler; both were dark with damp.

Alec stared fixedly at the west. "Just a . . . second longer . . ."

David followed his gaze back to the conflict in the heavens. The sun, he observed, had won free of the lowest battalion of clouds and had a clear drop to the horizon, which here was the topmost branches of a stand of pines half a mile away.

"Three . . . two . . . one . . ." Alec intoned.

Red disc touched black spear-points.

And the sound of vast wings flapping rode the low roll of thunder from the east.

David jerked his head around—and saw, as he'd expected, a dark shape drop from the heavier clouds on that side and dive toward the treetops. An owl, it had looked like: a very *big* owl. It lit in the forest a hundred yards to their left and vanished within the dense foliage.

What walked out of the woods went on two feet. But only by technicality was it human.

Oh, Snakeeyes wore man-shape, sure enough: tall and hard and well-muscled—as was revealed by the plain buckskin breechclout that was his only garment, the feather cloak he'd flourished earlier being nowhere in sight. But there was something too tight about his body: the cut-lines of those muscles showed too clearly, the veins and sinews that bound them were too sharply limned—especially for misty weather like this, which tended to soften forms. His waist-length hair—slicked back in a ponytail—was likewise too well-groomed, and too shiny, though not from moisture, David somehow knew.

His face showed nothing at all: no joy, no pain (though he'd been injured the last time they'd seen him), no anticipation, no regret. It was a face entirely devoid of emotion—and therefore of humanity. Only the eyes showed anything, and that was merely a grim yellow coldness: the dispassion of serpents.

David eased off the tailgate and stood, feeling his feet firm on the ground, even if his legs were shaky. Soft swishes to either side were his companions doing likewise.

Snakeeyes ignored them utterly, as though they were no more substantial than the raindrops that sketched arabesques on his chest and shoulders as he paced, in measured stride, straight toward the east-facing entrance of the asi.

Closer he came, and David realized that the witch's entire body was either subtly painted or tattooed (though if the latter, why hadn't he noticed it before?) with patterns that lessening distance revealed to be feathers and scales. They were almost the same color as his skin, too, the effect not unlike damask. And they alternated, one leg being feathered below the knee and scaled above, the opposite being patterned the other way round, and so on, all across his body.

The only ornaments he wore seemed to be a medicine pouch around his neck and a pair of dangling white earrings that David finally determined were skulls: a snake skull and a bird skull, most likely.

And still Snakeeyes proceeded toward the asi, the sun turning his skin so red he looked flayed, with the rivulets of rain transformed into blood. His eyes glittered like doubloons on the eyes of the dead. David nudged Liz and Alec with his elbows and plotted an intercept path: witch to the left, sweat lodge to the right.

When they were roughly twenty feet from either, Snakeeyes suddenly halted and swiveled his head to the right: a movement so swift and fluid it was like that of a reptile. "I'd stop right there, if I was you," he hissed. "In fact, I'd *leave*, if I was you. You might live longer that way. Then again, you might not. It might not make that big a difference."

"We're staying," David called back calmly, standing as straight as he could and trying to look taller than five feet seven.

"Your head, then," Snakeeyes spat. "But if Little Wizard in there gets to have partisans, I should, too, don't you reckon?"

David did not reply, simply tried to mask his confusion with a cold hard stare.

"I'm better at that than you are, white boy," Snakeeyes snorted derisively. Whereupon he closed his eyes, took a deep breath, and commenced a low, mumbled chant.

David tried to listen, but if the words were any language he knew (and he'd forced himself to learn a smattering of Cherokee), he didn't recognize it.

But something obviously did. For the woods were abruptly alive with noises: rustlings, and shufflings, and the soft thump of beating wings.

A bird landed on the limb nearest the meadow: a black bird with an ivory beak. A *raven*, David realized. Of which there were supposed to be but a few in Georgia, and none in Jackson County.

But as the chant continued, more appeared, all of them black birds of one species or another, so that the trees on the whole eastern side of the meadow were soon dark with their glistening bodies. The sunlit drizzle was like a veil of fire between.

A movement low down to the left caught David's eye, and he discovered that other creatures were likewise responding: lizards and snakes mostly, and not a few of the latter rattlers and copperheads: all the vermin of the Underworld, according to Calvin's ancestral myths. They coiled there among the grasses, tasting the air with forked tongues, beady eyes alert and hungry.

Eventually Snakeeyes stopped chanting. "*That* oughta be enough!" he snapped, his eyes flashing red as they caught the sunlight. A pair of strides took him to the edge of the outer Power Wheel, eight yards from the sweat lodge. With one sharp tug, he ripped the red-stained branch that marked the east from the ground and flung it with deadly accuracy into the remnants of the fire, where it blazed up, smoking.

And then he drew himself up to his full six-plus feet, leveled his right arm straight before him—straight toward the asi—and shouted, "Calvin McIntosh, come out of that hole and fight me!"

David held his breath, waiting. Five heartbeats passed, then ten. Fifteen . . .

On twenty the flap of blanket that served as a door twitched aside and a head of black hair appeared. Another breath, and Calvin eased out, rising to his feet in one fluid motion, to stand staring at his adversary.

The guy looked good, David handed him that. He wasn't as tall as his foe, of course—by a good six inches. But he was more gracefully built, without the exaggerated cuts and bulges that characterized the witch's body. Most of *his* body was visible, too: the buckskin loincloth David had been given at his naming ceremony in Galunlati his sole garment. The uktena scale and medicine bag around his throat, and the war club hanging carelessly from his right hand were his only ornaments. Though it had been hours since they'd last brought red-hot rocks to the lodge, his flesh was still sleek with sweat; in the cool drizzle, it steamed.

But where Snakeeyes's face looked cold and grim and distant, Calvin's was warm and human. A ghost of a smile even played around his lips. David wondered if he'd finally come to terms with this battle—and with the several others he'd doubtless been fighting with himself as well, most notably how to reconcile things with Sandy.

"So, Little Wizard," Snakeeyes growled, when Calvin had paced another step forward, so that the smoldering remnant of the campfire was the only tangible thing that lay between them, the ring of cedar twigs having been relocated to surround the asi itself. "So, Little Wizard," he repeated, louder. "It looks like you're a worse coward than I figured. For not only do you enlist women to fight for you, but you won't meet me without one weapon in your hand and another at your throat. I, as you can see, have none." He swept his arms away from his sides for emphasis.

Calvin glared at him. "I bear weapons only because I didn't trust you enough to leave mine unprotected— you, who seem to have no respect for either people or property."

"And is this place *your* property, that you would stain with fire and blood, magic and battle?" Snakeeyes shot back with soft precision.

"It's the property of good friends who once told me I was free to use it!"

("Is all this posturing part of the deal?" Alec murmured in David's ear.)

(He nodded. "I guess so. And ditto for the fancy talk, since neither of 'em speak like that normally. It's gettin' worse, too.")

("Hush," Liz muttered. "Pay attention.")

"And was that woman you stole from me also your property, to do with as you did?"

"She was her own woman," Calvin said flatly, "—which you know. No man can own another, or woman either."

"In the eyes of the state? Or the eyes of the strong?" Snakeeyes snarled back. "Myself, I prefer the strong."

"I prefer that people control their own lives," Calvin replied.

"And you'd enforce it with weapons?" Snakeeyes sneered, indicating the club.

Calvin dropped it neatly at his feet. "Now we're even."

Snakeeyes laughed derisively. "Are we indeed? *I* don't think so! For hear me now, Little Wizard: I am James Rainbow, called by my enemies Snakeeyes, and I am a *tskili*. I'm older than you, taller than you, stronger than you, meaner than you, more cunning than you, more learned in the powers of our people, and better hung. Men hate me and fear me; women lust after me on sight. What do you have to say to that? Can you claim any of those strengths as your own?"

Calvin looked him up and down, his face grim, his eyes narrowed arrogantly.

"Well, then, Vermin-eyes—for snakes, as we all know, are vermin—you can call *me* by my own name: Calvin Fargo McIntosh. Or you could call me by the name my grandfather foresaw at my birth: Edahi—He-Goes-About. Or you could call me Nunda-unali'i or Utlunta-Dehi, which names were given to me in Galunlati by the Red Man of the Lightning and the White Man of the Afternoon Thunder. Can you say the same of those who know *your* name? And if you can't, remember instead that I'm smarter than you and quicker than you, that I have more friends than you, and that my name is known in Worlds you can't imagine. Know that I fought the great uktena—and lived. I fought Spearfinger—and survived. I ventured to Usunhiyi, the Darkening Land to the West, and spoke to spirits—and returned alive. And now I prepare to fight you—and I *will* live. That's all I have to say.''

"Ah, yes," Snakeeyes purred. "You . . . prepare to fight me. Then perhaps we should agree on terms."

"Name 'em," Calvin said coldly. "You challenged, therefore it's my right to name 'em—yet I give up that right to show how little I fear you!"

Snakeeyes grinned. "The more fool you! Very well: battle will begin when the top edge of the sun falls behind that tallest pine, as seen by your own eyes. It'll end—if that be necessary—when the top edge of the sun greets the world again tomorrow morning. In between we'll do everything we can to kill each other. This ain't a fair fight, 'cause I'm not a fair man. I do what I want, and right now I want to fight you. After all, my friends are here—and my slaves. I could have 'em take you and never lift a finger. But since I intend to test your medicine as well as your body, we'll fight each other first as we are: as men; then as birds; and finally, as beasts of the field. If these terms are acceptable to you, so be it. If not . . . well then . . . *fuck* you!"

"They're fine," Calvin snapped, and closed the distance another step.

Again Snakeeyes laughed loudly. "Ain't you afraid, just a little bit, *Little* Wizard? After all, when the sun rises, you'll be dead."

"As long as I can fight you as a man, I'm not afraid."

"And when I'm *not* a man . . . ?"

"Fear," Calvin whispered, "is one of the things that keeps beasts and birds alive."

Snakeeyes merely grinned, then raised his head to gaze above Calvin's head toward the sunset. "Whenever you're ready."

Calvin ignored him, but walked straight toward him, past the fire and the edge of the inner Power Wheel—a distance of maybe four yards. Only when he was an arm's length from his adversary did he likewise turn to face the sunset.

("He's crazy," Alec gritted. "To turn his back, I mean.")

("Yeah," David agreed. "But it also shows Old Snakey that Cal's not afraid of him. It's a gesture of contempt.")

And then the sun reached the spot Snakeeyes had determined:

*"Yu!"* Calvin yelled and tucked forward into a roll that brought him upright again just past the fire. He snatched at something on the ground; then, as the witch sprang to meet him, whirled and charged.

Snakeeyes defused that assault by dodging left, which likewise brought him nearer the asi. He kicked at the embers of the fire, sending them straight into Calvin's face. Flame flashed bright, then faded. One caught in Calvin's hair and sizzled. He shook it free and kept moving. Closing . . .

Snakeeyes grabbed a still-smoldering limb and stabbed. Smoke writhed from his hand where he gripped it, though he nevertheless held on.

("Cedar, I think," David told Liz. "Interesting.")

Still half-blind, Calvin couldn't avoid the brand, and it grazed along his side. Flesh stank; blisters rose along his ribs.

Snakeeyes dropped the limb and retreated, easing left to put the fire between them. Calvin leapt again—not around, but *over*. His fist flashed out, straight at the witch's face. Snakeeyes deflected it instantly, as a fast upward counter with his right sent Calvin's arm arching skyward.

—Which was evidently exactly what he'd wanted. For just as it passed Snakeeyes's head, Calvin managed an awkward lunge—opened his hand—and slapped it atop the witch's skull. Something red showed there as Calvin ducked and dodged back. Even at his distance, David could see tiny dark somethings crawl onto the man's forehead. ("Fire ants," he muttered to Liz. "Smart thinking.")

Unfortunately the unconventional ploy delayed Snakeeyes but seconds before he moved again. Unbelievably fast, in fact, for Calvin was still regaining his balance when the witch smashed into him and locked his arms around Calvin's waist, slamming him hard into the trodden earth by the fire. One thigh flopped into the coals. Calvin used the resulting reflex to flip sideways—which set him atop Snakeeyes. His legs immediately clamped around his adversary's lower body, even as he sought to trap the larger man's elbows beneath his knees. Fingers found the witch's windpipe. Tendons tensed along Calvin's arms and back like mountains rising.

But then Snakeeyes worked a hand free. It shot up rattler-quick to clamp on Calvin's throat.

And the witch had reach. . . .

Calvin's face went pale from fear; his jaw muscles knotted and twitched as he sought to swallow—to *breathe* . . .

And then something very strange happened.

Snakeeyes simply stopped fighting . . . or so it seemed. His fingers slipped from Calvin's neck, and the entire arm flopped to the ground as if it had been struck numb. David dashed forward impulsively. His friends followed.

"*Stay back!*" Calvin warned between gritted teeth, his eyes wide and furious. "This may be a trick."

But it was not, David saw in an instant. No way any actor could mime the look of abject terror that contorted Snakeeyes's features.

And he evidently had reason to be afraid. For as Calvin held him close, and he struggled ever more weakly to free himself, it became obvious that every exertion left him weaker, as if he were being *drained* of strength.

But the worst thing was his face. Fear warped it, yes. But even beyond that, David could see that it was . . . aging. Bare seconds before, Snakeeyes had looked like a man in the very power of his prime—thirty-three, say. Now he seemed a man of fifty—and every ragged breath aged him further. His skin wrinkled and turned papery. Muscles lost their firmness and sheen, became flaccid and dull. Spots marred his skin's smoothness, wrinkles played havoc with the designs. His hair went gray, then white, then was gone.

The end came so quickly David gasped. Skin became skull became dust.

It was as simple as that. Calvin rocked backward abruptly, for he had suddenly found himself straddling nothing. A few fire ants crawled upon the well-churned earth. Already their fellows from the disturbed mound at the edge of the Wheel were assessing the worth of Snakeeyes's remnants as building stone.

Calvin swallowed hard and rose. David helped him. "Way to go, Fargo!" he cried. "Way to bloody well *go*, man!"

Liz stared at the place where the witch had died. Only his breechclout and the two skull earrings remained. "B-but . . . what *happened*?"

Calvin grinned at her smugly, but said nothing. The birds, David noted, were already dispersing—as good a sign as any that Snakeeyes's sovereignty had ended. "Maybe you'd better ask . . . Sandy," David chuckled, catching Calvin's eye.

Calvin's mouth dropped open. "How'd you know!"

David grinned back, then pointed to where the curve of Calvin's backside was revealed by his scanty loin-cloth. "I *didn't*—until now. But there's no tattoo on your heinie—or your shoulders—not even the ghost of one, which there oughta be. Shoot, just *think* a minute, folks: we saw Cal and Sandy go off together, but only one came back—Cal, so we thought. Even *I* thought.''

"And *I* think I see why Cal *thinks* so much of you,'' Sandy né Calvin replied. '' 'Cause you're right. I thought Cal was being an utter asshole about the whole thing, especially about not letting me stay here when he found out I was . . . bleeding. But then he said that warriors were forbidden to be around bleeding women, and I got an idea. And when he told me why: because a woman's body tries to compensate for her blood loss with the strength of others—well, that clinched it. The hardest part was convincing him to let me take the risk. The rest was easy, if you know some martial arts.''

"But you're in his *shape*,'' Brock gasped. "How . . . ?''

Once more Sandy/Calvin grinned. "You live together as long as Cal and me have, sooner or later you'll taste each other's blood—a cut finger, a love-nip, wild sex— you name it. And a taste was all I needed—that and the scale. The main danger came from not knowing whether me being in male-shape would screw up the prohibition—that, and the possibility of being recognized. And the danger of getting stuck in Cal's shape, of course— which could still happen.''

"And . . . ?'' Alec prompted.

Sandy/Calvin shrugged. "Once I changed, me and Cal did a little wrestling—enough to tell it worked, though apparently, the effect's only negligible in the real world. It's only when you come up against things like Snake-eyes that you get mondo reactions like we just saw. Magic amplifies magic, so to speak.''

"So where *is* Cal?'' Brock wondered slyly.

"Down by the river—I hope,'' Sandy replied. "I told him we'd toot the horn three times if I succeeded.''

"I'm on it!'' Brock volunteered, and promptly trotted off.

"This is . . . interesting," Sandy confided to Liz, glancing down her surrogate body. "You oughta get Dave to let you try it sometime."

Liz raised an inquisitive eyebrow in David's direction. "Actually," she giggled, "it'd probably do more to promote understanding between the sexes if he tried on *my* shape once in a while—preferably at a certain time of month."

Sandy/Calvin guffawed.

David simply rolled his eyes in resignation.

The Ranger's horn hooted three times.

"David," Alec gulped nervously. "Am I dreaming . . . or is a mist rising?"

# Epilogue:
# The Foggiest Notions

*(Jackson County, Georgia—
Wednesday, June 20—just past sunset)*

*Honk! Honk-honk!*

Calvin started awake from where he'd been dozing in a laurel thicket atop the eastern bank of the Middle Oconee River. Was that what he hoped it was? He hardly *dared* hope. Trouble was, he'd been going flat out for something like two days straight with only naps to stave off the worst fatigue—which meant that he wasn't certain about *anything* anymore: like whether he'd actually heard a car horn or only dreamed it; or could there maybe have been a bird that sounded like one, and either way, whether or not there'd been three honks. Dammit, why hadn't he anticipated that he'd be unable to avoid catching some z's and asked that they repeat the signal at five-minute intervals?

Twenty-twenty hindsight, he supposed. Of which he had God's plenty.

*Honk-honk-honk!*

That *had* been a car horn, and with that, he levered himself to his feet, noting how sore he was in odd places, how painfully hollow his stomach felt, and that a fox squirrel had been staring at him with wary interest until he'd moved. A pause to retrieve the backpack that contained most of Sandy's clothes—minus the jeans that were his only garment (too loose in the hips, too short in the leg, and so snug in the waist he had to leave them half unzipped), and he pushed through the screen of thick, shiny leaves.

And immediately got another shock, coupled, this time, with a chill.

He had stepped out into fog—a disturbingly *thick* fog that was oozing up the bank from the river very rapidly indeed. *So* rapidly, in fact, that it rose from ankle-deep to calf-deep even as he gaped at it. A glance west showed light but no sun, which meant he hadn't slept as long as he'd feared—but also revealed that the far shore was obscured by a bank of mist. Only his side was clear, and that not for long, for by then the fog had reached his knees, which finally set him moving.

It wasn't natural, he knew that already. Fog simply didn't act like this: flowing steadily up and out, with a tangible front that seemed to herd him on as he frantically stumbled upslope through more laurel, more generic undergrowth, and finally into the relative openness beneath a several-acre stand of hardwoods.

And always it moved faster than he—had *already* flowed around him, so that he now waded up to his waist and could discern the ground but dimly. Beyond— around—oaks and hickories rose out of the white like cypresses in a swamp. The sky beyond their branches was white, too, though it should have shown the richer shades of dusk, and the wind had kicked up and was blowing hints of cooler weather, and of serious thunder. The air at nose level was tense and nervous; that below his waist, cool, calm, and still. It was as if he was already in two worlds, he thought tiredly, and suppressed another chill.

Two minutes later, he could not see at all, but could still approximate his direction by the slope of the land and the relative quality of the light: pale to the west, darker to the east.

*Three* minutes later, he could see even less—hardly more than his hand before him, but the ground had leveled, and he got a sense of fewer trees.

And then he tripped on something solid and rough-barked, and fell forward onto another something that was soft and slick and moved beneath his hand. He jerked it away abruptly, but not before he glimpsed a thick-bodied serpent wearing scales in a diamond pattern. He didn't need to see the rattles as it slithered away.

He slowed then, both from fear of tripping again, and of stepping on something that might actually bite this time. Even so, he felt two more scaled shapes slide away from his bare feet before he found himself slogging through damp, knee-high grass, and an instant later, with no warning at all, stumbling across yet another log—and into clear air.

It was the Power Wheel that fronted the asi, he knew that instantly.

His friends were there, too: wary captives of a cylindrical wall of roiling white mist that rose twice as high as their heads. Still, he gasped out his relief as reflex identified Dave, Liz, Alec, and Brock, with enough joy on their faces to override the apprehension they likewise must be feeling. Snakeeyes was nowhere in sight—he'd pretty much expected that. But where was Sandy? And who was that other guy, who rose from where he'd been sitting wearily on a log, with his head propped on elbows that rested on knees? Only, he already knew; was already swallowing shock as his too-tired brain recalibrated enough to tell him that was Sandy, still wearing his shape—which was odd, given how spooked she'd said she felt when she first put it on. It took some getting used to, too; seeing his own body in three dimensions, from angles he never had—and seeing that body move and breathe without *him* being in control.

She looked up at him—but not with the relief he'd expected. Rather, her expression was one of despair—utter resignation.

"I'm stuck," she said simply, finally meeting his eye, though she didn't rise. "I tried just now to shift back, and couldn't." And with that she held out her hands. Both palms were crimson with blood, and that substance likewise showed as a red stain on the scale that glittered on his—*her*—bare chest.

Calvin was already reaching to enfold her, so sick at heart as to be almost in shock, when the whole world turned to light and heat and noise. *Lightning* he identified automatically, even as he felt himself flung forward—straight into Sandy's too-muscular arms and hard, unyielding chest. He *oofed*—or she did—but by then reality had stabilized. The air was thick with the scent of ozone.

But another odor rode an odd new wind as well: that of wood smoke, of distant campfire's burning. He'd smelled that before, too, and recently. But where?

But before he could decide, Sandy had thrust him away from her, and he saw.

A single bolt had struck the asi dead center, scorching blankets and scattering his friends like cordwood. As best he could tell from the way they were already picking themselves up, none were injured—which was fortunate, since by then he had other cause for alarm. For even as he stared at the smoldering rags of what had been the door flap, a figure emerged. He thought for a brief, despairing moment, that it was Snakeeyes born again, for all he could see initially was long black hair and piercing eyes in a dark face.

Only . . . the face was *too* dark and the eyes wrong. But before he could speak, the man stepped out among them, and Calvin knew him. It was Asgaya Sakani: the Black Man of the West. His face was grim, unreadable. "*Siyu*, Utlunta-dehi," he grunted tersely.

"*Siyu*," Calvin stammered back, stunned. "I—uh, that is—what brings you to the . . . the Lying World."

The Black Man's eyes flashed like distant lightning. "Lies! Lies are what bring me to the Lying World! You came into my Quarter unbidden. And there you wore shapes not your own, and practiced deception after deception on those who are sworn to uphold my commands!"

Calvin swallowed, but stood straighter, too tired to do aught but blunder ahead. "Yeah, well, we'll talk about that in a minute," he sighed. "But first, it might interest you to know that Sandy here's just destroyed a *master* of lies. One who stole lives and practiced deceptions, and would have one day been a threat to Galunlati—and perhaps to the Darkening Land as well. And besides, we came 'cause one of your . . . subjects asked!"

The Black Man's reply was to lock gazes with Calvin. And then, abruptly, the arrogance and accusation melted away—and the Black Man smiled!

"You trespassed in my Quarter without leave," he said, his voice like a fading storm. "You passed where no living man should have. Yet a moment ago, I heard a newly arrived soul screaming out its madness on my borders and cursing your name. Naturally, I hastened there, but on my way, I met many souls—many, *many* souls, all of whom had been trapped on the edge of my Quarter by their own uneasiness at having years of their lives usurped. Like your father they were, Utlunta-dehi: incomplete, and so unable—or unwilling—to go on. But when you caused Snakeeyes to be killed, those years came back to them, and they could rest. They will yet enjoy those unspent years, when they ride the wheel in your World again.''

Calvin could only nod out his relief. Behind him, he sensed the warmth of Sandy's body shadowing his own. David, Liz, and Alec looked wary. Brock was simply gaping, wide-eyed. ''I—I'm glad to have been of service,'' Calvin began. ''And I'm sorry if I've overstepped my bounds in your land. Yet—''

''*Yet what?*'' another voice thundered—this one from the fog-veiled east. That same mist had muffled it beyond recognition. Calvin swung around to face that way—and could just make out the dim outline of a tall man-shape darkening the swirls and tendrils there. It did not step through to join them, however, but remained where it was: a clotting in the mist.

''Yet what, Edahi?'' that voice repeated sharply. It was closer this time, and lower; and he recognized it.

''Uki!''

''Visitors,'' that voice rumbled back. ''I do not *like* visitors, Utlunta-dehi,'' it continued. ''I do not like them when they come from the Lying World without command or invitation. And I especially do not like them when they know *you*, whom I have forbidden to contact me until a year has passed, which it has not. Were I so inclined, I could accuse you of flaunting that prohibition.''

Calvin hung his head. ''I'm sorry . . . master. I was under an obligation. It seemed like the best thing to do at the time.''

''Best for you, perhaps!'' Uki snapped, still from the mist. ''Not necessarily for me!''

Silence. Then, from Brock. ''So, *screw* you!'' the boy cried. ''Cal did what he had to. If he hadn't sent 'Kacha away when he did, old Snakeeyes would've had her power to draw on and he might've been able to beat 'em then—or Sandy, or whoever. And if he'd done that, he'd have got Cal's scale and war club, and the ulun-*what*si, and there's no telling what he'd have done with 'em! 'Cept one thing I do know is that 'Kacha was afraid he'd try to use 'em to get where you were.''

''And if he had?'' Uki challenged from the fog.

Brock shrugged, shifted his weight. ''He'd—well, I don't *know* what he'd have done, but I know he'd have found out some stuff you might not want somebody like him to know. 'Sides, didn't you guys hide from us once already? Seems to me like you might even be *afraid* of us. And if you're afraid of folks like me and Cal and . . . and Sandy, what about folks like Snakeeyes, who're *really* bad?''

The boy broke off then, his sudden fury abated. He stood glowering at the darkness in the mist.

Silence, again.

And more silence.

Then: ''You are correct, boy—or at least in many ways you are—*as I would have said had you given me time!* But I wanted my student to taste the foul before I fed him the fair—except that you preempted me!''

Brock flushed. ''S-sorry.''

Unexpectedly, Uki laughed. ''Utlunta-dehi has spoken of you,'' he chuckled. ''He says you would learn the secrets you call magic. Is that still your wish?''

Brock glanced up warily, abruptly all attitude and bright eyes again. Calvin felt his heart skip a beat. What was Uki *doing*? No way he should offer something like that to a kid like Brock. *No way!*

But the boy squared his shoulders and shook his head. ''I—can't say I won't be curious,'' he murmured, and Calvin could tell the effort cost him, that he knew he was cutting himself off from something at once wonderful beyond imagining and dreadful beyond his darkest dreams. ''In fact, I'm gonna be curious,'' he continued, more loudly. ''But no, I think I've seen enough—for a while. I need to think about all this and then . . . I guess I need to think some more. And then''—he glanced at Calvin—"we'll see.''

"A careful answer that *wasn't*,'' Uki laughed again. Calvin saw the Black Man glower.

"You were about to speak, Brother-in-Thunder?'' Uki prompted.

The scowl darkened. "Will there be feast or fight?'' Asgaya Sakani asked sharply. "We promised these— most of these—a feast and a giving of gifts if they used the things they know appropriately during the last year. Part of me is not sure they have done so, yet another part thinks they have. A man should be of one mind about such things.''

"If it'll help any,'' Alec broke in unexpectedly, "it doesn't matter much to me either way—though I thank you for your hospitality and your honors in the past. But on the other hand, you just mentioned divided choices, and—well, isn't that what Cal's been putting up with here? He didn't want to teach Brock magic, but he'd made a promise, so he did—after a lot of soul-searching about the right thing—the *safe* thing—to teach. And everything he's done since then—well, he's tried to do the right thing, which I'm sure wasn't always the thing *he* wanted to do. I—''

"Sandy,'' Liz interrupted simply. "What about poor Sandy?''

Calvin felt his cheeks burning at having overlooked so fundamental a crisis in the midst of arguing dinner dates with demigods. His hand sought hers automatically—wincing but barely when he found it larger and harder. He swallowed, stared at the misty shadow that was Uki.

A grunt made him turn again. "I was not able to finish my message,'' the Black Man snapped. "Nor was I able to deliver one I was given by a certain soul I met.'' And with that, he reached to a pouch at his side and drew out something that glittered bright when he held it out in his palm. ''You father bade me send you this, Utlunta-dehi,'' he said—and passed Calvin a now-familiar uktena scale. Calvin, in turn, slipped it to his dopple-gänger. Her hands folded upon it, but she did not squeeze. Which showed admirable self-control. ''Thank you,'' she replied simply.

The Black Man nodded. The fog, Calvin noted, had begun to disperse. And he wasn't certain, but he thought he could discern the ruined dome of the asi through the Black Man's torso, as though through a thick cloud of smoke.

Thunder rumbled.

No! Not thunder: an engine—a healthy American V-8, if Calvin heard it right. An instant later, head-lights lanced through the fog. The engine roared louder—too loud; then, abruptly, brakes squealed—or tires did—and a low burgundy-and-chrome prow poked through the wall of mist. It swirled away. *Thunderbird,* Calvin identified automatically: *'66 Town Landau.* Could it be . . . ?

The engine died, a heavy door slammed, a figure took form, sprinting toward them. An instant later, it bounded into the open space. Calvin moved automatically to stand in front of Sandy, who had not yet resumed her own shape—and probably wouldn't until things died down a little. But then he was running forward, instead, to embrace . . . his cousin.

''Churchy!'' he gasped, as Kirkwood Thunderbird O'Connor bear-hugged him, then thrust him away.

''You son-of-a-bitch!'' Kirk gritted. ''What the hell's goin' on here, anyway?'' He indicated the fading wall of fog. ''This ain't natural, is it? 'Course it ain't natural when you wake up from your afternoon siesta and find a blessed peregrine falcon sittin' on the foot of your bed, either—one that screams out 'Calvin!' exactly once, then just sits and waits on you to finish dressing, and then flies out and lights on your hood, and *then* flies in front of you until—*Oh, shit!* What *the fuck?*''

Kirk staggered back automatically, having evidently just realized that the person whose face and body had heretofore been shielded by his cousin bore an uncanny resemblance *to* his cousin.

Calvin reached out to brace him, torn between concern and a terrible desire to giggle. ''Remember what I told you about the scale?'' he asked carefully. ''Remember when you asked if I could turn into a real pretty girl? Well, uh, Sandy thought she'd try it the other way round first—which just coincidentally saved our asses.'' He looked around at his friends for reassurance.

Kirk swallowed hard and slumped back against the hood of his car. ''I . . . hope so,'' he managed. ''One of you's plenty enough.''

''Gives a new meaning to 'walk a mile in my shoes,' though,'' Sandy laughed—which filled Calvin with vast relief. He squeezed her hand. ''Any time, babe.''

Calvin glanced around—which took his gaze to where Asgaya Sakani had last stood glowering. He was gone: dissipated like so much black smoke. A glance the other way showed the merest fading glimmer of the shape that had been Uki. ''One more for dinner—if there is one?'' Calvin called.

And from the fog came a voice, faint but clear. ''There will be, but in the meantime, I suppose I must consult the others concerning yet more war names. Perhaps I will consult the woman you sent me as well.''

Brock perked up. '' 'Kacha? What about her? You gonna keep her?''

''No,'' Uki replied, very faintly as the night wind began to unravel the fog, ''but I very well might marry her.''

Sandy looked at Calvin and raised an eyebrow dangerously. "If you say a word about Thundercats, I'll kill you."

"I won't," Calvin smirked. "Now, why don't you go change, and I don't mean just your clothes."

When Calvin met her in the woods a few minutes later, she was wearing starlight, and her eyes were shining.

Very soon he was wearing starlight, too.

And the only raptor that roamed the night between Lebanon Church Road and Athens was the emblem on the grille of Kirkwood O'Connor's Thunderbird, bearing weary travelers home.

**TOM DEITZ**, a north Georgia native, writes eloquently about the magic of his home state in such works as his fine series of contemporary fantasies, including *Windmaster's Bane*, *Fireshaper's Doom*, *Sunshaker's War*, and his most recent AvoNova hardcover, *Dreamseeker's Road*. His first hardcover, the near-future fantasy *Above the Lower Sky*, appeared last year to great acclaim. He is also the author of an ambitious dark fantasy trilogy comprised of *Soulsmith*, *Dreambuilder*, and *Wordwright*.

When he isn't writing, Mr. Deitz enjoys restoring classic automobiles, hunting, and drawing and painting, and dreams of someday building a small castle. He resides in Athens, Georgia.

There are places on Earth
where magic worlds beckon...

# TOM DEITZ

takes you there...

## DREAMBUILDER
76290-0/ $4.99 US/ $5.99 Can

## SOULSMITH
76289-7/ $4.99 US/ $5.99 Can

## WINDMASTER'S BANE
75029-5/ $4.99 US/ $5.99 Can

## DARKTHUNDER'S WAY
75508-4/ $3.95 US/ $4.95 Can

## FIRESHAPER'S DOOM
75329-4/ $3.95 US/ $4.50 Can

## WORDWRIGHT
76291-9/ $4.99 US/ $5.99 Can

### Coming Soon
## GHOSTCOUNTRY'S WRATH
76838-0/ $5.50 US/ $7.50 Can

Buy these books at your local bookstore or use this coupon for ordering:

Mail to: Avon Books, Dept BP, Box 767, Rte 2, Dresden, TN 38225          C
Please send me the book(s) I have checked above.
❑ My check or money order— no cash or CODs please— for $_____is enclosed
(please add $1.50 to cover postage and handling for each book ordered— Canadian residents
add 7% GST).
❑ Charge my VISA/MC Acct#_____Exp Date_____
Minimum credit card order is two books or $6.00 (please add postage and handling charge of
$1.50 per book — Canadian residents add 7% GST).  For faster service, call
1-800-762-0779.  Residents of Tennessee, please call 1-800-633-1607.  Prices and numbers
are subject to change without notice.  Please allow six to eight weeks for delivery.

Name_____
Address_____
City_____State/Zip_____
Telephone No._____                              DTZ 0395

# RETURN TO AMBER...
## THE ONE *REAL* WORLD, OF WHICH
## ALL OTHERS, INCLUDING EARTH,
## ARE BUT SHADOWS

## *The Classic Amber Series*

**NINE PRINCES IN AMBER** 01430-0/$3.99 US/$4.99 Can

**THE GUNS OF AVALON** 00083-0/$3.99 US/$4.99 Can

**SIGN OF THE UNICORN** 00031-9/$3.99 US/$4.99 Can

**THE HAND OF OBERON** 01664-8/$3.99 US/$4.99 Can

**THE COURTS OF CHAOS** 47175-2/$4.99 US/$6.99 Can

**BLOOD OF AMBER** 89636-2/$4.99 US/$5.99 Can

**TRUMPS OF DOOM** 89635-4/$4.99 US/$5.99 Can

**SIGN OF CHAOS** 89637-0/$4.99 US/$5.99 Can

**KNIGHT OF SHADOWS** 75501-7/$4.99 US/$5.99 Can

**PRINCE OF CHAOS** 75502-5/$4.99 US/$5.99 Can

Buy these books at your local bookstore or use this coupon for ordering:
........................................................................................
Mail to: Avon Books, Dept BP, Box 767, Rte 2, Dresden, TN 38225          C
Please send me the book(s) I have checked above.
❑ My check or money order— no cash or CODs please— for $_____is enclosed
(please add $1.50 to cover postage and handling for each book ordered— Canadian residents
add 7% GST).
❑ Charge my VISA/MC Acct#_____Exp Date_____
Minimum credit card order is two books or $6.00 (please add postage and handling charge of
$1.50 per book — Canadian residents add 7% GST).  For faster service, call
1-800-762-0779.  Residents of Tennessee, please call 1-800-633-1607.  Prices and numbers
are subject to change without notice.  Please allow six to eight weeks for delivery.

Name_____
Address_____
City_____State/Zip_____
Telephone No._____                        AMB 0395